ALSO BY A.M. PEACOCK

C

GRAVE INTENT

A.M. PEACOCK

Print ISBN 978-1-912986-44-6

For everybody who has helped along the way.

CHAPTER ONE

His breaths came in sharp, panicked gasps as he ran from the farmhouse. The rain was pounding down now, making it hard for him to see exactly where he was going. Stinging his face, as if scolding him for being out in such weather. His feet slipped in the muddy earth, nearly causing him to fall. He glanced over his shoulder, his eyes wide and fearful. He had to keep running. He just had to...

He hadn't expected anyone to be home. The wheat field had provided good cover and he'd been told that the farmer wouldn't be there.

'Wait until well after dark, approach from the east, and stay low,' they'd told him. 'Three scarecrows and you're there.'

He hadn't banked on a light turning on as he opened the door, nor the shrieking of rusted hinges announcing his presence. Such was his shock that, at first, he hadn't even seen the man with the shotgun sitting in the corner of the room.

That was when the growling had started.

The dog had lunged at him first, before the man had stood and cocked his gun.

He'd turned in sheer terror, feeling the warm trickle of blood moving down his leg as the Alsatian's jaws locked in place. He'd gouged at the animal's eyes and managed to wriggle free. He'd slammed the door behind him, and slipped on the wooden patio, smashing his chin against the damp wood.

And, so, he'd ran.

Cursing his luck, he moaned and carried on, dragging his injured leg away from the house in the pouring rain. He couldn't see him, but he knew the man was not far behind.

The barking grew in volume.

Each time his right foot made contact with the ground his injured leg screamed at him. 'Come on!' he urged himself, fishing out his mobile with shaky fingers.

Rain smeared across the phone screen as he typed in the wrong pin. He swore as the dog clamped its jaws over his leg, once again, dropping the device as he lashed out into the night. The dog whimpered and hurtled back towards the confines of the house.

He continued past the first scarecrow as a shot rang up around him.

The sound of screeching birds evacuating their nests rose above the noise of the retreating dog's barks. Allowing himself a stifled sob, he carried on past the second scarecrow.

'I'm coming for you, boy!' the farmer's gruff voice bellowed from behind him.

Why had he agreed to the job? He didn't know what was worse, having to go back to them without *it* or being chased through a field by a gun-toting maniac.

By the time the second shot came, he'd made his decision.

His adrenaline was up, blood pounding through his ears, as he passed the third scarecrow, which was sat askew on its frame. He could almost see the end of the field now as a set of headlights moved across his vision.

'Help!' he shouted.

The lights disappeared from view, leaving him alone with the man and his gun.

'Fuck!'

The field rose in a steady incline and he could feel his calves burning as he pushed onwards. The stitch that had been throbbing away at his side now burst through, sending shooting pains up his body. He could feel the injured leg lagging and knew he was slowing down. Every step proved more difficult than the last, his feet sliding in the sludge of the churned-up field. *Keep going,* he told himself. *Only one more scarecrow.*

Suddenly, the atmosphere thickened. So confused was he that he barely registered the absence of sound around him. There'd only been three, hadn't there? He'd passed all of them on his way to the farmhouse. Could he have been wrong?

He stood some fifteen feet away from it, its black cloak swirling around in the biting wind. Its head faced the ground, much like the others, with a pointed hat covering the upper features of its face.

He shivered, aware of how cold he now felt.

He could no longer hear the man, only the sound of heavy rain and his own thudding heart. He turned and looked back towards the house, noting that the light had now gone out.

He was alone in a field of four scarecrows when there should have only been three.

He snapped his head back around as the sound of a twig breaking cut through the silence. Sweat began to trickle down his back.

He edged forward. 'Hello?'

The scarecrow hung before him, unmoved by his presence. Reaching out, he took hold of the thick, black cloak and gazed up into its misshapen features. He exhaled a sigh of relief. It wasn't alive.

Thank God.

But he was sure there had only been three scarecrows, not four. How could...

Dread crawled up through his stomach as he realised. He'd been so distracted that he hadn't fully registered what he'd seen. The third scarecrow hadn't looked right, had it? It was askew on its frame. No, that wasn't quite right. What was it?

It hadn't been on a frame.

A blow to the head caused him to fall to the ground. The impact left the side of his face numb as he looked up and saw the third scarecrow staring down at him. It smiled a crooked smile, a thick, angry scar noticeable across its left cheek. He made to scream but was paralysed by fear. He tried to crawl away but his wounded leg wouldn't let him.

Slowly, the scarecrow man stepped forward, heavy boots slapping into the wet earth. The grin spread wider over his face as he brought a gloved finger up to his mouth.

Quiet now.

When the pitchfork broke through his skin he found himself unable to comply.

CHAPTER TWO

J ack Lambert rolled over in bed and tried to remember what dream he'd been having. The lack of sweat on his sheets told him it hadn't been a nightmare. He found himself plagued less and less by those in recent times. After last year's case, he'd initially been unable to shake the image of the Open Grave Murderer from his mind. After that, those dreams had been replaced with images of the Captain; the mysterious gangster who had threatened to find him at the beginning of the year. With the absence of a face, just about everybody he had ever known had appeared to him as the unknown criminal. With that threat unfulfilled, Jack had almost forgotten it had even happened now. He yawned, a satisfied yawn, and sat upright, correcting the crick in his neck.

'What time is it?'

Jack was startled. He still wasn't used to sharing his domain with another man. However, Ryan, a pharmacist in his mid-thirties, had entered his life, just a few short months ago—an internet dating success story, surrounded by a graveyard of failures.

Jack shuddered at the thought of graves. Perhaps some demons were harder to shake than others.

'Half seven,' Jack told him. 'Don't worry, just go back to sleep.'

Jack watched as Ryan buried his head in the pillow, bedraggled blond hair flopping from side to side as he groaned.

'How can I when you keep waking me up so early?'

Jack laughed. 'Sorry, occupational hazard.'

'Are you at least going to make me a coffee?'

'You hate the coffee I make,' Jack told him.

Ryan turned to face him, his neat features set in a fake pout. 'True,' he said, reaching over to trace the outline of the scar across Jack's stomach. 'That's because you're supposed to make a drink, not mix cement.'

'I—' Jack began before his phone buzzed, cutting through his thoughts. He mouthed a 'sorry' to Ryan and moved to the doorway to answer the call.

Two minutes later he re-entered the room.

'Problem?' Ryan asked.

Jack nodded. 'You'll have to make your own coffee, I'm afraid.'

Ryan sighed. 'Duty calls?'

Jack grabbed his jeans and wrestled with the left leg. 'Duty calls,' he mumbled.

Jack knelt in the wet earth and surveyed the scene.

'What do we know?' DI Russell asked, choosing to stay standing above him.

What did they know? Word had come in at around 7am that morning. The owner of the property, a farmer, had found the man in the field and made a panicked call to the police. Jack glanced at his cracked Rolex, a present from his late mother. It was now 9.13am exactly and the reality was they knew very little.

'Well,' he said, knees grinding as he dragged himself back up and brushed the mud from his white SOC suit. 'I know he's dead.'

DI Russell snorted and ran her painfully-thin fingers down her equally painfully-constructed fringe. 'Yes, I noticed that myself.'

Jack managed to stop himself before biting back. It was no secret that Jane Russell disliked him, she'd made that clear for the best part of ten years now. Despite her cutting remarks and general aloofness from others, though, she was a great detective. She was a stickler for formality, and Jack was pretty sure he'd never seen her in anything other than her drab, grey work suit with too-square shoulders. Quick to temper and impatient with bluster, she'd acquired her Bulldog nickname from her colleagues for good reason.

He pitied the officer that ever called her it to her face.

Gazing out of the tent, across the field, he took note of the three scarecrows sat on their perches. Jack shuddered inside. He'd watched *Worzel Gummidge* as a child. Creepy. 'Well we know what the murder weapon was, given that they've left it right next to him.'

'I'm beginning to see why they made you a detective.' DI Russell's sarcasm was just the wrong side of banter.

The SOC unit hadn't yet moved the pitchfork and the body was still in place under the recently-erected white tent. It wasn't pretty. The man's leg had been mangled by the fork but, having been the victim of something similar himself once, Jack was sure that the victim had also been bitten by a dog. The rock used to smash his head in lay next to what could only be described as a bloody pulp on the ground. The fact that the previous night's rain was still sodden in the man's clothes somehow made the whole thing seem even sadder.

'Guv.' DS Watkins strode over. 'We've found a mobile phone not far from the house.'

'Bag it up and put it in with the rest of the evidence.'

'Already done, sir.' Watkins was obviously pleased with his find, even the rain couldn't wash the beaming smile from his face.

Jack was a fan of the DS and was happy to see him starting to act on his own initiative. The gangly, ginger detective was growing into the role, even if his pipe-cleaner limbs still struggled to fill out his baggy clothes.

'The bloke has a shotgun in the house, can you believe it?' Watkins added, eyes flitting to DI Russell.

Jack almost smiled at the man's nervousness. Although an empathetic and social character, like many of his colleagues, he feared the wrath of Jane Russell. They'd never seen eye-to-eye and Jack knew that the DI didn't rate him.

Good job he was the boss, then.

'He's a farmer, Watkins. They all have shotguns.' He wasn't interested in the firearm. The victim hadn't been shot.

'We have an ID already, right?' Jane asked.

Jack nodded. 'Twenty-two-year-old Robert Norris. He still had his wallet on him.'

'Well it can't have been a mugging then.'

He gazed back towards the farmhouse. 'No, it looks more like he was the one doing the mugging.'

'So you think the farmer meted out his own form of punishment?' Watkins asked.

Jack bit down on his lip. 'It looks that way, at first glance. But why call us? Surely he'd know he'd become a suspect?'

The detectives exited the tent.

'Where is our vigilante?' Jack asked.

DI Russell pointed to the left of the house. 'Over there. I would have spoken to him but...'

Jack nodded. DI Russell only had a bad cop approach.

Jack looked up at the sky; last night's rain wasn't quite ready to finish, it seemed. 'Why is it whenever we get a murder it's always during a period of bad weather? It's as if people lose their minds and decide to kill because it isn't sunny,' he mused, fishing out two paracetamol and crunching them down. 'I'll go speak with him. You stay here and co-ordinate with the pathologist.'

DI Russell nodded her affirmation and cast a withering look towards Watkins, whose face was doing its best tomato impression.

Jack left them to it and made the short journey from the murder scene back to the house, moving adjacent to the marked-off area where a number of very distinct footprints had been found. One of them clearly belonged to Norris, and given one set of prints emanated from the house, Jack could only assume that they belonged to the farmer.

Who did the third set belong to then?

'Mr Fenwick,' Jack greeted a rather shell-shocked man who was sitting at the side of the farmhouse.

The man's eyes were as wide as saucers as Jack approached him. 'Name's Gus,' he said.

'I'll stick with Mr Fenwick, if it's all the same? I'd like to keep this formal.'

The man gulped, a protruding Adam's apple bobbing up and down on his loose-skinned neck. He had the look of a crane, albeit one with an extremely high hairline.

'I... I didn't do it,' the man protested.

Jack raised his hand. 'This doesn't look good does it, Mr Fenwick?' He took a knee in the dirt, lowering himself to the man's height. 'What happened here?'

'I told the other officer—'

'Tell me,' Jack interrupted. His voice firm, eyes unblinking.

'I can't explain it... But I damn well wish I had done it.'

'Excuse me?' Jack asked, taken aback.

'Trespassing on my property? He's lucky I didn't blow his head off.'

'Mr Fenwick...'

'I told you, it's Gus.'

Jack stood, his stocky six-feet two-inch frame looming over the thin farmer. 'And I told you I'm going to keep this formal. Mr

Fenwick, I'm arresting you on suspicion of the murder of Robert Norris.'

'You can't do that.' The old man stood, pumping out his chest. 'I have rights.'

He smiled. 'Of course you do, and I'm about to read them to you now.'

CHAPTER THREE

Watkins fidgeted with the recording device on the table as Jack motioned for Gus Fenwick to take a seat. Next to him sat Casey Clifton, smug duty solicitor and royal pain in the arse for all those who worked in the force. Jack hadn't seen him since they'd brought in the wrong person during last year's Open Grave Murder case. He forced the memory from his mind and surveyed the men before him.

Fenwick's initial shock had given way to a more robust response, one which Jack suspected was closer to the true nature of the man. He sat, arms folded, having refused a glass of water. Casey Clifton, on the other hand, had requested his with a slice of lemon. He sat, expensive watch clanging on the table as he made a show of opening his brown leather briefcase.

'Let's begin,' Jack said, trying his best not to grind his teeth.

Clifton nodded and Watkins did the introductions for the purpose of the recording.

'Mr Fenwick, do you understand why you are here today?'

'Not really,' came the curt response. 'I haven't done anything wrong.'

Jack pushed a hastily-printed picture of Robert Norris' dead body across the table. He noticed Clifton flinch, making to say something, before thinking better of it. 'This is Robert Norris. He was found on your property this morning at around—'

'Yes I know,' Gus Fenwick shouted. 'I was the one that bloody found him. Well done, detective.'

Jack attempted to swallow his dislike for the man sat opposite him and pushed on. 'He was found with multiple injuries including stab wounds from a pitchfork we found nearby and, although too early to tell, we believe he was killed by multiple blows to the head by a rock. What do you say to that?'

The tall, slender figure of Gus Fenwick leaned forward, eyes scanning the pictures without emotion. 'Nowt. Didn't know the bloke, didn't do it. He shouldn't have been on my property.'

'So you admit to having seen him on the farm prior to this?' Watkins asked.

Clifton tagged in. 'That's not what he's saying, at all, detective.'

Fenwick continued unruffled. 'Nah, never saw him.'

'Where were you last night, Mr Fenwick?'

'I was out.'

Jack could tell this wasn't going to be easy. 'Out where?'

The farmer sighed. 'Local pub. I went there around, oh I don't know, 7pm?'

'Alone?'

'Aye, although you're never really alone in The Black Horse.'

Jack noted Watkins scribbling down the name of the pub. 'So there will be people who can corroborate your story?'

'Aye, most likely.'

'And do you live alone?'

A pause. 'At the minute.'

'Meaning?'

Fenwick glanced at Clifton before answering. 'Wife is a bit unwell; she's in hospital, like.'

'Have you been visiting her?' Jack asked.

Fenwick rearranged his sleeves before speaking. 'Aye, from time to time.'

'You didn't put her there, did you?' Jack muttered to himself, frustrated by the farmer's lack of co-operation.

'What did you say!?' Anger flashed across Fenwick's already flushed face.

Clifton chipped in. 'That's out of order, detective. If you continue to show disdain for my client, I'm afraid I shall have no choice but to abandon this interview.'

Jack closed the space between them and rearranged the photos on the table. 'So you have no idea what Robert Norris was doing on your property?' He pushed the graphic images towards the fidgeting farmer.

Fenwick avoided looking at the more explicit pictures.

'I think it's clear that this Norris character was intending to rob Mr Fenwick.'

Jack smiled inwardly at the solicitor taking the bait. 'Maybe so. Let's say he did force entry and was there to rob you, like Casey here suggested.' He saw the colour drain from Clifton's well-moisturised face. 'And during this robbery, he was killed—'

Clifton attempted to intervene. 'Now wait a moment, detective, I never said—'

Jack ignored him. 'You tell me you live alone. So who killed him?'

Clifton whispered into Fenwick's ear.

Fenwick stared at the detective. 'No comment.'

Jack glanced at the duty solicitor. 'Really. No comment.'

Jack flicked the photos across the table at Gus Fenwick, one by one. 'Take a look, Mr Fenwick. You're facing a murder charge. Are you sure you want to give me no fucking comment!?'

The farmer finally exploded with rage. 'I don't give a shit what you think, detective! I'm telling you, it wasn't me that killed that low-life!'

Jack sat back, and studied his suspect. 'Look. You could argue that it was self-defence and you were protecting your property, but that argument won't carry much weight in court when they consider Norris was already leaving the property when he was brutally attacked.'

Clifton waded back in. 'If anything, detective, Mr Fenwick is the victim in all of this.'

Jack held a hand up to the solicitor. It was all he could do not to roll his eyes. 'I have a body in the morgue that's been pricked like a sausage, and has a rock where its brain should be. Don't tell me who the victim is, Clifton.' Jack turned his attention back to Fenwick. 'What time did you return from the pub?'

'After closing, around midnight,' the farmer said.

'And then...?' Jack continued.

Fenwick shrugged. 'Watched a little TV and went to bed around 1am, like I usually do.'

Jack took a good look at the yellows of the man's eyes. That was one story he could believe. 'And what about your dog?'

Fenwick started. 'My dog?'

'Yes,' Jack replied. 'The dog that took a chunk out of Robert Norris' leg.'

The farmer shook his head, the beginnings of a smirk appearing on his face. 'My dog died six months ago, detective.'

Jack leaned forward and held up the picture of Robert Norris' leg. 'Best think again.'

'Detectives...' Clifton followed Jack and Watkins out of the interview room. 'You can't hold on to Mr Fenwick indefinitely.'

Jack took a step back to avoid the pungent aroma of Clifton's Cool Water aftershave. 'I'm well aware of the rules regarding the law, Clifton. It's clear what has happened here. He'll be charged within twenty-four hours. If not, we'll apply for an extension.'

The solicitor removed his square-rimmed spectacles and made

a show of cleaning them whilst shaking his head. 'I guess I'll be seeing you both soon, then,' he said, before turning on his leather brogues and making a swift exit.

Jack watched the smug duty solicitor shuffle away with gritted teeth. He turned to Watkins. 'I want an update from DI Russell as soon as possible. I want boot prints, fingerprints, everything analysed to within an inch of its life. It has to be him. The proof will be there somewhere.'

The DS ran a freckled hand through his unruly ginger afro. 'I don't know, guv. He seems awfully cocky for somebody trying to get away with murder. Plus, what about the dog?'

Jack shrugged. 'Look into it. Check vet records to see if it's dead... And I want a thorough search done of the house, to see if there is any evidence of a dog having been there in the last few days.'

'And if there isn't...?'

'I dunno,' he cut in. 'Perhaps he was bitten earlier on in the night.'

Watkins raised his eyebrow. 'Bitten by a dog, then decides to go and rob a farmhouse? Seems a bit far-fetched to me, guv.'

The problem with Watkins' growing confidence was that he had a habit of asking pertinent questions which undermined Jack's theories. *Still,* Jack thought, *it makes him a better policeman.*

'Look, I don't have all the answers, Watkins. Let's just follow procedure and see what we find. If it isn't him, the evidence will prove it.' He made to leave. 'Oh, and we'll need to pay a visit to The Black Horse to see if his story checks out.'

'Jesus, guv,' Watkins whined. 'I'm already on a double shift. Can I get Christensen to give me a hand?'

'Good idea.'

Watkins offered a fumbled salute before turning on his heels and heading off.

'Guv...?' DC Claire Gerrard was bounding down the corridor, waving a piece of paper. 'We did a search on Robert Norris.'

'Let's go to my office.'

He led the way and motioned for Gerrard to sit down. He could tell she was full of nervous energy, her petite, lightly-freckled features beaming out at him. Her ponytail or, work hair, as she called it, swayed as she fidgeted in the seat.

In comparison, Jack felt tired. He slumped down on his office chair and glanced at the now clean whiteboard in his room. He couldn't help but wonder how long it would take to fill it up again.

Gerrard seemed to clock him. 'Still thinking about the Open Grave Murderer?'

He shrugged. Gerrard, perhaps more than any other of his officers, was always perceptive. And her unshakeable confidence meant she was never shy in airing her thoughts. Unlike DI Russell, she had a compassion for others that couldn't be taught. Gerrard was popular, intelligent and destined for the top. Given that being a feminist was no longer taboo in the force, Jack could see very little which would stand in her way.

They fell into contemplative silence. The truth was, last year's case now invaded Jack's dreams very rarely. He often found that when a case was closed he could cut it off and compartmentalise it. His old friend Pritchard would call it repression. He smiled at the memory of the now fully-retired criminal profiler. He'd not spoken to him in weeks, which was unforgivable given that the man's wife had died six months ago. He made a mental note to call him later that day.

'So, Robert Norris,' Gerrard continued, handing over the paper.

Jack noticed the excitement in her voice. 'Just paraphrase it for me.'

'Of course,' she said. 'I know how much you hate paperwork.' She cast a glance over at the corner he'd now dedicated to the shambles that was his filing system.

'Enough judgement from you,' he said, smiling. 'Facts, please.'

'Well he has previous,' she said. 'Burglary, attempted burglary,

GBH, drunk and disorderly, assault, the list goes on. Pretty impressive, given his age.'

'Interesting,' Jack said. 'Next of kin?'

'All on the system. I arranged for that liaison officer Watkins has been dating on and off to go and speak with them. Christensen is going with her.'

He laughed. 'Remind me again which of us is senior investigating officer here?'

She motioned towards the paperwork. 'You tell me. Once Edwards goes that sort of thing won't be allowed.'

He smiled. 'It will if I get his job.'

'Please,' she said. 'Attitude problem, PR disaster...'

'Alright...'

'A gay man no less!' she laughed. 'No, it would never do. It'll have to be a woman.'

'Oh really,' he replied. Claire Gerrard's staunch feminism was the stuff of legend round the station. 'And why is that?'

She rolled her eyes. 'We're just better. Anyway, come on, I'll buy you a coffee.'

'I'll take a water. I've given the stuff up.'

'Impressive,' she said. 'I wondered why you were so grumpy lately. If it's any consolation, you're looking good.'

'I hope you're not flirting with me,' he replied.

'Of course not, guv. I hear you're taken these days, anyway,' she said, leaning forward, her large, bright eyes boring into him.

Jack cleared his throat and picked up the Robert Norris paperwork. 'Where's this water I was promised?'

Half an hour and two waters later, Jack felt he had a pretty good handle on the kind of person Robert Norris was. Looking at his rap sheet, it was hard not to have the mental image of an angry young man with a taste for violence. He certainly wasn't somebody you'd want your daughter dating. He shuddered, his own daughter Shannon was approaching her teens and he had all of that to look forward to. Still, he'd already decided that being a policeman could have its uses there.

'What you thinking about?' Gerrard asked.

'Nothing,' he said, pushing the file to one side. 'Seems he was a nasty piece of work.'

Gerrard scooped a glob of natural white yoghurt in her mouth before responding. 'Indeed. Still, grim way to go isn't it?'

He nodded.

'Something on your mind?' she asked.

He frowned. 'I don't know... I just wonder about this.'

'How'd you mean? You don't think it was a simple robbery?'

He eyed her. 'Do you? Let's look at the facts; Robert Norris goes out in the middle of the night to rob a farmhouse? Why? Is it full of treasure?' That was a rhetorical question. Jack continued. 'He arrives, only to be confronted by the farmer who overpowers him, chases him into the field, tortures and kills him. That's not rational. No, there's nothing simple about this.'

'Maybe it wasn't the farmer? Maybe Norris was just dumped there?'

Jack exhaled and ran a hand through his recently cropped hair. 'That makes no sense. The boot prints, layout of the scene and blood spatter all point to Gus Fenwick.'

Gerrard paused to shake her slightly curled hair loose and rearrange it in a tighter ponytail. 'Okay, so now what?'

He finished off his third water and stood. 'We solve the crime.'

CHAPTER FOUR

The Black Horse was exactly how Jack pictured a pub in the heart of Northumberland. Certainly, when he and Gerrard entered, it was obvious to all involved that they were tourists. Unlike in some of the rougher areas of Newcastle, though, they weren't met with hostile disdain, merely a curious indifference. Given that it was barely 4pm, only a handful of hard-core punters were in the place. It had a dark, country feel to it, the thick, creamy smell of real ale seeping into its very foundations. In the corner a solitary fruit machine sat looking sorry for itself. As they entered, he could see Gerrard wriggle her nose in disgust.

Jack stepped up to the near-deserted bar and approached what could only be described as a giant of a man with an impressive set of dark eyebrows. 'Are you the manager?' he asked.

The huge barman finished wiping a still dirty half pint glass, a large, white apron spread across an impressive belly. 'Aye, that's me,' he said, his broad Glaswegian accent thicker than a pint of Guinness.

Jack sat and placed his palms down on the bar, instantly regretting it as he felt his skin stick to the wood. 'My name is DCI Jack Lambert, Mr...?'

'McCullagh. Brian McCullagh.'

'Nice place you have here,' Gerrard said.

The massive barman laughed, his belly straining against the apron, eliciting a wheezing cough that pointed to years of smoke abuse. 'Nay chance, pet,' he said, a slight twinge of Geordie creeping into his accent. 'Place is a shithole. But people seem to like it here.'

'I'll get straight to the point,' Jack said. 'Do you know a Mr Gus Fenwick?'

'Well of course I do,' the barman said. 'He's been a regular here for years.'

Jack waited for Gerrard to take out her notepad before continuing. 'And was he here last night?'

The barman's long tongue snaked out over his lip as if searching for a lost memory. 'Aye, I believe he was.'

'Between what times?'

'Must have been around half seven onwards. I know he stayed until around closing, always does.'

Jack shifted on the bar stool, aware that one leg seemed shorter than the others. 'Do you know if he was with anyone?'

'Gus? Nah, he never is. Although, in here, we're all friends; isn't that right, Vic?'

A grunted response came from a man at the end of the bar who looked about ninety years old, his nose bright red and pockmarked. He barely even looked up at them, white hair sprouting out of his ears as large, drooped eyelids gazed down at the dregs of his pint.

'So, just to be clear, Mr McCullagh, you can confirm that between the hours of half seven and twelve, Gus Fenwick was in this bar, drinking?'

'Yes, I believe I can.'

'Can you tell me what he's like as a person?'

The barman seemed to search his thoughts before responding. 'Can't say I can, really. He likes a drink, keeps to himself, never any bother. He'll chat if spoken to but doesn't usually make the first move.'

'Do you know his wife, at all?'

'Can't say I do,' he said, red-veined eyes wandering over to Gerrard. 'We don't get many women in here.'

Gerrard somehow managed to stay silent.

Jack motioned towards a CCTV unit in the corner. 'Seems unusual for such a close-knit community pub.'

The barman shrugged. 'Isn't connected anyway. It's just a precaution. We had a break-in a few weeks back. Say, you don't know anything about that, do you?'

'I'm afraid not,' Jack said, standing. 'Please, take my card and, should anything come to you regarding Gus Fenwick, do not hesitate to get in touch.'

The barman studied the card, his scourer-like eyebrows crunching down over his sunken eyes. 'Say, old Gus isn't in any trouble, is he?'

'I'm sorry, Mr McCullagh, I'm not at liberty to say.'

Gerrard waited until they were outside before speaking. 'Looks like he was telling the truth.'

'Only about being in the bar at the time he said he was. That still doesn't account for anything from midnight onwards—or before,' he added.

'Now what?'

He shivered and zipped up his jacket. It felt like deep winter had hit already and it was only late November. It didn't help that he'd lost nearly a stone in the last few months thanks to a new gym routine, courtesy of a personal trainer he basically paid to torture him. Once this was sorted he was determined to find the time to invest in some new clothes. 'Let's get back to the house and see what we can find.'

They arrived at the farmhouse some ten minutes later just as the first drops of that day's promised rain began to land. Scene of crime officers were out in force, going over every patch of ground in painstaking detail, still. Jack was met by a distinctly grumpy and windswept Jane Russell.

'Where have you been?' she chastised.

'What do you mean?' he said, unable to hide his anger. 'I've been questioning the suspect and we've been to the pub to see whether Fenwick's story checks out.'

Jane stood, hands on angular hips. 'And does it?'

'Yes, but that doesn't mean anything.'

Gerrard cleared her throat. 'I'll go see what's going on in the tent,' she said, leaving.

Brushing her fringe out of her eyes, Jane said, 'I've been trying to ring you.'

'Have you?' He fished out his phone. 'It's this blasted new phone I've got. It doesn't seem to work properly.'

She emitted a barely perceptible tut. 'I rang to tell you that we found evidence of dog hair in the house which, on its own, would seem to contradict the idea that his dog died some months ago.'

'Things like that have a way of remaining, though,' Jack said, playing devil's advocate.

'That's what I thought, but then it goes against everything else we've found in there.'

Jack motioned for them to head into the house. Getting a tongue lashing as well as being rained on wasn't his idea of a good time at this time of year. 'And what have you found?'

They suited up and entered through the main door. Jane motioned around the room. 'What do you notice?'

'It's spotless,' he said.

'Exactly. So, are we seriously saying that, although his dog died six months ago, he hasn't cleaned up any of the fur despite scrubbing everything else to within an inch of its life?'

Jack nodded. 'Good work. He clearly has a dog.'

'Yes but that is where it becomes more complicated,' DI Russell said. 'The vet confirmed that Gus Fenwick's dog, Chester, was put down six months ago due to old age. If he does have a new dog, the vet knows nothing about it. Plus, it begs the question as to where the hell it is.'

Jack scratched nervously at his freshly-shaven face. *It has to be the farmer,* he thought. 'I need to think about this,' he said, beginning to pace. 'We get a call from Gus Fenwick around seven this morning stating he has found a body in his field. The man, Robert Norris, known to us through previous criminal activity, is the victim. He has been tortured via a dog bite, pitchfork stabbing and, finally, killed using a rock. At least, that's how it looks at first glance. The evidence shows that Norris at least made it to the house before being chased away. We apparently know that Gus Fenwick was out between around 7pm and midnight. We don't know Norris' motive outside of the theory that he was simply looking to steal from the residence. We also don't know whether Gus Fenwick was even there or whether he does or doesn't have a dog.'

Jane cut in, 'I thought it was ironclad?'

He stopped pacing. 'It bloody well should be! How much more obvious can it be?'

DI Russell stopped dead in her tracks, clearly shaken by his outburst. 'I don't know.'

'I'm sorry,' he said. 'But this is ridiculous.'

'I agree,' she replied. 'But, if we can match any fingerprints and/or footprints to the murder scene then I think we have enough to put him there.'

Jack sighed. 'Except he admits to finding him this morning so he will be linked to the scene.'

'Oh.'

'And there is one further question we need answers to.'

'What's that?'

'If we can safely assume that two of the footprints belong to

Robert Norris and Gus Fenwick, who does the third set of prints belong to?'

DI Russell paused. 'The murderer?'

If that was the case, then the real killer was still out there and Jack's murder wall was about to be dusted off and put to use once again.

CHAPTER FIVE

Jack glanced at his wristwatch and groaned. Having spent a restless night tossing and turning over the murder of Robert Norris, he'd finally dragged himself up at 4.30am. It had been nearly a year since he'd suffered from such insomnia, but it wasn't new to him. What was new was operating without copious amounts of caffeine to help medicate him through the day.

His personal trainer, Rachael, had encouraged him to drop the substance as, in her words, 'your body should be your temple; you wouldn't put diesel in a petrol car, so why put that shit inside you?' He'd found it hard to argue with her logic, particularly once the weight had started dropping off. He didn't tell her about his continued love for whisky, but what she didn't know wouldn't hurt her. As it was, he was almost at his fighting weight from fifteen years ago and he still found he was able to enjoy a drink here and there.

Something told him he'd be having a few more of those before he was done.

He could feel the oppressive atmosphere as he entered the station just a couple of hours later. It hadn't taken long for

Watkins to appear, his usual chipper-self grating on Jack's frayed nerves.

'You gonna do the talking, guv?' Watkins asked.

Jack nodded. They'd managed to secure a twenty-four-hour extension on holding Gus Fenwick in relation to the murder, much to the chagrin of DSI Logan Edwards, Jack's boss and perennial pain in the backside. Even though he'd suffered a heart attack the previous year, he was clinging on to his job, despite the vultures circling.

He let out a frustrated breath. If they didn't find more damning evidence soon, Gus Fenwick would be let go. Hence their visit to Robert Norris' parents' house.

Angie Norris invited them into her semi-detached, three-storey home on the outskirts of Wallsend. 'I'm sorry there isn't anywhere to sit, detectives,' she said. 'But everything has been boxed up as we're about to move.'

'That's quite alright, Mrs Norris,' Jack replied. 'We sit down too much as it is anyway.'

She gave him a weak smile. 'I can't even offer you a coffee.'

Jack waved her away but Watkins appeared disappointed. 'Where are you moving to?'

He watched as Robert Norris' mother picked up an old photo frame, blew some dust off it, rubbed the corner, and placed it into one of the many boxes that had taken up residence in her sprawling living room.

'Ralph and I are downsizing.' She paused, wiping a worn sleeve across her face. 'Now that the kids...'

Jack sensed an intense sadness in the woman, not just at the loss of her eldest son, but something that ran much deeper. Her ill-fitting clothes suggested she had lost weight. She hadn't renewed her wardrobe and that suggested she had other things on her mind. Still, he couldn't comment. Her face also carried more lines than a woman of her age would usually live with. Everything about her screamed stress.

Not one to usually feel emotional around people, Jack couldn't help but feel for her. 'I'm very sorry for your loss.'

She met his gaze, as if suddenly shocked by his presence. 'Oh, yes, thank you.'

'Is your husband not home?'

'No, he's at work. They offered him time off but...'

Jack could relate. Sometimes work offered the only respite from emotional turmoil. 'We all cope in different ways.'

'Of course, Ralph isn't Robert's biological father,' she said, as if to explain it.

'Really? I didn't know that.'

'He adopted him when he was a teenager but they never saw eye-to-eye. Robert's real father was a piece of work from Liverpool. I haven't seen him in years.' She met Jack's gaze. It told him all he needed to know.

'And do you know whether Robert was in contact with his father?'

She snorted. 'I couldn't say. He was never bothered about him whilst he was growing up so I don't see why he would be bothered now.'

'And is he still in Liverpool?'

'No, he's lived in the north east for years but we haven't had any contact for some time.'

'And Robert's siblings?'

She sighed and took a seat on a nearby box, as if suddenly devoid of energy. Her eyes were somehow both striking and lifeless. 'Two boys, both in secondary school, both Ralph's.'

'And are they...' Jack began.

Angie Norris laughed without humour. 'Tearaways?'

He shrugged. 'For want of a better word.'

'No,' she said. 'But Robert's behaviour was starting to rub off on them, especially the eldest, Luke. I had to make a decision. We couldn't keep going as we were. Robert was non-responsive. We had to kick him out. You must think me a terrible mother.'

Jack knelt down beside her and took her slim hands in his own. 'Absolutely not. We all have a choice over how we behave and that always has an impact on others. You had the rest of your family to think about.'

'But he was my family and I let him down.'

'You did what you thought was best. This isn't your fault.'

'Thank you,' she said, taking out a tissue and dabbing her face with it.

'Mrs Norris, I know this is the worst possible time but I have to ask you a couple of questions about Robert to try and determine what happened.'

She tensed. 'I thought an arrest had been made?'

'It has, but we haven't pressed any charges yet. We are currently trying to piece together what happened. Do you know where Robert was staying and who he was mixing with?'

She shook her head. 'I have no idea. He came back a couple of months ago and begged for some money, said he was in trouble.'

'Did you give it to him?'

'No,' she said.

He saw the lie but decided not to push it any further. 'So you have no idea whether he was involved in any local gangs or anything like that?'

'No, I'm sorry, but it wouldn't surprise me if he was.'

He decided to be blunt. 'Do you know of any reason why he would be looking to rob a farm out in Northumberland?'

'Absolutely none. I'm sorry I can't be of any help to you, detective.'

Jack stood to leave. 'Don't worry, you've been more than helpful.'

Angie Norris saw them to the front door through the narrow passageway. Although sparsely decorated now, he could feel the history in the house—a history this family no doubt wanted to get away from. The ghost of Robert Norris' misdemeanours was clinging to the walls.

'They've invited us to view the body later on today,' she said.

Jack nodded. Based on the gruesome end that Robert Norris had met, it wouldn't be a pretty sight. 'Please, if you think of anything else, don't hesitate to contact me.' He handed her his card. 'Oh, and just before I go, what was Robert's biological father's name?'

'Les,' she said. 'Les Holding.'

They thanked her for her co-operation and made the short walk back to the car. He turned and saw Angie Norris stood, stock-still, staring into the distance, stuck in a tortured trance. She'd suffered an unspeakable tragedy and would no doubt blame herself for the rest of her life. Jack's sympathy was all dried up now, though. He had other issues to deal with.

'So he's a troubled teenager with a violent dad who gets kicked out of home nearly two years ago,' Watkins said. 'Not much to go on.'

Jack clipped his belt in and started the engine. 'I wouldn't say that.'

Watkins looked surprised. 'No? How come?'

'Les Holding,' he said, indicating to pull out. 'That's a name I know.'

'Really?'

He cleared his throat. 'Just from a long time ago. Buckle in, we've got an appointment at a fish shop.'

'Oh God, no.'

CHAPTER SIX

J ack pulled in just down the road from McGuinness Aquatics. 'Just wait here for now,' he instructed.

He hadn't had any contact with his former employer, Dorian McGuinness, since the previous year. He pulled his collar up to fight back against the cold and jogged towards the shop. After what had happened in the abandoned factory, he felt uncomfortable taking anyone else in with him when having to question the crime boss.

Jack's past never felt far away, and his time running with the crew as an impressionable young man had left deep scars that never quite healed.

He was sure McGuinness had committed murder that night in the factory. However, it would be impossible to prove. The dirt McGuinness had on him also made it difficult for him to push the matter further. He'd have to go after him sooner or later, though, before he became another one of his victims. That was how it worked. Since he had joined the force they had both danced around each other like two boxers sizing each other up. However, as with all fights, they'd have to engage sooner or later. Jack just hoped he could secure the knockout victory he needed when the time came.

'Here to see the boss?' Henry Stafford, Dorian's new right-hand man, greeted him at the till.

Jack nodded and was shown through to the back of the shop. Just last year Jack had attacked Stafford in a pub after being assaulted in his own home. As he walked through, he could feel the stale, warm breath of the hired heavy on the back of his neck, a warning that told him he hadn't forgotten. He wasn't frightened of Stafford, though. He'd fought bigger and won.

'Someone here to see you, Dorian,' the former George Michael lookalike said.

'Ah, Jack, what a nice surprise!' Dorian McGuinness greeted him, dragging his considerable bulk up from his immaculately-polished mahogany desk. 'I must say, it's been a while.'

'Dorian,' Jack said, taking a seat.

He looked over the crime boss and noted what difference a year had made to his appearance. Whereas he had lost weight and cleaned up his lifestyle, McGuinness had only grown fatter, with flecks of grey appearing around his temples. Jack couldn't help but wonder what battles he had been fighting in the last twelve months to have warranted such a change. Truth be told, he'd rather not know.

'How can I help you?' he asked, retaking his seat.

'Les Holding.'

Dorian's smile evaporated. 'What about him?'

'He still doing business with you?'

'Here and there.'

'And what about Robert Norris?'

He frowned. 'Who is that?'

'Holding's son.'

'Can't say I've heard of him.'

'So you can confirm that Robert Norris hasn't been working for you at all?'

'Have I not made that clear?'

Jack sighed and stood to leave. 'If you speak to Les before I do, tell him I'd like to have a word with him.'

McGuinness bristled, seemingly unused to being told what to do, before relaxing once more, his pointed features softening. 'I will do, detective.'

Jack noted the rolling of the last word off McGuinness' tongue, like a snake hissing as it closed in on its prey.

He made to leave before pausing, turning to face his former employer. 'I see your property development plans are moving ahead on the Quayside.'

McGuinness beamed. 'Ah, yes, a wonderful outcome for everybody involved. I must say, the good press on it has really helped.'

Indeed it did. David Robson, having also been rescued from the warehouse by Dorian McGuinness, had spent the last twelve months writing nothing but positive stories about the aquatic shop owner. It seemed at least one of them was paying his debt off.

As if reading his mind, Dorian said, 'Mr Robson has been most helpful, Jack. It seems he is keen to repay me for my generosity in saving his life. It makes me wonder when you will do the same.'

He didn't trust himself to stay calm so he turned on his heels and left McGuinness to it. Paying him back was what he was afraid of. Everybody knew that Dorian called in his debts sooner or later. Jack had done a good job of avoiding him for the last year but it seemed their paths were inevitably due to cross once again.

'I'll be seeing you,' Stafford called as Jack made his way out of the shop.

I'll be ready, he thought.

'How'd it go?' Watkins asked once he was back in the car.

'Holding is still doing the odd bit of work for him,' he replied. 'I'm sure he'll be in touch before too long.' He gunned the engine and pulled out.

'Seems a long shot.'

'Agreed. But what other choice do we have?'

'Now what?'

'We head back to base,' Jack told him. 'I want the team in the MIR.'

CHAPTER SEVEN

'Fuck you!'

'Calm down, Reaves.'

He watched as the scene unfolded before him. He'd seen it multiple times in the workshop at HMP Kirklevington. Reaves, frustrated by his lack of co-ordination, was hitting out at people around him. To be fair to the tutor, he always seemed to take it in his stride. He'd no doubt seen worse; they'd both been in Frankland and they made this lot look like a bunch of debutants. He picked up the chisel and got back to his project, kept his head down. Made them think he wasn't watching.

'Why the fuck should I calm down? I told you I couldn't do it!'

The tutor stepped forward, close enough to assert dominance but not close enough to threaten. A common technique the prison educators seemed to employ. He noticed that the man was wearing a particularly expensive-looking watch today.

'And I told you, Reaves, that I'd be with you in a minute, son.'

He smiled inwardly. If there was anything that was going to get Reaves' back up, it was being talked down to. He knew the man well enough to know his triggers. In fact, he made a point of getting to know everybody's triggers who he was spending time inside with.

'Don't you fucking call me *son!*' Reaves raged, spittle flying across the short space between him and the tutor.

The tutor backed up a step, clearly aware he'd made a blunder. He could see his eyes darting left and right, looking for help. He wouldn't find it here. The other inmates were a mixture of heads-down and excited at the prospect of a mini riot in the workshop. Sure, the blokes here in Kirklevington were deemed almost ready for release, but old habits died hard.

'I'm sorry, Reaves, I didn't mean any offence,' the tutor said.

Reaves reared up, squared his shoulders back. He wasn't a big fella but he knew how to carry himself as a threat. Being inside, you either acted the hard man or you kept to yourself, throwing in a little weirdness for a bonus point. Reaves had opted for the former approach but he wasn't buying it. He'd met hard men, hell, he was one of them. Real hard men didn't need to act the role, they just carried an aura. Nah, he wasn't buying Reaves' stunt. He'd seen him when the chips were down. Reaves wasn't the kind of man you could rely on in a fight.

'I should shank you right here, you fucking prick!' Reaves spat.

He was getting a headache now; his fellow inmates had a habit of doing that to him from time to time. He found himself unable to concentrate on his task. He looked up, clocked one or two of the boys moving in, saw where it was heading. He sighed, placed the chisel down, started walking.

'I... don't want any trouble, Reaves,' the tutor stuttered.

He knew the man was losing control. He'd shown weakness. He could almost smell it above the glue and sawdust of the workshop.

'Well you've got it now.'

He managed to take hold of Reaves' fist before he had the chance to launch it forward. The skin-headed criminal turned, sunken grey eyes turning wide as he clocked him.

'That's enough.'

'But this prick...'

He stayed silent.

'Aye, no bother, man,' Reaves said, his voice betraying the slightest hint of a tremor.

He turned to face the rest of the group, each one's eyes hitting the floor as he laid his own upon them. The implication was clear.

Get back to work.

'Thanks for that, Olsen,' the tutor whispered as he passed him by.

He shrugged, walked back to his work bench, picked up the chisel.

No problem.

He didn't give a shit about Reaves or the tutor. But, for what he had planned, he needed both of them.

CHAPTER EIGHT

The assembled officers quietened down into an intense hush as Jack entered the MIR. Such was the palpable tension he almost felt the urge to salute. DI Russell, DS Christensen, DS Watkins and DC Gerrard all looked to him as he cleared his throat to speak.

'Okay, let's start with what we know. Robert Norris, twenty-two, is found, we are told, by Gus Fenwick at around 7am two days ago.' He turned to the board behind him and placed a mugshot of both victim and suspect at the top. 'We know,' he said, turning to face the room once more, 'that Gus Fenwick was at The Black Horse, in Northumberland, the previous night between around 7.30pm and midnight. From there, Fenwick tells us that he went straight home and didn't notice anything untoward.'

'Yeah right,' Watkins snorted.

Jack pressed on, tossing each officer a photograph of Robert Norris' tortured body. 'We believe the victim was bitten by a dog and stabbed multiple times with a pitchfork before having his head smashed in with a rock.' Out of the corner of his eye he saw Gerrard wince. 'The pathologist's report is imminent on that, but she was willing to offer up a best guess at the time.' His mind briefly wandered to Rosie, still on the sick from the previous year's events. She would never have played such a guessing game. Jack hadn't spoken to his former lover since that time. Unfortunately, things between them were now so bad that any attempt at contact would undoubtedly be met with hostility. 'Gus Fenwick maintains his innocence and, amazingly, the evidence is currently inconclusive.'

'It seems obvious, though, doesn't it?' Watkins piped up.

'Indeed it does,' he agreed. 'But seeming obvious is not enough to get a conviction. Gerrard, what else do we know?'

The young DC sprang to her feet and dived straight in. 'According to the lab the rock we believe was used to kill Robert Norris had no prints on it.'

'Meaning?' Jack pushed.

'Four possible explanations as I see it,' Christensen chipped in. 'Either Gus Fenwick was in the house, wearing gloves, when he came across Robert Norris; or he wiped the rock afterwards; or it wasn't him. If it wasn't him then the person who committed the murder must have been waiting for Norris at the property for some reason.'

'What's the fourth scenario?' DI Russell asked.

Christensen turned to her. 'That Fenwick planned the whole thing and was waiting for Norris to arrive.'

The team took a moment to process the details.

'All of those options trouble me,' Jack said. 'If Fenwick knew he was coming, or somebody else did and was waiting for him, that points to something beyond a failed burglary.'

Jane Russell picked up the thread. 'And if that's the case, then we have to assume that both something specific in the house was worth taking; and that Robert Norris was set up.'

'And don't forget the dog,' Watkins added. 'Fenwick's dog died six months ago but we found evidence of dog hair in the house. A canine was definitely on the scene, so...'

Gerrard spoke up. 'So either he rented a dog for the night, he is lying about having a dog and is hiding it or...'

'Or somebody else was in the house waiting for him,' Jack said. The detectives looked to each other. 'We need to get back in that house.'

He took Christensen with him to the farmhouse on account of the others having already spent time there. He valued the Scandinavian's opinion and it wouldn't hurt to have a fresh set of eyes on the scene. Jane had stayed behind to co-ordinate things in the MIR, with Watkins and Gerrard going over details of the people closest to Robert Norris. He'd hesitated before that final instruction, aware that Watkins held some kind of attraction for the young DC.

For Gerrard's part, she seemed blissfully unaware of the DS's feelings towards her, no doubt putting his babbling nature in her presence down to his usual nerves. She hadn't seemed to realise that Watkins was generally a much more confident person these days.

He'd have to keep an eye on the situation. Workplace romances very rarely worked out; he could attest to that. Still, with his own complicated history, he was in no position to dictate what people did in their private lives.

Forcing it out of his mind he turned to Christensen. 'Tell me what you see; I've already been here. I want your opinion without any filtering.'

The squat DS nodded and limped towards the centre of the room. 'At first glance it seems spotlessly clean,' he said in his own, unique brand of Geordie-Scandi dialect. He ran a finger over a mahogany table. 'Not even a trace of dust.'

Jack watched as he made his way around the room. He could practically taste the smell of fresh wood polish, mixed in with the potent aroma of potpourri. He wriggled his nose. It reminded him of his mother and her obsession with the stuff, never mind that it caused him to violently sneeze as a child. He smiled at the memory.

'Neat as a new pin,' Christensen continued.

'I know that,' Jack said. 'Look beyond that, though. Tell me what you see.'

The DS offered up his usual no-nonsense brand of communication. 'I see nothing.'

They continued their tour of the house, with each room portraying a similar picture to the first. At the back of the property lay an open-plan dining room which led into the kitchen, complete with more mahogany furniture. Above the sink was a large, wood-framed window which looked out onto the back of the farm. The bench didn't have any pots or pans on it and Jack took the opportunity to touch two matching tea towels which were hanging over the sprawling white cooker in its brick alcove. They were bone dry.

'Something just isn't right with this,' Jack said. 'Where's the bedroom?'

They found what Jack assumed to be the master bedroom to the left of the property, just off from the living room. Again, everything seemed untouched. The bed was made and was cool to the touch. A single oak wardrobe stood in the corner; it looked like something out of an IKEA catalogue. Jack resisted the urge to joke about it, unsure how his colleague would react. Christensen had never displayed a temper but, then again, he never had to. His aura was enough on its own.

'This not seem odd to you?' Christensen asked, as he nonchalantly dimmed and undimmed the main light above the bed.

'This whole thing seems odd.'

'No, think about it,' he said. 'Let's consider this. Gus Fenwick usually lives here with his wife but she is unwell and is in hospital. How long has she been there?'

Jack shrugged. 'No idea.'

'Unless it's been years, I would say that the farmer has been living here alone.'

Jack started; the DS was right. 'Good observation,' he said, opening the wardrobe. An assortment of men's clothes were on the rack, all seemingly quite old. He also noted that there weren't many of them to start with. He brought a shirt to his nose and inhaled. It had the foisty scent of something not worn in a long time.

He furrowed his brow, as he often did when troubled. Rosie used to tell him it aged him ten years. The way things were going, this case would do that by itself.

'So the only thing living here, other than Gus Fenwick, is a dog that apparently died six months ago,' Jack said.

'It's got me stumped.'

'Me too,' Jack replied. 'Me too.'

CHAPTER NINE

'You seem pre-occupied.'

'I'm sorry,' Jack replied, forcing a smile. 'It's just this case.'

Ryan nodded and took a sip of wine. 'If you're not careful, you'll burn out.'

They fell into an easy silence as Jack ordered wholewheat pasta with a side of olives. Ryan went with steak.

Jack looked across the table at the man he'd been seeing for nearly six months now. His brief foray into the world of online dating had yielded few results, with more than one date leading to Jack having to remind the bloke that he was a policeman. In the end, he'd met Ryan just as he was about to give up on the whole process. Their early encounters led to Jack realising that they had quite a few things in common.

Ryan had also come out in later life, having also started a family first. He had two sons to an ex-partner, both teenagers now, but they were estranged. Things weren't quite so bad for Jack with his daughter Shannon but there was no denying he wasn't a firm presence in her life.

Unlike Jack, however, Ryan didn't have a dodgy background,

and had worked as a pharmacist for the last six years. After his failed experiment with the oddballs online, Jack had played it safe by using the domestic violence disclosure scheme to check out his background. Of course, he never told him that. Ryan would have taken a dim view if he'd known of Jack's intrusion.

'I know,' he finally said. 'But this is how it is for me. I expected to have this wrapped up by now but nothing is adding up.'

'You want to talk about it?'

He shook his head. 'No, I can't really.' He watched as his partner shrank back, as if slapped. 'I mean it's not exactly dinner talk, is it?'

Ryan laughed, the tension broken. 'Don't lie to me, DCI Lambert.'

'Never,' he said, not quite sure if he believed himself. Opening up wasn't exactly his strong point.

They settled down to their food and Jack felt an easiness in Ryan's company. *Could I love this person?* he thought. Having not allowed himself to be open about his sexuality until recent years, the idea of loving another man wasn't something that had even crossed his mind before now. However, being around Ryan brought a happiness to his life; the kind of happiness he hadn't realised he could still feel since the death of his mother.

'What are you thinking about?' Ryan asked, bringing his knife to cut through the rare steak, causing a wash of red juices to swell across his plate.

Jack chewed down on his pasta, noting the copious amounts of garlic and chilli it had been laced with. He coughed and reached for some water. 'Nothing.'

'That a good thing?'

'I think it is,' he replied.

They finished up their meals and set off on a walk through Jesmond. He felt Ryan take his hand and he found himself flinching.

Ryan leaned in, the light aroma of his Hugo Boss aftershave tickling Jack's senses. 'Don't worry, it gets easier.'

He softened and gripped Ryan's smooth hand. Physically, they were opposites. Where Jack was a brute of a man, coarse, dark-featured and broad, Ryan was of a much slimmer build and fair-haired, standing some four inches shorter than him. It wasn't really about physical attraction for him, though. Well, perhaps a little. For Jack, he was just happy to be living a more authentic life now.

The fact that Ryan was easy on the eye was a bonus, of course.

'Are you going to stay over?' he asked.

Jack shook his head. 'I'm sorry, I have to be up early tomorrow.' He noted the disappointment in Ryan's face. 'So you should stay at mine,' he added.

His face lit up and Jack felt a pang of affection for him. Ryan's smile was infectious. *Maybe I am growing to love him...* he thought.

CHAPTER TEN

'Alright, guv,' Gerrard greeted him in the MIR. 'Do anything interesting with your evening yesterday?'

'Why would you ask?' Jack shot back.

The DC's brow crinkled. 'I don't know, because we are colleagues and perhaps, some would say, distant friends?'

'I...' he stuttered. 'Apologies, I'm just tired,' he said, catching her eye. 'And let's keep it at acquaintances.'

He'd not introduced the topic of his love life to work colleagues yet. The likes of Edwards wouldn't have understood anyway. But, as Gerrard had previously mentioned, rumours were going round. He'd no doubt have to broach the subject at some point, despite his annoyance at the fact that heterosexual couples would not have to do the same.

'Fair enough,' she said, sarcastically. 'Well I went to a Ru Paul-inspired event and it was fabulous; you should get yourself along sometime.'

'Ru Paul?'

'Yeah, queens,' she said. 'I'd have thought it would be right up your street.'

He bristled. 'And why is that?'

She shrugged. 'Because straight men love it and gay men love it even more. You going to tell me you're a transphobic homosexual?'

He frowned. 'I have no idea what you're on about.'

Gerrard laughed. 'Don't worry, I'll send you an email. Oh, by the way, Edwards was asking for you earlier.'

'Thanks, I'll go see him now.'

His phone rang from an unknown number as he approached Edwards' office. He forwarded it on and tapped twice on the frosted glass before entering.

'If you value your life you would wait for permission before entering my... oh, Jack, sorry, come in,' Edwards spluttered.

'Still looking to get yourself on a disciplinary, Logan?' Jack said. 'I'll be sure to wait next time.'

'Nonsense, you can come in anytime,' he said, straightening out his crumpled off-white shirt. Jack wasn't entirely convinced it was the natural colour for the garment. 'It's the others I can't stand,' Edwards added.

'I'll be sure to let Jane know.'

The DSI coughed, sending paper flying over his desk. 'Don't mention the Bulldog to me.'

Jack pulled up a chair and sat opposite the burly detective. 'Trouble in paradise?'

Edwards snorted. 'Something like that. She does this job for about five minutes on secondment and now she thinks she can swan around as if she owns the place.'

'You should tell her that.'

'The woman is impossible!' he exploded. 'I need you to rein her in.'

'Seriously?' he said. 'You must be joking?'

The DSI fiddled with his belt, underneath a giant protruding belly complete with what looked like soup stains on his lower buttons. 'Well if you don't, I will, then I really will get sacked,' he said. 'And given Dalton's disdain for you she'll be up for DSI and you'll be answering to her.'

Jack felt his insides twist. 'I'll get on it right away.'

Edwards brought a meaty hand up to his sweaty brow and sighed. His health scare the previous year, during the Open Grave Murderer case, had done nothing to encourage him to change his lifestyle. He was still in dire need of a shave, as well as a general wash. Jack had heard on the grapevine that Edwards had dressed up as Santa Claus in the past. He didn't think the man would cut the mustard now.

'Something on your mind, Lambert?'

Despite their long history and, Jack believed, their friendship, he still wasn't stupid enough to tell the DSI what he really thought. Jack wasn't frightened of his boss, but he did value his career.

'Right, good,' Edwards said.

'Is that all, then?' Jack asked.

'Not quite. Have you seen today's paper?'

'You know I don't read that rubbish, Logan.'

The giant DSI shook his head and tossed a crumpled *Northern Chronicle* at him. 'Well you might want to start.'

The paper was folded untidily to the puzzle page, where Edwards had half (and incorrectly) completed the sudoku. Swallowing his irritation Jack refolded the paper so he could read the headline: *'Police harass man as he defends home from yob intruder.'* He didn't need to look at who had written the piece.

'I'll call Robson and get him told.'

'So the suspect has gone to the press via his solicitor?' Edwards asked. 'Or is it someone he knows?'

He read the headline again. 'Unlikely, he's only just been released.'

'What?' Edwards thundered, bloodshot eyes widening.

'We can't keep him indefinitely, can we?'

'We can if we bloody well charge him.'

'There's not enough to charge him with.'

Edwards grimaced. 'How exactly is there not enough to charge him with if the body was found on his property, having run from his house, with his footprints at the scene?'

That was the question Jack had been asking himself all along. 'There just isn't.'

The DSI stood and began stomping around the room. 'This is unbelievable,' he thundered. 'Jesus, Jack, what the hell is going on?'

'That's what I'm trying to find out, Logan.'

'I'm going to have to take a closer look at this.'

He stood and met his superior officer's gaze. Jack was big, but Edwards was bigger. 'I'll not have you poking your nose into my investigation. I've been doing this for long enough without you, I don't need your interference now.'

The DSI's posture shrank like a dried sponge, as it often did when Jack stood up to him. 'Dalton and Guthrie will have my head for this.'

Jack winced at the use of the PCC's name. Like most in a position of authority, Nadine Guthrie wasn't Jack's biggest fan. Ever since her election the previous year she'd been getting more and more involved in what was going on at the station. Jack had done his best to avoid her so far. It seemed Edwards wasn't having such luck.

'Just blame me,' Jack said. 'And, in any case, aren't you retiring soon?'

'I can't retire, can I?' he replied. 'The wife will leave me.'

After a conversation the previous year, Jack thought she already had. 'Look, I'm in control of this, just let me do my job.'

Edwards held up the newspaper once more. 'You call this control?'

'It wasn't the suspect who went to the press,' Jack said. 'For one thing, he states he never saw Robert Norris until after the murder.'

'Then who was it?'

The look that passed between them said it all. The leaks from the previous year were still ongoing. The mole strikes again.

CHAPTER ELEVEN

Jack saw Les Holding from across the way; the AWOL father of Robert Norris was nursing a coffee almost the size of his fists. Back in the day, Les had been pretty handy with those fists, Jack seemed to remember. He'd never spoken of a son; which wasn't surprising given that the Holding Jack knew was someone who cared about nobody but himself. And money, of course.

He'd received the call just over an hour before from a sombre-sounding Holding, and he'd agreed to meet him at the Quilliam Brothers' cafe, a swanky, hipster establishment just by Newcastle's old red-brick university. Both Jack and Les stood out amongst the youthful swagger of its clientele; he couldn't remember the last time he'd seen so many oversized glasses and tweed jackets.

He told the barista he was meeting somebody, ordered a large Americano, and sat across from the man who had once been something of a friend. More of an accomplice, in actual fact.

'Jesus, you haven't changed much,' Les said, his slightly high-pitched whining Scouse accent in marked contrast to the physical presence of the man.

He shrugged. If Les had seen him a year ago he might not

have had the same opinion. As for the bloke opposite, he'd changed immeasurably. Sure, there was still a liveliness behind his wide, grey eyes, almost like he was constantly on speed, and the same nervous tic of sticking his tongue out and playing with the stubble below his lower lip was present, but Les had put on weight. A lot of it. The old tattoos, a hangover from his days at sea, were now a faded blue, stretched across thick, grey-haired arms, and his hair had receded almost as far as Gus Fenwick's. Les, like countless others, seemed loath to get rid of it, with what was left clinging on like the remnants of a dusted cobweb to a garage wall.

'You look a bit rough, I must say,' Jack told him.

A flash across the eyes. There it was, the old temper. 'Well I have just lost me son,' he said.

Jack's coffee arrived. He thanked the waitress and took a sip of the warm, black liquid, feeling the instant kick of caffeine raise his pulse. He had to admit, the coffee here was good; just the right amount of bitter. You paid for it though. His self-imposed caffeine ban hadn't lasted long but, the way the case was going, he was going to need a lot more of it.

'I would express sympathy, Les, but from what I hear you haven't been around much.'

'Spare me your lectures, Jack,' he snorted. 'It wasn't that long ago you were just like me, so get off your high horse.'

Jack leaned in. 'I never hit women.'

Holding laughed. 'From what I hear, it's men you like to hit on.'

Jack snorted. 'Maybe you're forgetting who you work for?'

Les cleared his throat once, twice and shook his head. 'No offence meant.'

'Anyway, I'm not here to score points,' he told him. 'I'm investigating a murder. And whilst I might not think much of your character, or care for your lifestyle, I am sorry about what has happened.'

Les' eyes dropped to his coffee. Jack noticed that he hadn't yet taken a drink. 'Aye, well, I wasn't really in the lad's life much, but it's my own fault.'

Jack said, 'I've met his mother.'

Holding sighed. 'Yeah, she's alright. Deserved better than me. She's remarried now. Hopefully he's treating her alright.'

'Well he's not a gangster, if that's what you mean, Les,' Jack said.

'We gonna sit here and argue all day or have you got something to ask me?'

Jack paused, Holding was right. Talking about his past often brought out the worst in him. He needed to remember who he was and not fall back into old habits. 'Thanks for agreeing to meet,' he said in a feeble attempt to restore some professional balance.

Holding chuckled. 'You think I had any choice? You don't say no to Dorian McGuinness.'

'Either way,' Jack said. 'It's important that we speak.' Jack finished his drink and ordered another Americano. He probably wouldn't sleep for the next week but it was so good it felt rude not to. He motioned to Les, who shook his head in muted response.

'So what do you want to know?'

'When did you last speak to Robert?' Jack asked.

Holding cricked his neck and looked out the window, his tongue lapping away at his chin stubble like a dehydrated dog. 'I've had the odd bit of contact.' His eyes met Jack's. 'His mother doesn't know.'

'Jesus, Les, was he involved with the crew?'

Holding didn't answer, called a young waiter over and ordered another cappuccino.

'I need to know, Les.'

'No.'

'Don't lie to me,' he said. 'If you need protection from Dorian, we can offer it to you.'

He snorted. 'Are you having a laugh? Do you know what happens to people who cross McGuinness? I value my kneecaps.'

Jack knew only too well.

'Well what can you tell me?' Jack pressed him, aware that Dorian would have briefed him prior to their meet.

The waiter arrived back at the table and placed another drink down in front of Holding. The old one was taken away, and Jack noted it had barely been touched.

'He was going a bit off the rails. Said that he couldn't stand things at home anymore, that the husband was fine but a bit dull and he couldn't live such a boring lifestyle so he was acting out.' Holding puffed up his barrelled chest. 'Got too much of the old man in him... had.'

Jack started. 'That's not a good thing, Les, or hadn't you noticed that your line of work tends to get people hurt?'

Holding shrank back like a wounded bullock. 'Aye, well, I'm just saying.'

'Go on.'

'So, aye, I had a word with Dorian, asked him if I could bring the lad once in a while, just to help out with the simple stuff.'

'Moving fish and whatnot?' Jack asked, rolling his eyes.

Holding laughed. 'Aye, that kind of stuff.'

He leaned over the table and could smell the stale stench of Holding's sweat above the coffee. 'Did Dorian okay it?'

Les didn't flinch. 'No.'

'You sure?'

'Aye, I'm sure. Any involvement with the lad was strictly under wraps, not even Dorian knew.'

Somehow, Jack doubted that. 'Are you involved in this?'

Holding shook his head. 'That farm had nothing to do with us. He only ever got involved in things through me and I had nothing to do with it.'

Jack believed him. 'So what *do* you know?'

Holding's eyes hardened. 'I know that the bloke you arrested has been released despite killing the kid.'

Jack felt himself grab the table. 'We don't know that; he's been released under investigation but the evidence isn't conclusive.'

'I know it, though,' he said, leaning in so their noses were almost touching. 'And if you can't do your job, I'll do it for you.'

Jack retreated back into the trenches. 'I don't want that farmer touched, do you hear me? If we were sure he'd done it, he'd be in a cell right now. As it is, the evidence isn't stacking up.'

'That's not what I hear,' Holding said.

'And what did you hear?' Jack said, his mind immediately wandering to the leak in the force.

Holding laughed, but it was hollow and without humour. 'Lots of things.'

'So, what, you're going to take matters into your own hands?'

'That's what we do, Jack, or had you forgotten?' Holding replied.

'If I get so much as a whiff of you approaching him...'

'You'll what? You've got no power round here, Jack. But, then, you already knew that.'

His mind flashed back to the warehouse the previous year, when Dorian McGuinness had rescued him from what he was certain would be his death.

He tried a different approach. 'If you just let me do my job, I'll find the killer and bring him to justice.'

Holding shrugged. 'Maybe. The clock's ticking, though, Jack.'

The hired heavy pushed his coffee to one side and raised his considerable bulk from the table. 'I'll let you pay for the coffee, seeing as you've moved up in the world.'

'If you want someone to blame for what's happened to Robert, Les, maybe you should start by looking at yourself.'

His words were lost in the noise of the cafe as Holding left without looking back.

CHAPTER TWELVE

Jack's meeting with Les Holding the previous day had done nothing to stem his continued unease with regards to Robert Norris' murder. The fact that Norris had turned to crime was hardly surprising, given what they knew about both him and the situation, but any potential link to the McGuinness crew was a serious problem. Added to that, Jack also had to contest with Holding, clearly unhinged, and threatening Gus Fenwick. He was unsure of his next steps, but felt reassured of the fact that Holding wouldn't immediately go after the farmer. Plus, Fenwick was currently holed up in a hotel known only to the police whilst they continued a forensic search of his house and the surrounding area.

Still, Jack was anxious. On some level, he always knew his fate would be linked to that of his former boss. They'd danced around each other in a tense but workable arrangement ever since his defection from the crew. However, if they were involved, even indirectly, in Norris' death, he would be forced to act. What he couldn't predict was how McGuinness would respond.

One thing was for sure, it wouldn't be positive for Jack, either way.

McGuinness was a tactical man. He never made a move without first thinking it through. Jack's near-death experience the previous year being a prime example. Whilst McGuinness had never told Jack he was in his debt, he also didn't need to. The fact that he hadn't immediately gone after the crime boss after what had happened proved his point. That looked like it was about to change.

'Guv,' Gerrard collared him in the MIR. 'I've done some digging regarding Fenwick's wife. My cousin works in medical records at the hospital there and the story does check out; she has been in a couple of months now after suffering a severe stroke. Doctors aren't sure whether she'll ever fully recover. We have no way of knowing if he's been visiting regularly or not, but they do think somebody has been coming by.'

'It's probably not relevant,' Jack told her. 'Still, it's good to know one angle to this story checks out, even if it is of no use to us.'

'You alright?' she asked.

'Why wouldn't I be?'

Gerrard shrugged. 'You just have that distracted look you get sometimes.'

'I wasn't aware I had a look.'

'Yes,' she said. 'It's that look you get when you know something, decide not to share it, and then act of your own accord.'

Jack smiled. 'Thanks for the analysis. I'm not about to go rogue, though, if that's what you mean. I do, however, want to speak with you all privately.'

He gathered the team in his office. Christensen and Gerrard sat, with Watkins pacing behind them. DI Russell stood, off to the side, leaning against the wall whilst checking for something underneath her fingernails. It was a perfect portrait of his closest colleagues. Watkins, full of nervous energy, Gerrard and Christensen, confident and unflappable, and DI Russell, aloof from everybody around her.

Jack wondered what impression he gave off.

'What's up, boss?' Christensen asked.

'Robert Norris' father, Les Holding, contacted me. We met, earlier this afternoon, in Newcastle.' He looked up and noticed that DI Russell had stopped fiddling with her nails and was now glaring at him. 'Les confirmed that he had been in contact with Robert, despite the victim's mother believing otherwise. He also confirmed that Norris was loosely working with the McGuinness crew. Although,' he added, 'he maintains that this was unknown to Dorian himself.'

Watkins spoke up. 'Maybe we'll strike lucky and be able to bring McGuinness in.'

Jack shook his head. 'That would be some stroke of luck.'

Watkins frowned. 'So we are back to square one.'

'Not necessarily,' Jack said, before pausing. 'Holding made a not-so-veiled threat towards Gus Fenwick. I don't believe he is in any immediate danger, though, and there is no way Holding could know Fenwick's whereabouts at present.'

'That doesn't sound positive,' Gerrard piped up.

'No, but if something were to happen, it won't be at the order of Dorian McGuinness. Having spoken with Holding today, I believe he's most definitely unhinged enough to act individually when it suits him. If Holding is that much of a powder keg, what is there to say he wasn't involved in getting Norris to visit the farmhouse that night? We can't rule out his potential knowledge or involvement. I believe we should start watching him closely.'

'It still doesn't explain the reason for targeting the farmhouse,' Christensen said.

Jack paused. 'Who's to say Fenwick wasn't the target?'

'You think it was more than a simple robbery?' the DS replied.

Jack shrugged. 'I have no idea, but we shouldn't rule it out.'

'Okay,' Gerrard determined. 'So, potentially, Holding ordered Norris there for some particular reason?'

'It's certainly one theory. Anybody else got anything?'

'But if we assume, as we are now, that Fenwick didn't murder him, then who did? It still doesn't add up,' Watkins said.

Jack held a hand up to stop him. 'We are looking at the end game before putting the pieces into place. Nobody finishes a jigsaw without first working the edges and separating out all of the pieces. That's what we are doing now.'

'Good analogy, guv,' Gerrard said.

'Thanks, I've been working on it,' he replied. 'Now, let's get to work. Gerrard, look into Holding's background and movements, see if anything comes up. Christensen, speak with Norris' mother again, give her what we know, and see what she says.'

Christensen stood, nodded, and limped from the room.

Jack adjourned the impromptu meeting and made to leave, only to find his escape blocked by DI Russell.

'I see you're off on your own again,' she said.

He found his temper instantly rising. 'You want me to have accompaniment every time I follow up a lead?'

He could sense Watkins' embarrassment behind him. The DS hadn't been able to manoeuvre out before Jane had pounced.

She stepped towards him and raised an emaciated finger towards his chest. He could smell her perfume, the bitter aroma stinging his eyes. 'I expect you to treat your team with a bit of respect.'

He bristled. 'That's a hell of a thing for you to say, Jane. If anyone isn't a team player here, it's you.'

'Oh really? Why don't you ask your DS how he feels about it, then?'

Jack turned and was met with the bright red features of Watkins' face. 'I... keep me out of it.'

'Fine!' he shouted. 'The pair of you are coming with me.'

'Where to?' Watkins asked.

'We need to speak with Gus Fenwick again. If there was something in the house that was of value, he will have known about it. If the target was him, then there has to be a reason. Either way,

I'm assuming he knows, and in the spirit of teamwork I think it best we go together.'

The journey passed in a prickled silence. As the farmhouse and surrounding land were still an active crime scene, Gus Fenwick was now staying in a nearby hotel. The specialist crime unit were still there and, given the size and complexity of the area, it would be some time before the farmer was able to return home. If they could prove he'd killed Robert Norris, then the chances were it was a journey he'd never make.

He didn't need to see DI Russell to know she was glaring daggers at him from the back of the patrol car. Watkins, for his part, reverted to type and began jabbering on about nothing in particular.

'More rain, they reckon,' he said.

Jack mumbled a response and lowered himself down in the seat, taking the opportunity to take in the north-eastern country-side. Unlike Newcastle, which was a metropolitan hub of bridges, tall buildings and granite structures, Northumberland was as rural as it gets. Fields of lush green, laced with a layer of fine frost, passed them by as Watkins navigated the winding roads at a leisurely pace.

Out here, there were more trees than houses, and you were more likely to meet a tractor than a speeding moped as you drove across the undulating terrain. On some level, whilst Jack liked the idea of retiring to such a place, he knew he would miss the bustle and upbeat atmosphere of the city. He found himself wondering what Ryan's preference would be.

'Here we are,' Watkins said, indicating left and taking them down a short drive into the car park.

It was a local, family-run place, which looked like something out of *Pyscho*, one of Jack's favourite films. Net curtains greeted them from the twenty or so windows which sat above them over two floors. The walls were that awful pebble-dashed rendering, and the paintwork around the windows looked decidedly depressed.

'Not the nicest of places,' he pointed out.

Catching the Bulldog's face in the mirror, her scrunched up features told him she agreed.

'What room is it again?' Watkins asked.

'202.'

They made the short journey up the stairs to the second floor. Jack had never liked lifts and they didn't have a choice with this place as it was out of use anyway. He could feel his boots sticking to the busily-patterned carpet as they approached the room. From one or two of the off-white doors, he could hear the sound of booming TVs but, for the most part, the place seemed deserted.

'I'll do the talking,' he said, as they approached Gus Fenwick's room.

Jane snorted but remained silent.

He knocked twice but received no answer. He tried again.

'Maybe he isn't here,' Watkins suggested.

Jack put his ear to the door and could hear the faint sound of the TV playing out some kind of quiz show.

'The TV is on,' he said, turning back to the door and knocking again. 'Mr Fenwick, it's DCI Jack Lambert here, we need to speak with you.'

They were met with the sound of a buzzer going off on the show.

'He's probably just left the TV on,' Watkins said.

Jack could sense his nervousness. He shared it.

'Unlikely,' Jane piped up. 'Gus Fenwick doesn't strike me as somebody who leaves a TV on and goes out. Have you seen his house?'

'You're right,' Jack said. 'Stand back.'

He leveraged himself back and aimed his Doc Martens at the door—once, twice, three times, before the hinges gave in and the door swung open. He could hear Watkins spluttering as he pushed through into the motel room.

'We can't just go around breaking into places—' Watkins didn't get the chance to finish.

'Jane, get onto the station,' Jack said. 'Watkins, keep an eye on the rest of the residents.'

It was a reasonably-well decorated room, more modern than the outside anyway. Save for the net curtains, there was at least a well thought out colour scheme on the walls and a large, oak wardrobe in the corner. The double bed looked sturdy and, like most places, a complimentary tea and coffee set had been left next to a cheap Asda kettle. The only thing spoiling it was Gus Fenwick's body, hanging limp from the ceiling, attached to a piece of thick, coarse rope.

Somewhere in the corner of his psyche, Jack was aware that somebody had won £3,000 on the quiz show.

CHAPTER THIRTEEN

Watkins stepped into the room. 'Jesus...'

'Don't touch anything!' Jack shouted.

They could have been forgiven for thinking Gus Fenwick's death was a suicide, had it not been for the blood smeared around the room—up the walls, on the bedding, and the mirror above the TV. It looked like something out of *The Shining*.

Jack felt DI Russell tense beside him. 'Oh my God,' she said.

'Watkins, secure the corridor,' Jack repeated. He took out his phone and turned to DI Russell. 'Jane... Jane!' he shouted, bringing her out of her trance. 'Go and speak to the owner, make sure nobody comes in or out.' He looked back at the lifeless body of Gus Fenwick once more. 'And for God's sake, get onto the station!'

She paused, nodded without looking at him, and left.

It wouldn't be long before a team arrived. He slipped into procedure, and against all logic found himself checking for a pulse. Stepping carefully through the room, he raised his hand to the man's neck but was met with radio silence. Yep, definitely dead.

He resisted the urge to conduct a thorough search there and then. If he contaminated anything it could have dire consequences. Blood was visible up to the narrow hallway in the entrance to the room. Without proper overalls, gloves and boots on, it would be negligent of him to go running in.

Watkins stood nearby, his back to the room. 'How could they have known where he was?'

That is the million-dollar question, Jack thought. 'I don't know but I have a pretty good idea of who might have done this.'

'Holding?' the DS asked.

'Aye,' Jack replied. 'He has motive, already made the threat, and has connections.'

'He must have one sick imagination,' Watkins said.

The man Jack had once worked with most certainly did have a vivid imagination when it came to violence. If his memory served him right, Les Holding wasn't one to shirk a fight and certainly had it in him to kneecap the odd rival gang member. But murder? Torture on this level? Still, he was of the belief that Gus Fenwick had murdered his son.

Jack felt his insides lurch as he thought back to their previous conversation. He'd been sure Fenwick wasn't in any immediate danger. The scene laid out before him begged to differ.

Despite being stuck in the doorway, now, Jack was able to get a reasonable look into the room. Cream, damp-splattered walls were now covered in sporadic spurts of blood. It looked dry, which suggested that the killer had left some time ago. The experts would come to a firm conclusion on that, though. Fenwick's mouth was covered over with grey duct tape. Jack shuddered at the thought of the killer having tortured him, with Fenwick unable to scream.

He tuned into the room. The TV was blaring out the news now. News which would soon include details of Gus Fenwick's death—a suspect in a murder case who had been released. Jack's mind trailed back to the previous year, when an Open Grave Murderer suspect had turned up dead after being questioned by police.

History repeating itself.

Only the Open Grave Murderer was neat. This was an act of rage.

'I see you know how to pick 'em,' Bill Ivey's familiar voice called from the doorway.

'Bill,' Jack greeted him. He shook his old friend's hand. 'Thanks for getting here so quickly. Nothing has been touched and nobody has been in or out since we arrived.'

'Good,' Ivey replied. 'You know how I hate it when you contaminate my scene.'

Jack left as the junior pathologist arrived, her gasps permeating through the corridor. SOCO weren't far behind, with the team now in full flow. They reliably informed him that blood spatter was on the way. DI Russell had managed to stave off the curious onlookers from the other rooms with some stern words but it wouldn't be long before word got out.

'Come on,' Jack urged the detectives. 'Let's get back to the station.'

Jack could feel his stomach chewing itself on the drive back to police headquarters as he rolled the details over in his mind. Had his carelessness cost Gus Fenwick his life? He kept thinking back to his meeting at the cafe, the details of their discussion skipping through his mind on repeat. It hadn't even been a veiled threat.

It didn't take them long to make it back. Once there, Jack assembled the team in the MIR. Jane sat, stony-faced. Watkins' leg ticked with nervous energy. Even Gerrard looked flustered. Christensen sat stock-still, his features, as usual, unmoved.

'Alright,' Jack began. 'You all know what has happened. As if this case wasn't strange enough, Gus Fenwick has now turned up dead. The number one priority for us right now has to be the apprehension of Les Holding.'

Gerrard spoke up. 'Agreed. He has got motive.'

'He has,' Jack replied. 'He made a threat against Gus Fenwick when I met him yesterday.'

He could sense DI Russell tense out of the corner of his eye.

'It looks like it was a credible threat at the time,' Christensen said.

Jack paused. 'I suppose we have to view it as so.' The room knew what that meant. 'I'll take the consequences for that, obviously,' he added. 'But I'll be damned if he knew where to find him. That's what concerns me the most,' he sighed.

'You weren't to know, guv,' Gerrard interjected.

He waved her away. 'That's not important now. The way I see it we have three priorities now: inform Gus Fenwick's next of kin, locate Norris' father and re-search the house.'

'The house?' DI Russell asked.

He nodded. 'I think so but only once we've spoken with Gus Fenwick's wife. If Fenwick's murder was motivated by revenge, then that still leaves us with the conundrum of Robert Norris being there in the first place, not to mention his murder. We simply don't know what we are looking for. Here's hoping Mrs Fenwick's condition has improved enough so that she can shed some light on all of this. Everything is linked somehow, we just don't quite know how yet.'

The group paused for a moment. The low-level hum of computers churned over as they considered the details.

'I think you're right,' Christensen finally said.

'There's a first time for everything,' Jack replied. 'Okay, Christensen, you and I will speak with Margaret Fenwick; Gerrard, I want you and Watkins to co-ordinate the pick-up of Norris' father. You can reach me by phone should you need to.'

'I'll go to the house,' DI Russell said. 'Ring me when you know more.'

'Good idea,' Jack said, eyeing each of the team in turn. 'Now let's get to it.'

CHAPTER FOURTEEN

Olsen chipped away at his design. He'd been working on it for weeks now, each session involving a moulding of the odd section, followed by meticulous sanding. He was the dutiful student—quiet, focused and obliging. The tutor came over to appraise his work. They both knew the rules; tutors had to keep a professional distance from the inmates. They were criminals before they were students.

Olsen noted that the tutor was closer than usual today. That's because he wasn't seen as a threat.

The dutiful student.

Reaves was off on one again, everyone could see it. His eyes kept flitting to Olsen, who met his gaze with hostility. It told him all he needed to know.

Cut out the shit and get on with it.

'Your design should be ready soon,' the tutor told him.

Olsen could hear pride in the man's voice. He shrugged, he'd never been one to need praise. He knew his limitations and worked within them. He was good at some things, bad at others. He watched as the tutor moved towards Reaves, more of a shuffle than a stride, professional distance maintained on this occasion.

Reaves was clearly frustrated with his progress, but knew better than to act out once warned. It didn't help that Gibbons, a royal pain in the arse, was intent on jabbering on about how wonderful his particular piece of work was.

There was nothing Reaves hated more than other people getting praise over him.

The tutor was too long in the tooth to not understand that, though, and so hadn't said much to Gibbons. Reaves, ever watchful, seemed placated.

For now.

Olsen placed the coarse sandpaper down on the workbench and noted that he'd acquired a rather large spelk in his calloused hands. Gripping the end, he pulled, a momentary stab of pain followed by a trickle of dark, red blood. He watched it with some surprise: he hadn't bled at all since being inside.

His reputation went before him.

'Right, gang,' the tutor called out in his unnaturally high voice. 'That'll be all for today. Good work. Now, if you could just tidy the tools away we can get moving.'

Olsen moved towards the store cupboard at the back of the room and brushed shoulders with Reaves. He felt his fellow inmate stiffen before he realised who it was. Reaves stepped to the side. Gibbons was on Reaves' right, short and portly, carrying his tools in his thick, hairy arms. It was always a mad rush when tidying up. For some reason, prisoners seemed to have no concept of queuing.

They stepped out of the cupboard and Reaves immediately started playing up.

'Fuck you!' he screamed in Gibbons' face.

Gibbons, not one to lash out, turned, wide-eyed and mouth agape. 'W... what do you mean, like?'

Reaves' face lit up like a bonfire. 'I'm fucking sick of you and your fucking stupid fucking face!'

Olsen was two steps behind them as they faced off. Gibbons

wasn't much of a fighter, but if Reaves called him out he would have to respond. It wouldn't do to look soft in front of the lads.

Gibbons' eyes met Olsen's. Olsen stared back, unmoved. *No help here.*

The tutor heard the commotion. 'Right, lads, what is it now? Reaves, step away from Gibbons and calm down.'

Olsen almost smiled. If there was one thing Reaves hated, it was to be told to calm down. He could see the regret etched onto the face of the tutor as soon as the words came out.

'You fucking what!?' Reaves screamed.

'T... that's enough, Reaves!' he bellowed.

Olsen heard the tremor in his voice. The tutor looked behind him. The guards had appeared now, ready to step in. Unfortunately they were at least twenty yards away at the other side of the workshop. It wouldn't do for the tutor to back down either now. Once they show weakness to the inmates, they may as well pack up and go home. Olsen had seen it many times before. Staff turnover in this place was akin to that of reoffending statistics.

'I won't tell you again!' the tutor shouted.

Olsen watched as Reaves fumbled in his pocket. The tutor seemed unaware of the movement, instead his eyes flitting between Reaves, Gibbons, the guards and even Olsen.

'You're damn fucking right you won't!' Reaves shrieked.

The next few moments defined the whole interaction. Olsen watched, almost in slow motion, as Reaves' fist unfurled to reveal the chisel. The tutor, eyes wide, tried to lunge to the left, out of the way. The guards in the corner of the room were some ten yards away now, descending upon them. Gibbons, paralysed by fear, simply stood stock-still, unable to move. Olsen took a step back from the three of them and placed his hands on his head; *nothing to see here, officer.*

The lead guard was quick, and had stepped ahead of the others, baton raised. Olsen recognised the look in his eyes. Some officers see their work as a vocation, believing in the rehabilitation of offenders. Others just get a kick out of wielding power. This guy definitely fell under the latter.

Just to emphasise his point, Olsen fell to his knees, hands still by his ears. Being a day-release prisoner, it wouldn't do to get caught up in something like this.

Gibbons wavered. Olsen recognised the signs.

When the blood was up, many prisoners lost their minds, like kids in a school playground. Unlike school, though, people in here got seriously hurt. The handful of other students in the room were jumping on the workbenches, screaming. Olsen drowned them out as he watched Reaves raise the chisel in the air. He was too far away to influence the outcome. Plus, it wasn't his place.

The guards were on point, hurtling towards Reaves rather than seeking to placate the other inmates who were simply jumping around like agitated monkeys.

The lead officer was only three yards away now. Olsen could almost see the chisel in the man's pupils as Reaves brought it down, edge meeting neck flesh. He stabbed it in with grim force, dragging it down behind the windpipe for maximum damage. He ripped it back out and a spray of blood doused both him and the guard as he was tackled to the ground. The others had stopped screaming now, aware that this had moved beyond a mere confrontation. Gibbons fell to the ground in a crumpled heap amongst the sawdust.

'We need an ambulance!' the lead guard screamed. He tackled the now non-responsive Reaves to the floor, jamming his arm up behind his back.

'It's too late,' one of the others called. 'He's dead.'

'Fuck!' the lead guard shouted.

They'd left Olsen alone, aware that he hadn't been involved in the confrontation. Sure, he'd be questioned about events, but he'd been as frightened as the others and didn't know what to do.

Is that okay, officer?

Of course it is, son. You weren't to know and it's not your place.

He glanced at his hand and noticed that his own blood had been replaced by that of the tutor, who was now laying lifeless on the floor.

Gibbons had now regained his senses and was hyperventilating next to the work bench, under the gaze of one of the guards. His stare met Olsen's and Olsen noted tears forming in the man's eyes. Gibbons was too weak to survive in this sort of environment.

That's why Olsen hadn't approached him to do the job. Reaves was a much better candidate. He watched as they dragged him away, their eyes meeting. Olsen gave an almost imperceptible nod as a grinning Reaves was manhandled to his feet, dropping the chisel in the process.

Putting the tools away was always a cramped process. They didn't seem to understand the idea of queuing. That meant that inmates were often bumping up against each other.

Just close enough to hand over a chisel without being seen.

CHAPTER FIFTEEN

The drive to the hospital was spent in uncomfortable silence, with Watkins' on-off FLO girlfriend, Gemma, in the back sulking. Apparently she'd expected Watkins to be with Jack and, upon questioning, the revelation that he was chasing up a suspect with Gerrard hadn't sat well with her. For Jack's part, he didn't care about Watkins' relationship status as long as it didn't impact on his work. That line was seemingly close to being crossed.

He was still sure Gerrard was none the wiser.

They parked in one of the police bays and made the short walk to the entrance. The early winter slush seeped into Jack's socks as he walked, causing an unwelcome squelch with each step he took. Margaret Fenwick had been moved to ward four, on the first floor, and was expecting their visit. The exact purpose of their visit, though, was unknown to her.

Hence Gemma's presence.

A short navigation past some pyjama-clad smokers was followed by a lift ride with an elderly man with a chest like a broken car engine. One buzzer later, they were face to face with Gus Fenwick's wife. She had been given a private room, a luxury most didn't get, to help aid in her recovery from her stroke. As

Jack entered, he got the sense that Margaret Fenwick had once been beautiful but a mixture of illness and the hardships of life had put paid to it. Still, there was some fight in her sky-blue eyes and her hair looked like it had recently been tended to. She was sat looking out of the window as Jack entered.

He cleared his throat. 'Mrs Fenwick?'

She turned and motioned for them to enter. Jack had instructed the FLO to wait outside until called for. They wanted to speak with Margaret briefly before breaking the news of her husband's death.

'I expected someone shorter,' she said, bluntly, her speech slightly slurred as if she were a punch-drunk boxer. 'Like him,' she added, pointing to Christensen.

Jack smiled. 'I'm sorry to disappoint, Mrs Fenwick.'

'Is this the point where I'm supposed to say "please, call me Margaret"?'

'That's generally how it works,' he replied.

She nodded, dabbed her eyes with a crumpled handkerchief, and returned her gaze to the window.

Without prompting, Jack and Christensen took a seat. A flash of anger moved across Margaret Fenwick's eyes as Jack noticed she'd spilled her orange juice on her food tray, beside an untouched bowl of cold congealed chicken soup.

Christensen leaned over. 'Let me sort that for you—'

'No!' she spat. 'Just leave it, for God's sake.'

The DS shrugged and sat back down.

'Mrs Fenwick, I'm here to ask you a couple of questions,' Jack began.

'I gathered that,' she replied. 'Get on with it, I have things to do.'

Jack wasn't sure what things a bedridden stroke victim could possibly have on her agenda but felt it was best not to ask. 'Are you aware of the break-in at your residence, which led to the discovery of a body on your property?'

Margaret cleared her throat. 'I can still read the news,' she said, motioning to a copy of the *Chronicle* on the bedside table.

'I'm going to be frank with you,' Jack said.

Margaret Fenwick shrugged her right shoulder, the left one currently in a state of paralysis. 'Go on.'

'We have absolutely no clue as to what has occurred,' he said. 'I don't know why Robert Norris, the murder victim, was seeking to rob the property, I don't know what happened when he got there and I don't know who killed him.'

Margaret's eyes met his. 'Does one need a motive for robbery? Was that not the aim in the first place?'

'If it was, then that points to your husband as being the killer. However, I don't believe he was.'

'Why not?'

Jack chose his words carefully, avoiding the use of past tense. 'Well do you think he is capable of murder?'

'Aren't we all?' she slurred. 'Anyway, is it even murder if somebody is protecting their property?'

Christensen spoke. 'It is when the victim is found tortured.'

Margaret Fenwick didn't react.

'Mrs Fenwick, can you think of any reason why Robert Norris, or anybody else, would want to rob the farmhouse? It's very important that we know. I don't believe this was a straightforward robbery gone wrong. I think that there was something of value in the house that he, or somebody else, was after.'

She turned to him once more. 'I would have no idea, detective. Ask Gus.'

Jack tugged at his collar. 'There's no easy way to tell you this, but I'm afraid your husband is dead.'

Margaret Fenwick's eyes widened momentarily before righting themselves. 'I see.'

'I know this must be a big shock to you, Mrs Fenwick, but we have to ask you a couple of questions regarding Gus,' Jack said.

He motioned for Christensen to tag in.

'Mrs Fenwick, do you know of any reason why somebody would want to hurt your husband?' the DS asked.

They were briefly interrupted by the rattle of under-oiled trolley wheels and cheap crockery as a nurse, complete with plastic bib, appeared in the doorway.

'Any hot drinks?' she asked.

'No,' Margaret Fenwick shot back.

Despite the abrupt rebuttal, the nurse simply smiled and moved on. She was probably used to it.

'So, as I was saying...'

'How long is your arm?' she cut in.

'I beg your pardon?'

She turned and fixed her withering gaze upon Christensen. 'I'm sorry, do you not speak English?'

If Christensen was annoyed, he didn't show it.

'Mrs Fenwick—' Jack began.

'Oh, do be quiet,' she spat. 'I have no idea who would want to kill my husband but that's only because I wouldn't know where to start.'

'I'm not sure I'm following you, Mrs Fenwick,' Jack interjected.

Margaret Fenwick raised her one good hand as if swatting a fly. 'My husband was a charlatan, Mr Lambert. He was a drunk, a gambler, a liar and a thief. My only surprise is that he wasn't killed sooner.'

Christensen shifted. 'Mrs Fenwick, if you don't mind my saying, you don't seem particularly upset with this news.'

'First of all, I do mind you saying and, secondly, that's because I'm not.'

Jack was perplexed. 'Excuse me?'

'For a detective, you really aren't that bright,' she observed. 'My husband and I have been estranged for some time. I haven't seen him in a long while. The way I see it, whatever happened to him was a long time coming.'

She shifted her gaze back to the window. Jack could almost feel the anger spilling from her pores.

Jack, although shocked at the manner in which he was being spoken to, had to admire her guts. 'If you and your husband are estranged, Mrs Fenwick, then why has he been visiting you in hospital?'

She turned back to him once more. 'In case you haven't noticed, I have been rather unwell. So, I don't have any knowledge of who has been to visit.' Her eyes narrowed. 'But I'd be surprised if it were him.'

Jack ran a weary hand across his brow. 'Who could it have been then? Another partner?'

Margaret Fenwick cackled like a dehydrated hyena. 'Believe me, Lambert, when you've been married to that pig you learn never to have another partner again.'

'A friend, family member?'

She shrugged. 'Nobody in my age range. Looks like you've got another mystery on your hands.'

Christensen spoke. 'Do you have any idea as to whether or not Gus Fenwick had or could have had something of value in the house?'

'It wouldn't surprise me,' she said, leaning towards him, her left hand hanging limp. 'But you can bet that whatever it was it didn't belong to him. That barman, McCullagh might know. The pair of them were thick as thieves.' She coughed. 'Both of them *are* thieves, as far as I'm concerned.'

Jack stood. 'Thank you, Mrs Fenwick, you've been most helpful. I'm afraid we will need you to view the body once you are well enough to do so, unless there's anybody else?'

'No, we never had kids, thank God. But please, I'll view the bastard. After all I need to make sure he's finally dead.'

Jack nodded. 'We have a family liaison officer here to assist you.'

Gemma appeared in the doorway, her foot playing with the doorstop rather sheepishly.

Margaret Fenwick waved her away. 'I won't be needing any of that. In any case,' she said, squinting in the direction of the door, 'that lass needs a good meal. And she certainly won't get it here.'

CHAPTER SIXTEEN

Olsen slinked through the trees, looking left and right like some kind of extra in a road safety ad. Only, this wasn't about being safe in traffic, this was about staying unseen. Unseen because he had a job to do—a job that paid well, much better than the shit they had him doing in prison.

He smiled as he recalled how easy it had been. That was the beauty of being in Kirklevington. Aye, the coppers knew he'd had a violent past, but Olsen was a careful man. Too careful to be caught for rearranging some drug dealer's facial features. He frowned at the memory of what had been done for him, though. Petty theft. He'd been drunk, as he often was in those days. They'd banged him up in Frankland to start with, with the real bastards.

Far from being intimidated by the convicted murderers he'd been thrown in with, he'd relished the challenge of vying for the alpha position. The general rule was to either be loud and brash or weird enough that people left you alone. Olsen had perfected the third way. Silence. It had done the trick. Nobody bothered him. Perhaps it was his awkwardly shaped skull that had put people off, a defect he'd been born with and, at one time, ashamed of. Not anymore. Now he used it to his advantage.

A car passed him by and he shrank back, away from view. He had to wait for a break in the traffic before heading across to freedom. A freedom he thought he'd never feel once he was banged up in Frankland.

No, the killers didn't bother Olsen one bit; it was the paedos he couldn't stand. Like most people in prison, he'd nurtured a real hatred for that lot. In his view, they were almost as bad as the rats.

A second car passed him by and he saw his chance, stepping out into the road and moving swiftly to the other side. Head down, he ploughed on. He was confident nobody had seen him. Emboldened by his escape, he straightened his posture, each step one step further away from the rats, the killers and the paedos.

And ex-police.

He snorted. The prison service hadn't been daft. They knew to separate the bent coppers and the paedos from the rest of the criminals inside. He took great pleasure in knowing that the disgraced coppers had been put into a 'special section' with that lot.

Not that he could have acted on his feelings, anyway. He knew there was always the chance of another job. That was the beauty of the line of work he was in. The people that operated in his world employed men like him. That's how it worked. And if you wanted a job done properly, you employed the best.

And he was undoubtedly that.

He'd been good before, no doubt. But the stretch inside had taught him a discipline he'd not previously known. He had a lot to thank them for, when he thought about it. There was no doubt that the prison system had done its job in terms of changing him. He was a much more effective killer now.

That's why he couldn't have strangled one of the nonces. He'd had to bide his time and wait to be transferred to Kirklevington.

Minimum security, a world away from Frankland. Truth be told, though, Olsen preferred Frankland. In there they had rules, structure, all things that were missing from the category B prison they'd slung him in.

He made his way through the trees on the other side of the dual carriageway, confident that he hadn't been seen. The cars were travelling too fast to notice him anyway. Right now, he needed to avoid being noticed.

Not that it particularly mattered. Plenty of people had done a runner from Kirky whilst on day release; it had been exactly the same for him. Half the time the screws didn't even bother to raise the alarm.

He was different though.

He saw the way the other prisoners looked at him—the way the staff looked at him. They knew. He was a man of violence. That brought risks for him now. They'd flag it up, alert local police stations, and they'd be on the lookout for him. Those were complications he could do without.

Ultimately, it didn't matter if he was caught, as long as he got the job done. Worst case scenario, they caught him and did him for murder. He'd never rat on his employer, so he'd be banged up again, most likely back at Frankland. Only, this time, there'd be no release. He found himself cracking his knuckles at the thought. They'd never let him near the nonces, of course, but he'd be surrounded by rats. And people like Olsen excelled in pest control.

He was well clear of the road now, under heavy cover, with nothing but the clothes on his back and, more importantly, his list of names. His first port of call would be securing funds. They didn't exactly give you an advance and a pat on the back when you went on day release, so he'd have to improvise. Once he'd managed to get some coin, he'd need a burner phone to get in touch with the people who had contracted him—then the real work would begin. Proper work. The kind Olsen could make a killing out of. The kind people used him for to make a killing.

He smiled as a middle-aged bloke with too much tyre round his midriff broke through the treeline, carrying what looked like a cat-sized dog in his under-developed arms.

Easy pickings.

'Sorry to bother you,' Olsen called.

The man, no doubt surprised by the giant with the misshapen skull, offered a muted response as the escaped prisoner lengthened his stride towards him. Sure that they were alone in the woods, Olsen smiled and cracked his knuckles once more for good luck.

CHAPTER SEVENTEEN

The hunt for Les Holding hadn't gotten off to a good start. As Jack had expected, the goon had gone to ground. He was no doubt using his many dubious contacts which would mean he would prove difficult to find. They'd have to shake the tree and see what came loose.

McGuinness wouldn't be happy with the intrusion, but that wasn't Jack's concern. Gone were the days when he had to worry about managing that particular relationship. His old boss no doubt thought he had him over a barrel following events the previous year, but even he would have to accede control when it came to out-and-out murder. And he'd have to be completely thick to have had a hand in it.

And McGuinness was anything but stupid. Holding on the other hand...

Resources were stretched, something that Nadine Guthrie, PCC, noted with some concern. Although, in her own words 'there's nothing I can do about it.' So, a nationwide manhunt wasn't exactly going to ingratiate the Northumbrian force to the other regions in the country. Still, when it came down to it, they were all on the same team: good guys versus the bad guys.

And Les Holding was definitely a bad guy.

They had to assume he would either be in the local area, under the protection of somebody at least linked to the McGuinness crew, or in Liverpool, his home city. Those were big assumptions, however. McGuinness had contacts across the country, something Jack could attest to from his previous existence as a hired heavy. However, he didn't really believe that Dorian would stick his neck out for somebody like Holding, a ticking time bomb with a temper akin to that of a poked tiger. If Holding had killed Gus Fenwick, McGuinness would not be pleased.

So Jack decided to play the odds and speak with the crime boss first. He'd taken Gerrard along for the trip. She hadn't met the aquatic shop owner before and he was keen for the entire team to get a handle on the kind of operator he was.

He decided to skip the pleasantries. 'I'll get right to it, Dorian, Les Holding is wanted as a suspect for questioning over the murder of Gus Fenwick.'

McGuinness' oversized features were impassive. A trait he had perfected over many years. He paused, replacing his tinted glasses over his beak-like nose, before speaking. 'I don't know his whereabouts.'

Jack studied him. 'I believe you.'

McGuinness smirked. 'There's a first time for everything!'

He shifted. 'Don't get too excited, Dorian. Whilst you might not know where he is, I know you'll be looking for him. Somebody as loose-tongued and unhinged as Les Holding can't be good for business, right?'

The crime boss shrugged. His eyes flicked across to Gerrard.

'Don't worry about her, Dorian. She's a good cop. A very good cop.'

The implication passed between them; it said, *Don't even try it with her, she's incorruptible.*

'Thank you for that ringing endorsement, Jack,' she said, with only a tiny smidge of sarcasm attached. 'Mr McGuinness, when did you last see the suspect?'

A pause passed between them, the faint hum of tropical fish tanks cutting through the silence. McGuinness turned his considerable bulk and sized her up. 'Not as recently as your boss here,' he finally said.

Jack winced. The thought that he had been the last person to see Les Holding before he murdered Gus Fenwick would make things even worse for him. He'd end up a potential witness in his own case. He could imagine Edwards' response already.

'Sorry, sir,' Gerrard continued. 'But that isn't answering my question.'

Jack saw his old boss' eyes widen before correcting himself, the momentary lapse in temper now under control. That was the Dorian McGuinness Jack knew.

'I apologise, detective,' McGuinness replied. 'I saw him two days ago. I needed him for a job, you see.'

'I do see,' she shot back. 'And how did he seem?'

'How do you mean?' McGuinness asked.

'Well his son had just died, had he not? He had this information, surely he would have betrayed some emotion?'

McGuinness sighed and began tapping a long fingernail on his mahogany table. 'My employees know not to bring their baggage to work. It's sort of an implicit term we have in our contracts. You know, like not stealing from your employer or lying to them.'

Jack cut in. 'And had Holding lied to you?'

McGuinness stopped tapping. 'I didn't say that.'

He didn't have to.

'You're not going to make this easy for me, are you, Dorian?' Jack said.

He could see the cogs turning over in McGuinness' mind, weighing up the pros and cons of the situation. If he helped them find Holding, it would remove him from all suspicion in terms of helping Les, but he had to be worried about what the man would say. Holding was dumb, and dumb people say more than they should do. McGuinness surrounded himself with a number of dumb people so that they could carry out the dirty work no-one else would. Unfortunately for him, even the dumbest of dogs sometimes have to be put down. If Dorian thought Holding would implicate him to save his own skin, then he'd be conducting his own investigation and it certainly wouldn't be to help the police.

Finally McGuinness spoke. 'I really don't know what to say, Jack,' he said. 'I have no idea where he is.'

'But you're looking?' Gerrard asked.

McGuinness shrugged.

'If something happens to Holding,' Jack began, 'then you have to know all fingers will be pointed at you. But you're not stupid—'

'Thank you for that bit of positive feedback,' Dorian cut in.

'What I mean is,' he continued, 'you're in a difficult situation for a man in your position. If you help us, you risk him talking; if you don't you risk being an obstruction or, even worse, complicit in a very serious crime.' Jack nodded to Gerrard, and stood. 'I'll leave you to it,' he said. 'You've got my number. Let me know when you decide who's side you want to be on with this.'

Jack could hear the crime boss' teeth grinding long after they'd left the shop.

'You know,' Gerrard said, once they were back in the car, 'for two gay men, you don't half know how to throw testosterone about.'

'Being gay doesn't mean I don't have testosterone,' Jack told her. 'Besides, that's how McGuinness operates, everything is a game to him.' He indicated and pulled out of the cobbled street, heading towards the city centre. 'You did well in there, though, good job. He'll know not to mess with you from now on.'

Gerrard shrugged. 'I've dealt with worse.'

'Trust me,' Jack replied. 'You haven't. Did I ever tell you about the time Watkins first came with me to meet him?'

'No but I'm intrigued,' she said.

'Let's just say he isn't the best around dogs—'

Gerrard pointed to the Bluetooth screen as Jack stopped at a red light. 'Speaking of which...'

He answered the call. 'Watkins, speak to me.'

'We've just had a call to the station regarding Holding.'

Jack sucked in a deep breath. 'Is it credible?'

'I'd say so,' Watkins said. 'It was him.'

'What?' Jack almost stalled the engine as the light finally changed. 'Any clue as to where he is?'

'Not yet but we're analysing it as we speak. Oh, and Holding sounds very drunk.'

'We're on our way now,' Jack replied.

'Is Gerrard with you?' Watkins asked.

'Yes.'

A pause. 'Oh... hi, Claire, see you guys soon.'

Jack noticed a slight flush of embarrassment on DC Gerrard's face as he ended the call. Perhaps she wasn't as clueless as he thought? He weighed up the options of saying something, whether or not to be the bigger man in the situation.

He smirked. 'I'm just gonna crack this window,' he said. 'There's so much testosterone getting thrown about I can barely breathe.'

Out of the corner of his eye he could see Gerrard's face flash a red that was usually only attributed to Watkins. She remained silent, eyes on anything but him. He decided not to push it. Besides, if there was something blossoming between the pair of them, that would change the whole team dynamic, giving him a headache. Given his own chequered love life, he wasn't exactly a qualified expert on managing such a situation. Still, he was the boss and as SIO he couldn't have it affecting their work. *Maybe I should speak to them,* he thought.

For now, though, he had an important recording to listen to...

CHAPTER EIGHTEEN

Within the hour Holding's mugshot was plastered around various news outlets across the north east, including online via the force's social media accounts. It hadn't been a difficult choice. It was clear he was a major suspect; he wasn't at his residence; and those closest to him, namely Dorian McGuinness, seemingly had no idea where he was.

The call had been made from a payphone in Gateshead, which at least proved that he was still in the area. Patrol cars had been sent out but they'd had no luck. Jack wasn't surprised, though: people didn't have a tendency to hang around phone boxes all day after making calls. Holding had sounded slurred, and emotional, and had been blabbering on about the farmer getting what he deserved. There was no doubt now; Les Holding had killed Gus Fenwick in an act of revenge.

'I'll stay here and co-ordinate things,' Watkins offered.

Jack, realising he had been pacing for the last half hour, stopped dead. 'Good idea.'

The phone hadn't stopped ringing since the picture had been released. That wasn't a surprise. The difficulty they would have would be separating the wheat from the chaff. Given Watkins' patience for such things, Jack expected him to do a good job of it.

Christensen limped towards him. 'Guv, we've had a call from somebody who reckons they've seen Holding in the South Shields area. Apparently they recognised him after seeing his picture on the Facebook.'

'Just Facebook,' Watkins corrected him.

Christensen shrugged.

'Credible?' Jack asked.

'Who knows?' Christensen replied. 'Got any better ideas?'

Jack sighed. 'No. Let's check it out.'

'I can head it up if you like?'

'No,' Jack replied. 'I could do with the air.'

They left Watkins to it and began the journey towards South Shields. It was a place Jack was familiar with, having visited there many times as a child. The seafront was a spectacular sight by UK standards. Unfortunately, the weather didn't hold up its end of the bargain and people were only able to enjoy it for around two days every year.

'I'm assuming we need to be prepared for some resistance if we find him,' Christensen said.

Jack nodded. Given the brutal murder of Gus Fenwick, one could only assume he had it in him to cause a scene. They'd been careful to warn people not to approach him, but had stressed that he shouldn't be a danger to the wider public. After all, it was only Gus Fenwick that had been accused of killing his son.

So far.

'You worried about the blowback from this?' Christensen asked.

Pleased that they had made it through the Felling bypass without incident, Jack made a left turn off Whitemare Pool, and headed towards Shields town centre. 'Not on a personal level,' he finally replied. 'I'm more concerned with the repercussions of having not disclosed it or acted upon my instincts. Had I done that, Gus Fenwick may well still be alive.'

He could sense Christensen staring at him.

'There's always the possibility that it wasn't him,' the DS noted.

'I suppose you're right,' Jack replied. 'But then it does feel like he's gone to ground. Even Dorian didn't know his whereabouts and he always keeps tabs on his people. Why run if you have nothing to hide?'

Christensen shrugged. 'Who knows? We all have our reasons for acting as we do. Besides, McGuinness could have been lying.'

'Oh he always lies,' Jack said. 'The trick is being able to spot the major stuff from the minor. So what are your reasons then, Christensen?' he added.

He was met with stony silence.

They arrived in the town centre minutes later and Jack pulled the car into a narrow space on Ocean Road. The strip, not far from the seafront, was famous for its multitude of curry houses with the odd Italian thrown in for good measure. The smell of early-evening spices wafted through the air as they made their way up the steep hill of Henry Nelson Street on foot. Jack's stomach grumbled. He realised he'd gone without food so far today. It wouldn't do to get chewed up over a case and flush his new lifestyle down the toilet. He could already picture how that would go down with his personal trainer.

'Which number is she?' Jack asked. He noticed Christensen struggling up the hill. 'You okay?'

He waved him away. 'Fine, boss. We can't all be as fit as you. Number twenty-five.'

Jack felt brave so he took a punt on asking the DS outright. 'What's wrong with your leg, anyway?'

'Air rifle accident when I was a kid in Denmark.'

'Guns in Scandinavia?' Jack joked. 'I thought it was a socialist utopia out there.'

Christensen's shock of blond hair flapped across his reddening forehead as the wind picked up. 'Not real guns,' he said. 'In any case, socialists sometimes shoot people too.'

'Fair enough.'

Twenty-five Roman Road was about halfway up the hill, not far from the Roman Fort, another of Jack's childhood excursion locations. It was quite the tourist hotspot for people visiting the town, and Jack could remember digging up fake artefacts in a sandpit whilst visiting the place. He smiled at the memory; it was his mother that used to take him there.

Of course, once he'd turned sixteen, that had all changed and he was more likely to have hung about the place to get drunk and spray graffiti. He frowned at *that* memory.

Sylvia Thompson was an elderly lady with something of a twitch. As she opened the green door to her downstairs flat, two black cats came shooting out, causing Jack to have palpitations. She didn't seem keen on inviting them in and, given that the place was shrouded in darkness, Jack was pleased. In any case, they didn't have time to drink tea and eat biscuits; they had a murderer to catch.

'You the police?' she asked.

'Yes, Mrs Thompson,' Jack said.

'Ms will do,' she said.

Jack noticed an unruly tree in the front yard, which covered the majority of a flat, wooden-framed bay window. In the tree, two more cats sat, watching him with silent disdain. He shuddered. He'd never been one to like animals.

'We are just here following up on your phone call to the station regarding your potential sighting of Les Holding.'

Her dark, rheumy eyes met his, no easy feat given their height discrepancy. She couldn't have been any more than four foot six. Wiry hair wisped around her head in a tangled sort of bob, her face lined with deep wrinkles.

'Wasn't potential,' she said, face twitching. 'I saw him.'

'Was it outside here, Ms Thompson?' Christensen asked.

'That's an interesting accent you have,' she observed.

He smiled. 'I'm originally from Denmark.'

'Hmmm,' she muttered. 'I was coming back from King Street with my daily shop.' She motioned down the hill. 'I often go around that time as it's a bit quieter and I can move about in peace. I usually go to Herons, then Wilkinsons, then I head down to Savers before popping into Morrisons on the way back. Today, I went to Morrisons as I needed some cat food and their home brand does for my cats.'

'Indeed,' Jack said. He could feel his interest waning.

'Anyway, I was walking down Ocean Road when I saw the man. He was wearing a cap and looked shifty. It was when I saw his eyes that I knew who he was.'

'And you saw his picture on Facebook?' Jack asked.

She straightened up. 'Yes. Why, do you find it hard to believe that an eighty-five-year-old woman would be up to date with technology?'

'It is... a little unusual,' Jack stated.

'Well my niece set me up with an account a couple of years ago. I'm a member of the South Shields old photos group.' She eyed him. 'Plus, it's a good way of checking up on whether any of your friends or family have died. I don't get many visitors these days.'

Jack glanced up at the cats in the tree. He wasn't surprised. He fished out his phone and loaded the image of Holding on the screen. 'You're sure it's him?'

She nodded. 'Big fella he was. Awful tattoos. My cousin used to work away at sea back in the sixties. He was covered in those ghastly things too.'

Jack smiled and replaced the phone. 'Yes, it's a terrible habit. Are you able to tell me in which direction he went?'

She motioned up the hill and Jack could feel Christensen wither. 'He went that way, was in a hurry too. Although, it's taken you a bit of time to get here so God knows where he is now.'

'Thank you, Ms Thompson,' he said. 'You've been most helpful.'

They left Sylvia Thompson to tend to her cats and continued up the hill. They already had an officer presence in the area and Jack radioed them to convey the information. Sylvia was right, he could be anywhere by now, but there had to be a reason for him to head to South Shields. If you were making a quick getaway from the north east, you wouldn't head to a seaside town. The only reason he would head there was if he planned to lay low. Jack scoured his memory as to whether he knew of any safe houses or contacts linked to the McGuinness crew who were based in South Shields. It had been so long since he was involved with them that it would most likely be redundant information anyway. Still, not many people got out, so chances were if there was a contact here from back in the day then they would still be around.

'We should speak to the other neighbours and see if anybody else has seen anything,' Christensen stated.

'Agreed.' Jack turned to him. 'You stay here and co-ordinate that.'

'You off on an adventure again?' the DS asked. 'You do remember how that usually works out for you, right?'

Jack laughed. 'Don't worry, I'm not heading to any abandoned factories. And, in any case, the place is teeming with officers. I note your concern, though.'

Christensen raised a palm. 'Doesn't bother me,' he said. 'I'm just looking out for you. Once DI Russell finds out you'll be mincemeat, right?'

'That's two jokes in the last year,' Jack said. 'You going soft on me?'

Christensen shrugged. 'Just trying to fit in.'

Jack left the DS to head up the door-to-door enquiries and began the short, but steep, walk to the Roman Fort. Just beyond it was the river linking South Shields with its northern partner. Jack could remember many a trip with his parents on the ferry. It was a day out back then. Now most people used it as a way to get the DFDS across to Amsterdam for a cheap thrill on a weekend.

The road evened out as he passed the fort and he continued his walk until he reached a railing overlooking the river. Turning right, he made a loop along past The Beacon, a now closed pub. He'd never drank in there, himself, but it had had a reputation for having good craic at one point. It was sad to see it boarded up. The general consensus was that the smoking ban had put paid to the previously booming pub industry. Seeing old relics like this meant Jack was inclined to agree. It didn't stop his old man from going, though. That reminded him, he'd have to pay his father a visit in the not-too-distant future. Since his successful liver operation the previous year he'd been recuperating at home, grumpy but a damn sight healthier than he had been.

He carried on his walk until he reached a bend in the road and was faced with yet another boarded-up pub, The Harbour Lights. *At this rate, the people of South Shields will have nowhere left to go,* he thought.

He reached the crest of the hill, and was just about to head down the path adjacent to the North Marine Park, when he stopped dead. He turned on his heels and walked back over to The Harbour Lights. He was sure something hadn't looked right with the boarding. He inspected all of the window boards as well as the door before he was satisfied that it all seemed in order. He still found himself unable to shake the uncomfortable feeling, though.

He was about to head back to Henry Nelson Street when he twigged. It wasn't The Harbour Lights, it was The Beacon. He got on the radio. 'This is DCI Lambert, head towards The Beacon pub. If you go north of the Roman Fort it's just at the top of the road, I'll meet you there.'

'Roger that, guv,' a young officer responded.

He ran back towards the pub, thankful that his new-found fitness meant that he was barely out of breath. When he reached it, he realised what he had seen but not fully processed. Wooden slats sat over where the entrance had been, but they were skewed. There was also one missing, with a hole just about big enough that a large bloke could fit through it. He glanced at all the windows and noticed that one of them seemed to be skewed as well.

He had to make a choice. Go in now or wait for backup. Christensen was right, it never usually ended well.

The sound of screeching tyres made his decision for him. They'd picked Christensen up on the way and the DS sprang from the car before seeming to realise he had a bad leg. Instantly, he began hobbling.

'Christensen, nice to see you,' Jack said.

The DS greeted him. 'They were kind enough to give me a ride,' he said. 'What is it?'

Jack motioned to the entrance and window. 'I just have a feeling,' he said. 'Somebody has tampered with it.'

'Could be a homeless person,' Christensen mused. 'They do exist in towns as well.'

Jack nodded. 'Could be, but unfortunately I don't believe in coincidences. There's no easy way of doing this so just follow me in.'

The gap was fairly big but he still had to push the slat to one side to get into the pub. Turning, he held it so that Christensen could edge through.

'Dark in here,' the DS said.

Jack waited a moment for his eyes to adjust. If it had been summer there would have at least been some natural light in the place. As it was, the early-evening gloom was thwarting their progress. Jack took his phone out and switched his torch on.

'Can you feel that?' Jack asked.

'Feel what?' Christensen replied.

Jack kicked a pile of junk mail envelopes out of the way and stepped through the entranceway. 'Someone has been here.'

'How do you know?'

'Call it the benefit of experience.'

Despite the fact that the pub had clearly been closed for some time, it hadn't managed to shake the stench of real ale. Like most pub floors, it had kept its sticky texture. Resisting the urge to gag, Jack veered left, past the bar, and stepped into the main area. His torch beam wasn't the strongest, but it would do. Behind him, he could hear Christensen's laboured breathing as his own phone light added to the creepy atmosphere in the room.

'You sure somebody has been here?' Christensen asked.

Jack nodded and stepped further into the room. The torchlight cast a series of eerie shadows on the wall as he moved it over the various cobwebbed tables and mahogany chairs. He paused and listened intently for the sound of any additional presence. He was struck by how even the most abandoned of buildings still carried their own unique sound. The Beacon seemed to creak and groan like a Victorian hotel. It wasn't helped by the wind having picked up outside.

They moved to the back of the room, where a small, raised stage sat. Jack imagined the kind of bands that this place must have housed back in the day. Proper middle-aged classic rockers. Just his kind of music.

'Guv, you might want to see this,' Christensen called from the bar area.

He stepped away from the stage. 'What is it?'

The DS turned and held it up for Jack to see. He'd been right all along, somebody had been hiding in the abandoned pub.

There was no mistaking the red cap Sylvia Thompson had described to them—Les Holding's cap.

Jack cursed his luck; had he realised sooner then they might have caught Holding before he'd had a chance to escape. They had no way of knowing which way he'd fled, now.

He turned to Christensen. 'Get on the phone to Watkins and have him set up squad cars at all of the major exit points from the town, north and south.'

The Boris Johnson lookalike nodded, turned on his heels and made the call.

'Guv, look at this,' one of the local officers called.

He moved towards the end of the bar and saw what the officer was looking at. A broken string of pearl beads.

A thought struck him. 'Ring the local station and enquire about all robberies reported in the last twenty-four hours.'

Perhaps Holding really was on his own if he was reverting to petty crime to raise funds. They had to assume he had some cash on him. They'd had a hit on a local NatWest branch in Newcastle not long after they'd identified him as their main suspect. Holding, whilst undoubtedly angry, wasn't dumb. He was unlikely to keep making withdrawals from ATM machines if he could help it. Still, robbing people wasn't exactly inconspicuous either.

Christensen limped over to him. 'It's done.'

Jack nodded. He liked that about Christensen; no nonsense and straight to the point. It wasn't long before he'd make DI. 'It still won't be easy to find him.'

'Agreed,' the DS replied. 'He's bound to go to ground.'

Jack concurred. 'Still, we almost caught him once, we can do it again.'

They left the abandoned pub and stepped out into the evening light. Jack looked over towards the river. 'Make sure we have people at the dock for any DFDS ferries leaving in the next few days.'

Christensen raised his eyebrow. 'You think he's going to do a runner to Amsterdam?'

'Stranger things have happened,' Jack replied. 'We can't rule out the fact that he may have a fake passport on him. If that's the case,' he added, 'then special branch might not pick him up.'

Having said that, the fact that he had stolen a string of pearls pointed to a man without any sort of plan. That would make him both careless and dangerous. Jack hoped it'd be more of the former otherwise more people could get hurt.

'Come on,' he told Christensen. 'Let's do a loop around the coast, before heading back, just in case.'

A look passed between them; they didn't need to say anything. They'd missed their chance.

CHAPTER NINETEEN

'Alright, Les,' Olsen greeted him.

Les Holding looked up with an alarmed expression on his face before pulling his grey beanie down over his ears.

Olsen, without speaking, took a seat opposite him.

'They let you out early, like?' he said.

Olsen noticed the slumped posture of the man. Being on the run did that to you. Olsen hadn't hit that wall, yet, but he knew it'd come. In the meantime, he'd busy himself with the task at hand.

'No,' he finally replied. 'I jumped free on day release.' What did it matter to Holding? It wasn't like he could turn him in.

Holding looked up, shock etched onto his wide features. 'You jumped prison just before your release?'

'Aye,' he said. 'I've got a couple of jobs to do.'

They waited while a waitress came over to see if they wanted anything. Olsen ordered two beers and a cheese scone; he hadn't eaten in hours and this would be his first beer since going inside. Sure, roadside cafes weren't the greatest, but beer was beer.

'How'd you find me?' Holding asked.

Olsen shrugged and spread his body out across the booth. 'It's easy when you know how.'

Holding snorted. 'Aye, you always were good at that sort of thing.' He paused, looked him in the eye. 'Dorian send you?'

They paused again as the waitress returned with their beers. Olsen threw his back. It was warm but it'd do.

'Does it matter who sent me?'

'Nah, suppose not,' Holding said. 'So what you got planned now that you're out?'

Olsen detected the note of sarcasm in Holding's voice. He let it fly: the man was nervous, people often did stupid things when they were nervous. 'We'll just have to wait and see,' he said. 'See if any work comes up, maybe.'

'Pay a visit to your lass?'

Olsen stopped, stale beer half an inch from his mouth. Holding knew fine well 'his lass' wasn't on the scene anymore. Olsen recognised the attempt to push his buttons. Still, he didn't react, save for a small twitch in his left eye, the one that always set off when he got angry.

'Might do,' he said. 'I heard about your lad.'

Now it was Holding's turn to twitch. 'Aye... well, what can you do?'

Olsen glanced out of the window at the car park. Two lorries sat, their occupants snoozing on their breaks. Next to them were two, unmanned motorbikes. An old Ford Escort with rusted wheel arches was parked off to the side of them; no sign of the owners. He turned back to Holding and leaned in. He could smell the man's sweat as he spoke, and focused on breathing through his mouth. 'You could have been there for the fella, I suppose?'

Holding's head looked like it would pop, a thick, blue vein throbbing in the centre of his forehead. He glanced around the cafe and seemed to think better of making a scene.

Holding leaned in, himself, their noses almost touching. 'Aye but I made up for it, didn't I? And, in any case, you're hardly dad of the year.'

Olsen sat back, took another sip of beer. No point in having a cockfight in full public view. They were, after all, two fugitives. Holding was right, of course, he had been a lousy father. But, by doing this job and earning a tonne of money, it meant the bairn might grow up with more than he had done.

'I suppose you did, but that wasn't your place, was it?'

Holding shook his head. 'Bloke had it coming. I don't give a shit about Dorian's orders. Family is family.'

Olsen resisted the urge to inform him that, actually, his family were no longer his family at all. Instead, he said, 'How do you know the farmer did it?'

A flash across the eyes. Olsen noticed Holding's knuckles flex on the table, old, faded tattoos moving across his hands like dying snakes. 'He did it.'

Olsen shrugged. It didn't matter to him. Hell, had it been his boy, he'd have probably done the same thing. Still, it wasn't his kid.

And orders were orders.

'How'd you find him?' Olsen asked.

'I've got contacts,' he replied. 'Plus, it's easy enough to phone round local hotels.'

Olsen nodded. He suspected it was more pot luck than Holding actually having contacts on the inside. He wasn't important enough to have that kind of sway.

They finished their beers and Olsen cleared his throat. 'So, are we ready or do you want to continue reminiscing?'

Holding scanned the cafe, clearly weighing up his options. He didn't have many. He'd fancy his chances, Olsen knew that. But he also saw doubt in the man's eyes. Olsen, having always been reasonably fit, had gotten into fantastic shape whilst he was inside. So much so that his one beer would weigh heavy on his mind until he could work it off later. He looked over Les' ageing physique. Ten years ago he may have worked it off sparring with the bloke. He had been pretty good with his fists. But Les

Holding was a stupid man who fought stupid. Olsen tutted inwardly. He almost felt bad; it wouldn't be anywhere near a fair fight.

Holding drained his drink and the two men stood to leave. Olsen caught the waitress' eye, held up a crumpled tenner, and placed it on the table. They passed a man with a skin tight Harley Davidson T-shirt on and a ZZ Top-style beard that gave him a pot-bellied wizard look. He hadn't even bothered to take his sunglasses off. At least he knew who at least one of the bikes belonged to now.

'Where we going then?' Holding said, heading for the door.

'Up to you,' Olsen said, following suit.

They stepped out into the cold, northern atmosphere. Olsen breathed it in; it never failed to amaze him how much he'd missed free air. There was a crispness to it that being inside managed to suppress, even when on day release.

Holding turned and pointed between the two lorries to a break in the tree-lined clearing. 'There.'

'Looks good to me,' Olsen said.

As they passed the lorries, one of the drivers, a skinny bloke with a mop of grey-brown hair, peered over his cabin. Olsen nodded and moved on—*nothing to see here*.

Still, it wouldn't have mattered anyway. Olsen had a job to do and orders were orders. And when *his* boss gave an order, you followed through with it, unless you wanted people like Olsen to come after you. He smiled as he felt for the handle of the gun in his pocket. Sure, Holding would fancy his chances in a fist fight.

But Olsen didn't leave things to chance. He saw everything and planned accordingly.

Of course, even the best laid plans weren't without risk. Unfortunately for him, what he didn't see was the waitress, sure that she recognised one of the men's faces, move to pick up the phone.

CHAPTER TWENTY

Over twenty-four hours had passed and they'd still had no luck in locating Holding. They'd positioned vehicles on all of the major exit points out of the town and even called the helicopters in but it had been a fruitless exercise. Nobody had reported a robbery in relation to the beads, either, and the team were clearly frustrated. Jack noted that Watkins was unable to sit still and even Christensen's usual ice-cold demeanour was wavering, with two PCs cowering away from him in the corner of the MIR.

Watkins, all limbs, lumbered towards him. 'Seen this?' he asked.

Anything to take his mind off the Gus Fenwick and Robert Norris murders was a welcome respite right now. He snatched the *Chronicle* from Watkins' freckled hand and looked.

'Dayton Olsen,' he mused. 'I recognise that name.'

'Aye because we put him away for aggravated burglary.'

'Did we?'

Watkins beamed like the first kid finished in an exam. 'Well, I did, back in the day, like.'

'Good for you,' Jack said.

Jack read the report. Dayton Olsen had been in Frankland Prison in Durham for the best part of four years before transferring to the low-security Kirklevington establishment. He'd been due for release in the next few months and had been on day release when he'd done a runner. *No surprise there,* Jack thought. It was strange how many people did that once freedom became a distinct possibility. Chances were he'd resurface imminently and be banged up for a longer time for having broken the rules. Releasing him permanently would probably be more of a punishment than keeping him inside.

'Why is this of interest to me?' Jack asked.

Watkins' smile evaporated. 'Well... it says we need to keep a lookout for him as he is from this area and they believe that he might head back here.'

Jack waved him away. 'We have enough people on the run without worrying about some low-level idiot who's got the odd theft charge behind him.' He noted the wounded look on Watkins' face, which was currently doing its best Posh Spice impression. 'But... well done on catching him though.'

Watkins straightened up. 'Thanks, guv,' he said.

'Also,' Jack added, leaning forward. 'What happened to his head?'

Watkins chuckled. 'No idea, looks like his skull has been bashed in, doesn't it? Apparently he was born like that.'

Jack realised he had been clicking his pen on and off for the best part of ten minutes. He ran his gaze across the MIR. Every case suffered from this, a lull in proceedings. It was up to him as SIO to motivate his people. The problem was, he was having trouble motivating himself. They were no further forward with regards to solving the Robert Norris murder and the less said about Les Holding the better.

He gathered the team together. 'Right,' he said. 'We need to refocus our minds. Yes, it's important we catch Holding but we can't take our eyes off the whole reason this situation was triggered... the killing of Robert Norris.'

He pointed to the murder wall. Norris' mugshot beamed out at them. They'd have been forgiven for thinking that he was a model citizen rather than the petty criminal they actually knew him to be. Still, he'd been murdered and bad people deserved justice just as much as good people.

More or less.

'We should focus on Fenwick,' DI Russell said.

For once, Jack agreed with her. 'You're right.' He strode over to the wall and pinned up a picture of Gus Fenwick's estranged wife. 'Margaret Fenwick relayed some potentially interesting information to us regarding her husband, namely that they had been separated for some time. That throws up some unusual questions for us.' He motioned to DC Gerrard. 'Claire, provide us with an update.'

The vibrant DC jumped to her feet and danced to the front, ponytail swinging. 'Thanks, guv,' she said. 'Before he died, Gus Fenwick told us that he had been visiting his wife in the hospital. When spoken to, the nurses were aware that an older gentleman had visited Margaret Fenwick on occasion and we assumed this to be none other than Gus himself.'

'How do we know it wasn't?' one of the PCs asked.

Gerrard turned to him, her eyes alive with the adrenaline of holding the floor. 'We can't. However, Margaret Fenwick informs us that she hasn't seen her husband in nearly two years and that there was no way that he would have been in the hospital to see her. She also informs us that she does not know somebody of that age group who would visit her.'

Jack saw the room looking collectively confused so he stepped in. 'This poses two quandaries for us. Did Gus Fenwick lie about visiting her and, if it wasn't him, who was it?'

'How is this relevant to the case?' the PC asked.

Jack bit his tongue and fought the urge to throttle him.

'Because, as it stands, we do not know why Robert Norris was at Gus Fenwick's farm the night he was killed and the picture we were beginning to paint of Gus Fenwick suddenly doesn't seem so cut and dry. I can't help but feel there is something bigger at play, here.'

He just didn't know what it was.

'So now we are left with the question, "where do we go from here?"' Gerrard stated, eyes scanning the room.

The PC shrank back.

Christensen spoke up. 'We need to go over all of his known associates and see what comes loose.'

'Agreed,' Jack said. 'Margaret Fenwick informed us that he was close to the manager of The Black Horse pub, Brian McCullagh.'

Gerrard interjected. 'This wasn't something Fenwick mentioned when we spoke to him. Of course, he wasn't asked this outright.'

Jack cut in. 'But McCullagh was and he suggested he didn't know Fenwick particularly well.'

'Could be worth going to speak with him again then,' Watkins said.

Jack noted the blush on Gerrard's face. 'Yes, it could be.'

'Agreed,' Jack said. 'Watkins, you and I will take a trip out this afternoon and speak with McCullagh. Now that Gus Fenwick is dead, he may offer up some more information on the farmer's background that we can use. Christensen.' The blond DS looked up. 'I want you to stay on top of the Les Holding angle. Find out if we know of any associates in the area, liaise with the estranged family, even if just to keep their minds at ease, and report in with any updates. The South Shields branch should be more than open in co-operating but, if not, work some of that charm you have.'

Christensen almost smiled. 'No problem, boss.'

'Jane.' He turned to DI Russell. 'Margaret Fenwick has been released from hospital, I want you to go speak with her, see what more you can find out. We need any family names, no matter how distant; if she thinks that he may have had some interaction beyond a simple phone call once a month, I want to know about it.'

DI Russell, who was perched on one of the computer desks, slid off, with all of the grace of a drunken baby deer. 'Will do,' she said.

Jack smiled inwardly. An interaction between Jane Russell and Margaret Fenwick was something almost too good to miss. But miss it he would, on this occasion.

Watkins drove the route to The Black Horse and, once again, Jack found himself thinking of Ryan. He hadn't spoken to him for a couple of days and was feeling guilty about it. Ryan wasn't clingy, but he was affectionate. Jack was working on that. Unfortunately for both of them, he was also working a murder case and that had to come first. They'd already had 'the chat' about it at the beginning of their relationship.

'Something on your mind?' Watkins asked.

Jack's legs were jammed up against the glove box so he pushed the seat back and shuffled closer to the window. 'Other than your bad driving?' he replied.

He didn't need to look to know that Watkins' eyes were on him. 'Great deflection technique.'

Jack snorted. 'Okay, Watkins. Since when did you become so observant?'

'It's my job,' he said, in his usual cheery manner.

Jack turned to him. 'Seeing as we are having such a conversation...'

Red cascaded over Watkins features. 'No, it's okay.'

'No, let me finish,' Jack said. 'I don't know what's going on between you and Gerrard and, for the record, I don't care. But when it starts affecting our work that's where I'll draw a line.'

'I... don't know what's going on,' he said.

Jack jabbed a finger in his direction. 'Then you should maybe figure it out. Your current girlfriend knows something is wrong: it was written all over her face when we were at the hospital visiting Margaret Fenwick the other day. That's strike one.'

'W... what happens after strike three?' Watkins stammered.

'Full staff meeting,' Jack said.

They spent the next few minutes in silence as Jack seethed at Watkins' intervention. Deep down, of course, he knew that it was unfair to take out his own frustrations on the DS.

'You know,' Watkins said, a little too tentatively for Jack's liking, 'if we are talking about things affecting work, you might want to take a look at yourself.'

'What's that supposed to mean?' Jack thundered.

'I mean, yeah, things are okay at the minute, but do you remember the last two years?'

Of course he did. The Open Grave Murderer and Newcastle Knifer cases meant he'd never be able to forget. 'Yes,' he finally replied. 'I won't apologise for working hard.'

'I'm not talking about the case,' Watkins said. 'You know, your divorce from Louise, then the acrimonious split from Rosie and the admission about being gay.'

Jack baulked at the mention of his personal life. He couldn't help but wonder if it was a hot topic of conversation around the office when he wasn't there. 'Is there a point to this?'

Watkins indicated and turned off towards the village. 'I'm just saying that we all adapted around your personal circumstances and did the best we could because we understood that things weren't easy for you. How about you cut others some of the same slack?'

Jack stared at him.

'Just saying,' Watkins squeaked.

'I preferred the old Watkins,' Jack said. 'You know, the one who wouldn't say boo to a goose. What the hell has happened to him?'

Watkins straightened up. 'I learned some bad behaviours from me boss, like.'

Jack couldn't argue there.

'Here we are,' Watkins said, bringing the police car to a stop. He turned to face Jack. 'We can pick this up later.'

'We most certainly will n—'

Before he could finish Watkins had already scarpered from the car and was halfway to the pub entrance. *Clever move,* Jack thought.

If Brian McCullagh was pleased to see them then he didn't show it. The pub was almost as deserted as the last time Jack had been there and McCullagh, for his part, was a mirror image of the time before complete with stained apron and dirty glass in hand.

He greeted Jack as he approached. 'Detective.'

'Mr McCullagh,' he acknowledged him. 'This is my colleague, Detective Sergeant Watkins.'

The barman gave a curt nod. 'Here about Gus, are you?'

Jack pulled up a stool, with Watkins following suit. 'I'm afraid we are. But, seeing as I'll be taking up a bit of your time, we'll have two Cokes for your trouble.'

McCullagh grunted and turned to pour them their drinks. Jack noted that the old man from the previous occasion was there again, same seat, same vacant expression, same half-drunk pint. Aside from that, there was a couple in the corner of the room having a crisp buffet. Their Karrimor boots and bulging backpacks told him they were tourists. There were worse spots to visit, that was for sure.

The barman placed the Cokes down on the counter before them. 'So how can I help you?'

'I'm assuming you are aware of what has happened, Mr McCullagh?' Jack asked. It wasn't outside the realms of possibility that the barman hadn't seen the news.

The man's eyes narrowed, ever so slightly. 'I am.'

'It has come to our attention that you were close to Gus Fenwick.'

Jack noted a flash of anger swim across the man's eyes. 'Has it now?'

'Indeed it has,' Jack replied. He took a swig of his Coke, noted that the syrup had gone, but decided not to say anything. 'Which seems to run counter to what you told us before.'

'I don't recall what I told you before,' the barman responded.

'Do you know much about Mrs Fenwick?' Watkins asked him.

The barman turned to him. 'I know she's not on the scene these days. She's a nasty piece of work, that woman, mark my words.'

'How so?' Jack asked.

McCullagh snorted. 'She's got money, and people with money generally are. Gus couldnae stand her.'

'Did he talk about her often?' Watkins asked.

'Nah, not much,' he replied.

'And how close were you to Gus?' Jack asked. 'From what you can remember.'

The barman straightened out his apron, sighed, and took a seat opposite them. 'We played poker once in a while, shared the odd drink. He was a regular here. I'm close with all my customers, isn't that right, Vic?'

The old man at the end of the bar raised a thick eyebrow in muted response.

'Were you and Gus Fenwick involved in any business dealings?'

Jack noted the pause before McCullagh answered. 'No, can't say we were.'

'And are you aware as to whether or not Mr Fenwick had any

enemies? Would there be a reason someone would want to hurt him? Perhaps he had something in the house?'

Again, Jack noted the pause, this time accompanied by a twitch. 'No idea. I'm sorry, detectives, if that's all, I have a business to be running.'

Jack held the barman's gaze. The pub wasn't busy but the cool tone in which McCullagh was speaking to them told him all he needed to know. It was a marked contrast to their first visit to the bar. He'd clearly hit a nerve.

Jack stood to leave. 'Of course, Mr McCullagh. Oh, and one more thing,' he said, doing his best Columbo impression, 'your Coke is flat. You may want to change it.'

Brian McCullagh held his gaze. 'I will do, detective.'

Jack waited until they were out of earshot before speaking with Watkins. 'That was interesting.'

'Really?'

'I'd say it was very enlightening,' Jack replied. 'Last time we were here, he knew just about nothing with regards to Margaret Fenwick. Upon questioning, this time, he seemed to know a lot more. Plus,' he added, 'McCullagh is nervous.'

'Yeah,' Watkins said. 'I noticed the hesitation, and did you see the sweat on his brow? More than just a man in need of a drink.'

Jack nodded. And McCullagh was certainly a big drinker. 'The atmosphere in there was much more hostile than on our first visit. His eyes lit up when I mentioned that Margaret Fenwick had spoken about him.'

'Still no real answers, though,' Watkins observed.

'Don't worry about that,' Jack replied. 'You uncover enough questions and eventually an answer will present itself.'

Back in the bar, Brian McCullagh watched as the tourists finished up their drinks and threw their heavy backpacks over their shoulders. He smiled, offered a wave and watched them leave. He checked his watch. It had been two minutes since the detectives had left. He straightened up his apron, placed the glass on the bar, and waited for thirty seconds more, just to be sure.

That's when he made the phone call.

CHAPTER TWENTY-ONE

A knock at the door brought him out of his trance. He glanced at his watch—7.30am, a little early for the team to be on duty at this point. The double murder case landing on their doorstep meant it would be standard practice until it was either resolved or shelved, though. For Jack, the latter didn't bear thinking about.

'Enter,' he said.

Watkins appeared, stony-faced, coffee perched in his skeletal hands. 'Morning, guv.'

Jack could sense it. 'What is it?' he said.

'There's been a body.'

Jack inhaled and the fumes of Watkins' canteen coffee stung his nasal hairs. Another body was the last thing they needed. Given what had happened so far, this would send both the press and public into a meltdown. And Edwards would make it clear where the fault ultimately fell.

He motioned for Watkins to sit down. 'Details.'

The DS placed his Styrofoam cup on the table and wiped froth from his freckled upper lip. 'It's early days but we think it's Les Holding.'

Had Jack been drinking, he'd have spat it out. 'What the hell?!' he shouted.

'It gets worse,' Watkins replied.

Jack's stomach tightened. 'Explain to me how it could possibly be any worse?'

'We think the body was moved.'

Jack thought it through. Although not ideal, it did mean that there would be a chain of events that led to the discovery of the body. If they could work their way back through the mystery, they may find clues as to who the killer was. It wasn't necessarily the worst news in the world.

'Moved where?' he asked.

'That's just it...'

The police car manoeuvred through what was now becoming familiar territory to Jack. The idea that the Northumberland countryside could ever be a potential dream location for him and Ryan now seemed a distant memory. The fact that he was planning retirement at the age of thirty-six was a worrying sign in itself.

Jack motioned to a gap in the clearing. 'Pull in here.'

They stepped from the car and began the short journey up the pebbled driveway towards the farm. Gus Fenwick's farm. First Robert Norris had been found dead here, then Fenwick, the owner, had been murdered not long afterwards—a crime Les Holding had admitted to in a drunken phone call to the police. And now Holding himself had been killed, before being moved to this very spot. Jack knew the signs. It didn't take a genius to put the pieces together.

Someone was sending a message.

Jack had long since discarded the idea that this was a lone man on a mission of revenge. Something bigger was at play. Unfortunately for him, he found himself doubting his own instincts, something he wasn't used to.

DI Russell was already at the scene when they arrived. 'Jack,' she greeted him, thin lipped.

He nodded his reply and moved past her towards the crime scene tent. 'Show me.'

Once suited and booted, they made their way inside. The place was teeming with SOCOs, who were already going over every inch of surrounding ground.

He couldn't help but notice the placement of the body. Not too dissimilar from where they'd found Robert Norris. If it turned out that it was the same killer then that ruled out Gus Fenwick. It also meant Fenwick's death had been a terrible misjudgement on the part of Les Holding.

He scratched at the SOC suit; he never could get used to the claustrophobic feel of having to wear one. Not a great sign for a murder detective. He found himself sweating, despite the biting Northumberland winter weather outside.

'Just here, guv...' One of the PCs motioned towards the centre of the tent.

Jack stepped forward, careful to avoid straying into the cordoned-off area. He peered over Holding's body, taking in each detail. There wasn't much to see. 'It's him,' he said.

Minutes later Jack stepped back out into the field and wrestled his suit off.

'It's the same as before,' DI Russell observed.

Jack sighed. 'Except with one key difference.'

The DI raised a painfully-plucked eyebrow.

'It's a different killer,' he continued. 'Norris was tortured before being killed. His killing was messy. This is completely different.'

Watkins appeared next to him, slightly out of breath. 'Definitely. A single gunshot to the head? It's neat. Nothing like Norris' murder.'

'Still, they have to be linked,' Russell stated. 'The placement, and the fact it's Holding, for a start.'

'Yes,' Jack said. 'Someone is sending a message, we know that much. But who for? Was Fenwick protected? Was Holding involved in whatever Fenwick was linked to? And what about Norris?'

DI Russell shook her head. 'Jack, I have no idea.'

'Nor do I,' he responded. He glanced at the sky; the clouds were frowning on him, threatening to cry at any second. 'But we are fast running out of people to talk to in relation to this case.'

Watkins picked some dirt off his faded brogues. 'Maybe this is it,' he said.

Jack shook his head and ran a weary hand across his three-day stubble. 'No, something tells me this is just the beginning.'

Olsen looked the barman in the eye; hiding in plain sight was a skill. A skill he'd honed on many an occasion. Had he kept his head down, worn a cap, it would have looked out of the ordinary. *No wonder Holding had been so easy to spot. Amateur.*

He thanked the man, grabbed a bag of Quavers for good measure, and took a seat in the corner of the pub so that he could survey the entire room. Just two other punters, both old, sat propping up the bar. They looked older than his grandfather had been just before he died. He frowned at the memory; remembering how frail the old man had been just before cancer finally took him. It wasn't the grandfather he'd remembered from growing up, the one who'd taught him how to survive in the world he was now living in.

He grabbed a crisp, feeling the tangy cheese swirl dissolving on his tongue, and pulled out the paper. *The list was shrinking.*

CHAPTER TWENTY-TWO

J ack roused not long after 4am. It had been a broken sleep anyway. He looked to the empty space beside him and felt a pang of sadness at the lack of Ryan's presence. He'd asked to stay over and Jack had, once again, given him an excuse about work and sent him away. Ryan had been polite about the whole thing, he always was, but Jack wasn't an idiot. He could read people. His partner was becoming more distant, the rejections Jack dished out more and more common, with his reaction less and less emotional.

Not that he could hold it against him. He was only mirroring Jack's own behaviour; behaviour which had cost him most of the close relationships in his life up until this point. He wondered what Pritchard would make of that. He sighed, realising that he had once again forgotten to contact his old friend and check on his welfare. He knew the psychologist would understand, but that was no excuse. He had to be better.

He moved to the kitchen and made himself a double strong espresso from the machine Ryan had bought him for his birthday, knocking the thick, bitter liquid back in one gulp before rinsing out the cup and splashing cold water on his face. He could feel the anxiety of the situation creeping up on him. He needed to include the team, not go off on his own. Lives depended on it.

Of course, he'd had no credible threat made against him but he was the one heading up the investigation and it was clear that somebody wanted to tie off loose ends. It stood to reason that he would be at risk. Still, as SIO, he wasn't going to put police resources on his house out of some kind of personal fear. It was just a hazard of the job.

Except he didn't just have himself to think about now. He had Ryan to think about too, and Shannon. Gone were the days when the only person who would be impacted, should he come to harm, would be his estranged father and brother.

He moved to the front window and stared out into the early morning gloom. He could make out shadows moving across the way, inside Leazes Park—the park he had been kidnapped in last year. He shuddered at the thought and repressed the memory. He knew McGuinness would have tied up the loose ends. But McGuinness undoubtedly knew that Jack would never be able to pin anything on him. He'd never been involved in that kind of thing back in the day, but he knew how the business worked. He couldn't help but wonder what would have become of him had he not pulled his head out of the sand and joined the force. McGuinness rated him; that much he knew. The crime boss' disappointment at Jack's defection was only matched by his surprise at the fact that he was joining what the gang called 'the enemy'.

Those days were long gone now, though. He cracked his knuckles and looked over the faint scarring that was still left over from his fighting days, scars that would forever serve as a reminder of what he was capable of. His temper was under control, but it was always there, threatening to bubble over. If somebody close to him came to harm, and he had to make a choice between his old life and his new one, he couldn't say with any certainty which outcome would come to pass.

His buzzing phone brought him away from his musings. 'Ryan,' he answered.

'I knew you'd be awake,' he said.

Jack smiled. It hadn't taken the pharmacist long to get the measure of him. 'You know me,' he replied.

'I do, Jack, and that's what concerns me.'

Jack felt his jaw tighten. He didn't speak.

Ryan filled the silence. 'I don't know if I can keep doing this.'

Still Jack didn't speak.

'And you not speaking right now just proves my point. Look, we've gotten to know each other well over these past months and I've grown to... care for you...'

Jack's mind was whirring, thoughts overwhelming him, fighting against his default position of ignoring his problems.

'And I'm sure you care for me in your own way,' Ryan continued.

Jack was stunned. He hadn't thought that there was any doubt about his feelings for his partner.

'But this isn't healthy. I think...' he paused. Jack could hear him clearing his throat. 'Look I think we should take a break for a while, see how we feel in a couple of months and whether we really want to give this a go.'

When Jack finally spoke, his throat was dry and constricted. 'Is this because I didn't want you to stay over? I told you how it is for me. This job—'

'It's not the job, Jack,' Ryan cut in. 'It's you. Don't you see?'

No, he didn't.

Ryan continued, unbridled now. 'Do you know that you haven't even introduced me to your friends and family yet? You've met everybody close to me in my life but I am still a secret in yours.'

'I don't have friends and family,' Jack told him.

Ryan's tone stiffened. 'Yes you do, Jack, it's just that you choose to cut them off like you do everything in your life, including me.'

He had no idea what to say. Louise, Rosie and now Ryan. He'd managed to push them all away. And the worst thing was that he was so sure it was going to be different with Ryan.

He realised that Ryan had stopped speaking. 'Whatever you want, Ryan. With this case and everything that's going on, maybe it's for the best.'

'Right,' Ryan said.

Jack held the phone to his ear for some time after the line went dead. He knew Ryan had wanted him to fight for him. He'd given him the opportunity to do it.

But he hadn't bothered.

He finally lowered the phone, realising he was grinding his teeth, and felt tears forming in his eyes. He blinked them away, feeling the sting of repressed emotion not for the first time in his life, and reverted back to type.

The phone slamming against the wall took him by surprise, such was the force he launched it with. He glanced at his palms and noticed nail marks in the skin. The wall where the phone had hit, recently-painted, was now smudged with the debris of the cracked device.

He turned back to the kitchen, pushed the coffee machine to one side, and reached for his whisky.

The old Jack was threatening a return.

CHAPTER TWENTY-THREE

He'd spent two days without any communication with the outside world, save for a brief trip to the local Nisa shop round the corner from St James' Park, home of the now not-so mighty Newcastle United. Mr Grabben hadn't seemed very impressed when Jack had stumbled in, red-eyed and shoeless. He called him Mr Grabben on account of having known him since he was a child; a time when every adult was a Mr or a Mrs. Jack had mumbled an apology, thrown his change across the counter, and staggered back home to continue his suffering.

When he'd finally taken the time to look at his phone, complete with a newly-cracked screen, he saw he had sixteen missed calls and seven texts, one of which was from his ex-wife, Louise. Unable to see straight, he dragged sandpaper-like palms across his raw eyes, causing a clump of congealed sleep to come loose and tumble down his stubbled cheeks.

It wasn't long before somebody else called him.

'What is it?' he mumbled.

'Where are you?' Watkins shot down the line.

'I think I'm in Newcastle,' he replied.

'Very funny,' the DS said. 'I got your message the other night.'

Jack rolled over in his bed and gazed outside. It was still dark which, at this time of year, could mean anything in the north east. 'Message?'

'Aye, that you were unwell.'

Jack searched his mind for some memory of having contacted Watkins. All he found was TV static. 'Aye, well...'

'I've covered for you so far,' Watkins cut in. 'But people are going to start asking questions soon if you don't show up. You do remember we have a somewhat complex murder case on the go?'

Jack groaned as he made to stand, feeling every one of his thirty-six years. 'Alright, man, calm down,' he said.

'It's saying something when I'm the one cracking the whip with you, like,' Watkins said.

Jack was inclined to agree. Still, at this point, he barely cared.

'...or what?'

'What?' he said, having missed the first part of Watkins' sentence.

'I said are you coming in today or what? Edwards will stick the Bulldog in charge permanently if you don't pull yourself together.'

Jack detected a hint of the old whine in Watkins' voice. Like most of the Northumbrian force, he was still scared of DI Russell.

'How do you know I'm not well?' he shot back, wincing at his own petulant tone.

'You think I don't know a hangover when I hear one. Plus, you're never unwell. What's been going on?'

A heart-to-heart with his DS wasn't something Jack was interested in today. 'I'll be in within the hour.'

'Okay, but—'

Jack cut him off, lunged towards the bathroom, and threw up into what had, up until that point, been a reasonably clean porcelain sink. He watched as chunks of what looked like chicken chow mein swirled in the basin before clagging around the plughole. He couldn't remember having eaten. Good job he'd cancelled his previous session with the personal trainer.

Although he felt like a public-school boy after his first night on the lash, he still managed to put a clean set of clothes on and get on the move within the hour. He'd tested himself to see if he was over the limit before leaving the house, using a gadget he'd snagged from a colleague some years ago. As his old teacher used to say, 'it was close enough for jazz'.

As he made the drive to HQ, he couldn't help but be taken aback by how hard Ryan's rejection had hit him. Jack hadn't known for certain whether what he felt for the man was love.

He was certain now.

Like everything in his life, though, the job came first. Deep down, no matter how much he loved Ryan, he knew that the pattern would continue. He glanced at his beleaguered expression in the mirror. It was penance for his previous sins. His previous life running with the McGuinness crew was a scar that wouldn't heal. No matter how many criminals he caught, nothing could dampen his guilt at what he had once been. There was no doubt about it, he loved Ryan. But that didn't mean he would be able to put him first. Louise, his ex-wife, had labelled him selfish. Rosie, whose heart he had broken when coming out about his sexuality, had said something similar. Maybe they were right.

He suddenly remembered the missed call from his ex-wife.

He somehow managed to navigate his beaten-up phone to ring her.

'There you are,' she fired at him. 'What if it had been an emergency? You and that bloody—'

'Not now, Louise!' he shouted. 'What is it?'

'That's a fine way to talk to the mother of your child,' she said. 'Honestly...'

Jack allowed the tirade to wash over him. Over the years, he'd learned not to bite back. It wasn't a fight he was likely to win. He resisted the urge to inform her that, actually, in terms of ex-spouses, their relationship was probably in the healthy bracket.

More or less.

'Look, I'm really busy at work—'

'Well that's a lie as I can hear you're in the car.'

'I do sometimes drive on the job,' he said.

First Watkins, now his ex-wife, he didn't think the day could get much worse.

'It's about Shannon.'

Jack felt his chest tighten. Although semi-estranged from his only daughter, he would still have crawled across hot coals for her. Maybe even put her above the job.

Maybe.

'What is it?' he asked.

He heard Louise pause on the line, taking a deep breath, as he pulled into the car park for HQ. Parking in a space as far from the entrance as possible, he turned the engine off, leaving the key in the ignition so as not to end the call. He almost smiled to himself. He was learning.

Louise finally answered. 'She got into a fight in school.'

Jack was stunned. 'A fight? Details.'

'Don't harangue me, Jack Lambert, I'm not one of your suspects or police subordinates.'

'Sorry,' he said. 'Force of habit.'

'I had a call from the head teacher yesterday. Apparently, Shannon and a group of girls were caught spitting and fighting with a new girl at school.'

'I can't believe it...' he tailed off.

'The girl is Asian.'

Jack felt his jaw tighten. 'And was that a motivating factor?'

Another pause. 'According to the head, based upon what they were saying to her, he thinks so.'

'Jesus Christ,' he thundered, suddenly feeling very awake.

'They want to have a meeting this afternoon. I can go with Jeremy...'

'No!' Jack cut in. 'I'll be there. What time?'

They made the arrangements and Jack hung up the phone,

unable to move for a good two minutes. The Shannon he knew wasn't capable of such behaviour. She'd only started secondary school the previous year and her reports had all been glowing. He couldn't help but wonder what had changed in that time. He was wrestling with this dilemma when a knock at his window caught his attention.

'Alright, guv,' Gerrard said, her beaming face staring at him through fogged-up glass.

He opened the door and stepped out. 'For God's sake, Gerrard, you frightened the life out of me.'

She frowned. 'You sure you weren't frightening yourself? Jesus, Jack, have you looked in the mirror lately?'

He bit his tongue. Apparently the day could get worse. 'Spare me the lecture.'

'Don't mind me, guv, I'm just the hired help. Thought I would give you a heads-up, though, Edwards is looking for you. He collared Watkins earlier who wasn't much help.'

Something in Gerrard's tone told Jack that Watkins wasn't in her good books at the minute. He sighed, despite the personal growth Watkins had gone through in the previous year, he was still like a wet sandwich when it came to handling pressure from the boss. Still, it wasn't his fault. He couldn't expect the DS to put his neck on the line for him, nor should he have to.

'I'll see him straight away, get it over with,' he grumbled.

'You okay, guv?' Gerrard asked.

They began walking to the entrance just as the wind began picking up. Jack pulled his collar up tight around his neck and determined to start wearing his winter coat before the week was out. 'I'm fine,' he said.

'You had a falling out with your lad?'

He stopped short. 'My lad?'

She rolled her eyes. 'Come on, guv, everybody knows you've got someone on the go.'

Jack felt his stomach lurch at the thought of his colleagues talking about his love life behind his back. Not that he had a love life now. 'Don't worry about it,' he told her.

Gerrard placed a firm hand on his arm. 'Somebody has to.'

He pulled away from her and pushed through the door to the station. 'Consider it noted and, when I feel like I need to, I'll come and confide in you. Until then, let's concentrate on the case,' he said.

Gerrard straightened up and moved past him. 'That's what the rest of us have been doing while you've been AWOL.'

By the time Edwards had finished berating him for a lack of headway in the Gus Fenwick case, he'd long forgotten Gerrard's rant. Despite Robert Norris' still unsolved murder, as well as the disturbing discovery of his father, Les Holding, Edwards hadn't seemed nearly as bothered about them as he had about the deceased farmer. Apparently dead criminals weren't as important as everyday folk. Jack could understand the sentiment, and DSI Edwards was no doubt under the cosh from both ACC Dalton and PCC Nadine Guthrie. Still, though, background mattered very little to Jack. The way he saw it, three people were dead.

Plus, if they solved one murder, he knew the others would fall into place.

CHAPTER TWENTY-FOUR

J ack met Louise and Shannon at the school gates, all corrugated iron and rusted hinges. His daughter avoided his gaze, choosing instead to kick some dirt across the pavement.

'Louise,' he greeted his ex-wife, tersely. 'Shannon.'

His twelve-year-old daughter uttered a nonsensical response and they made the short walk to the entrance of Palmdale Comprehensive School. It was an imposing sight, old red bricks, giant wooden-framed windows and a strict uniform policy that included, amongst other things, a tie and blazer, which both boys and girls had to wear. Jack swallowed his guilt at having missed parents' evening the previous academic year, but consoled himself with the fact that he had been involved in choosing the school for his daughter. So far it hadn't academised, like many others in the region, and he quite liked that. His traditional stance on education would have sat well with his father. He shuddered at the comparison.

'Mr and Mrs Lambert,' the head greeted them in the reception area.

'Actually it's Ms Tully,' Louise corrected him.

Mr Corbridge's gaze swept across them, his eyebrows rising. They followed him into his office. Jack was impressed by the sheer size of it, but he couldn't help but feel that it would have served better as a classroom. The head sat down on what appeared to be an expensive mahogany chair, with ornamental carvings in it.

He could tell that Mr Corbridge was a man used to getting his own way. He reminded him of DSI Edwards, and the man's considerable girth made him his physical equal as well. Because of this, Jack was instantly on his guard.

The head placed his meaty palms face down on his immaculately-cleaned desk, thick black hair matting over the back of his hands and up what Jack could see of his arms. 'I'm pleased to see you both here,' he said, glancing at Jack. 'But I am sorry it is under such grim circumstances.'

None of them spoke. Jack felt like it was he who had been summoned for a telling off. Truth be told, he probably deserved it. His headache from lack of sleep and water had kicked in big time now and he was acutely aware of his tardy appearance. It wouldn't have cut the mustard in his old school.

It didn't really cut the mustard now.

'Unfortunately,' the head continued, a hint of Scottish creeping into his otherwise Queen's English, 'your daughter has been involved in a very serious incident here in school.'

Jack looked to Shannon, her head hanging down towards the maroon carpet.

'Yes,' Louise replied. 'And I want you to know that we also take this very seriously, don't we, Jack?'

His ex-wife's words pulled him out of his daydream. 'Yes, of course.'

The head nodded, and Jack noted that the man's pinprick eyes were sat too close together, dwarfed by his otherwise giant features. 'As do we, Ms Tully,' the head continued.

He paused, gazing out of his office window at the grey,

concrete lunch hall across the playground. Jack knew it was for dramatic effect. He'd done it himself, at work, a thousand times.

'Is the young girl okay?' Jack asked.

The head's beady eyes landed on him. 'As you can imagine, the student is very upset.' He looked to Shannon. 'It pains me to have to tell you this, but it would appear your daughter and a group of three friends have been bullying this student for some time. Her family only moved here in the last six months and to be faced with such behaviour is nothing short of a disgrace.'

Jack noted the boom in the man's voice. He made for an archetypal head teacher.

Shannon, still unmoved, continued staring at the floor.

'I just can't believe it,' Louise said. 'Our daughter, a bully!' She gazed at Shannon. 'You could at least look at people when they are speaking to you!'

Shannon was unmoved. Jack shifted in his seat, and waited.

'It gets worse,' the head stated. 'We have investigated this matter fully and it would appear that Shannon here is the ringleader.'

Jack was stunned. Shannon had never been the type to lead anybody. He glanced at her again and noted that her jet-black hair had been replaced with a lighter tint, her previously gothic clothes toned down for a more girly look. Just what was happening with his daughter?

'Are you sure?' Jack asked.

The head's jaw clenched. 'I am sure. Everybody involved in this process has pointed to it.' He turned to Shannon. 'Do you deny it?'

She shook her head.

Jack fought the urge to go into work-mode. He had to be a father right now. 'So what is she looking at in terms of a punishment?'

The head pointed to a mantra, printed and stuck to the wall above his head. 'Our ethos at this school is "respect, fairness and equality". I'm afraid your daughter's actions are in contradiction to those values. The poor girl at the centre of this now feels unable to return to school and her parents are rightly outraged. I have no choice but to put in place a temporary suspension.'

Jack had expected that. 'That seems fair to me.'

Louise shot him a harrowed look.

'And once your daughter returns,' he went on, 'she will have to be moved groups...'

'What?!' Shannon shouted. 'That's not fair!'

Jack watched as the head bristled. 'You'll find out, young lady, that a lot of things in life aren't fair! It wasn't fair when you decided to racially abuse a fellow student and begin a campaign of bullying and hatred against her now, was it?'

Shannon shrank back down, as if slapped, but not before Jack witnessed tears filling her eyes. Knowing what she had done, he had very little sympathy for her.

'And what about the other girls?' Louise asked.

'That is obviously something I cannot divulge,' the head replied. He leaned forward, the desk creaking under his considerable bulk. 'But you can rest assured that punishments will be handed down to all of those involved. I'll be making sure some of these issues are touched upon in the curriculum more rigorously, as well, from now on.'

After a firm handshake with the man charged with running the school, they stepped back out into the dim Newcastle afternoon. Darkness was setting in now, seeping into Jack's bones as they walked.

He was furious. 'This kind of thing is outrageous, do you hear me?' he lambasted his daughter.

Shannon's glare shot up towards him. 'Oh, so now you're bothered, are you?'

'What is that supposed to mean?' he shot back.

'Please,' Louise pleaded, running a hand across her brow. 'Can we just leave it for today?'

Jack had sympathy for her; she was basically tasked with bringing their teenage daughter up alone, and now she had found out that her only child was a racist. Her once striking eyes now carried the crow's feet that had dogged his own face for many a year. She was tired and Jack didn't blame her.

'We probably can't, Mam,' Shannon said, sarcastically. 'I doubt we will see Dad for a while.'

'You... know that isn't fair,' he spluttered.

Shannon rounded on him. 'Fair! What would you know about fair?'

He watched as his daughter marched towards her mother's car and stood, cross-armed, unwilling to engage further.

'Look,' Louise sighed. 'I'll find out what's going on and let you know.'

He turned to her. 'Has her behaviour been different lately?'

She bit her lip. 'For a little while.'

'And you didn't think to tell me?' He regretted the words as soon as he'd uttered them.

'I'll pretend I didn't hear that,' she told him. 'How about *you* call *me* when you want to know something?'

With that, they were both gone, leaving him to his own destructive thoughts. Just a few short days ago, he'd had a stable relationship, and a seemingly well-adjusted daughter. Now he'd lost one and was in danger of making it two out of two.

With one last glance at Louise's now disappearing Toyota, he turned, fished his mobile out, and rang Watkins.

'What's up, guv?' he asked. 'Daughter okay?'

'Yes,' he dismissed him. 'But meet me at The Black Horse in one hour.'

'Again?' the DS asked. 'Something come up?'

'No, just meet me there.'

He hung up the phone before Watkins could add anything else. He never had been any good at knowing when to shut his mouth.

He jammed his phone back in his pocket, sighed and got in the car. The school incident, whilst unsavoury, had served a purpose in that it had given him a thought with regards to the case.

Shannon was a bully. But she wasn't the only one. She had a network of support. Yes, she was a leader, but there were other players, including a victim.

Whatever was or wasn't in Gus Fenwick's property, he had to fall into one of those categories. Either he was the head bully, masterminding something and bringing others into the situation; or he was the victim, targeted by others for who he was or what he held. There was, of course, the possibility that he was a puppet in the whole operation.

Which meant somebody else was pulling the strings.

Jack indicated and pulled out of the parking space. Brian McCullagh had more to him than he was letting on. Multiple people had been killed now. As far as Jack was concerned, the time had come to put a little pressure on those who were still alive.

CHAPTER TWENTY-FIVE

'He's not 'ere,' the woman informed them in her broad Mackem accent.

Jack tried to hide his impatience. It wasn't her fault that Brian McCullagh had decided to go on leave. 'You seem a little far from home,' he stated.

She shrugged, pulling her bra strap up. 'Sunderland isn't that far. Nowt for me there anyway, like.'

Jack nodded. 'So when is he back?'

She sighed, her shoulders drooping. Jack had never seen such thick mascara on a woman's face. Her eyelashes stood out some three inches from her face and her lippy looked like it had been put on by a sugared-up toddler. She was certainly a character, of that much he was sure.

'No idea,' she said. 'He just sent me a text saying he was going away for a few days and could I watch the bar. The way I see it, a few extra shifts is no bother. Not that we're particularly busy.' She motioned across the room.

She was right. Even the old bloke hadn't made it in today.

'Are you acquainted with Gus Fenwick at all?' Watkins asked her.

Jack could see her sizing the DS up. Her lively eyes told him she liked what she saw. Unfortunately, she was about twenty years too old for him. No doubt Watkins wouldn't mind.

'Aren't you a pretty picture,' she said, causing a red flush to wash over the DS' face. 'Using big words as well!' She laughed. 'The farmer, aye? I know him a bit. Not on a personal level. He likes the curry we do 'ere.'

Jack was partial to an Indian himself from time to time. 'Have you ever seen Mr Fenwick and Mr McCullagh in a setting outside of the pub?' he asked.

'Not that I recall,' she said. 'We don't hang out, you know?'

Jack sensed sarcasm. He let it slide. 'Is it your opinion that the two men are... were close?'

The barmaid hesitated, just for a moment, but it was enough to give him the answer he needed. 'No,' she said.

'So as far as you are aware, the two men weren't in business together and they didn't have a close relationship of any kind?'

'I'd say that was about the top and bottom of it,' she told him.

He decided a direct approach. 'What is Brian McCullagh like?'

'Fine,' she said, quickly. 'He could pay more but he's alright. I've worked for worse people.'

Watkins said, 'So, to the best of your knowledge, Brian McCullagh is not a violent, dangerous or otherwise secretive man?'

'Old Brian!' she exclaimed with a nervous laugh. 'Don't be daft, lad.'

Back in the car Jack thumped the dash. 'This is ridiculous.'

'She was lying,' Watkins said.

'Of course she was,' he concurred. 'The question is, how much of it was a lie? I can't shift the feeling that McCullagh is somehow part of this in some way.'

'Well,' Watkins added, 'the goalposts do seem to shift every time we speak with him in terms of his relationship with Fenwick. Suggests he's got something to hide.'

A faint knock at the window caught their attention. It was the barmaid, carrying a bulging black bin bag over her shoulder like some kind of grim Father Christmas.

He wound the window down. 'Everything okay?'

'Look,' she said, her eyes darting left to right. 'I wasn't totally honest in there.'

Jack nodded. 'I got that impression.'

She shrugged. 'Gotta be careful, haven't you? Snitches everywhere.'

Jack didn't quite follow. He motioned for her to continue.

She gulped, looking him in the eye. 'I had to bring the bin bags out, he has the place rigged.'

'Rigged?' Watkins said.

'Aye, CCTV and that.' She pulled once again at her bra strap. 'And he watches it all the time.'

'Okay,' Jack said.

She cleared her throat before continuing. 'Gus Fenwick was always in the bar. Him and Brian were close. I wasn't involved in any of the conversations they had but I can tell you it went beyond friendly barman banter. Brian has... interests everywhere. They also held a poker night in here, once in a while. Super exclusive, four or five blokes and a woman.'

'A woman?' Jack asked. 'Any idea who she was?'

The barmaid replied, 'Older, really stern, didn't take any shit.'

An image of Margaret Fenwick flashed in Jack's mind. 'How do you know this?'

She shrugged. 'Someone's gotta serve the drinks, haven't they? And let me tell you, it wasn't just poker that went on.'

'What else?' Watkins asked.

She shook her head. 'I've already said too much. I'll have to get back. If he watches the tape and sees how long I've been out for...'

'Wait,' Jack implored her. 'I don't even know your name.'

'It's Patricia,' she told him.

'Why are you telling us this now?'

She gulped, her hands resting on the top of the rolled-down window as she leaned in. 'Some bosses are better than others,' she said, pausing. 'And some are worse than the worst.'

'I can help you,' he told her.

She waved him away. 'I'm a big girl, but thanks anyway. I'll be honest, though, if anybody ever asks me, I'll deny I ever said owt, do you hear? Not my job to catch bad people.' She pointed a gnarled finger at Jack, complete with chipped nail varnish. 'That's your job.'

She made to leave but Jack grabbed her hand. She jumped back, as if shot. 'I'm sorry,' he told her. 'I need to ask you one more question.'

'What is it?' she said.

'Did Brian McCullagh kill Robert Norris?'

Patricia looked to both of them. 'The young lad in the field? No idea, love. But if you're asking me whether he's capable of it...'

Jack pressed her further. 'Could he have been involved in Gus Fenwick's death?'

Patricia bit down on her lower lip and blinked twice in quick succession. 'That's more than one question, detective.'

CHAPTER TWENTY-SIX

'Listen up!' Jack barked to the assembled officers in the MIR. He turned to Watkins. 'You're a genius.'

The DS blushed. 'Well, what're you going to do?'

Jack smiled as the team turned to him. 'We've had a phone call from a witness, a credible one I might add, who states she saw two people leave a roadside cafe she works at off the A1, one of which matches Les Holding's description. The call was made days ago and had been lost amongst a myriad of other information. However, knowing what we know now, it seems that we may have stumbled across something.'

A collective intake of breath could be heard around the room.

'So who was the other one?' Gerrard asked.

'That's the killer question,' Jack said, wincing at his unfortunate choice of words. 'We believe, based upon the description from the waitress, that it's Dayton Olsen.'

Jack saw confusion on the face of some of the officers so beckoned towards Watkins to fill them in.

'Back when I was in CID,' the DS began, 'I was involved in the apprehension of Dayton Olsen, a known hard man from the Durham area. He'd been suspected of numerous acts of violence and, whilst he was convicted of aggravated burglary, we reckoned it was just the tip of the iceberg.' Watkins faced the room with a new-found authority. 'We believed that he was a hired hitman. We couldn't prove it, but we knew,' he said. 'Still he was put away and that was that.' He picked up a newspaper and waved it around for theatrical effect. 'It was revealed in the press the other day that Olsen had absconded whilst on day release from Kirklevington prison. Reports suggest that he was a model prisoner, not a hair out of place. He had been due for release in just a few months' time.'

'Then why abscond now?' Gerrard observed.

Jack placed a hand on Watkins' shoulder. 'That is the key question.'

'Fear of release? Wouldn't be the first criminal to jump ship just as he's due to get let out,' Christensen said.

Watkins shook his head. 'No, he's not that twitchy. He's one of the most calculating people you will ever meet. Nothing is done on impulse.'

Jack picked up the thread. 'Which means there can only be one other, possible, logical explanation.' He looked to each of the team in turn. 'He was given a job.'

'You think he was hired to kill Holding?' Gerrard posed.

Jack nodded. 'I do indeed. Also,' he said, turning to pin a mugshot up on the wall, 'this tutor, Mark Davison, was recently murdered whilst delivering a workshop session at the prison. Highly unusual in a low-security establishment such as Kirklevington.'

'I remember this,' Jane interjected. 'It was in the news! A chisel to the neck, wasn't it?'

'Yes,' Jack concurred. 'A man called Marshall Reaves has been charged with his murder but, as coincidence would have it, guess who else was in the class at the time?'

'Dayton Olsen,' Watkins said.

'Bingo.' Jack put pictures of both Davison and Olsen up on

the board. They couldn't have been further apart from a physical point of view. Olsen had angular features, sunken eyes and a lifeless look about him whereas Davison had a vibrancy about him that marked him out as somebody who must have loved life. It wouldn't have taken a genius to work out which one was the convict.

Then there was the small matter of the indent in the side of the larger man's skull, an indent which would surely make him easily recognisable to the wider public.

'You think he did it?' Gerrard asked.

'Well witnesses say Reaves clearly attacked Davison and that Olsen was an innocent bystander,' Jack said. 'In a sense, it is irrelevant to us; it's essentially a Cleveland matter, although Durham will be involved now too. However, it does matter to us in that Olsen, we believe, was seen with Les Holding, what could have only been hours, at most, before he was killed.'

'So what's the move?' Christensen asked.

Jack scratched at his chin absentmindedly. 'We need to establish the gaps in our information so far. The questions we need to be posing are: who hired Olsen to kill Holding; why did they do that; and is anybody else at risk?'

'That's a lot of questions to answer, when you add them to the conundrums we already have,' DI Russell sighed.

'It is, but it gives us something to go on,' Jack said. 'I'm going to speak to Oliver Tomkins and see if we can work together on this. Durham won't want us invading their patch but I don't see how we have any choice. If it's going to work we will need an open line of communication to share information. I'm led to believe that Olsen and Reaves were close on the inside. If we can speak with him, he may be able to help us out. I also want to know anything and everything about Dayton Olsen and his links to the outside.'

Watkins piped up. 'I can do that. I'll speak to some of my old buddies at CID and see what they know.'

'Good stuff.'

'And I can keep trying to locate Brian McCullagh, as well as dig a little more into Margaret Fenwick's dealings with him,' Jane said.

'Good idea,' Jack replied. 'Christensen, you and Gerrard co-ordinate the release of Olsen's image to the press and see what you can dig up with regards to his background.'

'Will do, boss,' Christensen said.

Jack nodded. 'Now, if you'll excuse me, I have a couple of phone calls to make.'

The team sprang into action. The first call, to Oliver Tomkins, would be straightforward enough. They'd known each other years and had often co-ordinated on various cases. The second phone call, however, Jack was not so enthusiastic about.

CHAPTER TWENTY-SEVEN

He could see McGuinness standing tall in a clear glass window above the dance floor as he entered the club. The smell of sweat, a permanent fixture since the smoking ban came into place, and the squelch of leather soles on drink-stained hard flooring, followed him as he made for the stairs.

Since McGuinness had gotten into the nightclub business, he'd been a roaring success. Jack glanced around the dance floor at the barely legal clientele; he'd certainly found his niche. Glow sticks, cheap shots and young girls in chaps and bikini tops adorned the bar, giving it a distinctly club 18-30 vibe.

Jack managed to push through the sea of bodies, each of them lost in their own intoxication, until he came to the foot of the staircase, which was blocked by a man similar to himself in terms of stature. 'I'm here to see Dorian,' he told him.

The man crossed his arms across a bulging black T-shirt and glared at him through tinted glasses. 'Why?'

He leaned in, trying to drown out the sound around him. 'He's expecting me,' he said. 'Jack Lambert.'

The man raised an eyebrow and looked at Jack's ID. 'No problem, up you go.'

He didn't know whether to thank the bloke or stare him down, instead chose to ignore him as he made his way up.

'Jack!' Dorian greeted him inside the office. 'It's good to see you.'

'Is it?' he asked.

'Always,' the crime boss laughed. 'Please, take a seat.'

This office had exactly the same layout, dominated by a mahogany table, as McGuinness' headquarters at the aquatic shop. Dorian always did have a fantastic attention to detail.

And a need for order.

'I was wondering if we could speak alone,' Jack said, aware of the presence of a younger bloke in the room.

'Oh, you mean Luke,' McGuinness said, his smile baring razor-sharp teeth. 'He's no harm, isn't that right, boy?'

The young lad shrugged, his painfully-plucked eyebrows barely moving across his well-tanned face. He resembled an orange pixie, and he couldn't have been much taller than one.

'Still,' Jack said, tugging at his collar. 'I'd rather do this in private.'

McGuinness sighed. 'As you wish, Jack. Luke, wait outside for me.'

'I'm not one of your hired goons, you know!' he pouted, before stomping across the room.

The track changed to another mind-numbing tune. Dorian's friend threw the door shut, leaving them with just each other and a dull thud throbbing through the walls.

'Really?' Jack said.

'What?' Dorian replied, laughing.

'The lad is about sixteen.'

Dorian scoffed. 'Actually, Jack, he's nineteen, but I don't discriminate. He's quite the party animal, keeps me young. You should try it.'

Jack shook his head. 'No thanks.'

'Already got somebody?' Dorian asked.

'No,' Jack answered quickly, Ryan's image flashing through his mind.

Amusement flashed across McGuinness' eyes. 'Fair enough.'

'Anyway,' Jack continued. 'I'm not here to talk sexual preferences, this isn't a personal visit.'

'Jack, Jack, Jack,' Dorian said, 'every visit from you is a personal one. Don't we go back many years?'

He didn't need reminding.

'How's the Les Holding investigation going?' Jack asked.

Dorian paused, threw open a drawer, grabbed an expensive-looking tumbler and an even more expensive-looking bottle of whisky and poured, before tossing it back. Unlike most men, he didn't follow it up with a rasp of the lips, merely a pleasurable groan, before pouring another.

'Can I offer you one, detective? You're surely not on duty at 11pm?'

'I'm not on duty now,' he said. 'But, if it's all the same, I'll pass.'

'Shame,' Dorian said, twirling the glass around in his huge palm. 'Very expensive stuff this. The Scots will tell you their stuff is the best, but you can't beat Irish.'

The pun wasn't lost on Jack. Dorian McGuinness had long been linked with the Real IRA. As with most aspects of his underworld, though, they were unable to pin anything on him.

'The investigation?' Jack repeated.

'Shouldn't it be me asking you that question, Jack?' Dorian said. 'After all... you're the policeman.'

'Seeing as we are alone, Dorian, why don't we be honest with each other?'

The crime boss leaned forward, peering over his Ozzy Osbourne glasses. 'Are you wearing a wire?'

'No,' Jack said.

Dorian narrowed his eyes. 'I believe you.'

'Good,' he said. 'Now, any updates?'

The giant hulk of a man leaned back, his office chair creaking under the strain of his immense bulk. 'Now, let's just say I was looking into it, I would probably have to say that I have come up with very little.'

'Don't lie,' Jack said.

Jack noticed the man clench his fists, ever so slightly, before responding.

'What would you have me do, Jack?'

He decided to play his cards straight. 'Does the name Dayton Olsen mean anything to you?'

McGuinness nodded. 'I've heard of him.'

Jack wasn't surprised. People like Dorian McGuinness and Dayton Olsen were part of the same world: undoubtedly they would have rubbed shoulders. McGuinness always knew what was going on in his patch, and that patch stretched to Yorkshire. Beyond that, if the rumours were true. He couldn't help but wonder whether that was where the mysterious Captain had been brought into the mix. During last year's murder case, Jack had been made aware of a new player in the Newcastle underground crime scene—a seemingly powerful new rival for McGuinness to contend with.

Priding himself on always having his finger on the pulse, Jack was sure that McGuinness would have known of Olsen's escape and his previous history.

The question was, had McGuinness hired him to dispose of Les Holding?

'Got many contacts in Durham these days, Dorian?' Jack asked.

The crime boss smiled. He never had been one to get straight to the point. The merry dance he and Jack always seemed to play was more his style.

'I know some people,' he said. 'What are you implying?'

Jack undid his top button and sank into his seat, motioned to the whisky, and happily tossed a tumbler back once McGuinness had finished pouring it. 'Olsen was due for release imminently,' he said. 'Yet he decides to abscond just when he can taste freedom. It makes no sense. Unless...'

'Unless?' McGuinness said, hurling back another glass before pouring Jack another.

'Unless he was somehow personally involved in Les Holding's business or,' he paused to finish his drink, 'he was hired to do a job.'

McGuinness clapped his giant hands together theatrically before undoing his garish purple tie and slapping a hand down on his thigh. 'And you think it's me?' he laughed.

Jack shrugged. 'Why not?'

'Because,' he said, pointing a slightly unsteady finger in Jack's direction, 'if I wanted him dead, I wouldn't need to have somebody abscond from prison to do it.'

Jack understood the logic. But if not McGuinness, then who? 'So you're admitting to having people on the payroll who offer such services?'

McGuinness' sharp, booming laugh, ended as abruptly as it had started. 'You sure you're not wearing a wire?' he said.

'Absolutely.'

'Good,' McGuinness replied, smiling. 'I'd hate for you to get into trouble. There was once a time you were on my payroll, remember?'

Jack suddenly felt very warm, and it wasn't just the light buzz the whisky had given him. He lowered his voice. 'I never killed anybody.'

McGuinness waved him away. 'But you wanted to,' he said. 'And, I seem to remember you being pretty handy at dishing out punishments to certain types of people.'

Jack held his gaze. 'That was a long time ago. It's not who I am now.'

'You keep telling yourself that, Jack. Henry Stafford?'

'That was personal,' Jack said.

'Personal? Without a shred of proof? I'd say it was more illegal, wouldn't you?'

'I'm not here to reminisce about the old days, Dorian,' Jack told him.

'Then make your point, detective,' McGuinness said, his tone flat.

'If you didn't hire Olsen to go after Holding, who did?'

The crime boss shrugged. 'No idea. But I'm hardly likely to tell you if I find out, am I?'

'I thought we were old friends?'

Jack watched as McGuinness picked up his empty whisky tumbler and held it up to the light, frowning, before removing a smudge from the side. 'Yes, we were old friends, Jack, but as you've pointed out, you've changed. With that in mind, I'm considering downgrading you to more of a current acquaintance.'

Jack stood. 'Enough people have died, Dorian, I don't want more bloodshed on the streets. You come to me if you hear anything.'

'Jack, Jack, Jack, don't be silly,' Dorian said. 'There are a number of police officers I would speak to before it even entered my head to come to you. Do you see what I mean?'

Jack was stunned. 'Who?' he demanded.

McGuinness smiled, teeth appearing once more. 'Everyone has a price, even you.'

Suddenly angry, Jack turned to leave, before remembering the other information he needed. He bit down on his tongue. 'There's something else.'

'For an acquaintance? Of course,' McGuinness said.

'I got word that Gus Fenwick was involved in a poker game, highly discreet, with a number of other players. Implication was that it wasn't just a game but some kind of secret club or society where other things went on. You know anything about that?'

McGuinness stood and walked over to the window overlooking the dance floor. 'A high-stakes game that I haven't been invited to? That's simply outrageous.'

'So you don't?' Jack said.

McGuinness clicked his fingers and turned to Jack. 'You sure it isn't just a harmless game?'

'At this stage, I have no idea.'

McGuinness nodded. 'I'll look into it. But, if I get you some information on this, I'm going to need a favour from you.'

Jack tensed. 'Dorian...'

'Before you get on your high horse about it, don't worry, when the time comes it'll be more or less legal, I promise.'

Jack didn't have much choice. Plus, chances were McGuinness wouldn't come up with anything anyway. He nodded. 'I reserve the right to refuse.'

McGuinness laughed before his features straightened up. 'You can ask.'

A heavy knock on the office door was followed up by the large bouncer from before appearing. 'Everything okay, boss?' the man asked, his voice even deeper than Dorian's.

'Shaved head, by the bar,' Dorian pointed. 'He's too drunk and is behaving inappropriately with the barmaid. I pay you to sort this stuff out,' he told him. 'If I can't rely on you, then what use are you to me?'

The man's posture shrank. 'Sorry, boss.'

'I won't have my club's reputation dragged through the mud by some drunken moron with loose morals—sort it out!' he boomed, before glancing briefly at Jack. 'Gently.'

The man's wide eyes landed on Jack, before returning to McGuinness. 'Okay.'

Jack turned to leave.

'Oh, and Scott,' Dorian stopped him in his tracks. 'Check that my old friend Jack here isn't wearing a wire. If he is, take him out back and break his kneecaps.'

CHAPTER TWENTY-EIGHT

'Where are we at?' he put to the team.

Jack glanced at Watkins; he looked as dishevelled as *he* felt. He hadn't told any of the team about his impromptu meeting with Dorian McGuinness as he knew what the reaction would be. Plus, he couldn't stomach the thought of one, or more, of them being on the gangster's payroll. There'd never been any indication that any of them even knew the man. As he nursed his third coffee of the day, something he'd now wholeheartedly reintroduced into his diet, he consoled himself with the fact that McGuinness always had a penchant for the theatrical and that he was a compulsive liar.

Not about the kneecaps, though. Luckily for Jack, he hadn't actually been wearing a wire.

Watkins stopped tapping the pen he'd been holding on to for the best part of ten minutes before responding. 'I spoke to some of my old uniform buddies; they remember Olsen well.'

'Good,' Jack said.

'Depends on how you look at it,' the DS replied. 'He's never been forgotten in their ranks. Known as a violent man, trained as a boxer before turning to mixed martial arts, but also a man with high restraint.'

DI Russell, who had up until that point been ignoring the pair of them, spoke up. 'Meaning?'

Watkins shrugged. 'It was always difficult to know what he was thinking. When he was in court, he barely spoke, save for answering to his name and address. When they passed the verdict, he didn't react.'

'Any known links to the McGuinness crew?' Gerrard asked.

'Not that they know of,' he replied. 'However, it's difficult to say as he wasn't thought to have a loyalty to any particular group. They reckon he made his name by offering his services for hire to the highest bidder.'

'That has to be the reason he absconded from prison,' Jack said.

Watkins nodded. 'I agree. Still begs the question as to who he was working for.'

Jack spoke. 'I'm not ruling McGuinness out. We never can.'

'It's a smart move,' Jane said. 'But where do we go from here with it?'

'His breakout occurred on Durham's patch,' Jack said. 'However, I have spoken with DI Tomkins and they are open to co-ordinating things with us. They are speaking with his fellow prisoners, tutors, even that bloke who stabbed Mark Davison in the neck, to see if anything comes up.'

'They letting us in on that?' Gerrard asked.

Jack smiled. 'Not yet but I'm working on it.'

'I think it's worth speaking with his old gym buddies down at the MMA training place,' Watkins said. 'I have the address. Apparently he was close with a few of them down there, including the owner.'

'Good idea,' Jack said. He turned to DI Russell. 'Jane, any further forward with regards to McCullagh or Margaret Fenwick?'

Jane sighed, and turned to face him. 'Still no sign of the barman.'

'Should we be worried?'

Jane chewed her cheek, as if deep in thought, before responding. 'Not sure. Nobody has reported him missing, and it's not against the law to go on holiday, it's not like he's a firm suspect or anything at this stage. I did a recce of his house; he's not married, and his neighbours haven't seen him in a few days.'

Jack processed the information. 'Speak with the barmaid again at the pub, see if we can find out any next of kin. I'd like to speak with him again, suspect or not. I'd certainly like to know his movements after our last discussion. There's more to Brian McCullagh than meets the eye.'

'I'll go with him,' Jane said, motioning to Watkins. 'Until something else comes up.'

Jack ignored the horrified look on Watkins' face. 'Good. Gerrard, you and me are going to pay a little visit to Durham.'

'Oh good,' she said, clapping her hands. 'I've always liked it there.'

Jack smiled. 'You won't like where we are going.' He scanned the room. 'Any idea where Christensen is?'

'Doctor's appointment, something to do with his leg,' Watkins said.

'Fair enough,' Jack said. 'Let's get to it.'

HMP Frankland hadn't carried the best of reputations in recent years. A number of high-profile suicides, coupled with obscene levels of violence and an almost thirty per cent positive drug test ratio, meant that the category A/B prison had come in for some stick in the press.

To be fair to them, it was an impossible job, not made any easier by a raft of private contractors botching things up. That, alongside the cuts the service had faced, meant the only surprise was that an attack such as the one that had killed Mark Davison hadn't happened sooner.

'Oliver,' Jack greeted DI Tomkins outside the imposing granite structure.

'Jack, good to see you,' he said.

Jack noticed that his stoop was even more pronounced than it had been, and that the man had lost considerable weight in the last year. Unlike Jack, he hadn't needed to shift any weight. He looked emaciated.

As if reading his mind, Tomkins spoke. 'Cancer,' he said. He removed his cap to reveal a balding, liver-spotted cranium.

'Jesus, Oliver,' Jack said. 'I'm sorry to hear that.'

The lanky detective coughed. 'Don't worry about it. It shouldn't kill me,' he said. 'Could be worse, I could be in here.'

'This is Detective Constable Claire Gerrard.'

Gerrard offered the DI a firm hand. 'Hi, pleased to meet you.'

'Likewise,' he said, smiling. 'This one not been working you too hard? He's an absolute grump sometimes.'

Claire shrugged, but Jack could see the laughter in her eyes. 'We do our best.'

Small talk finished with, the detectives made their way to the entrance of the prison. Jack shuddered. He'd visited the establishment on numerous occasions, but he found himself unable to get used to the oppressive atmosphere it carried.

High walls surrounded the entire outside of the prison, with many of them covered in what looked like black, fire-damaged bricks. Wiring trailed around the top of it, a stark reminder that this was a prison not a holiday camp.

The prison itself was surrounded by housing estates. Many people, Jack included, seemed to only picture prisons as being surrounded by derelict land, miles away from the general population and supposed 'good people'. The reality was quite different. A large number of terraced and semi-detached houses were dotted around the perimeter. Jack couldn't really see the appeal. It wasn't exactly the middle-class suburbia most people thought of when they visited Durham.

They could go and see the cathedral another day.

'I appreciate this, Oliver,' Jack said as they were waved through by a security guard in a dark navy ensemble, complete with cheap cap.

'Don't worry about it,' Tomkins said. 'You can just owe me a favour. Besides, it's not like the boundaries are clear on this one. The bloke just shanked somebody over at Kirklevington, after all. Cleveland have asked for our involvement so I take it as given that I can pass on the same access to you.'

Jack smiled. What Cleveland didn't know wouldn't hurt them. And, in any case, Olsen was inextricably linked to Les Holding now. That meant they had to be involved.

As they entered through the doorway to HMP Frankland, artificial air and lighting greeted them. Jack couldn't help but feel that he was going to owe a number of favours to people before this case was done.

After half an hour of bureaucracy, Jack found himself sitting across from the man who had stabbed Mark Davison to death.

'Marshall Reaves,' Jack said, making a meal out of reading the man's rap sheet. 'I'm DCI Jack Lambert and this is my colleague, DC Claire Gerrard.'

The prisoner glanced at Jack.

He didn't need to introduce Tomkins as the pair of them were already acquainted. The cancer-stricken detective was sat in the corner of the dank room, hands calmly placed over his thin knees, watching. The Oliver Tomkins Jack knew had always been a great reader of body language.

The meeting itself was strictly 'off the record' meaning that no recording equipment was set up. Knowing Reaves' previous, it was felt that it would only put him off speaking anyway. Whilst the man before them wasn't smart in any way, he was both violent and incredibly suspicious of those in power. Jack was keen to put the man at ease and that meant using Gerrard's skills as an interrogator. Somehow, he'd gotten himself into Kirklevington at some point, a much more light-touch prison than Frankland. Unfortunately for him, shanking a prison educator had landed him back in here.

'Marshall,' Gerrard began. 'May I call you Marshall?'

Jack watched as the man puffed out his chest, impressed at being given a choice. It was something these prisoners weren't often afforded.

'Aye, call me Marshall, like,' he said, smiling through yellowed teeth.

There was no denying that the man carried an aura. He was a slip of a bloke, barely an inch over five and a half foot, and looked as skinny as Tomkins. His shaved head and tattoos gave him a distinctly 'EDL' feel and, knowing that his fuse was shorter than a matchstick, Jack found himself unable to relax into the interview, despite Reaves' slim wrists being shackled to the metal desk in front of them.

'Thank you, Marshall,' Claire continued. She flashed her own smile, the complete opposite of Reaves'. Pearly white, million-dollar, and completely fake. 'I'm just here to ask you a few questions, if that's okay?'

Jack winced as Reaves' narrow eyes danced all over Gerrard. She remained unflustered.

'Fine by me, pet,' he said.

'Mark Davison.'

'Ha!' Reaves exploded. 'That prick got what was coming to him! Oh, sorry about the language.'

'Thank you for apologising, Marshall,' Claire said. 'So, you didn't like him much?'

Reaves shrugged, his handcuffs scuffing the table as he did so. Behind where they were sat, Jack could hear Tomkins shuffle. 'He was alright, I guess.'

'So why did you harm him?' Gerrard probed.

Jack watched as Reaves weighed up his options. He'd obviously decided he liked Gerrard, but was still unsure about them given their position of power. That kind of deliberation couldn't have been easy for him, given his IQ of eighty-four. They'd discussed tactics before going in. They'd begin by questioning him about the tutor, before bringing the conversation round to Dayton Olsen.

'Just had to, didn't I?' he finally said.

'You had to? Did somebody make you?' she said.

'No!' Reaves replied quickly. 'I never said that.'

For the first time since they'd arrived, Reaves couldn't look at Gerrard. Jack resisted the urge to step in.

'But you thought he was okay? Do you think I'm okay?'

'Yes!' he said, eyes back on her.

'And would you want to hurt me?'

'Not like that,' Reaves grinned.

Jack's stomach turned.

Gerrard continued unabashed. 'So why hurt Davison?'

Reaves began rocking back and forth, shaking his head.

'How many drugs are you taking?'

Reaves shot up like a NASA rocket. 'None! Why, who the fuck said I was?'

'Language,' Claire said.

'Sorry,' he quickly replied.

Jack almost smiled. Gerrard had him in the palm of her hand.

She leaned forward. 'The only reason I ask,' she said, voice barely above a whisper, 'is because I know how hard it is to get by when you need a fix.'

'You do?' he said.

'Yes,' she said, pulling up the sleeve of her blouse to reveal faint scars. 'We all have our secrets.'

Jack could see Reaves was baffled. 'I don't understand,' he said.

'I can help you,' she said, placing her hand over Reaves'.

Behind them, Jack could feel Tomkins moving, unable to see what was going on.

Reaves' greyish tongue swept over cracked lips like a lizard desperately in search of water. 'How?'

'They'll put you in solitary,' she told him. 'No access to anybody. And, when you lose access to others, you lose access to your supply.'

Jack could almost hear the cogs turning in Reaves' tiny brain.

'No!' he hissed. 'Not solitary...'

'Like I said,' Claire continued, finally removing her hand. 'I can help you.'

'Go on,' Reaves urged.

'Marshall, I need you to tell me what really happened with Mark Davison. I know you thought he was okay, just like you think I'm okay, and as we've already discussed, you wouldn't hurt me. So why hurt him?'

Reaves was rocking again. 'I'm not supposed to say.'

'It's okay, Marshall,' she soothed him. 'They can't get to you now.'

'They can,' he whined. 'He'll know.'

'Who will know?'

'Olsen.'

Jack felt his pulse quicken at the mention of Dayton Olsen's name.

'Did Olsen make you do it?' Claire asked him.

For the first time, he saw fear in the man's eyes. Reaves, a man low on intelligence and high on violent tendencies, was scared of Olsen.

Tears were forming now. 'Yes, he made me, said if I didn't, he'd keep taking the drugs and that he'd be paying me a visit twice a week.' He paused, tongue running over his lips again. 'But I wouldn't know when.'

'Visit you?'

'Yes,' he quivered. 'And he'd watch whilst they—'

He didn't need to finish the sentence for Jack to know what he'd been threatened with.

'So then what happened?' Gerrard asked.

'He told me he wanted somebody killed, but he wouldn't say who,' Reaves began. 'Then, one night, the night before it happened, he visited me and told me what I had to do.'

'And what did you say?' Gerrard asked.

Reaves shrugged and sniffed hard. 'Nowt I could say, like. You don't say no to Olsen.'

Jack could well believe it.

'What then?' Claire asked.

Jack could sense the excitement in her voice and silently urged her to remain calm.

'After the lesson, he handed me the chisel. I knew I had to do it, so I did.'

'Why did Dayton Olsen want you to kill Mark Davison?' Gerrard asked, her voice level once again.

Jack breathed a sigh of relief.

'I don't know,' Reaves said.

'There must be something,' Gerrard urged him.

'I... he had a list,' Reaves stuttered.

'A list?'

'Yes,' he replied. 'He kept it on him all the time. You'd sometimes see him scratch a name off or add one but he was always looking at it.'

'Names?' Gerrard said.

Reaves shrugged. 'Guess it was a hit list.'

'Do you know how many names were on the list?'

'You joking?' Reaves said. 'If you want your kneecaps taken off, you ask him those sorts of questions.'

Gerrard returned to flattery. 'But I'm guessing someone as smart as you found a way to look?'

Reaves smiled conspiratorially. 'Maybe.'

Gerrard whispered to him. 'How many names?'

'Not sure,' he replied. 'But there were at least a few.'

'Do you know where he got his information?'

Reaves shook his head. 'No.'

'One last thing,' Gerrard said. 'Do you recall seeing any names on the sheet?'

Slowly, Reaves nodded, eyes flitting around the room. 'One,' he said.

'Who was it?' Gerrard asked.

For the first time since they'd arrived, Reaves looked to Jack, before pointing a tattooed finger in his direction. 'Him.'

CHAPTER TWENTY-NINE

They were back in the car, screeching up the A1 at eighty-five before either of them uttered a word. Jack, being the SIO and commanding officer, knew it was up to him to break the ice.

'Those scars...'

'Really?' Gerrard cut in. 'That's all you've got to say?'

'Well it is a concern, given you have just told a convicted murderer that you used to shoot up.'

Gerrard shrugged. 'I was playing him, Jack. And, just so you know, I don't have a history of injecting heroin into my arms; I was a teenager once, dealing with the loss of a parent, reading a lot of glossy magazines at an impressionable time in my life.' Jack watched as she pulled the hem of her sleeve down over her wrist. 'I'm over it now.'

Suddenly, Gerrard's attention to detail, strict dieting and laborious exercise regime made sense to him. 'You were fantastic in there,' he said. 'I mean that. I thought Tomkins was going to have a fit when you touched him, though.'

He indicated and pulled off the motorway. They'd left Tomkins back in Durham, with a promise to co-ordinate further should anything come up. The fact that Olsen had coerced Reaves into killing the tutor meant that both Durham and Cleveland force would be kept busy trying to figure out why. Although good friends with the DI, Jack knew he'd been jealous at the fact that Gerrard had succeeded where his own team had failed. Namely, in getting Reaves to open up about what had happened. Jack wasn't bothered. The way he saw it, they didn't have time to squabble about who would do what. They now knew Olsen had a hit list of names. A list that apparently included him. Given Olsen was now clearly linked to the murder of Les Holding that meant he was everybody's problem.

As if reading his mind, Gerrard spoke. 'So, are we not going to address the actual elephant in the room?'

Jack bit down on his tongue as his fingers gripped the steering wheel. 'It's nothing.'

He could sense Gerrard staring at him. 'Nothing?' she spat. 'Are you kidding me? We've got three dead bodies, a violent prisoner on the loose and now, as if things couldn't get any worse, we know you're a target? We have to tell Edwards.'

'No!' Jack told her. 'We don't. We have no idea how credible Reaves' testimony is. The guy is coked-up and has about three brain cells. Until we are sure, I don't want Edwards knowing anything.'

'I can't believe you'd say that,' Gerrard replied. 'Actually, scrap that, of course I can. The great Jack Lambert, always running off to save the day on his own. You want to know what your problem is?'

Jack grunted. He didn't particularly want to know but he was also aware that Gerrard would tell him anyway. 'Go on then,' he said.

'You're punishing yourself.'

He raised his eyebrow in surprise. 'I don't know what you're talking about,' he said.

'Yes you do,' Gerrard continued, in full rant-mode now. 'So, what, you hung out with the wrong crowd as a teenager and got into some bother and now you're punishing yourself for it?'

You don't know the half of it, Jack thought.

Gerrard wouldn't be swayed. 'At what point are you going to cut yourself some slack?' she shouted, her voice rising above the roar of the Volvo's engine. 'Get over it. You're a decent person who was dealt a shitty hand earlier in life. We've all got problems.'

He remained silent.

'The worst thing is,' Gerrard went on. 'You're going to get the people around you hurt. Did last year not teach you anything?'

Jack turned to her. 'I'll not be lectured by you, Claire. I'm in charge and what I say goes,' he exploded. 'You nearly crossed a line in that interview: you're lucky Tomkins is a friend otherwise he would have filed a complaint, and it would be me you'd be relying on to get you out of it...' He let the implication of his threat hang in the air, regretting his choice of words almost as soon as he'd uttered them.

Almost.

Gerrard's rant ended as abruptly as it had begun. She crossed her arms over her chest and faced the window. Jack sat, fuming, as the tension continued to thicken.

They were at the station before she spoke again. 'Fine, get yourself killed,' she said. 'But if I even get a whiff that you've put somebody else in danger through this, it won't be Edwards you'll need to worry about...' With that she got out of the car and slammed the door for good measure. Jack watched as she marched past a couple of PCs who were out on a tab break, their easy-going smiles dissipating as they caught the look on her face.

He stayed behind, artificial air warming his hands and clogging his sinuses, as he processed what had happened. He hadn't needed to threaten Gerrard, really, but Edwards would boot him off the case if he thought Olsen was coming for him. He couldn't stomach that. He'd come too far now to back out. Plus, if somebody was going to get hurt, he'd rather it was him than one of the team. What he didn't yet know was why he had made the list.

Or who had given the order.

All troubling details.

Gerrard would forgive him, over time, but she wouldn't forget. He knew that their relationship had now crossed an invisible line and would never quite be the same again. In the long run, though, it would benefit her. Jack didn't need friends, he needed capable officers. Gerrard was certainly the latter and had been in danger of becoming the former. And, as she'd said, the people closest to Jack often suffered because of him. He couldn't risk that happening to her, not when she had her whole career ahead of her.

He had learned lessons from the previous year, though. Valuable ones. If he let people in, they got hurt. He wouldn't make that mistake again. Far from feeling fear at hearing he'd made Olsen's hit list, it had given him a new-found sense of clarity. His fate was now entwined with that of this case. And that of Dayton Olsen.

Only, Jack had the advantage of knowing he was on the list. Olsen wasn't aware that Reaves had ratted him out. As far as Jack was concerned, that gave him an edge. Sooner or later, the hitman would come for him. That much he knew. But he also knew something else.

That he'd be ready when he did.

CHAPTER THIRTY

J ack managed to avoid Gerrard for the remainder of the day. However, he could still feel her mood around the station. Watkins, for his part, clearly knew something had gone on— perhaps it was his new-found friendship with the DC—but had clearly felt it best to keep schtum.

The DS had spent the afternoon at a local MMA gym, speaking with the owner and one or two coaches who had known Dayton Olsen at one time or another. 'Quiet bloke, solid as a rock with a great ground and pound game,' was how Watkins had relayed the details. When Jack had enquired about what that meant, he was told 'it means strong enough to throw people to the floor and smack their head in without taking too much damage himself.' As Jack stared down his third coffee of the day, it didn't fill him with much confidence in terms of his own chances against the man—should they ever meet.

If, as they suspected, he had been the one to put Les Holding down, then he had already proved himself undeterred by reputation.

Jack was wrestling with the many permutations an altercation with Dayton Olsen would bring when his phone rang. 'DCI Lambert?'

'Jack, how wonderful to speak with you.'

He checked to make sure his office door was closed before responding. 'Dorian. Do you have news for me?'

'What, no chitchat?' the mob boss replied.

Jack snorted. 'Alright then, tell me about your day?'

McGuinness' laugh on the other end descended into a coughing fit before he composed himself enough to reply. 'Quite interesting, now you ask. I just wanted to let you know that I am considering running for councillor again, in the elections next year.'

Jack felt his grip tighten around his mobile. 'A political career? I thought that one was dead in the water?' He winced at his poor choice of words. It had only been a year since McGuinness' former employee, Liam Reed, had been found dead on the banks of the River Tyne.

'Of course not,' McGuinness replied. 'One must learn to keep trying when suffering a setback. I won't make the same mistakes again.'

The hardening of Dorian's tone left Jack with an uneasy feeling in the pit of his stomach. 'So, any news?'

'That's what I like about you, Jack,' he said. 'That impatience you carry around. It makes you more effective as a man. Not a great trait in a leader, I must add, though.'

Jack didn't need leadership advice from his former boss, he needed information, but knew he had to keep him sweet to get to what he wanted. If that took patience, he was willing to pretend he had some.

'I'll bear it in mind,' he replied.

McGuinness' voice moved away from the phone momentarily, and Jack could hear him barking an order at some lackey, before he came back on the line. 'My apologies, Jack. Some of my men do not know how to operate with any degree of independence.

It's quite draining. They don't have that quality that I saw in you once upon a time.'

'Things are busy here,' Jack lied. 'If you have any information, Dorian, I'd really appreciate it now.'

'Alright, calm down, Jack,' Dorian said. 'I've made some enquiries.'

'And?'

'I'm told there does exist such a group as the one you highlighted to me. I believe the poker game is a front for some rather... unsavoury activities. Brian McCullagh, I believe, was part of this—'

'Was?' Jack cut in.

'Apologies, slip of the tongue,' Dorian said.

The uneasy feeling wasn't going away. 'What kind of unsavoury activities?'

Dorian waited before responding. 'I don't know exactly... yet. As you well know, I can't be seen to be asking these questions directly and sometimes my men have to... persuade people to talk before we get the information we need. I'm told, however, that this is some kind of secret society. We are talking favours for members, illicit activities and the like. Exactly the kind of thing I will be looking to stamp out once I'm elected to public office.'

Jack noted down what McGuinness was telling him on a notepad and resisted the urge to laugh out loud at the man's hypocrisy. 'Anything else?'

'Not yet but I'll give you a call when I know more. I've got one or two irons in the fire. Let's see what comes up. They all talk in the end.'

Jack tensed. 'I don't want any violence.'

'Don't ask for my help if you are uncomfortable with my methods, Jack,' Dorian replied. 'But, just to put your mind at ease, I can confirm that no violence has yet been involved.'

Jack didn't believe that for one second. But, he'd known that when he'd first gone to McGuinness. The crime boss knew he was desperate and that put Jack in a very weak position. One he'd no doubt use to his own advantage at some point.

'Okay,' Jack replied. 'You have my number.'

'I do,' McGuinness said. 'You don't need to worry, though. I want to know what this secret group is about, what their influence is and why I wasn't privy to any of it.'

Typical McGuinness, Jack thought. 'Fair enough,' he said.

Jack began massaging his temples. He was tired, strung out, and no further forward.

'Just a word of warning, though, Jack,' McGuinness added. 'From what I hear, these people aren't without connections. What I don't yet know is who they are connected to. It's clear McCullagh is more than a barman. But I'm dubious as to how influential he really is. If he was at the top of this organisation, he wouldn't have been so easy to find. Leave it with me.'

Jack ended the phone call and ran through the details once more. McCullagh was definitely a man of interest, and it seemed the poker game was indeed a front for something more sinister. Just how far its influence spread was up for debate, though. If they could confirm Fenwick's involvement, things may start to open up for them.

And there were two questions that needed answering as a matter of urgency.

Who had hired Dayton Olsen to remove Les Holding from the picture and why was Jack's name on the same list?

CHAPTER THIRTY-ONE

'How's it going, old man?'

'Not so bad, Jack, yourself?'

He listened to Pritchard's withered voice down the phone, now a mere echo of the vibrant, chirpy presence it had once been. Perhaps last year's open grave case had taken more from him than Jack had thought. He swallowed his guilt at not having been in touch with him sooner and, through force of habit, told him all about the case.

Protocol be damned, he trusted Frank Pritchard with his life.

'Wow,' Pritchard responded to the details so far. 'Complicated, isn't it?'

'It is,' Jack sighed. 'Nothing seems clear at the minute.'

'So, let me get this straight,' the old man said. 'A young lad goes to rob a farmhouse, but ends up dead in the field, then the farmer, a suspect who is subsequently released, is found dead at the hands of the boy's father. Then the father ends up dead at the hands of an escaped assassin?'

'Yes,' Jack replied. 'Although we can't confirm with any certainty that Olsen killed Holding, it is the narrative we are currently running with.'

'Jesus,' Pritchard mumbled.

Jack concurred. 'The best bit is that Holding's body was dumped on the same patch of ground as that of his son, Robert Norris.'

'A message,' Pritchard mused.

Jack could sense some of the old life coming back to him. 'Yes, but to who?' Jack said.

There was a pause on the line and Jack could almost hear the cogs churning in the retired profiler's brain.

'There's something you're not telling me,' Pritchard said.

Jack frowned as he struggled to formulate the words. 'How do you know?'

Pritchard chuckled. 'Call it the benefit of experience.'

'We spoke to a witness who told us that Olsen, the hitman, had a list of names.'

'A hit list,' Pritchard observed. 'Go on.'

Jack hesitated before replying. 'Apparently I am on it.'

The profiler responded immediately. 'You told Edwards?'

'You mad?' Jack said, immediately wincing at his poor choice of words, given Pritchard's wife had recently died of complications arising from Alzheimer's.

'No,' Pritchard said. 'I'm quite sane, I think, but then I would say that. You should probably tell Edwards, though, either way.'

'Absolutely not,' Jack said. 'The only reason I can be on this list is because I'm investigating the case. Kicking me off it will do nothing but put somebody else in the firing line.'

'Maybe that would be a good thing,' Pritchard said. 'I don't know what it is with you and attracting violence.'

'You say that like it's my fault,' Jack retorted.

'The evidence doesn't lie.'

Jack tried to change tack. 'Anyway, less talk about work, more about you—how are you?'

'How do you think?' Pritchard said. 'Lonely, bored and old.

There are only so many pensioner walks and book clubs I can attend... I miss her.'

'I know,' Jack said. 'I'm sorry I've not called as often as I should have.'

'Nonsense,' Pritchard said. 'You're a busy man. I understand that better than anyone. I just wish I had dedicated more time to her than work over the years.'

Pritchard's comment didn't do anything to make Jack feel any better. Back when he was working full-time on the force, they'd formed an unshakeable bond. Pritchard hadn't had to say anything, but Jack knew it stemmed from his own relationship with his father. Between the old man's drinking, his put downs and the belt, it was no wonder he clung to the first older man he befriended and used him as a surrogate for his own absent parent. He was lucky that Pritchard was a good person. For his part, the profiler had accepted Jack as if he were his own son.

'I'm going to make more time for this from now on,' Jack said. 'You're not the only lonely one.'

'What about that fella you've been seeing?'

Jack swallowed the lump that was beginning to grow in his throat. 'Didn't end well.'

Pritchard must have sensed his tone as he pried no further. They ended the call with the profiler threatening to return to work and Jack promising to call him the following week. The silence in Jack's house suddenly felt overwhelming. He looked around—three bedrooms, two storeys, it was more space than one man needed. He had thought that either he would move in with Ryan, or the other way round, at some point in the not-too-distant future. Since he'd bought the place, following his split from Louise, he'd been reluctant to bring outsiders into his life. It was his sanctuary, a safe haven away from the world that so often made him feel claustrophobic. Even Rosie hadn't made the cut, with all of their time spent at her place. Keeping his house back then, he'd known that it was the ultimate safety exit from the relationship. His only regret was that he hadn't ended things sooner, before she'd gotten hurt.

Jack stood, his bones creaking from the effort, and glanced out towards Leazes Park. It was dark now, and he stood, without a light on, pondering. He often found himself able to think better when alone in the evening. He couldn't help but muse on Pritchard's words to him about how he was lonely, bored and old. Whilst Jack could hardly call himself old, he did carry around the burden of feeling like his best days were behind him. He was always lonely, an occupational hazard he'd convinced himself of some time ago, despite secretly knowing he preferred it that way as a barrier to intimacy.

As for boredom, that was a curse he always carried.

From the outside, those who knew him would have no idea that was how he felt. But, truth be told, he was often unfulfilled. He found the monotony of desk work dull as dishwater and he longed for action. That was partly why he threw himself into his job at the expense of the people around him. He got a thrill from it. And, although he'd never admit it out loud, he'd gotten a thrill from being in the presence of Dorian McGuinness just the other day. Jack flexed his fists and gazed out into the still night. In some ways, he missed the adrenaline rush of a job, missed the feeling of power he used to carry.

The fact that he missed the violence was the part that frightened him most.

He looked at his watch—it was nearly midnight. He was up for the early shift in the morning and the pool was widening in terms of the case. He could sense they were close to a breakthrough. It was building in his gut, so tangible he could almost taste it.

Yawning, he closed the curtains and made his way to bed. The last thing he remembered before passing out, fully clothed, was the faint passing of headlamps scything across his vision as he fell into an uneasy slumber.

The driver of the car moved slowly through the street, so as not to draw any attention to himself. As far as he was concerned, it was job done. It was very clear to him that Jack Lambert lived alone. That would make things easier, when the time came. He smiled, indicated left at the end of the junction, and turned towards the city centre. *Not long now, Jack Lambert.*

CHAPTER THIRTY-TWO

Jack woke the following morning with a light headache and what was clearly a developing cold. He wasn't particularly surprised; at this time of year the whole station made a habit of getting ill. If they ever found patient zero they would no doubt be offered one hell of a golden handshake to do one.

He fumbled for the bedside table and checked his phone—he had a text from Louise. His chest tightened as he jabbed the message icon, his mind instantly wandering to doomsday scenarios involving his daughter. When he saw the message, he groaned inwardly. 'J and I are going away this weekend. Your dad is ill so can't look after Shannon. She'll have to stay with you Fri and Sat night.'

It hadn't even been framed as a question. Despite Jack's unease at having to babysit for the weekend, he couldn't really complain. On some level, he felt an intense jealousy at the fact that his father had a better relationship with Shannon than he ever had. As a grandfather, he was a model citizen, something which irked Jack to the core.

He sent an 'okay' back to her.

By the time he got to the station, he'd convinced himself that he might be able to survive one weekend in Shannon's presence.

After a quick catch-up with Edwards, whereby he was told in no uncertain terms that Olsen had to be caught by the Northumbrian force, he found Christensen in the MIR.

'Boss,' the blond DS greeted him. 'I have news.'

Jack threw his coat down on the nearest seat and faced him. 'Tell me.'

'We've located some family members.' The DS shuffled some papers around on the desk. 'Brian McCullagh has an estranged daughter who lives just outside of Felling.'

'Excellent!' Jack said.

'Possibly,' Christensen said, his voice level as always. 'They haven't spoken in years, not since she married a bloke from Pakistan.'

'When was this?' he asked him.

'About twenty years ago,' the DS said.

'Still,' Jack replied. 'She may have something useful for us regarding his character and background.'

'Agreed,' Christensen said. 'And that's not all. We've located a cousin of Gus Fenwick's. They aren't what you would term close but they did keep in touch with the odd catch-up every couple of months, sent each other Christmas cards, that kind of thing.'

Gus Fenwick wouldn't be sending any cards out this year, Jack thought. 'Great work, Christensen.'

The DS shrugged.

He winced as another stabbing headache pain hit him. 'Let's start with the cousin.'

It turned out that Gus Fenwick's cousin, Paul Astley, lived not far from the Fenwick farm. What had once been a relaxing sight now only served as a source of anxiety for Jack, with every trip into the countryside seemingly bringing with it another murder. As they approached the driveway to Astley's cottage, Jack found himself praying for no more violence. He wasn't banking on it though.

Gus Fenwick's cousin greeted them at the front of the house.

'Mr Astley,' Jack said, extending a hand to greet him. 'This is Detective Sergeant Christensen.'

The man nodded. 'Paul will do.'

He invited them in and offered them a seat in an expensive-looking, albeit old-fashioned, lounge. The cousin's appearance, in some ways, couldn't have been further from Gus Fenwick's. Whereas the farmer had been obscenely tall and gangly, Astley's appearance was more akin to that of Christensen—namely, square. He had the same eyes and protruding Adam's apple as his now-deceased relative though.

'I suppose you're here about old Gus,' Astley said.

Jack shifted on the hard, leather three-piece that he was now perched on, noting the strong scent of jasmine, before responding. 'I'm afraid I am.'

Astley nodded. He looked slightly older than Gus had been. Retired, no doubt. Taking in his surroundings, Jack noticed a plethora of framed pictures around the room, which included a woman, presumably Astley's wife.

'As you will be aware by now,' Jack said, 'Gus Fenwick was murdered. We are, therefore, conducting an investigation into the circumstances surrounding his death to try and establish the facts.'

Astley bristled. 'Fat lot of good that was when you were hanging him out to dry over that rat's murder.'

Jack was shocked by the outburst, but carried on nonetheless. 'I would highlight that our investigation is still ongoing with regards to that.' He didn't need to say the words but the look that passed between them said it all. Fenwick hadn't been cleared of Norris' murder yet.

Astley leaned back in his armchair and let out a deep breath.

'We grew up together,' he said. 'Gus and I. Closer than brothers at one time.'

'But that changed?' Christensen asked.

Astley grunted in response. 'Mind if I smoke?'

Jack would have preferred he didn't, given his own troubles with kicking the habit, but it wasn't his house. 'No, go ahead,' he said.

They waited as Gus Fenwick's cousin stood, pulled an expensive-looking cigar case from a mahogany sideboard, and lit it with a novelty lighter pulled from his sleeveless, wool sweater. Thick, rich Cuban smoke swam around the room, working its way through Jack's blocked sinuses.

'Old Gus changed, not me. His old man,' he said, blowing a plume of smoke into the atmosphere, 'was a real hard bastard.'

Jack could relate.

Astley continued. 'Anyway, probably should have come as no surprise when he turned mean himself. When you have that start in life, what chance do you have?'

Jack understood perfectly. He'd been wrestling with his own daddy issues for years. 'It's never easy,' he said, realising as he said it how spurious the comment sounded.

'Gus was a soft clart when we were young,' Astley continued. 'I was the one always bailing him out of scrapes but, somewhere along the line, he started getting into situations that even I couldn't dig him out of. Once Rita came along,' he said, again glancing to the photo frame on the mantelpiece, 'I had to make a choice. Go down that path with Gus or grow up.'

The look that Astley gave him suggested it hadn't been an easy choice.

'And what path was that?' Jack asked.

'It all started when he worked at the Port of Tyne.'

'Port of Tyne?' Jack said. 'I wasn't aware he had worked there.'

'Aye, long before the farm, and Margaret's money.'

'Were you close with Margaret?' Jack asked, keen to get a

handle on the kind of woman she was.

Fenwick's cousin shook his head. 'By the time she came along we had already drifted. Hard as nails though,' he said, his eyes full of humour. 'Certainly, a match for old Gus. But, like I say, he changed. Sure, he charmed the pants off her—he always did have a way with the lasses.' He rolled his eyes. 'But she eventually got sick of him and kicked him out.'

Jack leaned forward on the chair. 'You say you drifted but you still maintained contact, yes?'

Astley nodded. 'Once my wife Rita was gone he reached out. We were both alone by then,' he said, his tone bitter. 'I guess after all these years of growing apart we finally found ourselves with something in common.'

'How long ago was it that Gus worked at the Port of Tyne?' Jack asked.

Astley's tongue protruded out as he seemed to search his mind. 'Must have been about twenty years ago now. He left there and bought the farm not long afterwards.'

'Seems strange,' Christensen said. 'Going from a job like that into farming.'

Astley stiffened before sarcastically saying, 'You'd have to ask Gus about that.'

'Except we can't now, can we?' Jack said, annoyed at the man's tone. 'I'll be straight with you, Paul, seeing as I believe that's the kind of person you are. If there is something you know then please tell us. Even the tiniest of details. It could be the difference between catching your cousin's killer or not.'

'I thought it was a revenge killing?' Astley stated.

Jack shrugged. 'It might have been, but I can't help but feel there's more to it. If I can paint a better picture of your cousin, it might help nail down just what has happened here.'

Astley took a large puff on his cigar before stamping it out into a glass ashtray, blowing on the end and placing it into his chest pocket. 'Sorry but I don't think I can be of any more help.'

'What about Brian McCullagh?' Jack said.

Astley raised an eyebrow, his Adam's apple bobbing. 'What about him?'

'How did they meet?' Christensen asked.

'Worked together at the port,' Astley told him. 'From what I gather.'

'Bit of a coincidence that they both left the Port of Tyne and ended up living and making their livelihoods a stone's throw from each other.'

Astley snorted. 'You'd have to ask Gus about that.'

Except we can't now, can we? Jack thought. He decided to press Astley further. 'Do you know anything about a secret society that your cousin may have been a part of?'

Astley's brow crinkled. 'No idea. Wouldn't surprise me, though. He liked to gamble, did old Gus. Don't see what it would have to do with any of this, though.'

'As I said,' Jack continued. 'We are just trying to piece everything together as part of our investigation.'

'Fair enough,' Astley said, his eyes already looking about the room as if he were tired of their company.

It seemed Paul Astley was done sharing information, his attention drawn to the photograph of his wife on the counter. When they'd stood to leave, Astley hadn't even so much as given them an extra glance. They saw themselves out and, as Jack threw the car into reverse to back out of the drive, he caught the outline of Gus Fenwick's cousin's silhouette in the window. He remained, unmoving, even as they manoeuvred out of the driveway and began their journey back to Northumbria HQ. It had been a productive discussion, Jack had felt. The many layers to Gus Fenwick's life seemed to be getting deeper. Jack was sure his instincts regarding Brian McCullagh were right. Now that he knew both men had worked together at the Port of Tyne, McCullagh could no longer feign further ignorance about his relationship with the man.

The question was, though, where the hell was he?

CHAPTER THIRTY-THREE

Back at HQ, the team were in agreement that the Port of Tyne could be a point of interest in piecing together the jigsaw puzzle that was Gus Fenwick's life. Given that he had met the pub landlord whilst working there, Jack was keen to know whether anybody had any information on the pair that could be of use in determining the course their lives subsequently took. Twenty years was a long time but, in that industry, there was every chance that there was still somebody there that would have worked with them and could remember them.

The second strand they still needed to explore was Gus Fenwick's estranged daughter. Luckily for them, Felling sat between South Shields and HQ, which meant they could make a detour on the way back.

'You must be Jack Lambert?' a sturdy-looking bloke greeted Jack and Watkins at the entrance to the giant warehouse at the Port of Tyne. 'I'm Tom Brown.'

Jack shook the man's hand, one of the firmest handshakes he'd ever felt, and took in the building behind them. The warehouse was huge, and seemed to be a hive of activity for men in overalls.

'Thank you for agreeing to speak with us,' Jack said as they followed him inside.

Jack noted that he limped slightly, not unlike Christensen, and that he carried the broad, firm physique of a swimmer. His hair had been shaved down to within half an inch of his considerably-sized cranium, which was criss-crossed with small scars.

'Just through here,' Brown said, motioning towards a small office at the back of the building.

They passed a number of warehouse operatives. Word must have gone around that they were coming, for everybody they saw held a wary curiosity towards them. Jack wondered whether any of them knew Brian McCullagh or Gus Fenwick.

Once inside the office, Brown offered them two stools. 'I've spoken with the lads,' he said. 'There's a fella on shift who used to work with the people you mentioned. I've only been here about six years so I'm not going to be of any use to you, I'm afraid,' he said, bringing a set of dirty fingernails up to scratch his deeply-creased forehead. 'Andy Henson has been here forever, though. If anybody knows these fellas, it's him. He'll be here in a moment. Can I fetch you lads a drink?'

They placed an order for two coffees and thanked the port supervisor, who left them to it.

'Seems a helpful bloke,' Watkins observed.

'They'll be nervous of any bad press,' Jack said.

A series of scandals had rocked the port in recent years. Firstly, there'd been a huge haul of cocaine found on a ship from the Netherlands. Then, a people-smuggling sting had been shut down. As a major employer in the region, it was vital that it carried a good reputation. The company had been doing its level best to try and restore faith in its operations in recent times. It had made charitable donations and set up a new link with a local further education provider. Jack's sources over in the drug squad weren't buying it, though. They were sure some high-level employees had been in on it and they were continuing to investigate, albeit on the down-low.

'So you and Claire have fallen out,' Watkins stated.

Jack raised an eyebrow. 'It's Claire now, is it?'

Watkins flushed red. 'Well, you know... like...'

'Don't worry,' Jack said. 'You can still work with both of us. We just had a professional disagreement.'

'Must have been pretty bad. She wouldn't say what it was about.'

Jack smiled. 'And you thought you could get it out of me?'

Before Watkins could respond Tom Brown returned with two Styrofoam cups of coffee and a man who looked like a squashed Brian Blessed. Jack thanked him for the drink, happy to have some warmth close to his fingers. He respected the kind of work these men did, but it wasn't for him. That was much to his father's chagrin.

'This is Andy, but we all call him Chip.'

'Chip?' Jack said.

The man smiled, showing off two serrated front teeth. 'Chipped off in a cycling accident I had a few years ago.'

'You not fancy getting them fixed?' Watkins asked.

The man shrugged. 'When you've been married as long as I have, son, you don't need to worry about stuff like that.'

Jack stifled a laugh at the man's matter-of-fact response. He decided he liked the bloke already. 'Thank you for taking the time to talk to us,' he said.

'It's nee bother, lad,' Chip said, pulling up his own stool alongside theirs.

'I'll leave you to it,' Brown said, giving a stiff salute before turning on his heels and leaving.

'So the gaffer tells me you want to know about Gus and Brian, aye?' Chip said, shifting on the seat. 'Sorry, piles, can't seem to shake the bastards.'

'Erm... yes, must be difficult,' Jack stuttered. 'Indeed we are. I know it was quite a long time ago but...'

The Blessed lookalike raised a hand. 'Don't worry about that. I have a canny memory. The wife jokes that it's like an elephant, and that I'm not far off looking like one,' he added, shaking his sizeable belly through his dirty blue overalls.

Again, Jack stifled the urge to laugh. 'So you did know them?'

'Aye,' he said, his eyes dancing between Jack and Watkins. 'Once upon a time anyway. Ain't seen either of them in years, mind, but I can tell you what I remember.'

Watkins took out his phone. 'Mind if I record this?'

Chip nodded. 'Knock yourself out, lad. Can't work the things myself.'

Watkins placed his iPhone on the counter and pressed record. Jack waited for the timer to start counting before continuing.

'What can you tell me about them?'

Chip, quick as a dart, began. 'I remember them well. They started here around the same time, just a couple of years after me. I'm the longest serving member of staff on site,' he said, puffing his chest out.

'And what were they like as people?' Watkins asked.

'Canny lads, for the most part,' he said. 'Gus was a quiet fella, Brian less so. They were both in the warehouse from the start. Thrown together by circumstance. Didn't take long for them to strike up a friendship. Of course,' he added, 'those were different times. Rumours went round, if you know what I mean?'

Jack did know what he meant. He reflected for a moment on how his life could have panned out had he entered a similar career path. 'So what happened then?'

'Ribbing, relentless it was,' Chip replied. 'I'm ashamed to say I took part in it somewhat. I wasn't an instigator by any means but back then you were either a part of it or you became a victim. It was vicious.' He turned from the detectives a moment, staring out into the workspace, lost in thought. Eventually, he spoke again.

'To be fair to the pair of them, they stuck together. Anybody could see they weren't *together*, you know? But that didn't stop the talk. Back then, we had a real nasty employee on the books, a bit of a ringleader. He cornered Gus one day, started having a pop. Gus wasn't a violent man, in my opinion, but he did have a moral streak that could lead to trouble. He wasn't going to back down, not that day.'

'What happened?' Jack asked.

Chip took a deep breath, as if to compose himself. 'The argument got heated and Gus gave as good as he got. Anyway, this fella wasn't the type to lose face; he was a well-known bloke in the local town, real rough family. So he gave Gus a bit of a slap across the chops. Nothing too serious, just a bloody nose. Enough to win the argument and save face in front of his mates.'

'Was that the end of it?' Watkins asked.

Chip shook his head. 'Unfortunately for everybody involved, Brian McCullagh wasn't as diplomatic as Gus was. He got word about what had happened and flipped his lid. Stormed into the canteen room that lunch-time and stuck a screwdriver into the fella's ribs before giving him a good hiding. It was shocking.'

'Were you there that day?' Jack asked.

Chip nodded. 'Yeah, I was there.'

'So then what happened?'

'Not long after that both Gus and Brian disappeared from the port. I guess you would call it a dishonourable discharge. They were probably given a bit of a payoff and told to do one. All I know is I never saw either of them again, until Gus appeared in the newspaper recently.'

Watkins leaned in. 'Do you know if they were on the take whilst working here?'

Chip scratched the back of his neck before responding. 'Everybody was, to some degree. No idea about them, though. All I would say is that if Gus had been on the take, Brian would have too.'

'So Gus was the alpha of the two?' Jack asked. He hadn't been thinking along those lines.

'Maybe not in terms of personality; Brian was the party animal with a big mouth. But, yeah, when Gus did speak, people listened, particularly Brian. McCullagh would have gone through a brick wall for the man. He basically did.'

'And you're sure they weren't involved in any business dealings whilst here?' Jack pushed.

'I can't say I know anything about that,' Chip replied. 'Sorry, fellas, maybe I'm not that useful after all?'

Jack straightened up. 'You've been more than helpful.'

'One other thing,' Watkins cut in. 'Is there any chance that this altercation could have anything to do with what is currently going on? An act of revenge from the bloke who was stabbed?'

Chip laughed, his tone hollow. 'I don't think so, lads. That bloke isn't around anymore.'

'How can you be sure?' Jack put to him.

Chip stood, his girth threatening to take over the room. He untucked his shirt, and pulled it up to reveal a small scar sat in between a sea of stretch marks on his hairy stomach. 'Believe me, I'm sure.'

They stopped off in Felling on the way back to the station but McCullagh's estranged daughter wasn't at home. Apparently, like her father, she had a habit of absconding at a moment's notice. Her husband, a man not too dissimilar in appearance from the pub landlord, bar his ethnicity, had conveyed this news to them in a bitter tone.

Screaming kids in the background had dragged his attention away from them so Jack had left a card and asked him to pass on the message that they would like her to call the station. The partner had nodded, picked at a clump of dried sick on his Gordon Ramsay apron, and said his goodbyes.

Back at the station, the officers in the MIR were operating with a spring in their step, due to the advent of new information in the case.

'So,' DI Russell said, 'we now know that Gus Fenwick was close to Brian McCullagh, indeed so close that he saw fit to lamp a bloke who called him a poof.'

Jack raised an eyebrow in surprise.

'Sorry!' she spluttered.

Jack couldn't recall ever having heard her apologise before and decided to make her squirm. 'Why?'

'I didn't mean...'

'Of course you didn't,' he cut in, resisting the urge to smirk. 'We can argue the merits of being PC later though. Right now, let's stick to the case.'

Watkins interjected. 'Everything McCullagh originally told us has proven to be false.'

'But they weren't involved in any shady activities whilst there?' Gerrard asked.

Watkins did a show of pulling his head from side to side, ginger afro remaining perfectly still. 'Andy "Chip" Henson told us he didn't know of anything like that going on but I'm not sure I entirely believe him.'

'How come?' Gerrard asked.

'There's clearly a code in that place, and this is a former hard man who isn't going to rat on his fellow employees, no matter what he originally thought of them. Also,' he added, 'he told us that most people were on the take in some way back in the day.'

'Yes,' Jack said. 'It stands to reason that he wouldn't want to implicate Fenwick or McCullagh in anything, particularly given the fact that he, at one time, terrorised them both.'

'Could he be involved?' DI Russell asked.

'My gut says no,' Jack replied. 'But I've been wrong before.'

'I don't think he is either,' Watkins said. 'But I do think there is more to their time at the port than Chip was letting on. The problem we have is that there is nobody else there from that time and there isn't exactly a record of who was doing what back in the early nineties.'

Jack saw the life drain from Gerrard and Jane's eyes. 'This isn't a dead end,' Jack said, keen to allay their fears. 'Think about it, we know more than we did at the start of the day. We know that Fenwick and McCullagh have a history and that McCullagh lied about this history for some reason. I don't buy that we weren't asking the right questions—he was holding back. I want to know why. The Port of Tyne has been involved in plenty of scandals over the years. I want to know whether they were involved in any criminal deeds whilst there or afterwards. To do that, we need to know who else was there at the time. Chip provided us with some names, I would suggest we begin by speaking with anybody who is still around.'

'I can dig up some info on that, guv,' Gerrard said, her previous frosty attitude towards him momentarily forgotten.

'Thanks, Claire,' he said. He turned to DI Russell. 'Jane, we still haven't spoken with McCullagh's daughter. Chase that up and see what information she can give us. Let's also check in on McCullagh's property from time to time, just to see if he returns at all.'

'What about the hitman on the loose?' Gerrard said, cuttingly.

Jack bit his tongue. He really didn't need Gerrard using that as a weapon against him right now. 'It's difficult to do anything until he resurfaces,' he dismissed her. 'However,' he added. 'We've released his image to the public, so he can't hide forever. I want us to keep working the Les Holding angle, see why their paths crossed, and keep digging into Olsen's past to see if we can locate any known accomplices or colleagues from over the years.'

'I'll look into it,' Watkins said.

'Good, that's settled then.' Jack ended the impromptu meeting before collaring Gerrard at the door. 'Look, Claire, I want to apologise for before,' he said. 'You're right, Olsen is dangerous and any potential threat against me is very serious. I'm not entertaining the thought of telling Edwards, though.' She made to pull away but he placed a hand lightly on her shoulder. 'But I promise that if I even get a whiff of him appearing anywhere near me then I'll be the first one to pull the plug. Compromise?'

Her face softened, albeit only slightly. She gave him a curt nod before leaving without further word. Jack breathed a sigh of relief.

He didn't like lying to his colleagues, but he needed everybody on side. The reality was, by the time he saw the whites of Olsen's eyes, it would be too late anyway. Claire wasn't to know he had no intention of removing himself from the case. But, if it kept her focused on the task at hand, he was willing to tell her what she needed to hear.

CHAPTER THIRTY-FIVE

By the time the weekend came round, Jack had managed to go through a rollercoaster of emotions—from convincing himself that Shannon's temporary stay with him would be a walk in the park, to it becoming an absolute disaster for everybody involved. It was with this trepidation that he greeted his daughter at the house. Her surly vibes were even more intense than when he'd last seen her. Evidently she hadn't been pleased with her mother's decision to dump her with him.

As for Louise, she seemed about ready to explode. He gave Jeremy, her fiancé who was sitting in the car, a short wave, before turning to her. 'How's things?'

She sighed. 'Fine.'

Shannon pushed past him into the house. Behind him, he could hear her bag get dumped on the floor as she began a heavy-footed ascent of the stairs.

'You sure this is a good idea?' he asked, instantly regretting his words.

Louise rounded on him. 'What, for you to actually spend some time with your daughter? Why would that possibly be a bad idea?'

'I didn't mean—'

'I've had enough of her attitude. Apparently the punishment at school has done nothing to change her behaviour.' She looked at him with pleading eyes. 'I am at my wits' end. I'm tagging out for the weekend.' She turned and marched back to Jeremy's black Rav 4, before turning. 'Try not to kill each other.'

Back in the house, Jack could feel the oppressive silence of his daughter's presence above him in the spare room. He'd painted the room pink a few years back, thinking she would like that. As it was, he couldn't even remember the last time she'd even slept over. The Shannon from the previous year would have hated the room, having been in the throes of a gothic phase. Judging by her change in attire, and highlighted hair, she probably wouldn't mind it so much now. The problem would be him, not the room.

He winced as she stomped around above him. He could hear the sound of the portable TV being turned on, channels flicking, before the sound cut dead and the remote was thumped on the floor.

He found himself at a loss. He'd always been one to soak up other people's emotions like an empathetic sponge. The fact that he was unable to vocalise his own feelings meant that he rarely dealt with it in an appropriate manner, though, hence the constant feeling of stress he carried around on his shoulders.

He decided to risk her wrath. 'I can rustle you something up for tea?' he shouted up the stairs.

A pause, followed by three footsteps and a creaking door. 'I'm not hungry.' The door slammed shut.

Jack spent the following two hours listening through his Led Zeppelin CDs. He'd picked up a new version of his favourite, *Led Zeppelin 2*, from the local flea market a few weeks before. He was proud at having managed to run his previous copy into the ground. Burning out a cassette was one thing, but it took a real effort to do the same thing with a CD. Watkins had been ribbing him about his love of discs, and had been trying to convince him to set up a Spotify account. Jack had told him he preferred to own the records and that surely it was better for the band to have people buy the music rather than stream it.

Plus, he quite enjoyed looking at his collection from time to time.

He sent Louise a message to let her know Shannon had settled in well—a lie but, like with Gerrard, it was one she needed to hear. Feeling somewhat productive, he set about rustling something up to eat before changing his mind and grabbing his phone.

'Shannon!' he called. 'I'm going to order a Chinese takeaway if you want any?'

Forty minutes later, they sat down to chicken chow mein with egg-fried rice and a carton of thick, creamy gravy. 'Good?' he asked.

'Mmm,' Shannon's reply came, followed by a shy wiping of gravy from her chin. 'Thanks.'

'It's no problem. Unfortunately, I'm not as good a cook as your mother. Don't tell her I said that, though.' Then he added, 'And certainly don't tell my personal trainer I did this.'

Jack waded through his food, and he could already feel the grease permeating through his pores as he did so. Still, if it meant spending some time with Shannon without a closed door between them, then it was worth it. By the time they finished, he was stuffed, and he had to resist the urge to spray air freshener to compensate for the oily stench that was in the air.

'That was great, Dad, thanks,' Shannon said.

'Watch a film?' he asked.

'Sure. You got Netflix?'

'I have a DVD player?' he replied.

After ten minutes of intense negotiation, they settled on Sean Penn's epic portrayal of Harvey Milk, the US gay rights activist. Shannon was keen to watch it, having heard good things, and he made her promise not to tell her mother about it, given that the age certificate was a fifteen. They'd agreed they would take it to their grave.

'Dad?' Shannon asked about half an hour in.

'Yes, sweetie?' he said, shuffling across the settee so that she could put her feet up.

'What was it like for you coming out as gay?'

He hadn't been expecting that. He made to speak but found that he was lost for words. 'I...'

'Sorry,' she said, turning her gaze away from him.

After a long moment he spoke. 'It wasn't easy,' he said. 'But, in the end, I had to do it. I wasn't happy.'

'And are you happy now?' she asked.

Jack could feel her gaze on him. Ryan's image flashed through his mind. He had been happy, to a degree. Now, he wasn't so sure. Still, to tell his nearly teenage daughter that her father was miserable wouldn't do. 'I'm as happy as an adult can be.'

She frowned. 'Does that mean I won't be happy when I'm an adult?'

He turned to face her. 'Of course not. It's just... complicated.'

'Are you not with that man still?'

'Man?' Jack asked, alarmed.

Shannon shrugged. 'I hear Mam talking sometimes.'

He'd have to remember to ask Louise to keep her thoughts to herself when it came to his private life. Still, it wasn't for him to dictate anything to anybody. 'That's... not a thing anymore.'

'That's sad,' she said.

'Anyway, who made you such an adult?' he asked, throwing a pillow at her.

'Dad!' she shouted. 'Watch the fringe.'

He watched as she stood up and meticulously put it back into place.

'The Shannon I knew a year ago wouldn't understand this obsession with hair,' he said. 'And she wouldn't approve of your new style.'

Shannon shrugged but he could see she was upset. 'People change.'

He nodded. 'Yes, they do, I suppose.'

'Like you,' she said. 'You became gay.'

'It's... not like that,' he said.

She sat back down on the settee, but Jack could sense a new distance between them. 'So you were always gay?' she asked him.

'Yes and no,' he said. 'It's complicated.'

'I don't understand.'

'Neither do I,' he said.

'You're just deflecting,' she told him, her voice carrying an air of mock authority. 'Mam says it's typical you.'

'Your mother talk about me a lot, does she?' he shot back.

'All the time. "He never calls, he's so unreliable, I'm sick of—"'

'Alright!' he called, holding a hand up to stop her. 'I get it. And, look, she's right. I'm not reliable and I should call more. It's not easy being a policeman.'

Shannon turned to face him once more. 'I'd like to be a policewoman,' she said.

Jack felt his insides twist, the undigested Chinese lurching in his stomach. The last thing he wanted for his daughter was for her to follow the same life path as him. Still, there was plenty of time to change her mind. 'It's not a straightforward job,' he said.

She shot him a wounded look. 'You don't think I'm smart enough?'

'It's not that,' he said. 'I... look I'm not good with stuff like this. Your mother is much better...'

'Yeah but she isn't here,' Shannon said.

'An astute observation,' he told her. 'If you want to join the force when you're older, I'll help you. But only if you're sure.'

'I'm sure,' she said, beaming. 'Fight crime, like Batman.'

Jack hadn't known when to broach the subject but now seemed as good a time as any. 'You have to be good to join the police,' he told her. 'That means sticking in at school and treating people with respect.'

She pouted. 'Grandpa says you didn't do very well at school and that you didn't treat people with respect.'

He ground his teeth together. Trust the old man to stick the boot in against him. 'Yes, well, Grandpa wasn't exactly the best teacher. I had to figure it out for myself.'

'You don't like him much,' she stated, her tone one of sadness.

'It's not that,' he said. 'We just aren't that close. I was always closer to Grandma when I was young.'

Shannon nodded. 'Like me with Mam and you.'

Jack bottled up his sadness at his daughter's comment. 'Kind of.'

'Well, I will stick in at school, you'll see!'

'About that,' Jack said. 'You can't bully someone if you want to join the police. People get in trouble for that kind of thing. They wouldn't allow it.'

He stopped short of telling her that, in actual fact, that culture did still exist in pockets across the force. Certainly, the reaction his own admission about his sexuality had carried was a case in point of the prejudice that others still carried.

Shannon's head dropped.

Jack decided to press it further. 'Why did you do it?'

'I dunno,' she whispered.

'There's always a reason,' Jack said.

'I just wanted to fit in,' she replied. 'I didn't want to hurt her. It just started with teasing but I didn't think it'd get worse, I promise.'

'I believe you,' Jack told her. 'But that doesn't make it right.'

They both jumped as the abrupt sound of a gunshot cut through the atmosphere. Harvey Milk had just been assassinated. He turned back to his daughter, only to be met with tear-filled eyes.

'I know it doesn't,' she said. 'I'm sorry.'

'It's not me you need to apologise to,' he told her, a little more firmly than he'd intended.

She nodded. 'I will say sorry. Will the school kick me out? I don't want to leave, I have friends there.'

'They won't kick you out,' he told her. 'As long as this doesn't happen again.' He shifted on the settee. 'It's hard enough for a person from another country to settle in in a new place without being abused by people at school. Do you understand?' She nodded. 'Imagine how you would feel if we moved to another country.'

'I'd be frightened,' she told him. 'I wouldn't want to go.'

'Exactly,' Jack said. 'Maybe this girl is frightened too. And, instead of making friends at her new school in this frightening new place, she gets bullied by a group of girls. Imagine how you would feel in her position.'

Shannon was openly crying now. 'I'm sorry.'

He pulled his daughter close to him and stroked her hair. 'I know you are, Shannon, it's okay.'

'It isn't,' she wailed. 'I'm a bad person.'

'You aren't a bad person,' he said. 'Sometimes good people do bad things. That's all that's happened. But you can make sure you do good things from now on, can't you?'

His daughter sniffed and dabbed at her eyes with a moist sleeve. 'I will.'

'Good,' he said. 'Now, this film is too depressing, let's watch *The Lion King*.'

Her eyes lit up. He might have failed her in many ways as a father, but teaching her that *The Lion King* was the greatest Disney film ever made wasn't one of them.

He watched as the detective got up and closed the curtains. The girl, presumably his daughter, was still there on the settee. He waited for another thirty seconds before making the call.

'Yes?'

'He's not alone,' he spoke down the line.

'And?'

'I think it's his daughter who is with him.'

There was a pause. Shivering slightly, he turned up the car's air temperature and sniffed. It always played havoc with his senses. He placed his hands over the vents and accepted the thin trickle of warmth they offered.

'That doesn't change anything.'

'It does,' he replied. 'I don't hurt children.'

'She's collateral damage, I don't care if...'

'I care,' he cut in. 'I've said no.'

He could almost sense the anger crawling through the phone line. He waited, aware he'd taken a big risk by refusing to obey a direct order. Everybody had rules, though. Not hurting children was his. He could live without doing the job if it meant keeping that intact.

'Fine,' came the reply. 'But I want this done... soon.'

He thumbed the call end button and tossed his phone onto the passenger seat. He took one last glance towards the window, but was unable to see any movement now. It was clear the girl wasn't going anywhere. *Never mind, he can't keep her around forever,* he thought. His research so far suggested that she wasn't a permanent fixture. He was a patient man. Another couple of days wouldn't matter to him.

He turned the key in the ignition and began a slow exit from the street. He'd have to be sure to pick up another car next time he came back. If he kept turning up in the same vehicle he would attract suspicion. And that was something he rarely did. He was a professional. Patient and precise.

Jack Lambert could wait a bit longer. When you were on borrowed time, what was a few more days anyway?

CHAPTER THIRTY-SIX

T he rest of the weekend had passed without incident, as far as Jack was concerned. Louise had seemed pleased to find Shannon still alive and Shannon, for her part, left a lot happier than when she had arrived. They'd promised not to tell her mother about the films they'd watched or the junk food they'd eaten but, given he'd not consumed such rubbish for months, his return to work on Monday felt like an early start after a night out on the lash. He wasn't counting the temporary meltdown he'd had after Ryan's phone call.

'Jesus, guv,' Watkins greeted him in the MIR. 'You look grim.'

'Too much sugar,' he grumbled. 'What's the latest?'

Watkins had managed to speak to McCullagh's daughter before work and had gleaned very little information. Apparently, her father was, in her words, 'a complete arsehole' and if they happened to come across him they should pass on her message for him to 'fuck off.'

Like others they had spoken to, it seemed that the daughter was unsure as to whether her father was involved in anything dodgy, but that it wouldn't surprise her if he was. She'd never heard her father speak about Gus Fenwick but, given that they hadn't spoken to each other for almost twenty years, that was no great surprise. Jack reflected on the weekend he had had with his own daughter. He prayed they would never end up in a similar situation, with her hating him, not knowing his whereabouts or, even worse, not caring.

Jack would have been frustrated with the lack of information they had found were it not for two key facts. One being that they had expected very little from the daughter and, two, they had another lead to follow up.

DI Russell had uncovered the names of three different employees who had worked with Gus Fenwick and Brian McCullagh, back in the day, at the Port of Tyne. Jack had sent Christensen and Gerrard off to one location, with Watkins and Russell chasing up the other. He decided to speak to the third person on his own. Jane had raised an eyebrow but it wasn't like he was running off into a firefight. He was simply speaking to somebody who may or may not have had information on people involved in the case.

'DCI Jack Lambert,' he introduced himself to Abdul Jamir, former colleague of McCullagh and Fenwick.

'Mr Lambert,' he said, offering his hand. 'It's a pleasure to meet you.'

They'd arranged to meet in a local Gateshead cafe, a request made by Jamir. As for Jack, he wasn't bothered where they met. He could understand the reticence the man had to inviting a policeman into his home. Many people preferred a public space in which to speak.

'Thank you for agreeing to see me,' he said. 'I appreciate it. We are keen to speak with people who know or knew both Brian McCullagh and Gus Fenwick.'

The man nodded. 'I can't say I know either of them now.'

Jack noted the ever-so-slight accent he carried. He sounded Pakistani but Jack didn't wish to pry by asking. It wasn't his business where the man came from and, in reality, it didn't matter. It was simply Jack's own nosiness that gave him the urge to enquire. He noticed the man's dark eyes were unable to stay still, his eyeballs seemingly on a fast spin from side to side. Perspiration was laced across his brow, despite the cold weather, with a thinning thatch of jet-black hair clinging on to the top of his cranium. He was dressed extremely smartly, with a shirt and tie combo, and looked freshly shaven, a small nick visible on his neck.

'Is something wrong, Mr Jamir?' Jack asked.

'Pardon?' he asked, surprised, as if he'd only just noticed Jack's presence. 'No, I—'

'I assure you, Mr Jamir, you aren't under any suspicion here. You can relax.'

'No, yes,' the man said. 'I understand.'

A waitress appeared and Jamir ordered a black filter coffee, with Jack deciding to restart his healthy living kick by ordering a water. The waitress smiled at Jack, warmly, a smile that carried a certain level of flirtation, before leaving them to fetch their order. Jack smiled inwardly at her poor judgement.

A screeching child came tearing past their table, causing Jamir to jump. A young mother, shoulders slumped, trotted by not long after, shouting at him to calm down and eat his chicken nuggets.

'I don't know how much help I can be,' he said.

Jack unzipped his jacket and placed it neatly on the back of his seat before replying. 'Why don't we start at the beginning? When did you first meet Brian McCullagh and Gus Fenwick?'

The man's tongue shot out, darting across his upper lip, as he rubbed his chin, before replying. 'It would have been in the early nineties at the port. I was a crane operator there for a number of years before... I left.'

'Okay,' Jack said. 'So, you met them in the workplace?'

'Yes,' Jamir said. 'It's a big workplace, you meet all kinds of people there.'

Jack paused as the waitress came back with their order. 'There you go,' she said, eyes dancing over Jack's appearance.

'Okay,' he continued, once the waitress had left. 'Did you get to know them at all, beyond being colleagues?'

'Like friends?' Jamir said. 'No, no, no. We were never friends.'

'Were you enemies?'

Jamir sat bolt upright and Jack could sense the man's leg tapping away under the table.

'No, not enemies.'

Jack tried his best to remain patient but the man sat opposite him wasn't making it easy. It wouldn't do him any good to frighten the man off. It was clear he had something to say. He wished Watkins had been there. He was always good at putting people at ease.

'Then how would you describe your relationship with them?' Jack asked.

'Different.'

'Different?'

'Yes,' Jamir said. He took a loud slurp of his coffee before grimacing and emptying a load of sugar into it. He sighed, stirred the murky liquid, and took another drink, following it up with a loud 'Ah.' 'I had a different relationship with each man,' he said.

'Okay,' Jack replied.

'I got on well with Brian,' Jamir said. 'Gus, not so much. He was not a nice man.'

'But Brian McCullagh was?'

Jamir frowned. 'He was abrupt, but was always kind to me.' He leaned in close to Jack. 'You have to understand, at that time, in that industry, things were not as they are now. I am a first-generation immigrant into this country. It wasn't easy.'

Jack could imagine. 'You encountered racist abuse?'

Jamir shrugged. 'Just the usual, you know, being called a Paki and whatnot.'

'And was Gus Fenwick racist towards you?'

'No, no,' he said. 'But he did not like me. Brian, on the other hand, was kind to me. He said, "Abdul, I don't care where you come from, only where you are going." I like that quote, don't you?'

Jack shrugged. It was alright.

'And,' Jamir continued, 'I didn't suffer much abuse once I became friends with Brian,' he said. 'You see, people were frightened of him.'

Brian McCullagh was a formidable man. He could understand. 'So he took you under his wing?'

'Ah, yes, a good saying!' Jamir beamed. 'Yes, I suppose one could say that is what he did. Mr Fenwick, though, he didn't like that.'

'He was possessive of Brian McCullagh?' Jack asked.

'Oh, yes, very much so,' Jamir replied, each syllable spitting out in a fast, syncopated rhythm. 'Mr Fenwick didn't trust me. He would tell Brian, "you must not speak with Jamir", but Mr McCullagh didn't listen.'

'Why wouldn't he trust you?' Jack asked. 'You were simply work colleagues. What was there to trust?'

Jamir licked his lips again. Jack could see sweat patches forming under his arms like a young child that had urinated itself. 'It was a different time...'

'You already said that,' Jack told him.

Jamir's shoulders dropped. 'Most employees in the port were... how do you English say, "skimming off the top"? We were no different to most.'

Jack took a gulp of water, and waited for Jamir to fill the silence.

'We were involved in people smuggling.'

Jack had suspected as much. There was so much cargo coming

in and out of the port that if there was something going on it was either that or drugs.

'Details,' Jack told him, his tone firmer than it had been.

'Brian McCullagh came to me and asked me if I wanted to get in on something; we were better acquainted by then so it seemed natural for me to say yes.' He nursed his coffee, the wisps of steam coming off in smaller strands now. 'I realise now that he used my colour to further his own interests. You see, I was the face of the operation. Because I looked like them, they would trust me.'

Jack could see the waitress coming back over so he waved her away. She pouted, a wounded look on her face, before turning and skipping away in the other direction.

'Go on,' he said.

'They came from all over, but Amsterdam via Italy mainly,' he said. 'Immigrants, who had bought passage through Europe, being ferried over. We were just near the end of the supply chain. We took a cut of the profits, and on we went.'

'How long did this go on for?' Jack asked him.

'A few years,' Jamir said. If Jack didn't know any better, he'd say the man was close to having a panic attack. 'I hold my hands up as having taken part, and I am prepared to go to prison,' he said, offering his wrists.

'Never mind that, now,' Jack said. 'How did it all end?'

'A supervisor found out and we were all paid off, told to leave,' Jamir said.

'I thought that McCullagh had been sacked due to punching another employee who had been abusing Gus Fenwick?' Jack told him.

Jamir shook his head, ran a slender hand through his greasy hair, causing it to stand on end like somebody had been holding a balloon to his dome. 'A convenient excuse, no?' He smiled, but Jack could sense no humour behind the grin. 'The port had a reputation to protect,' he told him. 'So, they swept it under the carpet.'

Jack took another swig of water as he pieced together the information Jamir had given him. So McCullagh and Fenwick had employed Jamir as part of a people-smuggling operation from mainland Europe. Jack felt sure it was all linked to what was going on now. He just had to find the right thread to pull and it would all unravel. It seemed McCullagh was the muscle behind the operation, with Fenwick, perhaps, the brains. As for Jamir, he simply had the right coloured skin and they had used him, just like they'd used all of the people who had come across for a better life in Britain.

Jack stood to leave. 'McCullagh was in charge then?' he asked Jamir.

'I don't know,' Jamir said. 'It was all very secretive. If they answered to somebody, it was beyond my pay grade to know who.'

Jack made to leave before stopping. 'Why come forward and tell me this now?'

Jamir pushed his coffee to one side and planted his gaze on Jack's. 'Like I said, it was a different time to now,' he told him. 'We all have to pay for our sins sometime. Perhaps the time has come for me now.'

'What happened to the people?' Jack asked him.

Jamir rubbed his forehead, leaving a red print across his frown lines. 'I don't know,' he finally said. He looked at Jack once more. 'But if you are asking me whether they got the better life they were promised in this country...'

Jack grabbed his jacket from the seat, spun on his heels, and marched off. 'Someone will be in touch,' he said over his shoulder.

CHAPTER THIRTY-SEVEN

'People smuggling!' Edwards groaned. 'You sure it's relevant?'

Jack shrugged. He was, but he couldn't prove it. 'At this point, I'm not ruling it out. Either McCullagh or Fenwick was the head of the operation, or they knew who was. I reckon they were in it up to their necks. They knew each other long before the barman let on, and were much closer than he had intimated. He lied. Why?' Jack leaned forward in his seat. 'Because he has something to hide. Something that I think is relevant to this case and can unlock the whole mystery.'

Edwards took a giant swig from a Dr Pepper bottle. Judging by the crimson colour of his face, Jack wasn't entirely convinced it was a soft drink he was chugging. As if reading his mind, Edwards thundered, 'Got something on your mind, DCI Lambert?'

'No sir,' he said, his body language suggesting otherwise.

Edwards cleared his throat and placed his bottle on the floor next to him. 'Anything useful I can tell the PCC?'

Nadine Guthrie was a much more hands-on PCC then her predecessor. Jack had successfully managed to avoid her, as of late, whereas Edwards clearly didn't have such luck. It was abhorrent to Jack that somebody who was supposed to be on their side constantly made swipes at the Northumbrian force in the local press. Maybe things were changing, though; Jack had to either adapt to survive or end up like Edwards—bitter and hurtling towards an early grave.

'Just tell her we are following up several enquiries,' he said. 'And that we are piecing together the different strands of the victim's life to try and find the trigger for recent events.'

Edwards nodded. 'Aye, but it won't fly,' he said.

'It should,' Jack told him. 'We've already solved two murders. Les Holding killed Gus Fenwick and, as of today, we have the evidence to prove it. His fingerprints were all over the scene. He hadn't even bothered to wear gloves or clean up after himself,' Jack added. 'And we are pretty sure that Dayton Olsen has taken Holding out of the picture.'

'That still doesn't explain the Robert Norris murder,' Edwards said. 'And we're no closer to bringing this Olsen bloke in. It's a fucking mess,' Edwards sighed. The giant DSI lumbered to his feet, placed his hands behind his back, and stood to face the window. Jack noticed a thick layering of snow-like dandruff on the man's tatty suit jacket. 'It's been suggested I retire,' he said.

'What, they're just suggesting this now?'

Edwards' furious gaze stopped him dead in his tracks. 'I'm only sixty-two years old,' he thundered. 'Have I not earned the right to go when I decide?'

'In my eyes you have, guv,' Jack said.

'Bollocks,' Edwards said. 'You're just like the rest of them.'

'That's unfair, Logan,' Jack told him. 'I've always supported you.'

Edwards shook his head. 'It doesn't matter now, I suppose. The decision has been made. This time next year I'll be gone.'

'Surely they'll have to give you a good package...'

'You think that matters to me?' Edwards shouted. 'I don't give a shit about the money. The mortgage is long paid off. It's the fact that they are throwing me out on the scrapheap before my time is up, like some kind of leftover meat, that's the problem!'

Jack understood what he meant. Edwards had given his whole life to the force and now, because he had refused to move with the times, he was facing extinction without so much as a thank you. Sure, there'd be an office whip around, but six months after he'd left, nobody would even give him a second thought—Jack included. That's just how it was in the force. One day, he'd be where Edwards was, facing an orderly exit or a drawn-out capability saga.

'There's still time to turn it around,' Jack told him, not even believing it himself. 'We can get to a satisfactory conclusion on this case and things will die down, you'll see.'

'Nah, I'm done,' Edwards said. He moved back to his desk and took a heavy-limbed seat. 'Sorry,' he added. 'Just one of those days. Good work on the case so far. And, just so you know, I'll be recommending you for the DSI role once I'm done,' he said.

Jack raised an eyebrow. Being a DSI wasn't on his bucket list. 'Thanks Logan, but I—'

Edwards raised his palm to Jack. 'I know, you don't want it,' he said. 'That's why I'm recommending you.' He smiled. 'One reference from me and that's the end of your promotion possibilities.'

Jack breathed a sigh of relief. 'Thanks, guv.'

'Don't thank me yet,' Edwards said. 'After you, Jane Russell is next in line.' Jack shuddered. 'My biggest regret is that I won't be here to see the chaos that ensues once she's telling you what to do.'

Jack laughed and stood. 'Nobody tells me what to do, Logan, haven't you learned that by now?'

The DSI raised his bottle towards Jack in a mock toast. 'Don't I know it? I won't miss your petulance once I'm gone.'

Jack watched as his boss gulped down the last of the drink, wincing after the last swallow. *Yep, definitely not pop.*

CHAPTER THIRTY-EIGHT

Jack brought everybody together in the MIR to debrief on his meeting with Jamir. The other detectives hadn't had much luck with their enquiries; it seemed that they either didn't know Fenwick and McCullagh personally, or were too nervous to give out any information. However, Jack's information had gone some way towards raising their spirits.

Jack moved towards the whiteboard and noted the extra information they'd been given. It was starting to look like a morbid family tree. McCullagh, the potential ringleader, heading up a people-smuggling operation at the port, with Fenwick his right-hand man. Jamir, the lackey, was used as a pawn in the operation. Rumour had it, they'd been found out and, when McCullagh attacked Chip, the port had the perfect get-out clause they needed to remove him. Not before giving him a good payoff, which Jack suspected had gone towards the purchase of The Black Horse pub. He wondered how much of Fenwick's payoff had been used in the farm.

As for Jamir, he'd left without a deal, but with a fear of retribution, should he speak out. His guilt had led him to come forward now, an admission which would lead to a severe punishment at a later stage no doubt.

That admission had also given them enough ammunition to bring McCullagh in for questioning, at least on the issue of people smuggling. The only problem was they didn't have any idea where he currently was. Jack just hoped that when he did surface, he'd not be found dead in a field. McCullagh had answers to questions they sorely needed to ask. It wouldn't do to have him turn up dead now.

'We need McCullagh,' Watkins said, echoing what everybody else was thinking.

'We do,' Jack said. 'But, in the meantime, let's keep digging into the people-smuggling. Claire...' He turned to face Gerrard. 'Look into any stories from the time and see if anything ever made the press.'

'On it, guv,' she said. Her moodiness towards Jack had seemingly dissipated since he'd told her his white lie.

'I'll have another crack at Margaret Fenwick,' Jane said. 'Hopefully I can get a look into her eyes to see whether or not she knew anything about the people smuggling. Given they were together around that time I would be surprised if she were totally in the dark.'

'Good thinking,' Jack said.

He left the team to it, with Christensen and Watkins continuing the search into Dayton Olsen's background. Somewhere along the line there would be a link to somebody who they could speak to so that they could attempt to place his movements. As for McGuinness, he had proved a dead end, although Jack doubted the validity of that. At least he was 'helping' Jack by looking into the existence of an underground group, based on information from McCullagh's disgruntled barmaid.

Too many questions and not enough answers, he thought. He just hoped something would come up before more people got hurt.

CHAPTER THIRTY-NINE

J ack tried not to look at the stump where the man's hand had once been, instead focusing on the mischievous grin on his face, complete with the same greasy moustache he'd been sporting since Jack had first gotten acquainted with him.

'David,' he greeted the journalist, throwing down a copy of the latest *Chronicle*.

Robson's eyes dropped to the front page, a familiar face smiling up at them. 'What?' he said.

'Really?' Jack said.

Robson chuckled. 'He's standing for election, that's news, is it not?'

'In May?' Jack shot back. 'Bit of a long run-up; also, I think you and I differ on what we class as the news.'

Robson shrugged. 'The incumbent isn't going to last much longer. A lot of scandal. I would expect a resignation any time now.'

Jack tutted. Dorian and his tentacles were everywhere. 'You are aware that the man is a criminal?'

'Keep your voice down,' Robson implored, leaning in so close that Jack could smell his stale, beer-bathed breath. 'This is a public place.'

'It's a pub, David, and, from the smell of you, I'd say you've been spending a lot of time here lately.'

Robson sat back, his face having taken on a wounded puppy look. Jack wasn't buying it.

'What I do with my spare time is none of your concern, Jack,' Robson told him. 'I'm just doing a friend a favour.'

'You do realise that Dorian McGuinness doesn't have friends, don't you? He'll use you until you're of no benefit to him and then he'll toss you out like he does everyone else.'

Robson shook his head. 'A high-profile local journalist will always be of use to a man like Dorian McGuinness. Besides,' he said, holding up his handless sleeve, 'I'd say we both owe him, wouldn't you?'

He had him on that one. Jack did indeed 'owe' him, as Robson had put it. However, they hadn't discussed the particulars of what that might mean yet. Also, with McGuinness acting as an undercover agent, of sorts, gleaning information for Jack, the debt was only growing.

'Why am I here?' Jack asked him.

'Do you not want a drink?' Robson said.

'I'm on duty and this isn't a social visit, so get on with it,' he told him.

Jack noted Robson's jittery body language, not too unlike Abdul Jamir. The last time they had engaged in an off-the-record chat Robson had been in much the same mood. That particular thread, once pulled, had led to the pair of them nearly being killed the previous year. Robson's index finger was scraping away at the cheap lacquer on the table and his hair was particularly unkempt today.

'I've got some information that may be of use to you,' Robson finally said.

Jack's patience was wearing thin. 'Spit it out then, man.'

'You're investigating some kind of underground cartel, aren't you?'

Jack gripped his leg, feeling his nails break flesh. 'How the hell do you know that?' he seethed.

Robson shook his head. 'That isn't important right now. What is important is what I'm about to tell you.'

The journalist brought his hand across his body and pulled out three sheets of A5-sized paper, placing them on the counter.

'Okay,' Jack said, his interest piqued. 'Humour me.'

'I took a look into it but I haven't found much I'm afraid,' he said.

Before Jack could respond, Robson pointed to the first sheet. Jack gazed down at the writing, which said, *'They have ears everywhere.'*

He looked at Robson's imploring eyes and gave a slight nod of acknowledgement. 'That's not much use to me then, is it, Robson,' he said.

'Lots of people play poker, so it's not like it's a big deal. But I can categorically say that the group you're looking for does not exist, as far as I'm aware.'

Jack waited as Robson pushed the second sheet along the table.

'They exist. They are known as the Syndicate. They are coming for you. They know who you are, where you live, everybody who is close to you.'

Jack felt his insides tense but did his best to remain calm. 'You could have sent this in an email, you know?' Jack told him.

'It's best to meet in person,' Robson told him, quickly glancing left and right once again. 'Besides, I do have one bit of information you can use.'

He moved the third sheet of paper across with his hand, but held it covered.

'Go on,' Jack urged.

'One of your officers is compromised,' Robson said.

Jack baulked. 'Not a chance.'

'You must not read the news; somebody has been leaking information for a long time,' Robson told him.

'I read plenty of news,' Jack said. 'And I'm aware of that. That doesn't mean somebody is compromised.'

Robson shrugged. 'Then don't believe me. I'm just the carrier of information.'

The journalist leaned forward and pressed his clammy palm into Jack's. Discreetly, Jack turned the paper over in his hand.

They've got people everywhere. Don't trust anybody. Why would they want you to know about a bent copper if they still had need for them? Think about it. You're all a target now. Destroy this.'

Robson made to stand but Jack dragged him back down and whispered in his ear. 'I can help you.'

Robson held his stump up to Jack's face and whispered back, 'Nobody can help me now.'

Jack waited until the journalist had left the bar, before making his own move. He opened his fist and folded the papers over before tearing them into small pieces. Then, he shuffled them up and placed half of them into one pocket before standing, wiping down his jacket, and leaving.

Once outside, he walked at a brisk pace along the street until he came to a bin, just on the corner before a set of traffic lights. He deposited one half of the papers into the bin and continued on along the road, before doubling back on himself and coming out on the other side of the road by a local post office.

He waited.

Three minutes passed before two men emerged from the bar. He watched as they moved down the street, only to be met by a third. They each looked between thirty and forty years old, and carried themselves in the same, authoritative manner. Black bomber jackets, heavy boots and short crew cuts. If Jack didn't know any better he would say they were triplets.

The third bloke motioned towards the bin. He could sense

they were arguing over which one was going to put their hand in and scour the contents. They looked about, eyes wandering, but not landing on Jack's position. He'd done a good job of blending into the background. Years of practice both in and out of the police had taught him well.

Finally, one of them placed his hand into the bin, only to pull out a few meaningless scraps of paper. He watched as goon two grimaced and began wiping his hand on his dark jeans. The other two were stifling a laugh.

More conferring.

Jack knew they were weighing up their options. Was there any chance of rescuing enough paper to put it back together so that they would know what the journalist had told him? They didn't deliberate for long. Goon three shook his head, and they moved on. He was the biggest and, Jack decided, the de facto leader. The reality was they were just hired goons, though, the real boss was somewhere behind the scenes, pulling all the strings. Was it McCullagh? Olsen? God forbid, McGuinness?

He waited twenty or so seconds, just enough time for the three of them to turn the corner in the opposite direction, before he took off in pursuit. Maintaining a healthy distance behind them, with his collar turned up, a perfectly normal action given the ever-darkening clouds that were threatening to have a tantrum, he followed as they waded through Newcastle City Centre.

Suddenly, one of the goons stopped and began to turn. Jack panicked and threw himself into a small cut to his left, pinning himself against the wall. He waited for a minute, trying his best to regulate his heart rate, before daring a look round the corner. He couldn't see them. Cursing, he took off and made an educated guess, heading right toward St James' Park. He gulped... not far from his house.

That was when he spotted them, shoulder-barging past a young hipster couple, complete with two skateboards and a mini boom box. Jack saw the fella go to say something, before catching a glimpse of thug three and deciding against it. They weren't far from the Gallowgate end of the stadium now, the end where Alan Shearer scored his record-breaking goal in a Newcastle United shirt, a happier time all round for those who followed the club. On match day, the area would be teeming with activity, with families, buskers and charity workers all congregating outside the ground. Today, though, all was quiet, and Jack was only too aware of how easy he would be to spot, should they turn round. He didn't fancy his chances of having to take on all three, but the main issue was the need to not be caught out. He needed them to think he was none the wiser with regards to their existence.

He'd blotted out all other sounds and images now, his focus solely on the men some twenty yards in front of him. That was, until a black sedan came screeching from behind him, pulling up not far from the St James' Park metro entrance. Jack watched as the three men stepped up, casually, and got inside the vehicle. He was too far away to see who was driving but it looked like a man. The windows were tinted, too much for him to get a grasp on who any of them were. As luck would have it, though, they passed by, not too far from where he was standing. He couldn't be sure whether or not he'd been seen, but he had come close enough to see the licence plate on the car.

The Audi, which housed the four mysterious men, sped off, screeching in second gear when it needed to be in fourth. Jack, eyes not once leaving the plate, took his phone out and made a note in his memo app.

Between them and Olsen, he was clearly a marked man. It was obvious he was getting closer to whatever was going on. The people in charge were getting nervous. Getting to Robson, and planting three heavies on them had been their first mistake. He knew they were after him now. What he would do with that information, he'd have to give some thought. One thing was for certain, however, he'd have to be sure to keep Gerrard out of it.

He glanced at his watch—4.15pm. He decided to head straight home.

On the way, he stopped to buy a magazine from a *Big Issue* seller with an emaciated-looking Staffy by his side. The man smiled a toothless grin in response and passed him over a crumpled edition with Benedict Cumberbatch's mugshot on the front. Jack thanked him and made to leave before a thought crossed his mind. 'You here often?' Jack asked him.

The man's eyes took on a look of panic before responding. 'I... please...'

'Don't worry,' Jack said. 'I'm just curious.'

The man licked his thick lips and glanced at the dog before answering. 'This is my patch along here. I spend most of the day in this area, sometimes into the evening. I'm not doing anything wrong, I swear...'

Jack nodded. 'I believe you.' He fished around in his back pocket and took out his wallet. 'What's your name, fella?'

The man's suspicion had not lifted, but he was at least engaging in conversation now. 'Raul. I'm originally from Spain.'

'Like the footballer?' Jack asked.

The man's olive-skinned face lit up. 'Yes, he is my hero! Real Madrid are the greatest team in the world!'

Jack snuck a glance at the stadium in the background. Fifty-two thousand Geordie fans would have respectfully disagreed. 'Okay, Raul from Spain. Now, tell me, how many magazines do I need to buy for you to do me a little favour?'

CHAPTER FORTY

J ack didn't enjoy the following morning. Suffering from about two hours of sleep, he had necked two double espresso shots and he could feel the caffeine pulsating through his veins. He'd called his personal trainer and put the workouts on the back burner until the case was solved, ending the call abruptly before she could admonish him.

He'd noticed Gerrard casting him a knowing look as he came into the MIR but he paid it no heed. He didn't have the energy to manage his peer relationships today. If that put him at odds with the DC then so be it. As for the others, Edwards always had his foot up Jack's backside, and there'd be no discernible change in DI Russell's attitude. Watkins and Christensen wouldn't say anything. Well, the new Watkins might, but he'd soon get in line.

He watched as the team threw themselves into the case, noticing that heightened tension that always preceded a break-through. Technically, Jack had already received news that would potentially blow the case wide open.

Yet he had decided to sit on it.

The fact that Robson had told him that one of his team was compromised had put him on edge. The issue of the mole from the previous year had never really gone away, but a lack of high-profile cases meant that there hadn't been much opportunity to wreak havoc on the force. Leaking information and being compromised were two different things, though. He was hoping that Robson, true to form, was simply full of shit.

Gerrard bounded over to him. 'I managed to pull up all the relevant information on people-smuggling cases from the nineties,' the DC told him.

Jack blinked, the dryness behind his eyelids scraping at his vision like windswept sand. 'And?'

'Nothing tangible,' she told him.

'So it's another dead end,' he muttered.

'Not exactly.'

'What is it?'

Gerrard handed him a set of notes before launching into a rundown of her findings. 'There was nothing on people smuggling, which only means they got away with it, not that it didn't happen. But I did find some stories involving McCullagh.'

Christensen limped over and they all looked as Gerrard spread the printouts over the table. It seemed McCullagh had been a busy boy in terms of press coverage at one time.

'Someone was popular,' Jack noted.

'So,' Gerrard continued, 'as you can see, the stories start with regards to his charity work.'

Jack looked at the first headline. McCullagh had organised a local dog walk for a cancer trust. His face, less rugged and noticeably leaner, smiled up at them from the sheet. He was quoted as saying he *just wanted to give something back.*'

'The walk is still going on now,' Gerrard said. 'But McCullagh has nothing to do with it.'

'Why is that?' Christensen asked.

Gerrard smiled. 'Because of this.'

She placed the next headline in front of them. This one was far less complimentary. According to the *Chronicle*, at the time,

McCullagh had been accused of siphoning off funds from the trust for his own personal gain.

'Interesting,' Jack mused.

'It gets better,' Gerrard said, pushing another headline towards him.

Former Port of Tyne worker and charity guru opens new pub

Apparently the good people of the north east had short memories when it came to Brian McCullagh's charity dealings. There, on the sheet, was a smiling McCullagh, surrounded by local dignitaries. He was holding a pair of scissors up next to a thin ribbon that was being held by two people, outside the pub.

'Maybe you need glasses,' Gerrard said.

'I see fine,' Jack told her, conscious of his need to squint as he looked at the image.

'See anything familiar?' she asked.

'Gus Fenwick,' Christensen chipped in. 'And Margaret Fenwick.'

He was right. On McCullagh's left, amongst the small crowd, were a smiling Gus and Margaret Fenwick, his long, spindly arms wrapped around her waist. Her eyes betrayed none of the vitriol they carried now. Clearly a happier time. Jack checked the date stamp on the article. September 12th 1998. Just over twenty years ago. Looking at that photo of those two people, he wouldn't have thought such a dramatic turnaround in relations was possible. Still, photos often told lies.

'So within two years of leaving the Port of Tyne, he manages to start up a charity, cause controversy by siphoning off funds from said charity, then opens the pub,' Jack summed up.

'I checked police records,' Gerrard said. 'Nothing on him. Looks like the charity accusation never went any further. Still,' she added, 'it was enough for him to step down from it.'

'Worried about reputational damage or the potential investigation that would ensue?' Jack said. 'Interesting stuff.'

'Not quite as interesting as who had written the final two stories,' Gerrard said.

Jack looked to the by-line and shook his head. 'David bloody Robson.'

'Yep,' Gerrard said. 'Doesn't mean anything, of course, but he may know something about McCullagh. It could be worth speaking to him.'

'I'll do that,' Jack said, a little too hastily. He noticed the glances offered from across the room. 'I mean, I have a reasonable relationship with him, so it makes sense for me to approach him.'

His colleagues seemed satisfied with that explanation.

'Okay,' Gerrard said. 'Knock yourself out. I'll keep digging, see what I can find.'

'Good work,' Jack told her.

'You sure you want to go alone to speak to the journalist?' Christensen asked him.

'Why would I not?'

The DS motioned for Jack to follow him to the corner of the room. He leaned in and whispered. 'Jane is on the warpath; she's already spoken to Edwards about it. The team are noticing that you are going off on your own again. Given that it's a simple act of talking to Robson, what harm is there in taking someone along? I know how you work, and it isn't a problem, but take someone to see him and it'll buy you some leeway for the next time you go solo.'

Jack understood what he was saying. He suppressed his annoyance at Jane once again complaining about his methods and nodded. 'Okay,' he said. 'You can come with me once it's arranged. Make sure they know we are going together; I'd hate for them to think I was doing anything independently,' he added, sarcastically.

He left the team to it and took some time in his office. He found himself in need of more painkillers, and was rewarded with a half-used pack in his middle drawer. Fishing them out, he chewed them down and massaged his temples. DI Jane Russell would be the death of him. He'd have to seriously consider his position should she ever replace Edwards. Jack had no real ambition of his own, save for that of catching the bad guys, and so it had never crossed his mind to go for the superintendent role. A hands-on DCI was a rarity these days; if he moved up to DSI he'd be sat twiddling his thumbs, waiting for Nadine Guthrie to tell him what a shit job he was doing. He was caught between a rock and a hard place. The longer Edwards stuck around, the better, as far as he was concerned.

He knew it would do him no good to confront Jane about it; for one thing, she was right, he *was* going off on his own. But he always had legitimate reasons for doing so, despite what his colleagues thought. If taking Christensen along to speak with Robson would shut her up for a couple of days, then he was willing to do it. Plus, the DS was right, he had no real reason to keep them out of the loop.

His phone pinged. He noticed the screen was grimy, scraped a bit off with his fingernail, and looked at the text. Louise was letting him know that Shannon had had a good week in school and the head was talking about reinstating her into her normal classes soon. Jack smiled: his methods had paid off. Having said that, he'd essentially bought off his daughter with Chinese food and unsuitable films. Still, it had worked, and he didn't care about methods as long as it yielded results.

And that went for both parenting and police work.

'Guv.' Watkins appeared in the doorway, before forgetting himself and walking back out to knock.

'Just come in,' Jack told him. 'Besides, you've seen I'm in and I already know it's you so it's not like I can pretend I'm not here.'

'You could,' Watkins said.

'Don't give me the option,' Jack told him. 'What is it?'

Watkins took a seat and Jack noticed the disgusted look he gave the ever-growing pile of paperwork that he had on his desk. Embarrassed, Jack moved to place some on the floor out of view.

If he ever did make DSI he would most definitely outlaw paper-work. Although, having said that, the thought of making Jane keep up to date with the pencil pushing did fill him with a certain amount of joy.

'You look happy,' Watkins observed.

'I'm always happy,' Jack told him.

'Hmmm,' Watkins grumbled, before letting out a shrill laugh. Jack was unmoved. 'Yes, anyway,' he said, 'I thought you might want to take a look at this.'

'What is it?' Jack asked.

Watkins pulled at his collar. 'It arrived at the station a couple of minutes ago.'

Jack picked up the brown envelope, addressed to him, and opened the edge. Whoever had shut it had used tape. He was glad. There was nothing worse, in his opinion, than having to run your nails over somebody else's saliva to open a letter.

'I never get mail here,' he stated, pulling the envelope open.

He emptied the contents onto his desk, which consisted of three clear, colour photos. It didn't take a detective to work out who was in the photos. He recognised himself immediately. The first image showed him sat at a table, in the bar, talking to David Robson. Feeling his fury rise, he turned to the second image. This showed them leaning in close, talking to each other. The third picture showed Jack holding Robson's hand, during the exchange of written notes, which made it look like they were transferring something to each other. Again, it didn't take a genius to work out what the implication would be.

Money.

A small piece of yellowed paper dropped from the images onto his desk. He placed the photographs face down and picked it up, before unfurling it. It had three, very simple words written on it in capitals...

TAKEN YESTERDAY. MOLE?

'It doesn't look good, Jack,' Watkins said.

'You've seen this?' he asked.

The DS nodded. 'Everybody has. We all received a copy moments ago. I thought I'd come to you now before anyone else gets the chance to speak to you.'

Jack bristled. 'You don't seriously think that I'm an informant, do you?' he asked.

Watkins couldn't look him in the eye. 'It's not for me to say.'

'Then who is to say?' Jack shot back.

His internal phone rang before Watkins could reply.

After a brief conversation Jack slammed the receiver down. 'I'm off to see Edwards.'

'Jack, I—'

He was already out the door before the DS could finish his sentence.

With every step towards his boss' office, he found his fury rising. By the time he arrived outside Edwards' room, he was positively spitting at the sheer audacity of somebody suggesting he was a mole.

He didn't knock.

'I'm here, thirty seconds early, granted, but I'm sure you can fit me in.'

As he entered the room he saw Dalton, the ACC, already sat at the DSI's desk. Jack noted the pile of paperwork that he'd managed to quickly shuffle out of the way. The red colour on Edwards' face was clearly down to more than just heavy drinking on this occasion. If Jack knew Dalton like he thought he did, then Edwards wouldn't have been immune from a beasting, despite it being Jack's neck on the block.

'Take a seat, Jack, please,' Edwards said, a pained look on his face.

Jack sat next to Dalton, acknowledging him with a curt nod. The ACC, a slim, lithe man in his late fifties, nodded back. He brought a hand up and pushed it through his immaculately combed hair, complete with just the right amount of silver at the sides to give him a distinguished look. Jack had never seen such good posture on another man. If he didn't know any better, he'd say he was an army man. Dalton acted like it, too.

'Jack,' he said, his northern accent as watered down as a cheap juice from a school tuck shop. 'I'm glad you were able to come at such short notice.'

Jack stopped short of informing him that he hadn't really been given much choice. 'No problem,' he said through gritted teeth. 'I'm assuming you've received a copy of the images?'

Edwards nodded, eyes flitting to Dalton. 'I have. I called the ACC here as... it... I...'

'It's okay,' Jack told him. 'It was the right thing to do, under the circumstances.'

'Good,' Dalton said. 'The question now is, where do we go from here?'

'Well, it's obviously false,' Jack told him. 'There really is nowhere to go.'

Dalton cleared his throat before speaking, his gaze hard and cold. 'We have no way of knowing if this will reach the press. Various officers in this station have received copies of it. It's not necessarily just a case of containment on this one.'

'Just spit it out,' Jack told him.

Only the slightest of twitches betrayed any emotion in Dalton. Jack had heard the stories about his famous bust-ups on the force but, given the way he was feeling, he didn't much care about the fallout. 'I'll remind you that you are sat here with your commanding officers, DCI Lambert,' Dalton told him. 'This isn't the murder squad and you aren't in charge here.'

Jack bit his tongue. He knew he had to keep Dalton on side if he valued his position. He may have lacked a certain level of personal ambition, but he didn't much fancy losing his job. 'So what do you propose?' he asked.

'We'll have to conduct an investigation, and it may go to a panel,' Dalton told him.

'Hold on a minute!' Jack shouted. He looked towards Edwards who seemed to be doing his best to watch the wildlife outside. 'It's just a picture. It could have been anybody.'

'Yes, Jack,' Dalton said. 'But the fact is it isn't just a picture— and it's of you.'

Jack met the ACC's gaze with hostility. 'I'm heading up a murder investigation, multiple murders actually. I am allowed to speak with people, and I won't justify myself for that.'

'It doesn't look good, though, Jack,' Edwards finally spoke, his voice barely above a whisper. 'We've been battling a leak in terms of information to that very journalist for some time now. We never figured out who it was. Now, we receive a photograph of you meeting with him, alone, with what looks like money being exchanged.'

'Bullshit,' Jack said. 'It wasn't money. He was handing me a note.'

'Saying?' Dalton asked.

'Warning me that people were listening, and that what he was saying wasn't true.'

'And what was he saying?' Edwards asked.

Jack paused. He didn't really want to highlight that Robson had told him there was a compromised officer. For all Jack knew it could have been one of the two other men in the room with him right now. 'He was just passing on information to me that he had looked into this underground syndicate theory we have been working on but that he'd had no tangible leads.' Edwards saw the lie, Jack was sure of it, but didn't speak.

'And is your team aware of this?' Dalton asked.

Jack shrugged. 'No. It wasn't pertinent information. He didn't give me anything.'

'Except the note,' Dalton cut in. 'Do you still have it?'

'No,' Jack said. 'I tore it up as I was conscious that we were probably being watched.'

Dalton pointed to the photograph on Edwards' desk with a tanned hand. 'Not conscious enough, it seems.'

'I don't know what you want me to say,' Jack told him.

'You don't have to say anything,' Dalton told him with a wry smile. 'But you know the rest.'

'This is outrageous. I can't believe you're questioning my professionalism.'

'Why?' Dalton rounded on him. 'Someone has consistently been giving out information for some two years now, perhaps longer, details which only those in the very middle of the case could know. Now, we see that you have been meeting with that very journalist, on your own, without the team being aware of it. How would you say that looks?'

'I don't give a shit what you think,' Jack told him. 'I won't have my loyalty to the force questioned by somebody who spends his entire time hosting meetings and throwing his weight around just so he can massage his own ego.'

Dalton leaned forward and spoke into Jack's ear, hot breath bearing down on him. 'Mark my words, Lambert, I'll see to it you're ruined for that. If I don't get you on this now, it'll only be a matter of time. You think you can outlast me? Let's see you try.'

Jack grabbed the ACC by the lapels. Dalton barely flinched, a perfect smile spreading across his face, almost daring Jack to hit him. He wanted nothing more than to plant one on the arrogant bastard.

'You have something on your collar,' Jack told him, releasing his grip and wiping his shirt down. 'There you go,' he told him. 'Almost clean.'

Dalton snorted. 'Almost.'

Edwards waited until Dalton had left the room before planting his head against the desk.

'What's your problem?' Jack asked him. 'It's not like you're being accused of malpractice.'

'Are you out of your fucking mind?' Edwards thundered. 'You just put your hands on the ACC, for Christ's sake!'

Jack waved him away. 'It's fine, I didn't hit him. Besides, he did have dirt on his collar. People like Dalton don't respond to reason,' he told him. 'You've got to show them you aren't afraid.'

Edwards shook his head, his entire frame struggling to burst out of his suit. 'You must have a death wish. That's your card marked now.'

Jack laughed. 'It's marked anyway. Your job? I don't want it.'

'It's your own job you need to worry about!'

'I can sleep soundly at night,' Jack told him.

That wasn't strictly true.

'Good,' Edwards said. 'And you're going to get more sleep in the short term. I'm suspending you until an internal investigation has been completed.'

Jack gripped the edges of his seat. 'Out of your hands?'

Edwards nodded. 'Dalton's orders. It was already decided before you even got here.'

Jack stood up. 'That figures. But, for the record, nobody is going to stop me from being involved in this investigation. I'll get the information regardless, whether I'm on active duty or not. Dalton doesn't frighten me, and neither does this bogus accusation. I've been set up.' He placed his hand on the doorknob before turning back to the DSI. 'And they want to pray I don't find out who.'

Edwards stood and leaned over his desk. 'Don't do anything stupid, you hear me?'

'Don't worry about it, Logan,' he said, before adding, 'unless it's you.'

The two men stared each other out for a good ten seconds before the DSI backed down. 'Don't make accusations you can't back up, Jack, it doesn't reflect well on you.'

'Unlike the person who did this,' Jack said, holding up the picture of him and Robson in conversation. He made to leave.

'Some would call that evidence, Jack,' Edwards called after him. 'And, for the record, if Dalton hadn't put the order in, I would have suspended you myself anyway.'

Jack was surprised the door didn't come off its hinges, such was the force he flung it with.

CHAPTER FORTY-ONE

His temper was still simmering by the time he got home. He slammed the front door, dumped the post on a side cabinet, and stormed through to the kitchen. Deciding that sobriety was overrated, he'd stopped off at the local off-license and stocked up on two bottles of single malt whisky. One sizeable shot later and he was sat on the settee, the only sound that of his neighbour's television mumbling through the wall.

He'd been set up. He didn't know what was more annoying, the fact that they'd done that to him, or the fact that he'd let it happen. The question he had burning in his head was: *did Robson know?*

If he did, then they'd managed to get to him. If Robson had been in on it, then it meant somebody with at least a similar pulling power to Dorian McGuinness had infiltrated him. Unless, of course, it *was* McGuinness. He dismissed the thought almost as quickly as it had arrived. McGuinness had no reason to pull him out of the game. If anything, he would have wanted Jack in a position of influence, which would mean keeping him where he was. Jack wasn't stupid, he knew McGuinness thought he could use him but there was no way he was going to abuse his position to help a known criminal.

So, that begged the question, if it wasn't McGuinness, then who? McCullagh? The Syndicate? Jack drummed his fingers on his cheap, IKEA coffee table whilst he thought. He needed to speak to Robson.

Urgently.

If Robson had been in on the sting, then that meant he'd broken with the script to tell him about the compromised officer. Why, though? The thought of one of the team being a player in this syndicate, or beyond, made Jack queasy. He couldn't fathom it.

He went to the kitchen, necked another shot of whisky, and grabbed a pen and paper. He ripped the sheet into six pieces and placed them in front of him. He was feeling a light buzz from the drink, now, which served to warm his insides against the cold that was penetrating the concrete walls of his Victorian house. He never had been one for putting the heating on.

He took the pen and wrote their names down. He was able to remove himself from suspicion, given that he knew he was innocent. That left only six names, one of whom was certainly wishful thinking on Jack's part. For now, he decided to treat the mole and compromised officer as one and the same person.

He decided to start at the very top, placing each bit of paper out in a sort of skewed family tree, placing Dalton's name at the head of it. Jack had trouble believing that Dalton was the traitor. Dalton, for all his faults, was loyal to the badge. Plus, he didn't have his finger on the pulse enough to be able to feed details of individual cases to the press. Still, he had considerable influence in the force. If somebody really wanted an inside man, there was no better person in terms of exerting influence over what went on.

And, given his threat to Jack, he would enjoy seeing him get his comeuppance.

Edwards was next. Jack thought he knew his superior officer well. But, then again, he couldn't say for sure with regards to the man. Since Jack's admission about his sexuality, Edwards had cooled towards him. Plus, he was on the way out, which meant he could have been creaming a bit off the top. He'd been drinking heavily, even more than usual, which Jack had originally put down to the pressures of the job and his crumbling home life. But, it wasn't outside the realms of possibility that he was medicating himself due to having been compromised by an outside source. He certainly knew details of the cases well, given that Jack often debriefed to him.

DI Russell. Jack allowed himself a smile at the thought that it could be her. Her attitude to him had never been positive and everybody knew her personal ambition. She wanted the top job. She didn't rate Jack and she had every reason to want to frame him. *But, was that enough on its own to allow her to become a rat?* Jack wondered. Somehow, Jack couldn't picture her betraying the force, despite her often aloof nature. Jack wondered if she really hated him enough to go through all that just to remove him from the picture.

DS Christensen. Jack's hand was already aching from having to write in freehand. He was a product of his generation, over-reliant on computers. He struggled to put pen to paper with regards to the DS. He thought, *what does anybody know about Christensen?* He remembered how Christensen had stood by while he'd roughed up Henry Stafford the previous year, and had never so much as uttered a word about it. That alone would have been enough to get him out of the picture. He didn't need to resort to this to take Jack out of the game. *Still,* Jack thought, *that would have involved revealing himself if he had grassed him up.*

DS Watkins. It was almost unfathomable to Jack that his closest colleague, his protégé, would betray him in such a way. But then, maybe that was the whole idea? Watkins had been like a younger brother to Jack for a long time. But, if Jack was being honest with himself, Watkins had grown more distant in recent times. He was certainly more assertive, and they no longer had a close bond. He thought back to when they'd spoken about the photos; Watkins hadn't even been able to look him in the eye. Plus, he'd made to continue the conversation but Jack had cut him off. *What had he wanted to say?* Jack wondered.

DC Gerrard. The rising star. Claire had ambition, but it wasn't a burning ambition like Jane's, one which would lead her to trample over others to get to the top—or so Jack thought. They'd argued recently, and she'd been keen for him to remove himself from the case once Jack had been fingered as one of Olsen's targets. Jack couldn't help but wonder whether that was to avoid having to set him up with Robson. Maybe that had been her way of trying to take the easy way out.

He lay back on the settee, realising he was now shrouded in darkness. He found he had a headache. Soon, he'd have to make a choice; drink more, or grab some water and go to sleep. He was shattered, emotionally drained and isolated from his own team.

Drink it was.

He looked once more over the names before him. The problem was, despite their individual personality traits, Jack didn't really know much about them outside of the workplace. That made it impossible to pin down a potential motive. He felt that they had to have been approached, whoever it was. And if they had been, then the perpetrator had been able to seize on a weakness. What that weakness was, Jack had no idea.

He found himself falling into an uneasy sleep but suddenly jolted awake. Something had crossed his mind. Dragging himself to his feet, he pushed the papers to one side and looked at the post. It was the brown envelope he'd seen on entering his house. It had his name on, but wasn't addressed. That meant someone had hand-posted it.

He turned it over, immediately recognising the seal at the top. He pulled it open and emptied the contents on the table. Just like at the station, it showed him in conversation with David Robson only, there was a fourth photo in the pile. Moving the other three aside, he flicked on his reading lamp and held it under the dim glow. It showed him, by the post office, looking towards the bar where he'd met Robson.

They knew he had been watching them.

Jack felt a shiver run down his spine as he studied the image further. It had been taken from his left-hand side, across the road, which meant that they had not been far from the traffic lights where he had crossed on the bar side. He scanned his memory as to whether he'd seen anybody but knew it was a dead end.

Another set of papers caught his eye on the table. He spread them out and held the lamp over them. It was bits of shredded paper, taped together. The words were nonsensical, but it showed that they had grabbed the ripped paper from the bin. He was glad that he'd had the foresight to only get rid of half the paper. He almost smiled at the thought of his assailants wasting their time trying to piece it together.

The final bit of paper had a single word written on it.

'Mole?'

The sharp ring of his house phone caused him to jump.

He picked up the handset. 'Jack Lambert.'

'I know what you did.'

He gripped the receiver. 'What?'

'The photo,' Louise's voice sang down the line.

He felt his gut twist in on itself. 'What photo?'

'You know,' she said, 'the photo of you and Shannon in the Chinese. I suppose you got your mate to take it and sent it when you felt brave enough? Very funny,' she added. 'Although it is a bit weird.'

'Listen to me,' Jack cut in. 'Go to the window and look outside now, but keep your lights off.'

'What?'

'Don't question it just do as I ask. Let me know when you're there.'

The change in atmosphere was immediate.

'I'm there.'

'Okay,' he said. 'Now, listen very carefully, I want you to tell me what you see.'

'Nothing,' she said, no hint of joviality left in her voice.

'No people?'

'Nobody,' she said. 'Look, Jack, what's going on? You're scaring me.'

'Good,' he told her. 'What about cars? Anything that looks unusual or out of place? Is there anybody sitting in a car, for example?'

'Not that I can see.'

Jack was in full police mode now. 'Where's Shannon?'

'She's out with Jeremy at the supermarket. They should be back any time now.'

Panic seized him at the thought of his daughter being exposed. Still, a supermarket in full public view at peak time was about as safe as a person could be.

'Listen to me very carefully; I didn't send that photo.' He heard the whoosh of his ex-wife's intake of breath. 'But the people that did know who I am, who you are and where we all live.'

'What the fuck, Jack?!' she screeched. 'You bring this to my door?'

'Listen!' he ordered. 'We can argue about it later. What I need you to do now is go and check that both doors are locked.'

Another pause as she followed his instructions. 'They are,' she said.

'Good. Now, I want you to use your mobile to ring Jeremy and see where they are, keep your voice calm, but encourage them to come home quickly. I'm going to stay on the line while you do it.'

'Okay.'

He waited while she muffled some words down the line to
Jeremy, before coming back on the line. 'They okay?' he asked.

'Yes. I said I was starting tea and that they should hurry. They
are on the way anyway.'

'Good,' Jack said. 'Now, I want you to ring the police and tell
them you believe there may have been a threat made against you,
based on a package delivered to your house, and that you don't
feel safe in the home. Again, I'll wait on the line.'

He waited until Louise had made the call before getting in his
car and arriving at the house some twenty minutes later. By that
time, both Jeremy and the police had arrived. Louise had asked
Shannon to go to her room. Despite some initial fightback, she
had acquiesced and done as she was told. Jack could tell Louise
was furious with him. *It's like being married all over again,* he
thought.

He could tell that the PC who had arrived on the scene wasn't
taking it seriously. His condescending tone didn't help matters so
Jack had put him right, flashing his badge to him in the process.
One stern dressing down later and the man's tone had changed.
Jack had made it clear that should any harm come to his family
due to the man's lack of due diligence, he could kiss goodbye to
any future on the force. He didn't like pulling rank in that way,
but it was his family. He didn't give a shit who he offended.
Besides, he was suspended from duty so technically he wasn't
abusing his position.

Or so he told himself.

He'd informed Edwards, as a courtesy, about what had
happened. The DSI had left the conversation with a promise to
let the team know, and keep it on their radar as part of their
investigations. Apparently, on its own, it wasn't enough to put
Jack in the clear.

He'd wanted to stay at Louise's but she'd shooed him out. If he
was being honest, he knew it was for the best. The reality was,
whoever they were, they wanted him. Targeting Louise would

have been to put the frighteners on him. If that was their aim then it had worked. He had never dreamed that his daughter would be dragged into his work but he should have foreseen it. He was a known figure, a high-profile presence in his field, not to mention his past dealings with the McGuinness crew. The only surprise really was that it hadn't happened sooner. Despite all attempts, conscious and otherwise, to cut himself off from the world, he'd still managed put those close to him in danger.

He arrived back at his house in a determined mood. The gloves were off now, as far as he was concerned. Whether it was McCullagh, some syndicate, a dodgy copper or even McGuinness, he was coming for them. He had to think clearly. He hadn't been when he'd left the house, clearly driving over the limit. It was reckless of him, but he'd not given it a moment's thought when he'd heard that they'd been to Shannon's house. Well, he was thinking clearly now. He slammed the door behind him, checked the latch, went to the kitchen, and poured the whisky out into the sink. He felt a rage he hadn't known he could carry burning up in him at that moment. He clenched his fists and thumped one into the kitchen counter, taking a chunk off the edge, and off his finger in the process. It stung, but he felt no real pain. Turning the cold tap on, he ran it over his finger until the bleeding stopped and then wrapped a plaster around the gash.

Edwards be damned. If the police wouldn't let him use their resources, he'd sort it out himself.

He didn't notice the black Mercedes parked on the edge of his street.

CHAPTER FORTY-TWO

He awoke the next day to a number of missed calls and texts —one of which was from Louise, just letting him know they were okay. He breathed a sigh of relief; whatever other news awaited him couldn't be as bad as something happening to his daughter. He managed to drag himself out of bed and poured himself a glass of water in the kitchen, all the while sifting through his messages. The office had been trying to get in touch with him. It hadn't even been twenty-four hours and they couldn't live without him, it seemed.

He sighed and dialled Watkins' number.

The DS picked up on the third ring, just as Jack popped some frozen bread into his toaster and managed to locate some barely in-date peanut butter. 'Finally,' Watkins said.

'You do know I'm not on active duty, Watkins?' Jack said. 'That means that, theoretically, I can get up whenever I like until I'm either sacked or told to return from gardening leave.'

The DS didn't bite. 'How's the family?'

'So, you've heard?'

'Of course,' Watkins said. 'Edwards briefed us this morning.

Jane is in temporary charge.' He lowered his voice. 'God help us all.'

Despite his annoyance over his suspension, and the mistrust he now had for all of his colleagues, he found himself smiling. 'So what can I do for you, detective?' he said, not even trying to hide the sarcasm from his voice.

'Have you seen the news?' Watkins asked.

'No, as we've already discussed, I have just woken up.'

'Stick *Look North* on now; they're running the story as we speak. Ring me back when you're done.'

The phone went dead. *Typical Watkins, always in a hurry,* he thought.

His toast popped out so he decided to have it dry, throwing it onto a plate, before grabbing the TV remote and switching to the local news.

The headline caused his hairs to stand on end.

'Nobody knows for sure the circumstances surrounding this senseless attack,' the news reporter at the scene said. 'But we do know that nightclub owner and former local political candidate, Dorian McGuinness, was in the club at the time. It is not known how many casualties there are but it is thought that the incendiary device went off after closing, with only a handful of staff in the building.'

Jack watched as the camera crew zoomed in on the burned husk that was McGuinness' nightclub, The Vibe. It was mainly smoke now but there was still a fire crew presence hosing a steady stream of water at the building. Once the building was secure, police tape would go up and the forensic team would do their thing.

Jack was speechless. He'd thought McGuinness untouchable. Certainly, by local gang standards, he was top dog. If somebody could get to him in this way, it signalled a much bigger turf war was at hand. *No news on casualties,* Jack thought. *Is he dead?*

He had mixed feelings at the thought of McGuinness dying.

Certainly, it would cut off the head of the snake in terms of local gang culture. It would also get him off the hook with regards to being in the gangster's debt. Still, he'd worked for McGuinness at one time and, despite his many faults as a human being, Jack was reasonably fond of him.

He chewed through his dry toast, clumps of congealed bread clinging to his windpipe, as the news reporter finished his segment. They returned to the studio, and the host's sombre expression soon changed to one of mild amusement as they began a new story about the Christmas Camel Parade in South Shields. Jack thought it an odd concept but then the people there were called Sand Dancers.

Watkins picked up after two rings this time. 'I told you you'd want to see that.'

'Alright,' Jack replied. 'I'm interested. Is he dead?'

'No word yet,' Watkins said. 'But he's seriously injured, we know that much. Clearly a murder attempt. There were a number of people in the bar and our early reports suggest at least three fatalities.'

Jack wondered whether or not the bouncer who'd been tasked with potentially breaking his kneecaps had been part of the carnage. 'I don't see what I can do from here,' Jack told him. 'As I previously said, I'm suspended.'

'Aye, about that,' Watkins replied. 'Edwards wants to see you, won't say why.'

He arrived at the station by midday. He gave a brief nod to the desk sergeant and headed straight up to see his boss. Thankfully, he managed to avoid any of the team. Knowing that somebody was potentially compromised had him on edge, and he didn't much fancy being privy to any accusatory glances in his direction.

'You're late,' Edwards said, after he'd entered the office.

Jack laughed. 'Really? Technically, given you've given me the boot, I'm actually canny early,' he shot back.

'Less lip from you,' the DSI boomed. 'Take a seat.'

Jack toyed with the idea of remaining standing, just to make a point, but thought better of it. He wasn't a child. Ultimately he wanted a return to work; if he had to suck up to the boss to do that, he was willing to swallow the bullet.

Plus, he had a mole to catch.

'How's the family?' Edwards asked.

'Fine,' Jack lied. Truth be told, Louise was furious with him. He didn't blame her.

'Good,' Edwards said. 'We will do what we can but it's tenuous at best at the minute. The force can't just plough resources into surveillance due to a photograph being delivered to a house.'

Jack understood his reasoning. The problem was, it was his daughter—so he didn't care. If they couldn't do anything about it, he'd make sure he could.

Jack cut to the chase. 'Why have you asked me here?'

He knew Edwards was itching to give him a dressing down but, at this point, Jack didn't care. As far as he was concerned, his boss hadn't even had the decency to back him up when Dalton had thrown his weight about. Plus, he no longer knew who he could trust.

'Because I need your help, Jack,' Edwards finally said.

Jack thought as much. Barely a day had passed and they'd already decided they needed him. Jack didn't believe for one second it was that simple, of course. McGuinness being targeted had repercussions, repercussions well beyond a tit-for-tat response. If the crew found out who had done it, there was no telling what the retaliation would be. Jack knew that as well as anybody. These people lived by a code; that code had now been broken. Things like that didn't go unanswered.

'I'm listening,' Jack said.

'For God's sake, man, are you going to make me beg?' Edwards erupted, jumping to his feet with a nimbleness Jack hadn't realised he'd had. He pointed a chubby finger at Jack's chest. 'And don't forget, you're suspended so less of the cheek. It's in your interests to do as you're told for once.'

Jack snorted. 'So, McGuinness gets targeted and suddenly I'm the golden boy again, is that it?' He knew he was being facetious but his patience had worn thin.

'Not likely,' Edwards told him. 'You're about as far from gold as you can get.' The giant DSI sighed before heaving his bulk back into his office chair. 'But you're perhaps the only person in Newcastle who can help stop whatever is coming.'

Jack took a seat. 'I don't have that kind of influence.'

Edwards shook his head. 'I've never pressed you on your past, Jack,' he told him. 'But it's common knowledge you know McGuinness on some level. At the very least, he respects you enough to listen to you.'

Jack wasn't sure how much listening Dorian McGuinness ever really did.

Edwards continued. 'We can't have this spill over onto the streets. Whatever you think of me, or Dalton, or whoever the fuck else you don't like, you're a policeman, a pretty good one according to some people. It's the city that's in trouble now, and Newcastle needs you.'

Jack was impressed, he almost asked his boss whether he'd rehearsed those lines but thought it best not to resort to any further sarcasm. He was right, though. Jack did care about the city, and they all knew the pressure pot was now likely to blow due to the attack.

'What about my suspension?' Jack asked.

Edwards pulled at his collar. 'You're still suspended... officially,' he said. 'But, a satisfactory conclusion to this can't harm your chances of a positive return.'

That sounded dangerously close to blackmail for Jack's liking. 'So, the ACC knows about this... arrangement?' he asked.

'Yes,' Edwards said. 'But... the others don't.'

Jack laughed. 'Are you mad? You want me to stop World War Three on the streets of Newcastle without any backup from the team? Also, McGuinness hasn't been murdered!'

'No,' Edwards said. 'But there have been multiple other fatalities. It's in everyone's interests that you look into it.'

'Are you kidding me?'

'Do I look like I'm joking?'

'What resources do I have?' Jack asked.

'Me,' he said. 'Whatever you need, just ask.'

Jack couldn't believe what he was hearing. His boss was asking him to go rogue. 'The team will be looking into this as well,' he said.

'Yes,' Edwards said. 'But they don't have the pull you have. The only way we stop this is to find out who orchestrated the attack and bring them in before it all kicks off.'

Jack resisted the urge to point out that an explosive planted in a nightclub had probably already pushed them past that point. 'I don't know,' he said.

'It's not a request, Jack,' Edwards told him.

Jack held his gaze. He believed him. His job was now on the line. Was he willing to throw himself back into that world just to keep the badge? He didn't even need to ask the question.

'I'll do it,' Jack replied, pretending like he'd had to consider it. 'But I'm still going to look into the Norris and Holding murders.'

'I'll pretend I didn't hear that,' Edwards said, grimly. 'You've got no jurisdiction to stay involved. If we find out you're interfering, we'll bring you in, and this arrangement will be off.'

'Understood,' Jack told him. He stood to leave. 'Anything else?'

'I've never questioned your methods,' Edwards told him. 'Because, ultimately, you get results. But if you balls this one up, there'll be nowhere left for you to go. Are we clear?'

Jack stopped at the doorway. 'Crystal, guv.'

'Oh, and Jack,' Edwards called. Jack turned to face him. 'Do whatever it takes.'

Jack managed to leave the station as he'd arrived—without being spotted. He got into his car, turned up his Deep Purple record to ear splitting volumes, and began to think. There was no way he was going to stop looking into the other murders. Whilst McGuinness would have any number of enemies willing to have a pop, Jack knew something the others didn't; namely, that he'd been looking into the Syndicate at Jack's request. Unfortunately for those involved, Jack didn't believe in coincidences. Through their collective efforts, they'd both managed to put themselves in the firing line. What they didn't yet know was who was aiming the weapon. One thing was for certain, though, they were all a target now.

CHAPTER FORTY-THREE

'What the fuck are you doing here?'

Jack shrugged. 'I see you haven't waited long to jump in the hot seat, Henry.'

Stafford started, as if he'd only just realised that he was sitting in his boss' chair. They both knew that McGuinness would be furious if he knew one of his underlings had sat on his throne. The goon was flanked by two heavies, neither of whom Jack recognised from the nightclub. The odds on the bouncer having made it just lengthened slightly, in Jack's mind. They both looked tense, their eyes on Jack, like he was a gazelle who had wandered into a lion's den. Technically, he had.

'I haven't got time for this, pig,' Stafford boomed. 'Get on with it and you can get on your way. I'll tell you what I told your colleague, that blond bastard, I don't know anything,' he said, the last syllable playing out over a good two seconds. 'We just sell fish, we have no idea why anybody would want to hurt us, or the boss.'

One of the goons sniggered. Jack watched Stafford's reaction. As opposed to McGuinness' demand for military precision, Dorian's number two just seemed pleased that somebody had laughed at his joke.

Jack wasn't impressed. 'Christensen?' Jack asked. 'He's a good officer.'

'Aye,' Stafford said. 'I seem to remember seeing him some place before.'

Jack's mind flashed back to the beating he'd given Henry Stafford the previous year. He didn't have time to feel guilty for that now. 'How about we talk in private,' he said, adding, 'unless you're nervous about that.'

Stafford was easier to read than a picture book. By playing to his ego, Jack knew he would get what he wanted. McGuinness would never have fallen for such a ploy. It seemed the drug lord was having problems finding the right staff these days.

'I ain't frightened of nobody, son,' Stafford said. 'Lads, how about you leave us to it for a bit. Jack will give a shout if he needs you,' he added, eyes dancing to the pair. Neither reacted and Jack could tell the man was wounded by their lack of response.

He waited until they'd left before continuing. 'Why don't we cut to the chase,' Jack said. 'Who made the hit on Dorian?'

Stafford tutted. 'You think I would tell you that?'

Jack read the man's features. 'You don't know,' he said, raising an eyebrow. 'I'm surprised.'

Stafford said, 'Do you know, like?'

That gave Jack what he needed. The crew had no idea, and they were rudderless without their leader. Perhaps it would be an opportune time for the drugs squad to swoop in and clean up.

Not before Jack was finished, though.

He decided to play things close to his chest. 'I don't know,' Jack said. 'But we both have an interest in finding out.'

Stafford laughed. 'You think I'm stupid? We help you out and you arrest them. Where's the revenge in that?'

'You really want a war whilst McGuinness is out of action?' Jack fired back. 'Worst case, McGuinness dies and you get run over by a rival,' he told him. 'Even worse case scenario, you get run out of town and McGuinness lives.' Jack leaned in. 'Who do you think he'll blame then?'

Jack saw the fear flash across Stafford's eyes.

'We have protection, numbers...' he stuttered.

'No, Henry,' Jack told him. 'How quickly do you think those people will turn on you once McGuinness is out of the picture? People in your business aren't loyal to McGuinness out of respect. They're loyal out of fear. If there's no longer anything to fear, why would they stay?' He knew he had him in the palm of his hand now. 'Sure, one or two would, such as yourself; but you just wait and see how many abandon you and before you know it there's just you, your two friends out there and a handful of fish tanks between yourselves and whoever has made the play. You forget, Henry, I've been in this world before. I know how it works.'

Henry laughed, but Jack could tell he was nervous. 'Yeah, but you betrayed him and joined the police. You're basically a rat.'

Jack shook his head. 'You're wrong, Henry. I'm anything but a rat. McGuinness and I have a professional relationship, an understanding. I'm no rat, I'm useful.'

'Whatever you need to believe,' Stafford replied.

'You warm, Henry?' Jack said. 'You're sweating.'

Stafford shrugged. 'Just a bit under the weather.'

Jack threw his card across the desk towards him. 'Give me a call once you've had a think about things. I can help put a stop to anyone else getting hurt, including you. It's what McGuinness would want.' He stood, before adding, 'And it's what you need.'

'Let's just see what McGuinness would want, once he wakes up, shall we!' Stafford shouted after him.

If.

CHAPTER FORTY-FOUR

It didn't take long for the call to come.

'It's me,' Stafford said. 'Can you talk?'

Jack finished stirring his coffee and took a brief sip. Hot, just how he liked it. It seemed his battle against caffeine was one he was destined to lose. 'Yes.'

'I've been having a think about what you were saying, like,' Stafford said. 'Maybe we can help each other out on this.'

Jack smiled. Stafford was almost too easy. 'I'm listening.'

There was silence on the line, broken only by Stafford's heavy breathing. 'They don't know if the boss is going to wake up. He's in an induced coma.'

'That's terrible,' Jack said, feigning concern. He'd already had the same news broken to him. It was surprisingly easy to find out information about a patient over the phone, just by telling someone you were a distant relative.

'Don't act like you give a shit,' Stafford said.

'Hey,' Jack replied. 'I used to work for him, too, don't forget. Just because we operate on different sides of the law doesn't mean I want him dead.'

'Solve a problem, though, wouldn't it?' Stafford fired back.

Jack was inclined to agree. However, Dorian dying at this point would only create bigger problems. So, as it was, he had to play ball and work with the gang once again. He only hoped that, when the time came, he'd be able to apprehend the culprit before they did. What he didn't know at this stage was whether that culprit happened to be Dayton Olsen, or not.

'Believe me, Henry, I've got many problems. Dorian isn't one of them,' he told him.

'Aye, so how do we do this?'

Jack had been preparing for that question ever since Edwards had effectively told him he was going undercover. He didn't much fancy working with the likes of Henry Stafford, but he hadn't been left with much choice.

'It's going to take a collective effort.'

'What does that mean?' Stafford asked.

Jack had to bite his tongue and remember he wasn't ordering his investigation team around anymore. He had to treat Stafford like the idiot he was.

'It means it isn't going to be simple,' he told him. 'We need to track his movements and the movements of every gang member that was with him that day, particularly at the club. We also need to review the CCTV.'

'So you can spy on the lads?' Stafford coughed. 'No chance, mate.'

'No, Henry, not so I can spy on the lads. It's so we can catch the bastard that did this to your boss.'

'Alright,' Stafford relented. 'I'll get the CCTV footage, provided it ain't damaged. And I'll check the rotas and get the lads' movements to you so you can take a look. Anything in particular you're after?'

'No,' Jack told him. 'But in my line of work you learn to look at everything and dismiss nothing. We're looking for anything suspicious. Any changes in movements, any irregular behaviour.'

'You think it was an inside job, like?' Stafford asked, his pitch rising as he finished the sentence.

'Tell me something, Henry,' Jack said. 'Has Dorian slipped?'

'Nar,' Stafford said. 'No chance.'

'Then how does someone get close enough to him to almost kill him?'

'Jesus.'

Jack's mind tracked back to the mysterious letter he'd received —*mole?* If the Northumbrian police force could suffer such a betrayal then it was hardly bending reality to assume the McGuinness crew could have suffered a similar fate.

'All I'm saying,' Jack told him, 'is that you should trust nobody, apart from yourself and Dorian. And I would only trust Dorian on the account that he hasn't tried to have himself killed.'

'You forgot to mention yourself,' Stafford chuckled.

'What would be the point?' Jack said, grimly. 'I'm not here to make friends, I'm here to stop a war.'

'Aye,' Stafford replied. 'But, just remember, I'm here to start one.'

CHAPTER FORTY-FIVE

It took Stafford less than twenty-four hours to get Jack a copy of the CCTV footage, alongside a staff rota list. He looked at the names of the three henchmen who had been in the club with Dorian. Ordinarily, they'd have had a much heavier presence, but once the club was closed, it was felt that McGuinness plus three others was enough muscle to have adequate cover.

In Stafford's words.

Something told Jack that, should McGuinness live, that number would rise somewhat.

Scott Morris, Ian Graham and Leeroy Yates were the three bouncers that Dorian had been surrounded by. They knew already that both Morris and Yates had died. That left Graham as the only one alive, and from what Jack had gleaned, that was still touch and go.

As was Dorian's condition. Jack had contacted the hospital that morning, a concerned cousin, and had been given an update.

So far, there'd been no contact from Edwards and, as far as Jack was concerned, no news was good news. He'd already decided that he was in it for the long haul now. Edwards could pull him from the case all he wanted but Jack would be damned if he was going to sit this one out. Everything was linked, he could feel it in his bones.

Not that he'd told Stafford that, of course. The way Jack saw it, he'd use the inside information to further his own cause, and nothing more. McGuinness and co. could sort their own backyard out.

According to Stafford, all three henchmen were trusted associates. Jack had no reason to doubt that. Two of them were in body bags now anyway so they'd have to have been idiots to betray McGuinness and be in the club when the bomb went off.

The CCTV was much more interesting and, unfortunately, Jack didn't have an analyst at hand to help him. That meant using his laptop to laboriously pore over movements from earlier in the night, which wasn't easy given it was a busy club and there was some five hours of footage to go over.

He could feel his eyes stinging. This was why he wasn't cut out for an office job. He knew he needed glasses but had been putting it off for some time now. Ryan had worn them, and looked quite distinguished, Jack thought. A pang of sadness hit him as the thought of his former boyfriend washed away from his mind. Perhaps he was destined to be alone. Given the fact that they'd already approached his daughter's house, he had to assume anybody close to him would always be at risk. As it was, Ryan was no longer close to him and he'd been very secretive about their relationship.

In some warped way, that made Jack feel worse.

He noticed he was hovering over Ryan's number on his mobile. *Focus,* he told himself. *You've got a job to do.*

It was no use; he'd looked through the first two hours of footage and nothing had stood out, save for a couple of Geordie Shore-types squaring up to each other which had led to one of the bouncers manhandling both out. Jack had recognised him. It was the kneecapper. Scott Morris, now deceased.

Stafford hadn't seemed bothered by the need to organise help but Jack had informed him that, as of right now, it was his job to sort out the muscle. The problem was, Henry wasn't smart. Jack almost felt like he was doing the man's job for him. He had to be careful on that; he was still a detective, after all. Still, the gang needed to keep up appearances otherwise rivals would soon pounce and the whole point of being involved was to avoid Newcastle going up in flames.

He decided to take a break. He walked to the kitchen and found some leftover lasagne from the previous day. He gave it a sniff; *close enough for jazz,* he thought. He popped it into the microwave and heated up a couple of pittas to have with it. So consumed had he been by everything that he hadn't even made the time to eat today. His stomach protested loudly until the microwave pinged and the pittas popped almost simultaneously. His trainer wouldn't approve, but the pittas were wholewheat and he'd scrimped on the cheese. The way he saw it, he'd at least made some effort to minimise the damage to his insides.

The lasagne was hot, just how he liked it. Crispy bits of cheese burned the top of his tongue as he tore into it, washing it down with water. He thought of McGuinness, lying in the hospital, unable to eat. There was no doubting he had some sympathy for his old boss. But, that was the life he had chosen. He was loaded, and could have gotten out at any time. The problem with Dorian was that he was greedy. When was enough, enough? Never when it came to him. It would be his downfall.

Still, Jack felt partly responsible. He'd dragged McGuinness into the Holding and Norris case, asking him to find intel on the supposed syndicate that was operating in Northumberland. Had they found out about Dorian's snooping and then put a plan in place to stop him prying further? Jack couldn't shake the feeling that it was linked. Jack wasn't aware of a rival powerful enough to do what this person, or people, had.

There was the Captain, of course. The previous year, he'd heard of the Captain operating in the north east, but they'd not had any inkling as to who it was or what the operation entailed. He glanced at his side cabinet. He'd kept the letter he'd received the previous year, sent by the Captain, informing him that he'd be in in touch. *Was this his way of sending a message?* Jack wondered.

He finished the last of the lasagne and mopped up the luke-warm tomato juices with his pitta bread. As usual, the problem was that he had too many questions and not enough answers.

What he really needed was to speak with McGuinness. Currently, he was still in an induced coma, but the hospital had informed him that they were hopeful that he would be brought out of it before the end of the day. Of course, that carried no guarantees. Jack had heard countless tales of people remaining in comas for weeks, or even months, before waking up. Something told him they didn't have that kind of time. He'd pay a visit to the hospital tomorrow and see if McGuinness had woken up.

He took another look at his laptop. They'd gotten so close to McGuinness. In all his years, Jack had never known anyone even come near to harming a hair on the mob boss' well-oiled head. He sighed. He knew he'd never sleep now. His head would be whirring with potential scenarios throughout the night. He decided that if he was going to chew over the case, he may as well do something productive.

Jack rinsed his plate in the sink and left it on the counter to drip dry. He opened the cupboard and grabbed his whisky. If he was going to pull an all-nighter, he may as well have some good company, health be damned.

CHAPTER FORTY-SIX

By the time he'd reached the Freeman Hospital, at the 2pm visiting time, he'd felt sicker than most of the patients looked. After many hours re-watching footage, he'd given up and fallen asleep on the settee. He'd then found himself wide awake, two hours later, with a crick in his neck and a sore back.

That meant he hadn't been in the mood to be faced with two McGuinness henchmen, who were stood guard outside the ward.

'Are you for real?' he snapped. 'You're not police, you can't just camp out here.'

'No,' the taller of the two, although both were of considerable size and bulk, said. 'But you're police. And I don't like your kind.'

'Good for you,' Jack told him. 'But we're in a public hospital and it's visiting time so I won't ask.'

Jack pushed past them and marched into ward two, where the mob boss was being housed. He could feel the heavies' gaze burning into the back of his skull as he made the short journey to McGuinness' room.

Despite his considerable size, Jack noted how frail the man looked. It was hard to believe he was looking at the same person who had terrorised the Newcastle underground with a steely determination and a penchant for the macabre when dishing out his own particular brand of violence. Jack shuddered at the memory of his own involvement in such matters.

McGuinness' bed was surrounded by a plethora of whirring, white machines. He looked vulnerable in his mint-green hospital gown. Jack noted his hair had been pulled back neatly. Judging by the bandages on his hands, his money wasn't on Dorian having done it himself. Jack could smell the sweet scent of burnt flesh as he approached him.

'Jack,' a weak, yet coarse voice spoke to him from the bed. 'How nice of you to come.'

He leaned over and placed a straw at his lips. McGuinness twitched, obviously uncomfortable at showing any kind of weakness, before accepting the offer. He gave a sharp cough as Jack drew the glass away from him.

He waited until he'd calmed down before speaking. 'How are you feeling?' Jack said.

McGuinness turned his burned features towards him. 'Like somebody tried to kill me.'

'That's why I'm here,' Jack said.

McGuinness nodded. 'Police business?'

'Not quite.'

He saw the mob boss raise a singed eyebrow. He'd always been perceptive. 'I suppose you're wanting to know who did this?' he said, his voice barely above a whisper. 'Don't we all?'

Despite McGuinness' weak state, those last words still carried the stinging threat of violence.

'Do you know who it was?' Jack asked.

McGuinness briefly closed his eyes before opening them again. He shook his head. 'No.'

'I'm working with Stafford,' Jack told him. 'Trying to piece this thing together.'

McGuinness nodded. 'I know.'

It seemed news had travelled fast. Jack pulled up a seat by

McGuinness' bedside and made himself comfortable. The view out of the window was pleasant enough, showing an internal hospital garden that was neatly kept. Regular patients often had to share wards in the NHS but it seemed McGuinness' reputation had preceded him.

'Look, Dorian, we have different end games here. You want revenge, I want justice,' he told him.

McGuinness boomed a throaty laugh. 'Where I come from, it's the same thing,' he said. 'Where you come from, too.'

Jack shook his head. 'No.'

'You've got the footage already, you have the staff list, I'm sure you'll figure it out.'

'I won't though, will I?' Jack said. 'Because you're lying to me.'

McGuinness smiled, then winced. 'Always so perceptive, Jack. Tell me, how do you feel about returning that favour to me, calling it even, so to speak?'

He didn't like the sound of that. 'I don't do blackmail, Dorian.'

'Yes, but I do,' Dorian told him. 'So you don't have much of a choice now, do you?'

'What do you want?' Jack felt like he already knew the answer.

'You find the people that did this and you bring them to me.'

Jack scoffed. 'You've got goons to do that sort of thing. Don't drag me into your dirty work.' He noted that with each passing sentence, McGuinness' voice, and resolve, was getting stronger.

'I seem to remember you dragging yourself into this line of work. You sought me out.' McGuinness brought his tongue across calloused lips. 'You don't just get to decide when you leave.'

Jack stood. 'This conversation is over.'

'It's over when I say it is.'

'You can't bribe a policeman, Dorian!' Jack snapped, causing a nurse passing the room to jump in fright. He raised a hand in apology and she tutted before striding away.

'I'm not bribing you,' McGuinness said. 'I'm offering you nothing. Therefore, by definition, it can't be a bribe.'

'Enough games,' Jack told him. 'I haven't got time for all this.'

'From what I hear, detective, you have a lot of time at the minute.'

Jack rounded on him. 'And what is that supposed to mean?'

Dorian remained unflustered. 'Not all officers are as incorruptible as you, Jack. Hearing rumours is what I do. And, from what I gather, you aren't operating with any kind of authority now.'

Never before had Jack felt so close to wanting to punch his former boss. Of course, that wouldn't end well for him. He spoke through gritted teeth. 'I'm not doing your dirty work.'

McGuinness said, 'No, but you're currently suspended, so that begs the question—whose dirty work are you doing?'

'I'm not doing anyone's dirty work. We've a case that needs solving. Plus, I won't have war on the streets.'

'Jack, Jack, Jack,' McGuinness tutted. 'You say that like they're your streets.'

He decided to prod. 'If they were your streets, then how come you're in here whilst the culprit runs free, quite possibly planning further attacks on your operation?'

Jack could see the fury in McGuinness' eyes but his voice remained composed.

'Nobody is impenetrable,' McGuinness said. 'Sometimes, we need a jolt to wake us out of our slumber. I've been taking my eye off the ball, what with my juggling of businesses and my run for office.'

Jack rolled his eyes. 'There isn't even an election.'

McGuinness laughed once more, this time his old booming timbre shaking the bed and walls. 'Things change.'

'So you're blackmailing the sitting councillor?' Jack asked.

'I'm offended by such a slur, Jack,' McGuinness said. 'The only reason a councillor has to stand down early is through ill health or scandal. In both circumstances, they are too weak to continue. I'm merely offering my own services to the good people of

Newcastle in response to such unfortunate events. Nobody wants the burden of public office, least of all me, but we do it because we care.'

All Dorian McGuinness cared about was profit and his own legend. *Whatever is going on, it won't end well for anybody else tied up in the situation,* Jack thought.

'I've got places to be,' Jack told him. 'I don't suppose you've actually got any useful information for me? You've been awake a matter of hours yet you seem to have the inside scoop on everything.'

'Bring them to me, Jack, and we're even. I'll not ask anything of you again. We'll be even with regards to my saving your life, you leaving my employment and for coming to me for information recently. I told you the price—this is it.'

'Why do you even need me?' Jack put to him.

McGuinness raised a dismissive, bandaged hand. 'Because Stafford is an idiot. I am surrounded by strong people, but I'm not surrounded by smart people. You, Jack, are smart, you always were.'

Jack didn't know whether to thank him or run from the room. Instead, he merely shrugged. 'You picked them.'

'Indeed,' McGuinness said. 'And they are loyal, for the most part. Stafford is no use, though, really.'

'Maybe it's him?' Jack said.

McGuinness shook his head. 'Stafford isn't that smart or stupid. I need you on this, Jack, one last time. Bring them to me.'

'I don't know who "they" are,' Jack said. 'And I'm not lining somebody up so you can throw them in a lake.'

'You don't have a choice,' McGuinness said.

'Don't think you can threaten me.'

'I'm not threatening you,' McGuinness said. 'Not yet. Think about it, if they can do this to me, imagine what they can do to you. You're not even on active duty now,' he added. 'They'll know where you live, who your friends are, your family. Do you really think you'll be safe now? They know you've been investigating them. You'll be next.'

Jack processed what McGuinness was saying. Did that list belong to Dayton Olsen, or somebody else? The image of the black Audi shot into his head. He still hadn't run a check on the plate, which was sloppy of him. Not that he expected them to have left a trace. They'd been smart enough to outfox him when he met Robson, they weren't going to be that daft, surely? Still, he'd get Edwards to run the check.

Then his mind drifted to the photograph they'd delivered to his ex-wife's house. He felt his fists clench at the thought of anything happening to them. There was nothing he could do now, though. They knew where they lived. He couldn't exactly ask Louise to up and leave their home. *Scrap that,* he thought, *that's exactly what I'm going to do.*

'You've brought this on all of us,' Jack told him.

McGuinness snorted. 'No, Jack, you brought it on yourself when you decided to become a detective. Did you really think there wouldn't be consequences? Look at me,' he said. 'I am barely-living proof of what can happen. We aren't that different you and I and, deep down, you know it.'

Jack pointed a finger at him. 'I'm nothing like you,' he said. 'You don't frighten me.'

'That's good for you,' McGuinness said. 'But you should be frightened of these people.'

Not for myself, Jack thought. 'Okay, I'll do it,' he told him. 'But not for you. For my family and the people of this city. I'm not going to let any more innocent people get hurt. And, I want no involvement in what happens afterwards.'

'Good,' McGuinness said.

'I need your word on that, Dorian,' Jack said.

'You have it.'

Despite what he knew about the man, Jack believed him. 'Good.'

'Henry has already been briefed. Whatever you need, just go through him. There won't be any problems.'

Jack was astounded at the arrogance of the man. He'd already assumed his co-operation before they'd even spoke. It was always that way with him, though. One way or another, he always got his way.

'I could do with being pointed in the right direction,' Jack said.

'Henry knows everything I know, speak to him,' he said. 'I'm tired now, and there's a young, male nurse on duty who makes wonderful cups of tea so make yourself scarce.'

Typical McGuinness, Jack thought. 'I'll see what I can do.'

'I know you'll do your best, Jack,' McGuinness said, before pausing. 'You'll get it done. But, can I make one suggestion before you go?'

'Go ahead,' Jack said.

'Begin by taking a look at who wasn't there that night.'

'What do you mean?' Jack asked, but McGuinness was already asleep before he could reply.

He stopped by the end of the bed and glanced over at a loose pillow. *How easy it would be,* he thought, *to end the hold McGuinness has on me and the rest of Newcastle.* If only he were brave enough. Unfortunately for Jack, he wasn't a cold-blooded killer. Unlike whoever had bombed the club and threatened his family. Those people were serious, which told Jack they had something to lose. His job would be to find what they were so scared of being without. McGuinness clearly felt it was all linked, and Jack was in no position to argue.

'Hello, Dorian,' a young voice chirped from the doorway, followed by the clattering of tea cups. Looking at the male nurse the crime boss had referred to, it was clear that McGuinness had a type. Slight and Latino. 'Oh, he's asleep. I'll come back later,' he said.

'He wanted a cup of tea,' Jack said. 'I'm sure if you made it he'd appreciate it—just in case he wakes up again.'

The man's vibrant eyes smiled at him. 'No problem.'

Jack smiled back and he noted, inwardly, just how easily he'd fallen back into the McGuinness trap. Now he was sorting out cups of tea for him. The sooner he returned to active duty, the better. Without the team and his badge behind him, he felt exposed to the kind of life he'd spent years running from.

'I'll get going, thanks again,' Jack said.

'Bye then,' the nurse said, picking up the stray pillow and placing it on the chair Jack had been sat in moments before.

He gave a curt nod to the heavies in the corridor before making a swift exit from the hospital. He was halfway across the car park before it hit him. *Look for who wasn't there.* Jack smiled. Dorian most certainly did have a type. And, on his last visit to the club, he'd gotten to see just what that looked like, first hand. Interestingly, though, there was one person missing from the CCTV footage he'd trawled through.

He glanced up at the windows to the hospital, the ominous structure looming over him, causing a shudder to run through his spine. Memories of his mother hit him but he forced them from his psyche. He had a job to do now. At least he knew where to start, even if he was unsure where it would end.

One thing he did know, though, was that there was no way he was delivering anybody into Dorian McGuinness' clutches.

CHAPTER FORTY-SEVEN

Jack spent ten minutes on the phone with a somewhat flustered-sounding Edwards, giving him an update on McGuinness' condition. He hadn't thought it possible to sound both disappointed and happy at the same time but somehow the DSI had managed it. Jack could relate. A world without McGuinness was a better place but the vacuum it would leave could be catastrophic in the fight against organised crime in the area.

He took great pleasure in asking his superior officer to run a car registration check for him but he'd done his best to hide the glee in his voice. Edwards, on the other hand, had made no attempt to hide his disdain for being asked to undertake such a menial act.

Edwards informed him that the car was rented from a service operating near Newcastle airport. They had a name for the man who had requested the car but Jack already knew it would be a dead end. Edwards promised to look into it and get back to him.

Jack then played his trump card and gave over the name of McGuinness' olive-skinned lover—the man who had previously thrown a huff with him at the club. Jack had secured his name from Stafford who, much like Edwards, was not best pleased at being ordered about like a lapdog. Jack, on this occasion, had made no effort to hide his happiness at being in such a position of power. Still, orders were orders and Stafford, whilst pretty dumb, wasn't stupid enough to go against his boss' wishes.

Edwards had then mumbled something nonsensical about a meeting with PCC Nadine Guthrie and DI Russell. Strangely, at that moment, Jack had felt pleased to be suspended. The DSI promised an address and any information the system had on him as soon as he could.

As it was, he'd already secured the address from Stafford, himself, but Jack had withheld that information from his boss. Even though he'd been given quite a bit of free rein to undertake the investigation, he didn't think the fact that he was essentially working with the McGuinness crew would go down well with the DSI.

He parked his Volvo across the street to the flats and surveyed his surroundings. All was quiet, save for a couple walking their dogs, their Montane Outlet puffer jackets betraying an affluence that was well-placed in this area. It seemed McGuinness' lover had expensive tastes. He wondered whether it was Dorian who was putting him up here, or whether he paid his own way.

Or perhaps he was on the take from someone else.

McGuinness clearly thought so. If that was the case, Jack was hopeful he could persuade him to give up his source. If the attack was a reaction to McGuinness prying into their business, then it seemed impossible that his lover had been in on it from the start. It was far more likely that they'd approached him. For him to potentially betray McGuinness, he must have had something to lose. *Why not tell Dorian?* Jack thought. Surely then he would have been offered protection. That led Jack to believe they had something on the boyfriend that McGuinness didn't know. What that was, at this stage, was anyone's guess.

There was still the possibility that McGuinness was wrong, of course.

Jack left the car and made the short journey across to the luxury apartment complex. Luke Barrera lived on the second floor, according to Stafford. Jack had been clear with the henchman that he wasn't a person of interest, as such, just that he was keen to follow up every potential witness and person close to McGuinness to help piece together what might have happened. That had been enough to call off the dogs.

Walking through the main entranceway, Jack caught a look at himself in the window pane. He looked haggard. Hell, he felt haggard. He still wasn't sleeping and running around playing undercover cop with a criminal gang was taking its toll on his psyche. Still, he had no choice. He was being blackmailed by Dalton, Edwards and McGuinness, none of whom he was particularly fond of right now.

He made the short journey to the second floor and approached the door to number twelve. The flats, overlooking the Quayside, looked too upmarket for a nineteen-year-old socialite. *Perhaps dating a gangster has its perks,* Jack thought.

He found the door to the apartment and gave it a firm knock.

Silence.

He placed his ear against the door and listened for any signs of life.

Nothing.

He weighed up his options. A policeman couldn't just go barging in without due diligence having been done, as well as securing a warrant. Having said that, he *could* smash the door in if he felt there was an imminent danger posed to somebody. He looked left and right. Nobody around. Technically he wasn't on duty, and securing a search warrant through Edwards could take days.

Choice made.

He returned to the door minutes later with a screwdriver in

hand. It was an old trick he'd used back in the day. Push it under the lock, apply force and, providing it's the right kind of door, hey presto you're in. Once the internal mechanism had snapped, he was able to gain entrance to the flat.

He stepped forward and noticed it was reasonably tidy, save for the odd glossy gossip magazine. 'Hello?' he called out. 'Police.'

There was no response. Jack moved through the living room, spacious with paintings adorning the walls. A cream corner settee faced a massive mounted TV. Jack guessed it to have been somewhere around sixty inches. It dominated the décor of the room, like a giant, black birthmark.

There was a hint of vanilla in the air and, at the far side of the room, a window sat, overlooking the River Tyne. The whole place appeared almost unlived in.

He did an about pivot and looked into the modern, open-plan kitchen space, complete with two-seater dining table off to the side. Not a crumb in sight. Off to the right of the living room sat the bedroom. Whilst tidy, the occupant hadn't taken the time to make the bed. What they had done, though, was more or less clear out the wardrobes, leaving the door open.

As if the person living there had left in a hurry.

The bathroom yielded much the same result—clean, tidy, missing a few key items. Everything he'd seen so far played into the narrative which McGuinness had planted in his head—namely that his young lover was somehow involved in what had happened. It certainly looked like Luke Barrera had made a quick getaway.

McGuinness had been helpful enough to provide names and addresses of his partner's associates. Apparently, Luke had no idea McGuinness had this information. It was silly of the boy to think that McGuinness wouldn't have done his homework on him. Although, if he had betrayed the mob boss, then perhaps Dorian hadn't been as switched on as Jack thought.

What had led him to betray the boss?

Jack was about to leave when his phone rang. It was Edwards. The ID used to rent the car had been fake. No trace, then. Edwards had been unwilling to push further on getting any CCTV footage from the area. Jack could understand that stance. He was basing it on the fact that he saw three men get into a car. Hardly compelling evidence of a crime.

The DSI had also provided an address for Luke Barrera. Jack had thanked him, leaving out the bit about him already standing in the man's apartment after having jemmied the door.

He was faced with Plan B. It took less than half an hour to drive to the outskirts of Hebburn and find the terrace house where Luke Barrera's parents lived. Many of the homes in the area were former council houses which had been left to dilapidate as time went on and budgets were slashed. The street had a gritty feel about it, one Jack actually welcomed, given his own background.

Luke Barrera's mother, Rosa, greeted him at the door with a nervous glance and frayed temperament. Her hair, although combed, was wild and standing at all angles above her head. She was squat, no more than five foot tall, but with an aura that no doubt struck fear into those who would oppose her.

'Who are you?' she demanded. 'What do you want?'

'I'm here about Luke,' Jack said. 'May I come in?'

When he flashed his credentials he thought she would have a heart attack. Her wide-featured face registered shock, then terror, then she turned on her heels and muttered something in a foreign tongue. Jack took it to mean he should follow her into the living room.

Although the outside of the building was nothing to shout about, he could tell that Barrera's mother was house proud. There wasn't a speck of dust about the place, and she had more ornaments than an episode of *Cash in the Attic*.

He sat himself down on a leather three-piece as she threw herself into a rocking chair, her bare feet barely touching the busily-patterned carpet as she began moving backwards and forwards.

'He's not here,' she said, curtly.

'Mrs Barrera,' Jack said. 'Are you aware of your son's current... social situation?'

'You mean the man with the shop?' she said. 'Yes.' The woman folded her arms across her sizeable chest and continued rocking.

Jack nodded. 'I see. And are you aware of the... business that your son's partner runs?'

'Fish, yes?' she said. The look in her eyes told him she knew.

'Something like that,' he said. 'Mrs Barrera, are you aware whether or not your son was in communication with a potential rival of Dorian McGuinness?'

The rocking continued unabated as she replied. 'I will tell you what I told the gentleman who approached me earlier on, I have no idea who my son speaks to. He only comes here when he needs something.'

Jack's heart skipped a beat. 'Who was this man?'

She stopped rocking abruptly and leaned forward. 'Why, is Luke in trouble?'

'Not necessarily,' Jack said, choosing his words carefully. 'But any information you can give me will help in piecing together what is going on.'

'Oh,' she suddenly wailed. 'It's that fire at the club, isn't it?'

'Yes but, don't worry, Luke wasn't there,' he told her. He noted the blank expression on her face. 'But, then again, you already knew that, didn't you?'

'I don't know what you mean,' she told him.

'Mrs Barrera, it's my job to know when people are lying,' he said. 'And you're lying to me right now. Whatever trouble Luke is in, I can help him. But if I don't know where he is then there is nothing I can do.'

Tears filled her large eyes. She shook her head and let out a sob before dabbing at her face with a cotton handkerchief. 'The man told me not to speak. He said you would come.'

'Which man?' Jack urged.

'I don't know this man's name. Quite short, stocky, angry look on his face. He was looking for Luke, said he could help him, but that the police were looking to arrest him because he had been involved in the fire. I said there was no way my boy would be involved in something like that.'

Jack leaned forward and took her warm hands into his own. 'Mrs Barrera, I can tell you right now that this man does not have your son's best interests at heart. Now, think carefully, did you tell him where Luke was?'

She shook her head.

Jack breathed a sigh of relief. 'Will you tell me?'

'No,' she said, 'but I can tell you where he is going to be.'

'Tell me,' he implored her.

Only a few times had Jack seen true horror on a person's face. It was disconcerting, to say the least. As he left the Barrera house, he knew he would carry the look she gave him to his grave. It was clear what he needed to do. He had to find Luke Barrera before somebody else did.

CHAPTER FORTY-EIGHT

Given Rosa Barrera's description of the mysterious man who had visited her it had to be none other than Henry Stafford. Back in the car, Jack pondered what to do. He could have it out with the goon, but felt it would achieve nothing. They would fall out, Jack would be ignored, and they'd know that he had spoken to Luke's mother. He briefly toyed with the idea of ringing McGuinness as well but it would be of no use. He knew that McGuinness wanted results and he'd enlisted Jack in achieving this. McGuinness wouldn't care who brought him the culprit, just that he had achieved the desired outcome.

So, as it was, Jack was faced with acting alone, without a team, and without approaching Stafford, McGuinness or any other associate. He was jumping into the unknown, with nobody to rely on but himself. However, he knew that the best chance of catching whoever had killed the bouncers, and attempted to kill McGuinness, was to intercept Luke Barrera before anybody else could.

If they hadn't already.

First, though, he had a few hours to kill. Rosa Barrera had told him that Luke had arranged to meet a friend at a club in

Newcastle that evening and was lying low until then. That gave Jack more than enough time to pay a visit to somebody he'd been meaning to catch up with for several days now.

'I swear I didn't know.'

Jack's gaze remained unmoved as Robson, perched at his breakfast counter, squirmed before him. He was holding back, Jack could tell and, on this occasion, his tactic was silence until Robson gave him something that was actually useful.

'Look, what do you want me to say?' he whined. 'Everything I told you was true.'

'So which one of my team is compromised?' Jack said.

'I don't know, I swear.'

'And you couldn't have just come to the station, or invited me here, to tell me that?' he thundered. 'Instead, you invite me to a public place, which ends up in my being framed as some kind of double agent? That's a little convenient, David.'

Again, Jack let the silence grow between them. Robson was sweating.

'I don't mix my private life and professional life, Jack, you know this,' he said.

Jack waited while the journalist moved to an oversized fridge and pulled out a cold bottle of Bud. 'Want one?' he asked.

'Water is fine,' Jack told him.

Robson poured him a drink, deposited it on the breakfast island he was now sat at, and pulled the top off his bottle with his teeth. Jack winced, he could think of nothing worse than ripping bottle tops off that way. As a young lad, he'd tried, but a deep laceration and a lengthy dentist appointment had put paid to any further ambitions he had with trying to show off in front of his mates again in that way.

Robson seemed more at ease now that he had a drink. 'I can't be seen to be wandering into a police station,' he said. 'Not a man in my position.'

'Bullshit,' Jack told him. "Fess up.'

Robson smiled, some of his arrogance having returned to his person. 'There's nothing you can threaten me with, Jack. Don't you understand, you have to play by the rules?' He pointed towards the window. 'The people out there, they don't have rules —and that makes them dangerous. More dangerous than a copper with a God complex.'

Jack necked his water and launched his glass above Robson's head. It smashed on impact, causing the journalist to spring from his seat, his missing hand slipping on contact with the table. He almost fell, but righted himself at the last second.

'Jesus Christ, what the hell is wrong with you!?' he shouted.

Jack stood, towering over the slightly-built man. 'Because of you, I've been suspended from duty while they investigate whether or not I have been leaking details of major cases to the press for the past two years.' Robson's eyes were wide as Jack loomed over his quaking body. 'Only we both know that that is complete and utter bollocks.' He jabbed a finger at Robson's chest. 'Now I've got nothing to lose, so you're going to tell me what is going on before I do something we both regret.'

'Y... you can't threaten me!' Robson stammered. 'I've got rights!'

Jack picked up one of the many newspapers that had been lying around the counter and rolled it up. 'Have you ever been hit with a rolled-up newspaper, Robson?' Jack said. 'It's surprisingly painful, especially when jabbed into sore or broken ribs.'

The journalist scrambled backwards towards the kitchen sink, falling amongst the broken glass. 'I'll make a complaint.'

Jack shook his head. 'You won't, because I was never here,' he said. 'Don't worry, though, I'll be back on active duty soon enough and, believe me, when I am I will be sure to drag you in for questioning in full view of the public. What do you think that will do for your image?'

A small sob emanated from Robson's throat. 'You can't do that, they'll kill me!'

'Who?' Jack said. 'Last chance, David.' He raised the paper high above his head, ready to strike.

'I don't know, okay,' he said. 'It's always a go-between. They approached me months ago, and have been feeding me information.'

He lowered the paper. 'Go on.'

Robson picked himself up and buried his head in his hands— his hand. 'Originally, it was insider info on goings-on in the area. I thought, "Great, this gives me even more of an edge than I had before". Local news is old hat, I want to get in with a national newspaper, like the *Mail* or something.'

Jack couldn't see the allure. 'I'm not here to discuss your professional ambitions, Robson.'

The journalist continued. 'Things started to change about four months ago, though. They started demanding information from me, started getting heavy-handed.'

'Threats?'

He snorted. 'Then some. They knew where I lived, they knew where my family lived, all of my associates. They said they'd pick them off one by one until it was just me left and then, when I had nothing to lose, they'd finally come for me. What the fuck am I supposed to say to that?'

'You could have come to the police,' Jack said.

Robson raised his stump. 'Like last time. Fat lot of good that did, didn't it? And look at you now, the great Jack Lambert, about to beat up on a defenceless man in his own home. You want to take a look at yourself. Maybe I'm not the only one Dorian got to.'

'Surely he could have protected you?' Jack said. 'All of those stories in the press, supporting his business expansions for the last year. Aren't the two of you best friends?'

Robson pulled at the corner of his moustache. 'I do what he says, which usually amounts to the odd nice story once in a while —it's no big deal. I'd say it's a pretty good return for saving my life. More to the point, what has he got you doing?'

Jack remained tight-lipped.

Robson continued. 'If I'd gone to Dorian, they'd know I talked and the reality is I don't know who the head guy is. All I know is that nobody is bulletproof and they had me by the balls. I couldn't risk it. And now, look, it turns out Dorian McGuinness isn't as immortal as he'd have us all believe. If they can do that to him, what would they do to me?'

Jack glanced down at the crumpled-up newspaper in his hand. McGuinness' face was plastered over the front, complete with an image of the burnt-out nightclub in the background.

'It's him, isn't it?' Jack said. 'The Captain?'

Robson sighed and pulled up a stool. 'They'll kill me.'

'I don't need you to tell me,' Jack said. 'Just don't correct me.'

'Fine,' Robson said. 'Then consider yourself uncorrected.'

'I've been played for a fool,' Jack said, gripping the paper.

Robson elicited a hollow laugh. 'That's what Dorian does, though, isn't it?'

'He had me believe it was linked to something completely different.'

Robson nodded. 'The Norris and Holding murders?'

Jack waved him away. He'd already said too much. 'Never mind that. What about this syndicate, then?'

Robson's moustache began twitching. 'The worst of the worst,' he said. 'People smuggling, prostitution, you name it. Only, their ambition got the better of them. They've moved into McGuinness' territory now; drug peddling and protection, hence the conflict. But, believe me, nothing happens without His say so.'

It was as much as Jack had suspected. 'How do you know these things?'

'It's my job to know things, Jack. Now, get out,' he pleaded. 'I think you've done enough damage.'

He glanced once more at the newspaper. 'I'm going to keep this,' he said.

'Hey!' Robson shouted. 'What about all this mess?'

'Send me the bill,' he said, turning. 'Oh, and for the record, I never was going to hit you, David. Even though you make it easy for me to want to.'

Jack left Robson to clean up the smashed glass. His mind was already elsewhere. Robson's information had thrown a spanner into the works, well and truly. He'd assumed that the McGuinness attack had been linked to the murders in Northumberland. The reality was, it had been a play by the Captain. And now McGuinness was using him to do his dirty work.

Unfortunately for him, he was under orders, although strictly under the radar, to get to the bottom of the McGuinness hit and stop a turf war exploding. He had hoped to kill two birds with one stone. However, it seemed he only had one bird to kill now, with his bare hands.

Luckily for him he was used to getting his hands dirty.

CHAPTER FORTY-NINE

J ack moved through the club, a heavy, bassy beat thumping out of the speakers around the dancefloor. The place was rammed, despite the fact that it was early, and the clientele appeared to be having the best of times. The tunes were of a distinctly eighties vibe, in keeping with the decadence of the time in relation to the gay scene. Despite being a gay man himself, he felt ill at ease. There were far too many fishnet vests and men in mascara for his liking.

This didn't help him in his approach to keeping undercover as he attempted to locate Luke Barrera. He could feel people's eyes on him as he pushed through the sweat-fuelled dancefloor, his feet sticking to the tiled surface with every step.

Barrera's mother had given him her son's whereabouts for the evening. The man was clearly nervous, although seemingly not nervous enough to avoid being seen in public. Rosa Barrera was adamant she hadn't told anybody else about where he'd be. That didn't mean that they wouldn't know. If McGuinness had been as thorough as his reputation suggested, they would know all of his usual haunts. Jack could scarcely believe the young lad's stupidity at putting himself in such a vulnerable position.

Of course, that wasn't accounting for the protection he may be under, Jack thought. If that was the case, he may have a harder time getting Luke out of there than he thought. Still, in situations such as this, Jack had learned two things; keep your wits about you, and take one step at a time.

Step one was almost complete, given he'd just spotted him sitting towards the back of the bar on a battered red armchair. The lad was with what looked like a couple of friends and, judging from their attire, they definitely weren't hired muscle.

Unless they were deep undercover.

He pushed his way out of the dancefloor, not giving much thought to who he was bumping into. He was keen to close the distance as quickly as possible before being noticed—to avoid Barrera doing a runner. Jack was reasonably fit, but this lad was younger and about four stone lighter than he was. Over any length of distance, Jack didn't particularly fancy his chances. If he got away on this occasion, he might then prove impossible to find.

Luckily, he didn't register Jack until he was stood above him. He could hear squeals of delight in the background, but blocked them out, as he eyed McGuinness' boyfriend's pals.

'Get out of here,' he told them.

He could see their urge to answer back but one look at Jack's face, all business, and they merely shrugged and apologised to a now pale-faced Luke Barrera.

'We need to talk,' Jack told him.

'Wha...' he slurred, eyes dancing at angles a GCSE maths exam would be proud of.

It was clear Luke Barrera was trashed. Jack needn't have worried about him making a quick escape. This lad was going nowhere in a hurry. Jack leaned over him and placed his hands on his oversized collar.

'Let's get out of here.'

'No way, man,' he said, wriggling under Jack's grasp.

He dragged him to his feet. 'What have you had?'

Barrera pursed his bottom lip. 'Just a few beers.'

'Don't lie to me,' he growled.

'Alright!' Barrera pleaded. 'An E, okay, an E.'

'Idiot.'

Jack didn't have time to check his peripherals; he needed Barrera out of the club but the nearest exit was through a sea of people and dragging a semi-conscious young lad out would draw attention to himself. Plus there was the logistical nightmare of carrying the dead weight.

He glanced left and right, noticed a men's toilet on the far wall. He weighed up his options and realised he didn't have much choice. Toilet it was.

'Alright, mate,' he greeted the toilet attendant, a concept he'd never get used to.

'Spray? Towel?' the man beamed through abnormally white teeth, motioning to an array of perfumes and soaps on the counter.

Jack ignored him and checked the toilet cubicles. Empty. 'Listen, how many other bathrooms are there in here?'

'Nothing wrong with this one,' he fired back.

'Just answer the question.'

The man recoiled, as if wounded. 'Two others.'

'Look, I need to have a word with my friend here,' Jack said, gesturing towards a rapidly sobering Barrera.

The man winked. 'I know what you mean.'

'I'm pretty sure you don't,' Jack said. He noticed a 'cleaning in progress' sign propped up in the corner of the room. He picked it up, handed it to the attendant. 'I need five minutes. I want you to put that outside and stand guard so nobody else comes in here.'

'What? I can't do that!' he protested.

Jack fished out a twenty-pound note and placed it in his pocket. 'That help you at all?'

The man beamed once again. 'No problem; I tell you what, I'll make it six!'

He waited until the attendant had left the toilet before running the cold water tap and holding Barrera's head under it in an attempt to wash some sense into him. The pungent smell of piss and cheap bleach made Jack's eyes water, but he hadn't had time to book them a plush room at the Ritz.

'Hey!' Barrera gurgled, thrashing about. 'Don't hurt me...'

'I'm not here to hurt you,' Jack said, lifting him back up and throwing him a paper towel. 'I'm here to help you.'

Barrera's eyes were starting to look more human now. He looked to the towel before dabbing it on his face and throwing it on the floor. 'The cop?' he spluttered, looking at Jack as if he had only just noticed him.

'Detective,' Jack said. 'I'm not American. And pick that up,' he ordered.

'Well I'm not fully British,' he said, placing the used towel in an overflowing silver bin.

'Fair enough. I'm here because you're in danger. Dorian knows you double-crossed him.'

Barrera's head shook like a novelty Churchill dog on a tractor. 'I don't know what you mean.'

'Yes you do, Luke,' he said. 'And, more importantly, Dorian knows. If you had nothing to hide, why leave your apartment and move back in with your mother? Why go off the radar when your fella is critically ill in hospital? They know you've not been to see him.'

'I...'

'Time to start giving answers,' Jack cut in.

'You've been to my mum's?' Barrera said. 'Oh my God.'

'Yes,' Jack told him. 'She's a formidable woman. You can worry about that fallout later, though.'

'Look....'

Jack saw Barrera's expression change as door hinges creaked. Heavy footsteps made their presence known, followed by the scuttling of the cleaning sign skidding across the black and white tiled floor. Jack tensed as it landed at his feet, eyes darting left to look into the mirror. Two of them, both big, both from the bar he'd met Robson in just days before. Neither of whom he knew. If there were two in here, that meant the third bloke was elsewhere. Jack looked to them again and shrugged inwardly. The third one was bigger.

'Nobody needs to get hurt,' one of them spoke, a deep, Yorkshire accent reverberating off the walls. 'We're here for him.'

'Well you can't have him,' Jack said. 'I'm police.'

'We know who you are,' the other one replied, similarly deep but with a more southern accent, somewhere outside of London, Jack felt. Hell, once you got beyond Manchester, it was all the same to him.

'Then you'll know to walk away and leave him be,' Jack said.

'It's not him we're after, though,' Yorkshire said.

Jack motioned, discreetly, for Barrera to move back against the wall. Maintaining his calm breathing, he looked for something useful. He couldn't exactly tickle them with a toilet brush.

The clock was ticking.

He sensed the pair of them move closer now. He tensed, looked in the mirror again. They were still at least four paces away. That gave him plenty of time to come up with a plan. Although he'd never understood the concept of a toilet attendant in a club, he now found himself eternally thankful that such a role existed.

He waited until Yorkshire was almost within touching distance before picking up a bottle of Lynx Africa deodorant and spinning round, unleashing it into the man's face. He screamed, and the other heavy had little time to register surprise before Jack launched the container off his face, causing him to stumble back.

Turning back to Yorkshire, he raised his leg and slammed a heavy boot into the inside of his leg. He yelped in pain, and fell to one knee, eyes streaming. Jack finished him off with a knee to the face, grabbing the nearest glass soap dish and spinning with it, the ashtray-like holder crunching against London's temple. He called out and staggered into the toilet cubicle. Jack waited until the door had swung back towards him before throwing his entire weight against it, wrenching it from its hinges.

Once done, Jack surveyed the damage. Both men were out for the count, one lounging by the sink with a serious case of pink eye, the other a bloodied mess under the cubicle door. He checked both for a pulse—good to go.

'What the fuck was that?' Barrera shouted.

Jack turned to face him. 'I don't know, yet, but you're going to tell me.'

Lunging forward, he grabbed Barrera by the lapels and dragged him out of the toilets, stopping to give the attendant another twenty. 'There you go,' he said. 'Keep the tip; there's a fair bit of rubbish to clean up in there. Sorry about the mess.'

The man, speechless, watched on as Jack headed straight for the exit, Barrera muttering obscenities all along the way.

Once outside, he raced to the car and threw Barrera into the drivers' seat, pushed him across, and got in after him.

'Where are we going?' Barrera said.

Jack gunned the engine and made a screeching exit from the street, not bothering to see if he was being followed. If London and Yorkshire had been there, chances were the third goon wasn't far behind. He wasn't interested in hanging about to find out. 'Someplace safe,' he finally said.

He kept his eyes on the speed dial—whilst keen to get out of there, he wasn't exactly enamoured with the thought of getting pulled over by the police. Every second wasted was time he could be spending interrogating McGuinness' lover.

'Fuck, man,' Barrera said. 'You messed those guys up good. Dorian was right about you.'

Jack gripped the steering wheel, indicated left, and pulled out into the dual carriageway. 'And what exactly did Dorian say?'

He noted that Barrera was about as far away from him as he

could get. He was practically crushed in the gap between the seat and the window.

'Just that you were badass once upon a time, a good boxer with a mean streak.' He paused. 'Looks to me like you still are.'

'Don't concern yourself with my past, present or future,' Jack told him. 'Right now, you've got more important things to worry about.'

'We going to the police station?' he asked.

Jack shook his head, noticed he was doing eighty-five on a seventy road and brought it down to eighty. 'No, it's not safe.'

'What the fuck?' he spluttered. 'How can a police station not be safe?'

Jack didn't answer him. He was only half lying. The reality was, he was suspended, he needed to question Barrera off the record and, perhaps most importantly, they had an officer working for the wrong team. He'd dismissed the idea of going to the station almost as quickly as he'd thought of it.

'Shut up and let me think,' Jack said.

He'd been driving blind, but he needed a plan. He cursed himself for not thinking of one prior to arriving at the club but he hadn't banked on being faced with a spun-out Barrera and two unknown thugs. Now, he found himself driving aimlessly around at ten above the speed limit, with a semi-conscious nineteen-year-old in his passenger seat, who, in all honesty, had been forced into leaving with him. Not only was he suspended, he was now actively breaking the law.

Desperate times.

He glanced over to Barrera, who was sat stock-still, wide eyes staring out into the cold winter night. 'Is there a safe place you know of?' he asked him.

Barrera shook his head.

He racked his brains; it was a risk, but he felt there was only one place they didn't know about.

CHAPTER FIFTY

'Jack? I wasn't expecting you...' he said.

'I'm sorry, I had no other choice,' he told him. 'Can I come in?'

Ryan's eyes drifted to Luke Barrera, who by this point was on a serious comedown from the drugs. His mood had plummeted. No doubt this was linked to what he'd witnessed in the club toilet.

Ryan beckoned them inside. 'Yes, of course.'

Jack thanked him and helped Luke into the living room, popping him down on one of Ryan's expensive, grey recliners.

'Can we get some water?' Jack asked.

'Yes,' Ryan said, leaving them momentarily.

Jack flicked the lights off, moved to the front of the room and pulled the heavy drapes slightly across. He peered out into the night. He saw no signs of movement but that didn't mean they weren't there. Once he'd settled on bringing him to Ryan's he'd made the journey in record time, being sure to check for signs of being followed. He hadn't seen any. But, then again, there were many things he hadn't seen with regards to the situation he was now in.

He closed the curtains and turned to face Luke, but found

Ryan standing between them. He recognised the look in his eyes. An argument was brewing.

'What's going on?' he said, his voice even, with a hint of anger simmering just below the surface.

'It's... complicated,' Jack offered.

He made to move but Ryan stood before him, looking up at him. Jack felt uneasy with the man's penetrating gaze—he always had done.

'Don't you dare give me that!' he said. 'I don't hear from you for days and this is how you get in touch, rocking up on my doorstep with some coked-up teenager!'

'Hey,' Barrera called. 'I'm nearly twenty. And it was E, not coke.'

'Shut up,' Jack chided him.

'Don't take your mood out on him,' Ryan said. 'I want answers, now, otherwise you're out, and you can face whatever it is that is waiting for you out there.'

Jack was torn. He'd never gone into much detail about his cases with Ryan, mainly because he didn't want work to infect what they had. But, the man was right, he did owe him an explanation.

'I'm sorry I haven't called but I've been busy,' he told him, omitting the part where Ryan had made his feelings clear the last time they'd spoken.

'Nothing new there then,' Ryan snorted.

Jack didn't bite. 'I've been suspended.'

'Jesus—'

'Long story,' he said.

'I have time.'

'I don't,' Jack told him. 'But the short version of it is that I've been set up to look like a mole. It's not true though. They're investigating me but in the meantime, Edwards has asked me to look into the attempted hit on Dorian McGuinness. That is what has brought me here.'

'Jesus Christ, Jack,' Ryan said, placing his hand on his arm. 'Why would he ask you to do that whilst you're suspended?'

Jack couldn't meet his ex-partner's gaze. 'Because he knew I would, because he knows I get results and because rules don't apply in this world.'

'He's using you,' Ryan said.

'You're probably right,' Jack said, turning to Barrera. 'But I don't have the luxury of being able to dwell on it right now. I'm sorry, Ryan,' he told him, 'I should never have come here but I didn't know where else to turn. They know where Shannon lives, they know where I live, I can't go to the station, and I didn't know what else to do. I've put you in harm's way.'

Ryan made to speak before shaking his head.

'I'm going to need some time alone with the lad,' Jack said.

Ryan nodded. 'Will you hurt him?'

Jack didn't reply, but his look gave the pharmacist the assurances he needed. Ryan nodded, turned on his heels, and left the room.

Jack wasn't going to lay a finger on the boy, but it didn't hurt to have him think otherwise. Barrera, who hadn't seen the look Jack gave his ex-partner, began babbling away in nervous starts.

'Shut up,' Jack told him. 'It's just you and me now; and you're going to start giving me answers.'

He pulled a stool around and sat directly opposite Barrera, just above his position. It was important to intimidate. One of the advantages of not playing by the rules anymore was the ability to drag answers out of people. Above his head, he could hear Ryan pacing around the bedroom, a room they'd shared for months, until recently.

'Please don't hurt me,' Barrera wailed, head in hands.

'Stop whining,' Jack told him. 'It's just the drugs making you paranoid.'

'So you won't hurt me?' he implored.

'I never said that,' Jack told him. 'Now, start speaking. Who were the goons in the club?'

'I don't know.'

'Don't lie!'

'I swear, I don't,' he recoiled.

'Next question then; who approached you to betray McGuinness.'

He shifted on the seat. 'I don't know what you mean.'

Jack launched forward and grabbed his hand, holding it in an iron grip. 'Tell me, Luke, do you know how many bones there are in a human hand? Let me tell you; twenty-seven bones in total. How many do you think I need to break before you start telling me what I need to hear?'

'Okay, okay!' he shouted. 'I'll tell you.'

Jack sat back, relieved. If the lad had called his bluff, he didn't know what he would have done. As it was, Barrera was frightened of him and he needed to keep it that way. 'Go on, then.'

'It was a woman,' he said. 'She came to me a few weeks ago, said there was something I had to do.'

Jack resisted the urge to step in with more questions; it was important that Barrera was allowed to tell his story.

'I told her where to go at first and she just shrugged and walked away. But then she came back, this time with a big fella.'

'One of the blokes from the club?'

Barrera shook his head. 'Bigger, scarred face.'

Goon three, Jack thought. 'And then?'

'I told her that her fella didn't frighten me, that I was protected. Said I'd go to Dorian and he'd make sure they both went away, good and proper, like, you know?'

Jack did know. 'So what changed?'

Barrera began tearing up. 'The big fella threatened me, said he'd make my face into a canoe. The woman stopped him, though, said it was no use. She knew that whatever I promised out of fear of violence would be useless once they left. Plus, Dorian would know they had come to me. So she left again.'

'But she came back?' Jack asked.

Barrera nodded. 'This time alone again, though. She... threatened me, gave me no choice.'

'How did she threaten you?' Jack put to him.

'I can't say...' he cried. 'Especially to a cop.'

'A detective,' Jack corrected him. 'And, the way I see it, Luke, you'll be looking at some serious jail time, not to mention retribution from the McGuinness crew for your involvement. You think they can't get to you in prison? They'll come for you and everybody you ever loved.'

'I know, I know!' he exploded. 'Don't you think I don't know that?'

'Then do yourself, and your family a favour, and tell me how they got to you.'

'If I tell you, then you have to promise not to use the information.'

'I can't promise that,' Jack said. 'But it can't hurt your chances.'

'My dad and uncle are... complicated people.'

'Go on.'

'Okay,' he sobbed. 'They do what they can to get by—drugs, women, that sort of thing. I don't care about me,' he said. 'But I care about them. The woman, she knew all about them, said she'd ensure they went away, permanently and, once they were gone, they'd come for my mother.' He put his head in his hands. 'Then my father had his kneecaps smashed up in a bar. That's when I knew... They gave me the device and told me what to do.'

Jack pitied the boy. Stuck between somebody like Dorian McGuinness, and a threat like that, it's a wonder he didn't lose his mind. No wonder he'd turned to drugs.

His sympathy didn't stretch to the boy's male relatives, however.

'They'll know I've told you,' he suddenly said. 'Oh, God, they'll come for me, my family, my mother!'

'Calm down,' Jack said. 'They don't know anything yet.'

'You just roughed up two of their men, they'll know about that!' he said.

Jack began pacing. 'Then they'll know a policeman has the details. They have nothing to gain by going after you right now, save for more bad publicity. These people thrive on secrecy. They don't make rash decisions.'

'How can you know?' Barrera said.

Because these were his people. 'If it makes you feel any better, ring your mother and ask her to go to a friend's house,' he said. 'Do it now.'

Jack waited whilst Barrera made the call, half the conversation in a foreign language. Two minutes later, Barrera exhaled, placed his phone back into his expensive, tight jeans, and slouched in the chair.

'She's going to go to my aunt's house—well, not my aunt but, you know?'

Jack did know. A curiously British thing, to name people aunty and uncle when they were, in fact, neither. 'Good. Now, I need you to tell me what you know about the people that approached you.'

'She was a woman, older, grey hair, slim, really cold eyes, you know?'

Margaret Fenwick's face popped into his head. 'Did she give you a name?' he asked.

'No,' Barrera told him.

'You're sure?'

Barrera paused. 'I'm sure.'

Jack processed the information. The description matched Margaret Fenwick, but that didn't necessarily mean it was her. He'd been told that the Captain had organised the hit on McGuinness, by David Robson. McGuinness had said it was the

Syndicate. Either one was lying, one was mistaken, or they were both and the same.

Jack couldn't help but wonder if the Captain had been involved all along. Robert Norris had been known to the McGuinness crew, via his father. Perhaps they had organised the move on the Fenwick farmhouse because the Fenwicks had links to the Captain. If that were true, then they'd been wrong this whole time. Jack did the sums. If Holding didn't know about the hit on the farmhouse, then that meant he'd still acted out of revenge, taking out Fenwick for the murder of his son.

That still left Dayton Olsen. They were sure he'd taken Holding out. The Captain obviously had Olsen on retainer, hitting back at a member of the McGuinness crew for taking out one of their own.

He sat back down and scratched at his stubble. He'd been spending the last few days running around trying to avoid a turf war when one had already broken out. He had to ring it in.

'You alright?' Barrera asked. 'You look ill.'

Jack shrugged it off. 'I just get headaches sometimes. Wait here, I need to make a call.'

He moved into the kitchen and called Edwards, bringing him up to speed on what he'd found out, missing out the details about taking out two henchmen in a nightclub toilet. He found Edwards reserved, tense and out of sorts on the phone, as he often was when Jack called him outside of office hours. They'd left with an agreement that they'd keep it under wraps for now but that Edwards would immediately call Dalton about it.

Good job Jack had kept his fingers crossed. He'd ended the call, made a split-second judgement of trust, and dialled another number.

'Jack? Jesus, it's good to hear from you. Look—'

'No time, Watkins,' Jack told him. 'Get a pen, note this down.'

He waited whilst the DS fumbled in the background. 'I've been speaking to a witness who has confirmed that he was

approached by a woman, matching the description of Margaret
Fenwick, to betray McGuinness and help organise the hit on him.
I think this secret syndicate goes much further than we thought,'
he told him. 'I believe the Captain is at the head of the organisation and that the Norris murder is inextricably linked to a turf
war between the two. I also think McGuinness has known this all
along.'

Watkins exhaled. 'Jack, you're supposed to be suspended.'

'Never mind that for now,' he cut in. 'Do you trust me?'

'Of course,' Watkins said.

'Then you know I'm not a rat,' Jack told him. 'I've given you
what I know, now go use it.'

'Jack, there's absolutely no evidence to back this up.'

'There's the witness. And, by this time tomorrow, I'll have
more.'

'Wait, what...'

Jack cut him off and replaced the phone in his pocket. He
moved back into the living room to find Barrera snoring away on
the recliner. Turning once more, he made his way upstairs and
called out to Ryan.

'You get what you need?' Ryan asked.

Jack nodded. 'Thank you.'

'This can't happen again.'

'I know,' Jack said. 'It won't.'

'Look... I don't think we should have any contact from now
on,' Ryan told him, arms folded across his chest.

Jack stood at the top of the stairs, dumbfounded. 'Not even as
friends?'

Ryan turned away from him. 'Just go, Jack.'

'But...'

'I don't care,' he said. 'I want you to leave. I won't have you
bringing this to my doorstep again. I'm done. You can stay here
with the boy tonight but then that's it. I want you out of here and

out of my life for good. I was stupid to think that this could ever work.'

Jack made to speak but found his voice had deserted him. He nodded and turned on the stairs, only to be faced with a weary-looking Luke Barrera. 'I might not know her name,' he said. 'But I do know where she might be.'

CHAPTER FIFTY-ONE

Five minutes later and they were in the Volvo once more, heading out of the city. Jack had parked a short distance from Ryan's house, just in case somebody spotted the car. He was as certain as he could be that they hadn't been followed. He struggled to focus; he needed his head in the game. He hadn't exactly left on good terms with his ex-partner. Hell, they'd left on no terms at all, with the pharmacist making it clear that they were done in all forms.

After a short time, Barrera spoke. 'So, he's your boyfriend, aye?'

'That's none of your business,' Jack said.

'Just making conversation,' he said.

'Well make a different one.'

Being in the presence of McGuinness' boyfriend hadn't been quite as irritating as he'd thought it would be, but he still wasn't in the mood to talk about himself.

'Forgive me for saying,' the young lad continued. 'But you don't seem very... gay.'

Jack sighed. 'What's that supposed to mean? Am I supposed to be camp or something?'

Barrera shrugged as Jack indicated and pulled round the roundabout in Newcastle City Centre, taking the exit through to the centre of the city. 'It's not that, I... no, forget it.'

'Well you've brought it up now,' Jack told him, 'and we've got at least a half hour drive ahead of us.'

'It's nothing to do with your lack of being camp,' Barrera told him. 'You just don't give off much of an aura. Most people, once they come out, their life makes sense. It was like that for me,' he said. 'But you, you just seem miserable.'

Jack laughed without humour. 'You can be gay and miserable, you know? My misery has nothing to do with my sexuality,' he told him.

'Whatever you say,' Barrera said.

Jack noted that now the drugs were seriously wearing off, the cocky, mouthy young lad that he'd previously met at McGuinness' club was back. 'And what about you?' Jack said. 'How does a young bloke such as yourself get mixed up with Dorian McGuinness?'

Out of the corner of his eye, he could see Barrera's body language slump, and he turned his head against the window.

'I met him at the club, didn't I?' Barrera said. 'He treats me okay. I never want for anything.'

'So you bagged yourself a sugar daddy, is that it?'

'It's not like that,' he mumbled.

'Looks that way to me,' Jack said.

'He's a powerful man, isn't he?' Barrera said. 'That's attractive in a person.'

'He's certainly powerful,' Jack said. 'And now you're mixed up in this you might find out just how powerful he really is.'

'He's in the hospital,' Barrera said. 'So it's not like he's bulletproof.'

'No,' Jack said. 'He most certainly isn't. Dorian McGuinness, like the rest of us, is just an ordinary human.'

'He'll kill me,' Barrera said.

Jack shook his head. 'You don't know that. Anyway, you can't go around just killing people. We can help.'

'No, you can't,' he said.

They fell into a silence for the remainder of the journey. Despite Jack's battle with his own sexuality, he could safely say he'd never found Dorian McGuinness attractive whatsoever. To him, he looked like a bloated Val Kilmer in a *Saturday Night Fever* costume. Still, Barrera was right, some people were attracted to power, and gravitated towards it, thinking they needed protection.

Jack didn't need protection.

'Not far now,' Barrera said.

Jack nodded, and continued on towards Ashington. The bustle of the city had once again given way to the quiet of the country-side. In the still night that surrounded them now, Jack felt trepidation at what stood before them.

'You sure you know where this is?' Jack asked.

Barrera nodded. 'I have a good memory,' he said. 'My mother always comments on it. If you turn left up here, it's not far.'

Jack nodded and did as he was instructed. His mind wandered back to Watkins. There was no denying he'd taken a risk in contacting the DS. For one thing, he didn't know if he was compromised; not to mention, he was disobeying his superior officer by involving the team—at the same time as conducting a covert investigation whilst suspended. When all was said and done, Jack couldn't see any positive way out for himself.

But he was determined to put an end to the killings and uncover who the Captain was.

'Here,' Barrera said. 'It's just along this road.'

Jack performed a three-point turn and pulled over onto the verge of the country lane. He figured they may need to make a quick getaway at some point and he wasn't keen on performing such a manoeuvre if they were strapped for time. Plus, parking a distance from the house drew less attention.

The element of surprise was about all he had left.

They stepped out of the car.

'What should I do?' Barrera asked, charcoal eyes wide in the moonlight.

Jack took a look up the lane. Two options: take him with him, or leave him in the car.

'Can you drive?' he asked him.

'No,' Barrera replied, kicking at the dirt in the road. 'Never needed to.'

'Okay,' he said, tossing him the car keys. 'You wait here in the car. Keep the lights off but if you stick the keys in the ignition you'll be able to run some hot air if you get cold.'

Barrera nodded and re-opened the door.

'What if you don't come back?' Barrera asked.

Jack turned to face him. 'Then you might want to learn how to drive.'

CHAPTER FIFTY-TWO

He continued the rest of the journey on his own. The temperature had dropped even further, and Jack could feel the slippery beginnings of frost underneath his feet. He blew into numb hands, his own breath doing little to combat the icy feeling in his fingertips. Still, it was only a short walk to the house. He put his head down and moved towards the side of the road, facing oncoming traffic. He was wearing dark jeans and a black jacket, which would help him stay unnoticed.

Barrera had pointed the way and, knowing how sparsely populated this area was, Jack knew he'd have no problem spotting the house. Unlike in the city, people round here weren't jammed together like a tin of spam. He gritted his teeth as the lane widened out and sloped up, feeling a slight burn in his calves as he kept on. He'd made his decision—retiring into the countryside definitely wasn't for him.

The house was just up ahead on the left. He was near the brow of the hill when he heard the motor. He moved further to the right, into the tree-lined edge, and stayed motionless. Two small pinpricks appeared at the top of the bank, growing in size until they were nearly upon him. He held his hands up to his eyes as it passed, translucent spots dancing around his vision as it whizzed by. He blinked away the stars and watched as it continued on, its high beams disappearing into the distance.

He waited until he was sure it had moved past the Volvo before continuing on. Looking left and right, he held his ears against the night, listening for any sounds of another presence.

There was just him, and the hammering of his heart.

Sure he wasn't being watched, he crossed the road and entered the front of the property. The house was set back from the edge of the drive, as all houses were in this area, which meant he had cover until he was closer to the main building. He checked his peripherals, and noted shrubbery on both sides, evening out into a field the closer you got to the house. *Eeni meeni miini moh*—he went left, crouching as he did so.

He'd forgotten all about the cold now, only slightly conscious that his hands were stinging. He was focused on the house ahead of him. He could see it was a three-storey property, old and sprawling, with a black Range Rover parked outside.

He could see a light on at the right side of the house, possibly a living room. He stopped, waited and looked for some sign of life. Nothing. On he kept, his eyes never leaving the window. Approaching this way gave him more cover. If it was just one woman in the property, then Jack was confident he'd be okay, unless she was armed. However, he had no idea what he was dealing with and whether she had protection. If that was the case, he'd have to reassess his options.

None of those options included turning back around, however.

A sharp snapping sound to his left dragged his attention away from the house. He stopped dead, crouched down further and listened. His eyes, despite being clear of the headlamp stars, played tricks on him as he gazed into the night. Every shadow was an assailant, every noise an indication that they were moving towards him.

Pull yourself together, he chastised himself.

Turning back around, he felt a tremor run through his body as he noted that the light had now gone off in the house. Given that the car remained unmoved, whoever had been in the living room was still there. And it confirmed that someone was home.

He was beyond the trees now, moving into the shorter grass. He was only too aware how exposed he was. A light went on at the left side of the house, its glare almost reaching him. Panicked, he threw himself to the ground and began a military crawl.

Part of him wanted to return in the daytime, and flash his police ID, but something told him these people knew he was suspended from duty and that they didn't care who he was.

Convinced he was taking the best course of action, he continued on.

He was mere metres from the house now. He watched as the second light went off. Jack could feel the damp earth beneath him as he continued to crawl. If the same light went on again now, he'd be easily visible from another window.

He was parallel to the back of the Range Rover now. It had a private registration attached, but Jack couldn't make out what it was trying to spell. Certainly not 'Captain'. He had no way of knowing whether the woman who had approached Barrera was the Captain but his gut told him she wasn't. He felt it was a man.

The light remained off. He was so close to the house now that he could almost reach out and touch it. Grass turned to gravel and he continued, even slower, aware of every crack of body against stone, each movement feeling like a thunderstorm in his ears. He'd made it to the flowerbed underneath the window. The windows had wooden frames, which would potentially make it easier for him to hear what was going on inside. As it was, he couldn't hear a thing.

He had to make a decision. Scout out the front and look for a way in, or move round to the back of the property.

He edged round the building as quietly as he could. He felt his hand scrape along the cool, jagged brickwork as he stuck rigidly to the wall, keen to make himself as small a presence as possible.

What he also didn't know, at this point, was whether or not the property had any automatic lighting. There definitely hadn't been at the front of the building. He had no choice but to risk it. Whoever was inside, they couldn't know he was coming. These people were secretive, an underground cell, operating outside of the law. They were cool, confident and sure of themselves. People like that took risks.

He just hoped he could capitalise on their arrogance.

The sound of a crash jolted him upright. He tensed and pinned himself against the wall, holding his breath. The wheelbarrow he'd walked into lay strewn across the side lawn. He tried to regulate his breathing again and focused on listening for any reaction from inside the house.

Time stretched on. He felt sure that they had to have heard him. Seconds stretched into minutes as he stood, waiting for them to come.

But nobody did.

Satisfied that he hadn't been heard, he jimmied on until he reached the edge of the building. In his mind, he'd broken the journey down into segments, ticking each one off as he reached the next stage. He had two left. Survey the back of the house and, what would perhaps be the most difficult part, find a way inside.

He was about to round the corner when a voice broke through the silence.

'Boss says he wants it done tonight,' a man said.

Jack instantly recognised the Yorkshire accent. It seemed his mate from the club had recovered.

He heard a muffled response from inside the house. He couldn't make out the words but he was sure they belonged to a man. That put at least two heavies inside the house as well as, presumably, the woman that Barrera had told him was living there. He had to assume the other man was the Londoner.

'Having a tab, aren't I?' Yorkshire responded.

Jack could smell the faint aroma of menthol cigarettes.

'Alright,' the man said, followed by the sound of heavy boots stamping down on concrete.

He heard a door pull across, with the two voices fading away. He waited another minute before daring to look round the corner. There had been no light when the goon had stepped outside. Safe in the knowledge that he wouldn't trip any alarms, he veered right and shuffled along the back of the property.

A sprawling garden spread out before him, like an unkempt bowling green, as he continued his journey towards the door. A window passed above his head and he ducked down and edged beyond it. The door was a mere five yards away now. Although freezing, Jack could feel sweat dripping down his body.

Three yards.

His mind began playing tricks on him, telling him he was wrong to go in without backup. He knew it wouldn't have been possible, though. Edwards had made it clear that this was his mission alone. His suspension had put station resources outside of his reach; plus, he had nothing to go on apart from a hunch and the word of a drugged-up teenager living in fear for his life.

Two yards.

He could almost reach out and touch the handle now. He took a deep breath and focused on the task at hand. He had to go through with it. With three people dead, and an attempted hit on Dorian McGuinness, the north east was on the cusp of gang warfare.

One yard.

He began to reach out with his hand, surprised by its steadiness as he leaned towards the door. It had often been this way for him. Back when he was boxing, he'd managed to find an internal calmness in the most stressful of situations. He didn't know what waited for him on the other side of the door; all he knew was that they were powerful people, and that they'd apparently infiltrated the very centre of the Northumbrian police force.

He dragged the door open.

The man on the other side clearly hadn't been expecting somebody to be looking at him from the garden. Jack, buoyed by the element of surprise, lunged forward, the bridge of his forehead crunching against nose. The bloke grunted and staggered back, blood dripping down his face.

Although dark, he instantly recognised him as Yorkshire. Using insider knowledge to his advantage, Jack brought his foot up and jammed it into the side of the man's leg. He went down with minimal fuss, barely having time to call out again before Jack landed the crucial blow to his face, sending him to sleep. Satisfied that the goon was out for the count, he moved on through the kitchen.

'Trev, mate, you alright?' a voice called out.

The Londoner.

Jack didn't have time to dispose of the mess he'd left. His best hope was to work his way through the house, taking them out one by one, until he found her. Or, if she wasn't there, until one of them told him where she was.

'Trev!' the voice called again.

Jack could hear the shuffle of boots coming down a rickety staircase. He retreated back into the kitchen, hiding just behind the doorway.

'Trev?'

More trepidation now.

He could hear the slowing of the man's steps, each clunk growing louder as he moved towards Jack's position. Fumbling with the bench to his right, he found the handle of a pan and brought it up to his chest.

'Trev, what are you...' The voice stopped dead in the doorway. 'What the fuck?'

Jack flicked the light switch on and swung the pan around

with as much force as he could muster. There was a split second between stainless steel meeting bone and the sound of the goon hitting the floor. He was out cold. Jack waited a few more seconds to see whether or not anyone else was coming but all went quiet.

He'd heard two of them on his approach to the house, and he'd put two down. Confident he was now over the worst, he turned the light back off and moved on through the living room. Shadows around the room caused shapes to form, each one a potential assailant. Jack found himself frantically searching about his person. Suddenly he didn't feel so alone. He could see out of the window now, could see the field which he'd crawled through to reach the house. Had anybody been standing where he was, they would have definitely spotted him.

He turned away from the window and moved across to the left of the room. A large, wooden staircase stood before him. As quietly as he could, he placed his foot down on the bottom step, the creak which came from it feeling like a shriek in the otherwise silent house. He winced, stopped, and waited. It wasn't until he was about to move to the second step that he heard her.

'Detective Lambert, how kind of you to join us.'

He barely had time to speak before the gun cocked.

He looked up the staircase. A third goon, bigger than the other two stood staring at him, a lopsided smile spreading across his stretched features like a science experiment gone wrong.

'Why don't you sit down,' the woman said. 'We've got much to discuss.'

CHAPTER FIFTY-THREE

He sped through the city, aware that he was pressed for time. With the best will in the world, committing murder meant that your face was likely to be recognised sooner or later.

And he had a recognisable face.

They'd given him the car, and the instructions for where to go. Heading out of the city centre, he just hoped there was enough time to get the job done before he was caught—because he would be, in the end. He'd known that from the moment he'd absconded from prison. People like him didn't stay out indefinitely and, the way he saw it, he preferred it inside anyway. They had rules—rules that were followed. Sure, they played politics, but he was at the head of the tree. Out in the real world, it was a different ball game.

He had somebody to answer to.

Not that he minded too much. This was about securing his son's future. Nothing else mattered to him now.

He glanced down at the clock. It had just gone 8pm. His grip tightened on the wheel, his leather gloves squeaking against his knuckles.

He was aware that things had progressed. The detective was

moving closer to the centre of the story. That meant he had little time to get it done before things became public. Too public for his boss to allow.

He slowed slightly as a police car approached. He saw the lights begin to flash, followed by a sharp, brief siren as it sped into life. He maintained his speed, all the while keeping his eyes on it. Whilst he didn't want to hurt anybody that he didn't have to, he knew that he would be willing to if cornered.

He placed a hand on the passenger seat; he was glad he'd brought his tools. Two trained policemen would be no easy task but he had to assume he had the element of surprise. He tensed as they pulled up alongside. He watched as the passenger momentarily looked his way. He turned his head ever so slightly to the left in an attempt to hide his features. He had to make a choice now, fight or flight. It wasn't in his nature to run, but he still had a job to do and didn't need complications. However, if they'd spotted him and he ran, it wouldn't take long for them to catch up with him. He moved both hands to the left of the wheel and prepared to make a hard right into the car.

He'd made his decision.

Just as he made to turn the wheel, the patrol car shot off past him into the night. He exhaled a sigh of relief. They weren't looking for him. He waited until the car was out of sight before adding three miles per hour to his speed. Knowing you could get away with ten per cent over the limit, he kept within a safe zone, eager to arrive but still in control.

And he was a man who liked control.

He didn't know how much Lambert knew at this point, or who he had told. All he knew was he had a job to do and, thanks to his own, meticulous planning, he was about to complete it. He could feel the serene sense of satisfaction building in him. The feeling he always got when he was about to finish his work.

Not far now.

He indicated and took the exit towards Ashington, happy to

be accelerating onto a quicker road and into a quieter area. Fewer people lived in the leafy Northumberland suburbs and fewer people meant fewer police. Exactly what he needed.

Seeing he was completely alone on the road, he added an extra five to his speed.

Not long now.

CHAPTER FIFTY-FOUR

J ack sat as the head goon pointed the gun to his head. He felt his stomach muscles jerk as the man applied further pressure on the muzzle, practically stabbing it into his cranium. The lack of a silencer on the end told him they were confident that nobody would hear what was about to happen to him.

'You fancy asking your guard dog to calm down?' Jack said.

The woman gave a faint nod and, after one final push, the man did as he was told, stepping back from them.

'I'm afraid you've made quite a name for yourself, Jack Lambert,' she said.

Jack was sat opposite her on a faintly warm leather armchair. He hadn't been tied up but then, given the gun pointing at his head, he obviously wasn't seen as much of a threat.

'Unlike yourself,' Jack told her. 'It seems I know very little about you.'

'My name doesn't matter,' she replied, her cool, watery eyes unwavering in their gaze upon him.

Jack shrugged. 'I suppose not.'

She smiled, baring a set of sharp teeth, not too unlike Margaret Fenwick. In fact, so sure was he that the mystery fourth woman in the Syndicate was Margaret Fenwick, he found himself somewhat surprised by the woman sat before him. Although dark, he could make out her angular features. *A face well-worn,* he thought. There was something familiar about it, but he found himself unable to place her.

'You've been quite the nuisance to my men,' she said, motioning to the kitchen.

The two henchmen he'd put down were now on their feet but they hadn't interfered in the scene.

Yet.

Only their eyes betrayed any hint of malice towards him.

'My apologies,' Jack said. 'But I don't appreciate being cornered in a toilet.'

He sensed a small shift in the one he'd kneecapped but the woman was on it in a flash. 'Both of you,' she said, 'fetch the boy. He won't be far.'

Jack tensed. Barrera would be a sitting duck in that car. He found himself hoping that the lad had scarpered but, given he didn't live in the area, he would have nowhere to go. He could live with putting himself in danger, but an innocent nineteen-year-old was another matter.

He reminded himself of the fact that Barrera's actions had led to multiple deaths. Still, he didn't deserve to die at the hands of the very people that had blackmailed him so that they could get to McGuinness.

As if reading his thoughts, the woman spoke again. 'Dorian McGuinness is a powerful man.'

Jack nodded. 'Yet he's lying in hospital now.'

'Yes,' she said, 'but hardly fighting for his life, now, is he?'

He decided to play it evasive. 'I wouldn't know.'

'There's your first lie,' she said. 'Once you hit three, my friend here is going to pull that trigger. He won't kill you, but it will hurt, I can promise you that.'

'Bullets have a way of doing that,' he told her.

'I admire your spunk,' she said. 'Unfortunately, your sarcasm is wasted here. You're not long left for this world, Jack Lambert.'

Jack believed her. 'And why is that?' he asked.

'McGuinness is a fly in the ointment of everything we've been trying to achieve. You are his puppet, a puppet in a position of power and influence. Once we strip away all of his influence, he will be left with nothing. Then, he will be removed too.'

'I'm not his puppet,' Jack told her, firmly.

'A second lie,' she chuckled. 'Jack, don't say you weren't warned.'

'I'm not lying,' he said. 'As far as I'm concerned, you're a bunch of charlatans and should all be behind bars. McGuinness is no different.'

The woman scoffed, but Jack could see doubt in her features. 'So you didn't work for him previously?'

The rumble of the returning Range Rover could be heard, its headlamps sweeping across the living room, temporarily lighting up the woman's features. He was sure he recognised her. They waited as the doors slammed, followed by the sound of shoes dragging over gravel. Seconds later, the front door was opened, with a visibly shaking Barrera thrown to the floor in the process. The lad looked up at Jack, fear etched across his face, along with snot and tears.

He turned to face the woman once more. 'I used to work for him, years ago,' he said. 'But I got out of it a long time ago. I'm not on the take with anybody, so get your facts right.'

'Yet you visited him in hospital?' she said.

Jack shrugged, wondering how she managed to know all of his movements. 'I'm a policeman, and there'd been multiple murders in the blast.' He looked to her. 'Your handiwork, I assume?'

She raised a well-shaped eyebrow as she spoke. 'Perhaps.'

'Yeah, well, it didn't work,' he told her. 'And now you'll never get to him.'

'Yes,' she said. 'And that is what has brought us here.' She turned to Barrera. 'Thank you for your service, young man. Delivering Jack Lambert to us almost writes off your failure to complete the job on Mr McGuinness.'

Jack turned to Barrera. 'What?'

McGuinness' partner struggled to his feet. 'I'm sorry...' he choked. 'I had no choice. They... they threatened my family, said I had to deliver you.'

Jack did the maths and realised he'd been played. 'The club?' he said. 'You made sure I knew to find you there? You knew I'd speak with your mother and you fed her the information.'

Barrera nodded, eyes at his feet. 'Yes.'

'But how...' his words trailed off as he realised.

Barrera let out a sharp sob. 'When you left the room at your bloke's.' He motioned to the woman who remained impassive on her chair. 'I called her.'

Jack began to panic. The whole journey to the house had been a setup. They knew he'd come. She'd been waiting for him the whole time. They hadn't needed to watch from the window because Barrera had already given them the heads-up. He felt sick. Not at the lad's betrayal—he barely knew him, but at the fact that he hadn't seen through it.

'Don't worry about it,' Jack told him. 'I'm sure you had no choice.'

'That's the difference between people like us and him,' the woman said, steadily rising to her feet. Jack noted she was extremely tall for a woman, and stooped ever so slightly as she moved. 'We know that everything is a choice, and with it comes a consequence. Now, what should we do with the boy?'

She was speaking to the muscle but her attention was locked on Jack. He had to remain calm, find a way out of the situation. The front door was still open, with one goon blocking the exit. It was the one he'd kneecapped, though, which meant he had a weakness. The problem was the heavy with the gun. The scarred man. Jack knew they'd make it no further than the doorway before he put a bullet into at least one of them.

He had to keep them talking.

'What does it matter?' Jack put to her. 'It's me you want.'

The woman leaned over Jack, her jasmine-infused perfume tickling his nostrils. 'And you tell me you aren't working with McGuinness...'

'I'm not.'

She straightened up. Out of the corner of his eye, he saw the lead goon relax the tension in his shoulders. This woman was important, of that there was no doubt.

'I believe you,' she said. 'But I'm afraid that doesn't matter now. You've seen my face, you already know too much.'

Jack scoffed. 'I'm pretty sure I know very little of what you lot get up to.'

'Even so,' she said. 'You're a problem. And I like my problems dealt with quickly.'

Jack turned to Barrera, who was staring intently at him. He aimed a wink at the boy, receiving a faint nod back. Good, he needed him switched on for what was coming.

'That's where you and I do have something in common,' he told the woman.

She cocked her head towards him. 'What do you mean?'

Jack shrugged. 'Only that I'm the same; I too like my problems sorted quickly. Take my problem of being here.' Jack saw a break in the woman's confidence. 'You think I haven't rung this in?'

She laughed in his face, close enough for her perfume to hit him once again. He fought the urge to sneeze and resisted the urge to grab her. Something told him that was a hostage situation that wouldn't end well. He knew she could see he was weighing up his options. This was a woman who was cold, calculated and entirely vicious in her dealings.

'I happen to know, Jack Lambert, that you are suspended from the force. In fact, it was our people who made sure your superior officers were made aware of your... indiscretion.'

'It is true,' he said, 'that I am currently suspended but, as you probably know, I'm still investigating the McGuinness hit.'

The woman smirked. 'We know everything.'

Jack chalked up his second victory. Robson's theory about a compromised officer had to be true. The next bluff, on his part, relied on him betting on the right officer not being dirty.

'But did you know that I rang in my whereabouts to one of my team, just before setting off for this location.'

'Enough of this,' the kneecapped goon grumbled. 'Let's just waste the bastard, he's stalling for time.'

The woman turned her fury upon him. 'You shut your mouth!' she screamed. The man stumbled back as if slapped, wincing as his knee buckled. 'Did I say you could speak?'

'No, ma'am,' the man mumbled.

'You don't believe me?' Jack said, keen to regain her attention. 'Take a look at my phone.'

He motioned for them to fumble in his trouser pocket. London stepped forward, then paused, waiting for the go ahead from his boss. She nodded. He took the phone out and handed it to her.

'What am I looking at?' she said.

'Check the call list.'

He watched as she scrolled, her eyes scanning the dim screen. 'DS Stephen Watkins,' she read out loud.

Jack waited for it. If Watkins was compromised, then this was the end of the road for him. The look on the woman's face told him otherwise, though.

She tossed the phone back at him. 'I don't believe you.'

He bent slowly to pick it up, making it clear he wasn't planning anything funny. 'What, that I called him? It's there in the log. I thought you people were meant to be clever? A syndicate, yes?

This all powerful, secret, underground society that operates in the shadows? You're not the only one who knows things.'

Her face twisted in on itself. Jack almost recoiled, such was the ferocity of her anger. 'You're lying!'

He motioned to Barrera. 'Tell her.'

Barrera, picking up on his thread, looked her in the eye and responded. 'It's true, I told him before we arrived here. I... felt guilty about everything, came clean to him.'

'You see,' Jack said. 'It's me who's played you. And any second now a team will be here, ready to pick you up. How'd you fancy your chances then?'

Jack watched as the woman's piano-player fingers clenched in on themselves. 'We pay people in high places so that this kind of thing doesn't happen.'

'How much you willing to bet on that?' he said.

She turned to the scarred goon and nodded in Barrera's direction. 'Kill him.'

The man stepped forward and Jack took the opportunity to act whilst his attention was elsewhere. Spinning right, he lunged for him, taking hold of his wrist as he made to bring the gun up towards the boy. The man let out a wail as Jack wrenched his hand back, disarming him. He aimed a blow to his head with the butt of the gun, knocking him to the floor, before stepping away from him and into the centre of the room.

'Nobody move,' he told them.

The woman laughed. 'You're bluffing,' she said. 'If you really aren't Dorian's puppet, then you won't kill us.'

Jack tutted. 'Who says I'm not working with McGuinness? Like you said, I have links to the crew, I visited him in hospital, I've been running around with Luke here all night, and he told me in advance what I would find here. So, you tell me, how's my poker face?'

'I'm willing to take my chances,' she said, motioning towards kneecap.

Jack shrugged, took aim, and pulled the trigger, planting a bullet in the man's leg. He fell to the ground, howling in pain. Jack would chalk it up as self-defence. Unfortunately for the goon, he was 0-3 in the space of about two hours.

'You should find some better help,' Jack told the stunned woman. 'Now, pass me the keys.'

London didn't even wait for the woman's permission before handing over the keys to the Range Rover. He motioned for Barrera to follow him and backed out of the house, gun pointed straight between her eyes. The biggest goon was back on his feet now, and Jack could tell he was itching to take a shot at him.

'You do realise we will kill everyone you ever loved,' the woman told him, calmly. 'Nobody will be safe.'

Jack had never taken a life before but, he paused in the doorway, feeling his finger run over the trigger. Barrera was tugging on his arm but he shrugged him off and turned to face the woman once more.

'Yes, your daughter, your ex-wife, the man in your life; oh, yes, we know all about him. And then, when you've lost everything, we will come for you, just like we'll come for Dorian McGuinness in the end. You think killing me will change any of that?' She laughed. 'You have no idea.'

He took a deep breath and raised the gun.

CHAPTER FIFTY-FIVE

The city was long gone now, and he found himself enjoying the country roads. He settled into the journey, mapping out the many permutations of what was to come in his head. He'd nearly finished his job; that meant his boss would be pleased. Not that he was particularly bothered. He was more worried about his own reputation than the happiness of the man who'd contracted him.

He checked the dash once more, noticing his adrenaline had pushed his speed up. He exhaled heavily, brought it back down, and made a left turn. He glanced at the clock—8.39pm.

By his calculations, he would arrive at 8.56.

CHAPTER FIFTY-SIX

Jack stepped on the accelerator. Barrera sat next to him, quiet as a mouse, unable to look him in the eye.

'You alright?' he asked. 'Luke! Are you alright?'

The lad nodded. 'I thought you were going to kill them in there.'

As did he.

'I'm a policeman, that's not what we do. Besides,' he added, pulling his phone out. 'We've got her on record admitting to all of it.'

'You recorded her?' Barrera asked, dumbfounded.

Jack nodded. 'Misdirection. Always works a treat. I was recording everything whilst working my way through the house and, once she handed my phone back, I got the rest of it.'

'So you lied?'

Jack laughed, his brush with death causing a wave of euphoria to wash over him. 'Yeah, at least three times which, according to her, is the limit.'

'They nearly shot me.'

'You're right,' Jack said. 'But they would have anyway. I needed their attention on you, needed the big guy to make a move.'

'Misdirection,' Barrera repeated.

'Correct.'

'Why didn't you arrest them?' he asked.

Jack shrugged. 'You can't drive,' he said. 'Which means you would have to sit facing four of them in the back of this car holding a gun to their heads. No offence, but I don't think you have it in you.'

'Fair enough,' Barrera said. 'But won't she get away?'

Jack shook his head. 'Where will they go? I've already rung it in to somebody I can trust and they are in a secluded area without transport. Besides, I don't think that woman is the running type.'

'That guy's knee is pretty bashed up,' Barrera said, smiling.

'Self-defence,' Jack said, returning the grin.

Barrera stretched out and yawned. 'So where are we going now?'

'To finish the job,' Jack told him.

'What?' Barrera cried.

'I know who she is,' he told him. 'Which means I know who else is involved.'

'How?' Barrera asked.

Jack smiled. 'Her perfume.'

Barrera looked puzzled. 'Perfume?'

He nodded and changed up a gear. 'Now, if you'll excuse me, I need to make another call.'

CHAPTER FIFTY-SEVEN

Jack arrived at the house within minutes. He glanced at the clock—8.51pm. He turned to Barrera. 'Wait here; oh, and give me your phone.'

Jack took the boy's mobile and got out of the car, slamming the door and pressing auto lock. He didn't expect him to do a runner, but he couldn't take the risk. Ultimately, he was looking at a murder charge. His life would be ruined, but at least he'd have a life inside—potentially. If he stayed out, it wouldn't be long before he disappeared, another victim of the McGuinness abyss.

Jack made his way up the drive, nonchalantly, until he reached the door. At the side of the house, he noticed the kennel—home to a sleeping Alsatian. The first time he'd visited here, he hadn't noticed that detail.

Unlike the last house he'd visited, he felt a more direct approach was in order. He gave it three firm knocks and waited.

'That you, Brian?'

When he answered the door, a look of shock registered on his face, before a different, altogether more sinister expression appeared. A face that had been hidden when Jack had first met him.

This was his real face.

Jack raised the gun and aimed it between his eyes. 'Aren't you going to invite me in?'

CHAPTER FIFTY-EIGHT

'Is my wife okay?' Astley said.

Jack considered making the man sweat before deciding there was nothing to be gained by it. 'She's fine,' he said. 'But we're bringing her in.'

They sat down, almost a mirror image of the first time Jack had been in his presence. He wriggled his nose, once more, in discomfort at the jasmine smell in the air. It wasn't air freshener, it was perfume.

'So now what?'

'You're going to fill in the blanks,' Jack said, leaning back but with the gun lying across his knee, facing Astley. 'And, it looks like you're expecting a visit from somebody I'm keen to talk to. I'll be sticking around for a bit if that's okay?'

'To what end?' he said. 'You have no idea what you're letting yourself into.'

'I think I'm already in it,' Jack told him. 'And I'm tired. So how about you give me what I need before we arrest you.'

Astley sat back and folded his arms across his barrelled chest. Jack watched as his face took on a purple hue of anger. 'Whatever,' he muttered.

'Good,' Jack said. 'Now, how about we start with your involvement in the Syndicate? What I don't get is how you got tangled up in it. The port was the link, right? McCullagh and your cousin were founding members?'

'Founding members!' Astley erupted. 'Listen to yourself. You don't get it, do you? We're just pawns.'

Jack leaned forward. 'If you're a pawn, who is the king?'

Astley smiled, running his tongue along the edges of his yellowed teeth. 'You know who.'

'The Captain?' Jack asked.

Astley laughed in his face. 'He told you he'd find you.'

Jack replied. 'He hasn't found me, though. I'm sat here with his lackey.'

'Oh he has,' Astley said. 'You just don't know it yet.'

Jack tried to do the sums in his head. It would explain why they had been caught up with McGuinness.

'You told me that your wife, Rita, was gone,' Jack put to him.

Astley tutted. 'I had interests to protect. She's more of a silent partner now in all of this.'

Jack decided to up the aggression. 'Seems to me that she must be somebody important to be given that kind of secrecy. More important than you, anyway. Perhaps she is more than just a pawn?'

Astley didn't twitch. 'Maybe.'

'You murdered Robert Norris,' Jack said. 'Admit it.'

Astley sat back. 'I'll admit nothing. None of us will.'

Jack raised the gun towards Astley. 'Let's see about that, shall we.'

'You won't use that,' he said, dismissively.

Jack lowered the gun once more. Going around forcing confessions out of people at gun point wasn't what he did. If he wasn't careful, he'd become the man he'd always feared he would, running around doing gangsters' dirty work.

'What I don't understand,' Jack said, trying a different

approach, 'is why you were at the farmhouse that night and not Gus. It was his house, after all.'

'That's because Gus wasn't involved,' a broad Glaswegian accent boomed through the room.

Jack spun round to find himself face to face with Brian McCullagh.

'Brian,' he said. 'You're a difficult man to find.'

The giant barman grinned, shotgun planted firmly on Jack. 'You obviously haven't been looking hard enough,' he said. 'I've been here the whole time.'

Jack turned back to Astley. 'You're both under arrest.'

Astley laughed. 'I don't think we'll let you arrest us today, detective.'

McCullagh took a step forward.

'So, what, you're just going to kill a policeman?' Jack stated.

McCullagh nodded, and took another step.

He weighed up his options. By the time he managed to spin the gun around to face him, his head would have been blasted off and plastered all over Astley's garish wallpaper. Plus, there were two of them to his one.

'So who was the fourth member of the Syndicate, then?' Jack asked.

McCullagh held firm. 'Gus backed out of the group years ago.'

'What are you doing?' Astley chided him.

'What does it matter?' McCullagh responded. 'He's a dead man. I've got the car out back. We'll be gone before he even stops breathing.'

Jack didn't much like the sound of that. 'Did you cut him out?'

'Nah,' McCullagh replied. 'Old Gus left for love—not that it did him any good. The bitch left him in the end anyway. Gus never got over it. Up until the day he died it was like he still thought she would come back to him. After she'd left, Gus tried to get back in but it was too late by then. That was long before we became what we are now. He got out at the right time,' he added. '*He'd* never let him leave now.'

'Yet he was targeted by Norris,' Jack said, conscious that every second he bought was a second closer to help arriving. 'Forgive me if I don't believe a word you say,' he added. 'You've done nothing but lie so far.'

McCullagh scoffed. 'I'm sure you'll get over it, in the seconds you have left.'

'Then at least tell me what happened,' Jack said. 'Call it a final wish.'

'You know what,' McCullagh said. 'I think I'll grant it.'

Astley looked fit to burst.

'Gus left,' McCullagh said. 'He was too soft for that life, anyway. He was a good man; a better man than us.' He motioned to Astley. 'That bastard, though, was hard. And his wife,' he continued. 'If you think Gus' Margaret was tough, this woman is in another league altogether.'

Having met her, Jack was inclined to agree.

'But even though he wasn't involved anymore,' McCullagh went on. 'That didn't mean he wasn't without his use. It was through him we were able to hide it.'

'Hide what?' Jack asked.

'Information,' McCullagh said. Jack saw the sadness spread on his face. He clearly had an affinity for Gus Fenwick that went beyond the professional. 'We all had access to it. Masses of information on important people in the UK and beyond. Leverage that allowed us to keep our business interests running. Only, nothing is fool-proof. There was a leak and, once we knew that McGuinness was aware of it, we decided to lay a trap. It worked well until...'

Always Dorian McGuinness, Jack thought. It seemed the crime boss knew more about Robert Norris than he had originally let on. He'd sent the boy to pick up the intelligence—with devastating consequences.

'We weren't to know what would happen to Gus, later.'

Jack couldn't believe it. After everything that had occurred, Gus Fenwick had indeed been an innocent party all along. Well, save for his initial involvement in the smuggling at the port. Jack cast his mind back to the initial interview with the man. The farmer had told them that he had been visiting his wife in hospital. Margaret had been adamant that it wasn't him. It now seemed like the actions of a desperate man. He met Brian McCullagh's eyes. Tears for his old friend were streaming down his face.

'I'm sorry,' Jack said, almost meaning it.

McCullagh brushed him off. 'Too late now. But that McGuinness bastard will get what's coming to him.'

'Who was the fourth member of the Syndicate?' Jack repeated. 'And who is the Captain?'

McCullagh shook his head. 'You're all out of questions, detective, and I'm out of time. You might want to close your eyes for this.'

Jack did as he was told this time. He'd timed it all wrong. Nobody had arrived to save him and, finally, his rogue approach to policing had caught up with him.

He waited for it.

It was the gurgling sound he noticed first, followed by a startled cry from Astley. By the time Jack opened his eyes McCullagh had already fallen to his knees in a pool of his own blood, his neck slit. Astley retreated into his seat, as a man Jack recognised stepped out of the shadows.

Dayton Olsen.

He looked into the eyes of the hired hitman but saw only evil staring back at him.

Olsen, satisfied with his work, stepped over McCullagh's body, bloodied knife outstretched.

'You can kill me,' Astley raged. 'But it won't change a thing. You're all dead.'

'Tell me where it is,' Olsen demanded.

'I'm no rat,' Astley spat back. 'You don't frighten me.'

Olsen shrugged. 'You know I won't stop until I have you all.'

Astley rounded on him. 'You're a fucking animal. Mark was a good man. I told him not to go into the prisons. But he wouldn't listen to me. He always did have too much of a conscience.'

'He was one of you,' Olsen said, pointing the knife towards Astley. 'Hardly a good man. In any case, it isn't for me to judge; I just do my job. Boss' orders.'

Jack was stunned. The horrific realisation that Olsen had used Reaves to kill the tutor because he was a Syndicate member hit Jack like a punch to the solar plexus. None of them had made the link. Jack had been sure Olsen was working *with* the Syndicate. Jack looked on in horror at the barman. McCullagh's now lifeless body told a different employment history.

That left one man.

Always Dorian McGuinness.

Jack watched as Olsen moved towards Astley, his catlike speed a dangerous contrast to his considerable bulk.

He remembered the weapon. 'Stop!' he called, firing a shot above Olsen's head.

The assassin flinched. He clearly hadn't expected Jack to be armed. Jack knew he only had moments to react. Surprise always wore off. Once the plaster dust settled, Olsen would realise that Jack was unlikely to shoot him. Once that happened, the odds would lengthen on him bringing things to a satisfactory conclusion.

Olsen took a step forward. Jack tensed and raised the gun. He could almost see the cogs turning over in the hitman's mind. Olsen smirked and lunged at Jack. Another shot rang out as Olsen grabbed Jack's wrist. Conscious of the fact that the escaped prisoner wouldn't hesitate to shoot him, Jack launched the gun to the other side of the room.

He managed to wriggle free from the man's grasp, and took the opportunity to throw his weight into him before Olsen could use the knife. The hitman stumbled back, knocking Astley over in the process. Jack lunged again, taking him down this time, before landing heavy blows to the man's face.

Having been a boxer, and standing at a stocky six foot two, Jack was confident in his own strength. But he wasn't prepared for the force with which Olsen took hold of his wrists and bent them back. Jack howled in pain and thrust his head down onto the bridge of the man's nose. Olsen grunted and released his grip enough for Jack to unlock his wrists from his grasp. Then, as though they were in a movie, they both glanced across to the floor on their left, noticing the knife. Jack scrambled for it, only to find himself pulled back by the giant hands of Olsen. The hitman pinned him to the carpet and planted a forearm on his neck. Jack wheezed as the air was forced out of him. He realised he only had a matter of moments before it was over. Again he caught the look in Olsen's eyes, a look with no hint of malice—simply a void where emotion should be. Despite his predicament, Jack found himself shuddering.

His vision was clouding now as Olsen leant into the manoeuvre. Jack was in full panic mode as he frantically scratched at the hitman's hands and arms. He was unable to get traction, and clouds began forming over his vision.

Somewhere through the fog, he heard Olsen speak. 'The boss will be pleased.'

He knew he was heading into the abyss and, rather than some kind of light, felt the strange sensation of snow landing on him. *That's funny,* he thought, *I don't remember it snowing.* Black then turned to red, to orange and then to yellow as he found himself staring at a ceiling light above him. He brought a shaking hand up to his face and found it wasn't snow, but glass, that had fallen onto him.

His ears throbbed, like he was on a particularly rocky long-haul flight, and he was aware of a lack of oxygen, a deep, burning pain attacking his throat.

'Fucking bastard!' the voice called.

He turned over, his ears returning to focus, along with his vision, to see Astley standing over a furious-looking Olsen. Through his haze, he was aware of blood seeping out from the side of the assassin's misshapen head. A trembling Astley stood above him, remnants of the tumbler he'd used to attack the man still in his hand.

Jack managed to drag himself to his feet just as the sirens started. Olsen pushed Astley to one side and attempted to stand. The Syndicate member appeared too angry to notice the net closing in on them.

Astley began launching wild haymakers at the felled Olsen, who put his hands up in defence, before sweeping the man's legs from beneath him. Jack continued his crawl towards him as a giant fist reared back, ready to splatter Astley's head across the floor. With one final effort, Jack launched himself at the man, knocking him over before he was able to connect. Jack winced as Olsen's head cracked against the mahogany coffee table but he seemed unperturbed, immediately springing forward towards him.

Then it was over as abruptly as it had started. Jack, expecting an onslaught from the thug, found himself suddenly without resistance. Multiple hands grabbed the hitman and dragged him back. Olsen, whose eyes now carried a burning fury in them, attempted to fight them off in a vain attempt to get to him. Jack scrambled backwards and leaned against a toppled seat, his breath raspy and shallow. He watched as the officers, four of them in total, dragged Olsen to his feet. Jack was aware of Astley being manhandled to the ground, somewhere to his right, but found himself unable to look away from the cold eyes of Dayton Olsen.

They made to move him.

'Wait!' Jack called. 'Wait, I said!'

The officers gave each other a nervous glance before acquiescing.

Jack approached them. 'It's finished, Olsen,' he said. 'Admit it, you're McGuinness' man.'

The thick, purple veins in Olsen's neck settled down, like snakes retreating into the ground, as he simply smiled at Jack.

Jack resisted the urge to slam his fist into the man's face. 'Read him his rights and get him out of here.'

The officers dragged the strangely-compliant Olsen from the room, leaving Jack with a now handcuffed Astley.

He leant down in the shattered glass, and held the man's head up to him. 'Soon, Astley,' he told him, 'you and I are going to have a conversation about all of this. And, believe me, whether you talk or not, you're going down for a very long time. How about you think on that and let me know how co-operative you want to be. People smuggling, protection racketeering, prostitution rings, drugs, it's all coming out.'

Jack watched as they pulled the dejected man from the room. Moments later, Watkins arrived with Gerrard in tow. Jack picked the gun up from the carpet and handed it over.

'Jesus, Jack, what the hell is all this?'

He shrugged and resisted the urge to plant a kiss on the man's freckled face. As it was, Gerrard ignored all professional boundaries and threw herself at Jack in a hard embrace.

'You bastard!' she said, thumping him on the chest.

'Ouch,' he winced. 'Careful.'

'I don't care,' she said. 'You could have gotten yourself killed.'

Jack held his palms up in an act of surrender. 'We can talk about it later,' he said. 'Technically I'm still suspended which means I wasn't allowed to contact the team.' He gave Watkins a knowing look.

Gerrard raised an eyebrow. 'It also means you aren't supposed to go rogue on us all, as well,' she chided him.

'Let's leave that for later, Claire,' Watkins said, placing a hand on Gerrard's arm.

Jack watched a moment of affection pass between them,

before averting his eyes, as if he'd stepped into an awkward moment without permission. Watkins and Gerrard were good officers, and good people. If they wanted a relationship, he was in no position to stop them.

Watkins cleared his throat and turned to Jack. 'We picked the woman up at the address you gave us. The big bastard with the scars was with her. They didn't resist.'

Jack nodded. 'What about the other two?'

Watkins laughed. 'They were hobbling down the lane, about four hundred metres from the drive. Didn't take us long to track them. Looks like they were hit by a bus; you know anything about that?'

Jack shrugged. 'No idea, officer.'

He brought a bruised hand up to his neck and groaned in pain as it touched his throbbing skin. The adrenaline had left his body now, and he felt shattered at the thought of continuing. But, unfortunately for him, the night wasn't over.

'Where are you going?' Gerrard asked as he moved past them.

'I've got to go see somebody.'

'This about the case?' she asked. 'You can't—'

'No,' he cut her off. 'Not this time.'

'What about all this?' Watkins put to him.

Jack reached the doorway before turning. 'It's a crime scene,' he said. 'And I'm still suspended. I'll be going and you two can do your jobs. Let me know when you need a statement. Until then, I'll be seeing you.'

Jack left them to it and headed outside. Barrera was still in his car, which was now guarded by a PC. The young man caught his eye, offered a limp smile and nodded. Jack nodded back; he'd grown reasonably fond of the lad's company, all things considered. However, the truth was that he had committed murder—albeit under extreme duress. He was looking at a long stretch of jail time.

If it weren't for the seriousness of the situation, Jack would have laughed. The Syndicate, a rival to McGuinness' empire, had more or less been disbanded in one night, with the man responsible for his attempted murder under arrest. Meanwhile, the gangster was recuperating in a warm hospital bed, while the man tasked with carrying out his dirty work under arrest and unwilling to talk.

Olsen, Jack felt, was the kind of man who longed to be banged up. They'd be more likely to get a confession out of him if they offered to put him on the outside. People like him didn't belong in the real world.

He had little time to consider that now. He checked his watch —9.45pm. His body was crying out for rest but he couldn't contemplate that until he'd made one more house visit.

Perhaps the most important one of the night.

CHAPTER FIFTY-NINE

'Jack,' he said, an intense sadness in his tone, lathered on like cream-cheese on a dry bagel. 'I suppose you best come in.'

Jack followed him into the kitchen and took a seat at the breakfast diner, allowing the silence to stretch out between them.

'Can I get you a drink?'

He shook his head. 'I'm not here for a social visit,' he told him. 'Mona not about?'

Edwards' eyes locked on his. Jack saw the fear in them.

'She's not been about for a while,' he said.

The DSI's shoulders slumped as he spoke. Jack, despite his anger, felt sympathy for his boss. He'd known about their marital problems from the previous year but he hadn't been aware that they were living separate lives. He gazed about the kitchen; the place was a mess, a mirror image of Edwards' work life. Despite the considerable girth of the DSI, he looked smaller than Jack had ever known, lost in a world that had moved beyond him.

'How long have you been working for them?' he said.

'It's not like that,' the DSI replied.

'How long?' Jack reiterated.

Edwards stood, pulled open the fridge, grabbed a Heineken,

and popped the ring pull, downing what must have amounted to half of a can within twenty seconds. He placed the tin on the counter, and retook his seat.

'About two years. How did you know?'

Jack shifted. 'I'm a detective, Logan, it's what I do.' His mind shifted back to the call he'd made to Watkins earlier in the night. 'Call it the power of deduction. Plus, I've spent some time with Rita Astley. Something she said made me think. When I threatened her with backup, she told me that they paid people in high places so that things like that didn't happen. That meant it had to be somebody above my pay grade. I figured it was either you or Dalton. An ACC doesn't have his finger on the pulse the way a DSI does, though. And, so, here we are...'

'You always were good, Jack.'

Jack refused to speak. This was Edwards' burden to bear, and bear it he would.

'I made a mistake,' Edwards finally said. 'And they used my weakness against me.'

'What did you do?' Jack asked.

'Mona and I have been apart for some time now. It's been years since we've been a proper couple. The dregs of our relationship was all that was left and, now, I don't even have that.' He drained the rest of his can, stood, and grabbed another. 'I was drunk, at a bar, met this woman. She said she was twenty and I was flattered,' he said, adding, 'I mean, look at me, who wouldn't be?'

'They set you up?' Jack asked.

Jack watched as Edwards began picking away at a piece of dislodged lacquer on the counter top. The DSI sighed and, when he looked again at Jack, tears were streaming down his face.

He nodded. 'They had me hook, line and sinker. About two days later, a man came to me, big bloke, scarred face. They gave me a set of photos, told me she was fifteen and, on top of that, an illegal immigrant.'

'Shipped in at the Port of Tyne?' Jack asked.

'I don't bloody well know, do I!' he thundered. 'I was so panicked about myself, still living in hope that Mona and I would work things out, that I didn't stop to ask. Most likely, though.'

'So it was self-preservation?'

Edwards pointed a thick finger at him. 'Save your self-righteousness, Jack.'

Jack ignored him. 'So, what, they used you on the inside?'

'It wasn't like it was an ongoing thing,' he replied. 'They just told me they needed people to take a blind eye from time to time, is all. I arranged that for them.'

Jack threw his chair back and lurched forward, grabbing Edwards by the collar. 'But that wasn't it, was it?'

Edwards recoiled. 'No, alright, no!'

Jack released his boss, who didn't even bother to straighten out his shirt. A mess, just like the rest of his life. 'Tell me.'

He knew Edwards was wrestling with how much to say. At this point, it didn't matter. If Jack had to beat it out of him, he would.

'They told me you were bought and paid for by the McGuinness crew. I told them that was madness, they were wrong. They didn't believe me. I...'

'Don't clam up on me now, Logan,' Jack said.

'They told me you used to be involved with him, that you were his go-to guy in the force, and that you were a threat that had to be removed.'

Jack rose, watching as Edwards shrank back once more. Instead, he moved past him and got his own beer from the fridge. Once he was sitting back down, he motioned for his boss to continue.

'I told them I couldn't do that, that there was a murder investigation ongoing, and that you were in charge of it.'

'What happened then?'

'They told me I either got you out of the picture, or they'd make sure I was scrubbed out, permanently. It was the bloke with the scars again. Always him.' Edwards shuddered.

'So you knew I wasn't the mole,' Jack said, a statement, not a question.

'It was the only way to get you pulled from the case,' Edwards said. 'They needed you out of the picture to continue their move on McGuinness. They thought you were protecting him. They roughed that journalist up a bit, put him out there to set you up.'

'My kid, Logan.'

'I didn't know...'

Jack roared and threw his beer against the wall, wisps of cheap lager froth spraying across the floor. 'My goddam kid!'

'I'm sorry, okay!' Edwards cried. 'I didn't know they'd do that.'

'But they did,' Jack replied. 'And, still, you did nothing.'

'You're right, I'm a piece of shit,' Edwards said.

'No, you're worse than that,' Jack told him. 'You're a bent copper, and that's about as low as you can get.' He stood to leave. 'Was the undercover gig their idea, too, an attempt to get me permanently removed?'

'No, Jack, you have to believe me,' Edwards implored. 'That was my idea to get back at them. I knew I couldn't touch them but if you were seen to be going rogue, then I wasn't culpable. I knew you could get to them and stop it all.'

'Dalton?'

Edwards shook his head. 'He was on board with my suggestion, but knew nothing about the reasons behind it.'

Jack paused in the doorway to Edwards' kitchen. 'You've got a few cans left in the fridge. I suggest you drown your sorrows now or, better yet, drown yourself altogether.'

'Jack!' He stopped but refused to look back at him. 'The Captain controls all of it. He sees you as a threat now and the taking down of the Syndicate will only harden his resolve.' The DSI sighed. 'I don't know who he is, but he knows who you are. He won't stop.'

'Neither will I,' he shot back.

'We all have bosses, the Syndicate is no different,' Edwards said.

Jack stared him down. 'I used to, but not anymore.' With that, he turned and left Edwards to his disgrace.

CHAPTER SIXTY

'There he is!' Watkins beamed. 'The hero of the hour!'

His return into the MIR was met with a firm applause. From the corner of his eye, he noticed DI Russell with her hands firmly clamped by her sides. He felt like anything but a hero.

'Is that prosecco?' Jack asked, surprised.

'Not quite,' Gerrard said. 'We aren't allowed to drink on duty, apparently, so it's fake. Still, it's the thought that counts.'

He took an offered glass and raised it to the room. Christensen stood and offered him a nod. Jack acknowledged him with a nod of his own.

'Speech!' Watkins chanted.

'No,' Jack waved him away.

'Oh, go on, guv, we went to all this trouble,' Gerrard told him.

'Fake prosecco?'

'And a banner,' she said.

Jack turned to see a welcome back banner tacked to the ceiling above the door, one corner already hanging off.

'At least tell us how you did it?' Watkins implored him.

'That would be a long speech,' Jack said. 'Maybe another time.'

He thanked them for their support and left a rather wounded-looking Watkins to tidy things up. Once back in the safety of his office he slumped himself in his seat. His neck was sore, an after-product of having nearly had his windpipe crushed just a few days prior by Dayton Olsen. He'd had a few close calls in the past, and the fight with the hitman was undoubtedly up there with the best of them. He was thankful that there were still some people he could trust in the force. The gamble that Watkins hadn't been dirty had literally saved his life.

Not to mention the wiping out of the Syndicate in one fell swoop.

Olsen had admitted to committing the murders of Les Holding and Brian McCullagh, as well as orchestrating the killing of Davison. What he wouldn't admit to was who had enlisted him. He kept repeating his mantra that he didn't work for anyone and that he was simply acting in his own interests. Jack wasn't buying it. They both knew he was McGuinness' man. But, without a hard evidence trail, and the non-co-operation of Olsen, it would yet again be difficult to pin anything on the aquatic shop owner. Jack recalled his last conversation with Olsen. The only thing he'd expressed regret for was the fact that he hadn't been able to finish Astley off and retrieve whatever it was he was looking for.

During the altercation at Astley's, those involved had admitted to information being the end goal. Jack assumed it was some kind of USB stick or hard drive. Just who, and what, exactly was on there was anybody's guess. There was at least one person who would be appearing on it, that much Jack knew. His now former boss, DSI Edwards, and all his indiscretions were no doubt on there. Information that valuable carried a heavy price, a price that had resulted in the deaths of Robert Norris, Gus Fenwick and Les Holding. McGuinness obviously didn't yet know who the Captain was, but his dismantling of the Syndicate suggested he was getting close to the centre of the mystery.

The deaths of Norris, Fenwick and Holding all carried a

sadness for Jack. In their own ways, all three were bad people. Norris, a petty thief and school dropout; Holding, hired muscle for the McGuinness crew and Fenwick; a one-time people smuggler but, as Jack had found out, not involved in the Syndicate. The irony that all three had died because of it, yet none were directly involved in it, was not lost on Jack.

Olsen had taken out Brian McCullagh, and, with a little help from an unhinged prisoner known as Marshall Reaves, Mark Davison had also been dealt with. The Astleys were both in custody. Both were refusing to speak; as was the scarred man. However, the two lackeys who Jack had put down in the club weren't so tight-lipped. With a promise that it would reflect favourably on them, they'd admitted to knowing that both Astley and the scarred man, known as Martin Cutler, had orchestrated the murder of Norris. Both had been in the field when it happened. Jack smiled as he glanced at the photograph of Cutler, taken just outside his house, clearly watching Jack's movements. The Big Issue-selling Real Madrid fanatic had done a sterling job, and all it had cost Jack was a cheap camera phone and an extra magazine.

Faced with mounting evidence, Cutler was starting to twitch.

And Jack was willing to bet a hefty sum on the dog hairs at Fenwick's farm matching Paul Astley's Alsatian—affectionately known as Lawson.

Watkins appeared round the door. 'Got a minute?'

'Of course.'

'Probably isn't worth much now but I came across this.'

The DS placed an old newspaper cutting in front of him. A team of workers, all in dirty blue overalls, smiled out at them. There was no mistaking Gus Fenwick, his arm draped round a slightly slimmer Brian McCullagh. Next to him was Mark Davison, which didn't come as a surprise, given DI Tomkins had confirmed that he'd been plucked from industry to work at the prison. Davison's links to the Syndicate were never looked into, mainly because they'd had no reason to suspect him. Had they known earlier, Jack felt that they may have been able to put a stop to events before things began spiralling out of control.

Jack looked again at the newspaper cutting. The headline on the story was about some new piece of machinery. There were twenty or so workers in the shot.

Watkins must have seen the look on Jack's face. 'What is it?' he asked.

Jack ignored him and pulled his desk lamp across to shine it on the image.

'What?' Watkins repeated.

Jack pointed to the image of one man, just off to the left of McCullagh, somewhat aloof from the others, as if hiding from the camera despite being in the picture. It was a face he recognised, but couldn't place.

'Nothing,' he muttered. 'I'll keep this, if that's okay?'

'No problem,' Watkins said. 'Fancy a cuppa?'

Jack declined. 'No thanks, I've got a meeting with the ACC.'

'Sounds important.'

'To him, perhaps.'

CHAPTER SIXTY-ONE

'Jack, come in.' ACC Dalton beckoned towards the empty seat at his desk.

He did as he was told, and nodded a greeting to PCC Nadine Guthrie, who was sat, cross-legged, adjacent to him. Jack could sense the tension in the room, something which suggested a difficult discussion had taken place prior to his arrival. It wasn't hard to fathom what it was about. He'd been under strict orders to keep what he knew about Edwards under wraps, a pre-condition of the lifting of his suspension.

He enjoyed watching the two of them squirm. Dalton looked like he had a rod stuck firmly up his back. Nadine Guthrie, for her part, was unable to meet his gaze—not out of embarrassment, he felt, but of pure rage. Ever since the previous year, she'd made clear her dislike for him, telling him in no uncertain terms that she'd be keeping a close eye on his career progress. Her wiry, black hair was impeccably-styled, much like her suit, not a crease out of place. As for Dalton, judging by the dark look across his face, their recent confrontation was still fresh in his memory.

Jack was tired and fed up with waiting. 'Well?'

Dalton tensed, before wriggling his shoulders and placing his palms across his neatly-arranged desk. 'Thank you for agreeing to see us, Jack,' he said.

He resisted the urge to tell him he didn't really have a choice. 'It's fine,' he told him.

'The Police and Crime Commissioner and I have been speaking at length with regards to this situation...'

'Oh, get on with it, Richard!' Guthrie demanded, uncrossing her legs before shifting her body further away from him.

Dalton stiffened but didn't react to the admonishment. 'Yes, quite,' he said. 'First of all, let me just start by saying how pleased we all are that this question of your loyalty has been ironed out.'

'My loyalty was never in question,' Jack said.

Dalton nodded, pausing briefly, before getting to his feet. He began pacing left and right, arms clasped behind his back like an academic professor delivering a lecture on quantum physics. 'Unlike Logan Edwards,' he said.

Jack glanced at the PCC, who met his gaze with hostility.

'Don't worry,' Dalton said. 'She knows everything.'

'*She* has a name,' Guthrie spat. 'And I'd thank you to use it.'

'My apologies, Nadine,' Dalton said, turning back to Jack. 'Needless to say, this is a sensitive matter. DSI Edwards was a pillar of this community, a stalwart in the Northumbrian force and a man who commanded the public's respect.'

'It sounds like you're delivering a eulogy,' Jack remarked.

Dalton nodded. 'Perhaps I am.' He paused whilst he retook his seat once again. 'What I'm saying here, Jack, is that we can't allow that information to come out.'

Jack laughed. 'You want to cover this up?'

'It's not about that,' Guthrie said. 'We will not have scum like him drag our names through the mud. We've worked too hard to build all this.'

'You've been working for one year, and I'm still not sure what you do,' Jack told her. 'Forgive me if I choose to ignore what you have to say.'

Guthrie made to speak before Dalton cut in. 'That's enough!'

Jack could tell they were both seething.

'You were saying?' Jack put to the ACC, barely containing his contempt.

'As of today, DSI Edwards is no longer an employee of the Northumbrian Police Force.'

Jack scoffed. 'And how big was the pay out?'

Dalton didn't bite but the skin around his chiselled cheeks stretched taut across his face as he ground his teeth. 'That's none of your concern, nor is his involvement in what has occurred.'

'Are you kidding me?' Jack said. 'Because of him, I nearly died. My daughter was made a target!'

'Calm down, please,' Dalton implored him. 'I'm aware of that and, as part of Logan's...' Dalton seemed to search his mind for the most PC term, 'retribution, he is fully co-operating with us.'

'He doesn't know who the Captain is,' Jack told him. 'And we have accounted for the others. So, what exactly is he offering?'

'I'll be the judge of that,' Dalton said.

Jack threw his chair back. 'Is that all?'

Dalton and Guthrie glanced at each other. 'Not quite,' he said.

Dalton pushed a badge across the table towards him. He noticed PCC Guthrie staring out of the window, unable to watch. 'What's this?' Jack asked.

'I need people I can trust, Jack,' Dalton said. 'I might not agree with your methods, or your attitude,' he added, 'but there's no denying your results. The team here respect you; there's nobody else suitable for the job.'

Jack stood. 'I can't believe this,' he said. 'You're buying my silence?'

'It's—'

Guthrie turned to face him. 'Whatever you need to hear, detective.'

'Nadine—'

'Oh, shut up, Richard,' she scolded the ACC. 'You can believe what you want, Jack, but either way your silence is taken as given. Why not earn a few more pennies whilst you do it?'

Jack leaned over the desk and pushed the badge towards Guthrie. 'You can't buy me,' he told her. 'Why don't you do it, seeing as you've been working so hard?'

He slammed the door on his way out before either of them could add another word.

CHAPTER SIXTY-TWO

Jack entered the room without knocking.

Christensen looked up from his desk. 'Alright, boss?' he said, mouth half full of apple.

'Not a bad time is it?' Jack asked him.

The DS shook his head. 'Just finishing up some paperwork.'

He motioned to the newspaper on the desk. 'That today's?'

'What? Oh, yes,' Christensen said, holding it up. 'It's an interesting read.'

Jack nodded. The papers were filled with headlines alluding to the taking down of the mysterious crime syndicate, with various pictures and tenuous sources alluded to. Perhaps, more interesting, was the story at the top of the page regarding Dorian McGuinness. It seemed the incumbent Newcastle councillor had been the victim of a shocking exposé into his sordid sex life. McGuinness, now out of hospital, praised the work of the emergency services in saving his life, castigated the councillor for his lack of judgement and announced his intention to run in the upcoming by-election. It seemed McGuinness' ambition knew no end.

'Not quite as interesting as this one,' Jack told him.

He pulled out a copy of the newspaper he'd pilfered from Robson's house and placed it into Christensen's hands.

He frowned. 'What's this? It's from over a week ago.'

'Yes it is,' Jack told him. 'I picked it up at a mutual friend's house and thought I'd bring it along with me.'

'I don't understand...' Christensen said.

'They say a picture tells a thousand words,' Jack said. 'I wonder what words this picture tells.'

He pointed to the image of some barely known celebrity at the top of the page, complete with drawn on glasses and moustache. 'Christensen,' he said. 'If you're going to collude with the enemy, at least get rid of the evidence. We've spent the best part of two years wondering who the mole was. I never dreamed it would be you.'

The DS blanched. 'I—'

'Save it,' Jack told him. He snatched that day's paper from him and held it up. 'I'd call that a perfect match,' he said, pointing to the near-identical glasses and moustache he'd scrawled onto the face of the disgraced councillor. 'It was right there in front of me the whole time. I spotted it last year but never made the connection.'

'I can explain...' the DS stuttered.

He met Christensen's shocked gaze. 'Say hi to Robson for me and give him this.' Jack threw a pound coin down on the desk. 'I owe him for the paper. If it's any more than that, he can take it out of your next payment.'

CHAPTER SIXTY-THREE

The club was alive with the bustle of workmen, moving in and out, carrying various bits of debris and heavy boxes. Given what had happened, Jack was surprised that nobody had stopped him on entry. The smell of charred furniture still laced the air, choking his lungs.

Surveying it all from the middle of the room was a revitalised, suited and booted Dorian McGuinness.

Jack brushed past one of the burnt-out tables and stepped over the ash to face him. 'Dorian.'

'Jack!' he greeted him. 'How nice to see you.'

'Is it?'

McGuinness stopped to bark an order at a pair of hired hands who were carrying out an old table. 'It's always a pleasure, Jack. You really should call ahead, though; I'm a busy man—what with the upcoming election.'

'So I heard,' Jack replied.

'Yes,' he said, frowning. 'Nasty business with that Syndicate, don't you think? Once I'm councillor I'll be sure to crack down on that type of thing. People smuggling, prostitution and racketeering! It's a disgrace.'

Jack ignored the irony. 'I didn't think you were the political type.'

McGuinness laughed. 'Jack, everything is politics.'

Jack grumbled a response and motioned to their surroundings. 'You going to try and rebuild this?'

'No, no,' McGuinness said. 'It's too much of a ruin now. It'll have to be pulled down, unfortunately.'

'I'm sure the insurance money will more than compensate.'

'Quite,' he replied. 'I'll rebuild elsewhere, start again. These things are unfortunate but you live and you learn, don't you?'

Jack moved a step closer and lowered his voice. 'Not everybody has lived, though, have they? Robert Norris, for one.'

McGuinness towered over him. 'Speak plainly, Jack.'

'I thought you liked the theatrical.'

McGuinness laughed, a boom which echoed across the room, causing nervous glances from nearby workmen.

'Something tells me we're beyond that now,' he said.

Jack snorted. 'You're damn right we are. I know you sent Robert Norris to the farmhouse that night and that you employed Olsen to track down members of the Syndicate so you could get your hands on information.' Jack moved another step closer. 'And I know you had Holding killed because he knew about the whole thing and was a loose cannon waiting to blow.'

For a moment, Jack thought McGuinness would headbutt him. His eyes narrowed, and he reared back, before seemingly thinking better of it. When he came close to Jack once more, his hooked nose was practically touching Jack's.

'From what I gather, Jack, that boy was a tearaway. Who he decides to rob is no business of mine. And, as for Holding, why would I kill my own employee?' Jack watched as something flashed across McGuinness' eyes. He didn't know what it was, but he didn't care much for it. 'Dayton Olsen is a criminal,' he continued. 'It's my understanding he is now back behind bars, refusing to talk.' He placed a heavy hand on Jack's shoulder. 'I know that must be frustrating for you, to know you'll never get to the bottom of it all.'

Jack shrugged him off and stepped away from him. 'The boy shouldn't be harmed, it's not his fault,' Jack told him.

McGuinness smiled. 'Betrayal comes in many forms and I'm a big believer in karma.'

'If something happens to him, so help me God, Dorian...'

'Don't get so wound up, Jack,' he said. 'Nobody can ever truly know what will happen to any one of us. I mean look around you,' he said, motioning to the burnt-out husk that was his club. 'Nobody could have foreseen such an incident occurring.' He fixed Jack with a hostile stare. 'People have accidents all the time.'

Jack felt sorry for the boy. He'd gotten caught up in something he had no control over and now he was in a cell, charged with a host of crimes including murder. Both Jack and McGuinness knew that he was the one variable nobody could control. If Barrera spoke, it could lead to Dorian McGuinness finally being brought down for the crimes he'd committed over the years. Keeping Barrera alive and safe, and getting him to talk, was all that mattered now.

Jack finally spoke. 'You're right,' he said. 'People do have accidents all the time, even those who think they are untouchable. I'll be seeing you soon, Dorian.'

McGuinness remained unmoved. 'I look forward to it.'

He watched as Lambert left the club, standing still amongst the carnage long after he'd gone, pondering. Whilst they'd always had their issues, he felt that there had at least been a grudging respect between them. Nobody stood up to him the way Jack Lambert did. Granted he was a policeman, but something told him that it didn't matter what profession Lambert worked in, he'd still be just as assertive, just as fearless. He'd always respected that. But there was a new look in Jack's eye now. A hostile one. McGuinness knew it was only a matter of time before Jack came for him. Things were at a crossroads for both of them. He was so close to achieving it all, nothing could be allowed to stop him now. He clenched his fists, still unmoved. First Barrera, then Jack Lambert.

Then Him.

'Alright, Mr McGuinness, where do you want these?' she said, holding out a set of leaflets for him to peruse.

He put on his best fake smile. 'Patricia, how many times have I told you, I have people who can handle all of that? You just keep an eye on things, let me know if anybody steps out of line. And, it's Dorian to you.'

The woman smiled, fiddling with her pink bra strap. Everything about her made him sick, but there was no doubting her use to him. No doubting it at all.

'You're too kind, Mr... Dorian,' she said, her broad Mackem accent grating on him. 'You're so much nicer than Mr McCullagh ever was.'

'I reward the people who are useful to me,' McGuinness told her. 'You've done a great job so far, Patricia. Now, run along, I want to hear that beautiful voice of yours screeching at those removal men; it's not the same around here without it.'

She smiled. 'Yes, sir!'

He watched as she bounded off, happy in her fragile bliss. He almost gagged. It was pathetic how far a little charm went on some people. She'd been easy to nab, in the end. Still, fake charm had its merits. He would use it to win that vote. Not winning hadn't even crossed his mind. It was just a question of who would dare run against him.

His hand moved to his pocket. He briefly panicked, unable to locate it, before breathing a sigh of relief. There it was. He moved his finger over the surface of the small plastic device. Ensuring nobody was watching, he took it out and turned it over in his hand. He smiled. Yes, Patricia had been more than useful to him.

He found it curious how such a small device could carry so much power. The mistake the Captain had made was to trust his lieutenants with copies of it. He would never have made that error. And now he had background information and all of the dirty secrets the Captain was in possession of. The leverage he would now have on some of the most influential people in the country was untold. No wonder they had been willing to kill to keep it safe.

And, as for Olsen, two out of four Syndicate members was a fine job and, having delivered Holding exactly as he'd asked, he would make sure the hitman's boy was taken care of. Of course, it hadn't been a perfect job. He hadn't managed to secure the USB. No, that had come from Patricia. His research had paid off. The disgruntled barmaid with the big mouth had delivered for him spectacularly. The Syndicate hadn't banked on their biggest threat being a part-time employee with no criminal links. That's what helped him stand apart from the rest. He was careful. They were amateurs. He'd never have discussed business in front of the help at a poker game.

McGuinness' mind wandered back to Olsen. There was still one other person he hadn't given him.

He placed the device back into his pocket. Gazing outside, he noticed the bleak Newcastle weather worsening, cement-like clouds churning over like grey butter. A storm was coming. His storm. No, scratch that, he *was* the storm. And nobody would be safe from him.

First Barrera. Then Jack Lambert. Then Him.

Information was power, and now he had it all.

CHAPTER SIXTY-FOUR

A stley seemed unfazed to see him. The man one quarter responsible for the group known as the Syndicate merely observed Jack with a mild curiosity. Whilst they knew the identity of all of the Syndicate members, they still had no clue as to who it was that had been in charge of the whole operation.

The Captain.

The PC outside of the room began a nervous shuffle. Jack could tell he was on edge. Turning up alone, without a recording device, meant that he wasn't exactly playing things by the book. Given the plethora of rules he'd already broken this week, Jack didn't see the harm in bending one more.

Astley remained still, eyes straight ahead. The man betrayed no stress, anger or upset at his predicament. He seemed completely accepting of what had happened to him. From what he had heard about Rita Astley's attitude, she was less stoic.

Given his previous interaction with the woman, Jack wasn't surprised.

Jack had hoped that Astley would start speaking once the seriousness of his predicament hit home. That now seemed unlikely. He stood, moved to the corner of the room, and flicked on the light. He retook his seat, and placed the picture in front of him.

'This,' he said, pointing to the Port of Tyne newspaper cut out. 'Who is it?'

Astley's face remained unmoved, but his eyes briefly flitted towards the image. Silence.

'I know his face,' Jack pushed him. 'McCullagh's bar, yes?'

When he made to speak, Astley's voice was ropey, as if he hadn't used his vocal chords in some time. 'Then you know who he is,' he said.

'Funny that,' Jack said. 'Brian McCullagh told me he was a regular customer at The Black Horse, and that he was there every day.' Jack replaced the photo. 'Yet he's not been seen since McCullagh stopped turning up for work. That would suggest to me that he's less of a regular punter and more of an acquaintance to Brian McCullagh, wouldn't you agree?'

'An astute observation, detective,' Astley said.

Jack placed his forearms on the table and edged forward. 'Vic here is clearly an employee at the Port of Tyne. Yet,' he said, 'it's the strangest thing...'

Astley remained silent.

Jack continued. 'When I presented this photo to them, they'd never heard of any Vic, or Victor, going by this description. They gave me a name, but it doesn't match any records we have, which means he must have changed his identity at some point. Or, at the very least, gone off the grid.'

Astley shrugged.

Jack leaned back. 'So, yeah, Vic doesn't exist. But they said this guy had a nickname.' He pointed to the photo once more. 'Care to venture a guess as to what that was?'

A sly smirk spread across Astley's face. He shifted slightly, handcuffs clanging against the desk as he did so. He motioned for Jack to lean in, whispering in his ear, before adding, 'he told you he'd find you.'

Jack threw his chair back, stood, and banged on the door. Moments later, the PC opened it, but not before Astley finished his say...

'You can run, Jack Lambert, but you can't hide. You have no idea what's coming, none of you do—you and your gangster friend, you're all finished!'

It wasn't until he reached the station reception that he realised he was shaking.

'Guv?' said the desk sergeant. 'You alright?'

He let out a deep breath and turned to the officer. 'Pass this on to DS Watkins for me, will you?' he said, placing the newspaper clipping on the counter.

'Err... no problem, guv,' she said.

He thanked her and left the station, pausing in the car park to glance up towards his office—an office he'd more or less lived out of for the best part of ten years. Policing was all he knew, apart from the life he'd left behind previously...

It had started snowing now, a sure sign that winter was really kicking in. Somewhere in his psyche, he was aware of a biting wind whipping up. But he wasn't cold.

He dragged himself into the Volvo and turned the key, the engine kicking in on the second try. Jack gritted his teeth in grim determination at the thought of what he would now have to do. He manoeuvred out of his parking space, and began a steady journey towards the centre of Newcastle, without even so much as a cursory glance behind him at Northumbria HQ.

She felt her ageing heart skip a beat as the knock at the door came. Like clockwork, he always arrived at the same time. Despite knowing this, however, she still felt the familiar pang of anxiety that his absence brought to her.

She danced towards the door, and flung it open, only to be

met with a giant bouquet of red roses. 'Oh really, you shouldn't have!' she beamed.

He stepped through the doorway and placed the flowers on the floor with a heave of effort. She reached out and touched his face and he brought a hand up to his cheek, holding her fingers there.

'Of course I do, Margaret, you're my number one after all.'

Margaret Fenwick thought she would faint, such was the power this man carried in his words. Everything he said, she knew he meant. 'I read the news; it's just terrible what happened to them all.'

She watched as he eyed her. He knew fine well she couldn't stand McCullagh, owing to his loyalty to her husband but, for his part, he never picked her up on it. She'd taken a risk hanging the barman out to dry over his previous involvement with Gus. However, if the man before her was angry, he didn't show it. She felt relief wash over her. Everything would be alright. She knew he still loved her. But she also knew that love complicated things. Leaving Gus for him would have put everything in jeopardy. And, so, she'd done what she had thought was best, forcing her husband to abandon the group, paving the way for her and Vic to be together.

And so Brian's loyalty to his old friend had brought about a powerful enemy for her.

'Never mind that,' he replied. 'Every setback provides us with an opportunity, and I have some ideas for our next move.'

She threw herself at him with all the vibrancy of a lovesick teenager. 'Oh, Vic, you always know what you're doing.'

The Captain, after a moment's hesitation, placed his arms around her, and looked to his reflection in the hall mirror. He allowed his mask to fall, revealing who he really was underneath— the face nobody ever got to see in public. It was a good job she was wearing a cardigan; it allowed her to remain blissfully unaware of his nails digging ever so slightly into her back as he fought back the rage that was building within. The Syndicate had existed to protect his identity. Without them, he was more vulnerable than he had been.

He brought his hands up to her neck.

Back at the station, word had gotten round about Jack's conversation with Astley. Watkins, nervous as ever, was on the lookout for him. He made straight for the DCI's office but found it empty. He glanced around the room; unlike outside, the office was warm, but that didn't stop him from shuddering. He moved to the window overlooking the car park but Jack's car was no longer there. Fishing out his mobile, he scrolled down to Jack's number, but hesitated before ringing him.

He didn't need to press call to know that his boss wouldn't answer.

By the time the desk sergeant found his police badge on the counter, Jack was already halfway across Newcastle, with Astley's whispered threat still ringing in his ears...

'Nobody close to you, Jack Lambert, will survive.'

He gripped the steering wheel with his left hand before turning his phone off with the right. Sacrificing his closest relationships to protect them was a small price worth paying, as far as he was concerned. Robson had told him that these people, drug dealers, people smugglers and pimps had no rules, and that somehow made them more dangerous. Well, the Captain wasn't the only one who could go off grid.

This network of criminals was about to find out just how dangerous Jack Lambert could really be.

ACKNOWLEDGMENTS

Since Open Grave was first published, I've had the pleasure of meeting and becoming part of an entire writing community. With that in mind, I would like to thank a number of people who have helped me along the way and been a part of my own journey through publication.

I would like to thank all of the staff at Bloodhound Books for their efforts in creating what you now see before you. Betsy, Fred, Heather, Sumaira, Tara and Clare have all been invaluable to me throughout my time as a published writer and I can't thank them enough for what they do.

Glenn Upsall remains a constant support to me, putting up with my many Facebook ramblings about realistic dialogue and characterisation. I'd also like to thank Jaclyn Wrightson, again, for providing me with procedural advice when requested. I'm also very grateful to Amy Pearson for being willing to read over the manuscript at very short notice!

I'd like to thank Fiona Sharp for her enthusiasm and willingness to promote my work across the region in Waterstones, as well as for creating an amazing crime community within the Durham branch. A big shout out to the Durham Crime Book Group!

Vic Watson and Jacky Collins have also supported me along the way and have been kind enough to either host my own events or invite me along to theirs. They are both wonderful people who have taken the time to help me. I am forever in their debt.

I've met many authors in the past year and I will no doubt forget to name many of them here. A number of current and former Bloodhound authors have been extremely welcoming and helpful to me and I would like to thank all of them for their advice and time, in particular: Liz Mistry and K A Richardson. I would also like to give a mention to both Robert Scragg and Howard Linskey for being there to offer advice and encouragement whenever I needed it.

None of this would be possible without the many volunteers that get involved at writing events, the book bloggers who read, review and promote my work and anybody else who has bought, borrowed or read my writing. I've had many kind comments along the way and it is very much appreciated. Libraries are so fundamental to our society that it pains me to see how many of them are now struggling with a lack of funding. With this in mind, I'd like to give a mention to my local library in South Shields, as well as to all of the staff who have played a part in helping me host events there. The Word is a truly fantastic place and the work that they do in the local community is truly astonishing.

And, finally, to all of my friends and family, as well as all of the members of my local writing group, the South Shields Fiction Writers, thanks for the support.

Lightning Source UK Ltd.
Milton Keynes UK
UKHW010155151220
375229UK00004B/1253